Time After Time

mikki daughtry

putnam

G. P. PUTNAM'S SONS

G. P. PUTNAM'S SONS
An imprint of Penguin Random House LLC
1745 Broadway, New York, New York 10019

First published in the United States of America by G. P. Putnam's Sons,
an imprint of Penguin Random House LLC, 2025

Copyright © 2025 by Mikki Daughtry

Penguin Random House values and supports copyright.
Copyright fuels creativity, encourages diverse voices, promotes free speech, and creates a vibrant culture. Thank you for buying an authorized edition of this book and for complying with copyright laws by not reproducing, scanning, or distributing any part of it in any form without permission. You are supporting writers and allowing Penguin Random House to continue to publish books for every reader. Please note that no part of this book may be used or reproduced in any manner for the purpose of training artificial intelligence technologies or systems.

G. P. Putnam's Sons is a registered trademark of Penguin Random House LLC.
The Penguin colophon is a registered trademark of Penguin Books Limited.

Visit us online at PenguinRandomHouse.com.

Library of Congress Cataloging-in-Publication Data is available.

ISBN 9780593533826 (hardcover)
1 3 5 7 9 10 8 6 4 2

ISBN 9798217110865 (international edition)
1 3 5 7 9 10 8 6 4 2

Printed in the United States of America

BVG

Design by Kathryn Li
Text set in Criterion

This book is a work of fiction. Any references to historical events, real people, or real places are used fictitiously. Other names, characters, places, and events are products of the author's imagination, and any resemblance to actual events or places or to persons, living or dead, is entirely coincidental.

The publisher does not have any control over and does not assume any responsibility for author or third-party websites or their content.

The authorized representative in the EU for product safety and compliance is Penguin Random House Ireland, Morrison Chambers, 32 Nassau Street, Dublin D02 YH68, Ireland, https://eu-contact.penguin.ie.

*For everyone who believes in love,
and for everyone else who wants to.*

I seem to have loved you in numberless forms, numberless times . . .
In life after life, in age after age, forever.

RABINDRANATH TAGORE

Prologue

DECEMBER 31, 1925

The light from the oil lamp gleamed off the mahogany Victrola. Elizabeth opened the phonograph and unscrewed the tiny knob on the tapered arm. Excitement coursed through her as she fished out a new needle, dropping it twice before finally securing it into its tiny clamp. She opened the lower cabinet and sifted through albums, pulling one record free from the others. "Auld Lang Syne." Days Gone By. The unofficial anthem of New Year's Eve.

She placed the record on the green velvet disk and cranked the mechanical arm. With the quick flip of a switch, the disk began to turn. Elizabeth settled the needle into the outermost groove of the spinning record. Static, then music, filled the room. She hummed along to the melody as she looked for something else to do, anything to keep her hands occupied. The fire had nearly burned itself out, so she reached for the fireplace poker and shuffled the pointed end through the dying coals. The embers flared, their amber light dancing across her silver beaded dress.

At that moment, one of the red-hot coals cracked, right down the middle. Elizabeth stared at it uneasily. *An omen.* The thought curled inside her belly, tried to take up residence, but she refused it shelter. She would not allow a silly cracked coal to ruin what was meant to be a night of joy, of celebration. It was New Year's Eve, after all, and she intended to be light and carefree!

But that burning coal watched her from its bed of ashes, its red glow pulsing like a living thing, like the hell that was preached from the pulpit, like the brimstone that awaited all sinners. She stared at the ominous thing, then she shoved the poker right into the coal, rending it fully in two. The pieces lay open in fiery judgment. *Guilty guilty guilty*. She swung the poker again, pulverizing the ember, crushing it beneath the steel tip of the poker. She refused to believe that any love could be wrong. Especially *this* love. *Her* love.

She leaned the poker against the hearth, then deliberately turned her back to the fire, as if daring it to pop again, daring it to try and ruin her good mood.

She focused instead on the room, her very favorite room in the house, especially this time of year, when it was decked in all its holiday frippery. Wreaths and garlands adorned every window; the huge mantel hosted a handcrafted Nativity scene, little models and figurines passed down from her grandmother's grandmother; and an eight-foot tree stood in the corner. All would remain, fully decorated, until the end of January, as was Post family tradition. It was as perfect this year as it had been for all her nineteen years.

Still, she felt the heat from the embers behind her, pictured that cracked coal in her mind. She whirled round to the fireplace, searching the fire, searching for that coal. She had crushed it. She had destroyed it. Hadn't she? Her eyes searched and searched, seeing no sign of the coal but sensing that somehow it was still there, lurking, hiding, waiting to—

She heard the beastly motor of the roadster outside roar to life. Then a cold snap of air brushed over her as the front door opened.

She pulled her eyes from the embers and turned to see Patricia walking through the foyer, toward the fireplace. Toward *her*. Elizabeth had never seen her look as beautiful as she did that very moment, in her shimmering gold gown, briskly rubbing her arms, her cheeks flushed from the cold, and with a smile that, Elizabeth knew, was just for her.

Snowflakes dotted Patricia's wealth of bright red curls. Elizabeth looked past her to the dark night outside, where the snow was softly coming down. It was that snowfall, thick and silent, peaceful and pure, that finally banished any thoughts of sins or omens or preachers bellowing brimstone and fire. That, and the young woman who stood before her.

"Are you ready?" Patricia asked, her accent lilting every word. Patricia reached for her, and Elizabeth knew the only thing she would ever need was standing right here, gazing at her with so much love, squeezing her fingers with winter-chilled hands.

Patricia.

Nothing else mattered. Only this woman and this night, this glorious night . . .

1

LIBBY

My foot holds down the brake of my hand-me-down Camry as I idle at the curb, staring out the car window at the run-down Victorian. It sits heavy on its brambly, unkempt lot. The Mulberry house is mine. And I can't quite believe it.

"Oh, Gammy," I whisper, "don't be mad. Please don't be mad."

Gammy didn't have much while she was alive, but after my grandpa died, she sold their small house and moved in with us (the very best years of my life). She put the money from the sale into two accounts. One for me and one for my brother, Peter. Half and half. My family is middle-middle-class; we're not rolling in dough. Even though it's not a fortune, Gammy's gift was meant to give Peter and me enough money to go to college and graduate without a ton of debt. A gift that only the most privileged kids have. A gift I just spent on something that is definitely not college.

But I'm sure, I'm absolutely certain, that the Mulberry house is my future. I think about my Saturdays with Gammy. About our movie days and our walks and our talks and the Mulberry house and my wanting it so badly that it carved a hollow ache in my belly. A dull ache that's been there ever since. I think about the little girl who was me, staking my young, foolish claim on that house, as if mere wishing could make dreams come true.

Now, every night, ever since I saw the For Sale sign in the yard, I've been having different dreams. As soon as I fall asleep, the images start: the house, big and bold and pristine. Pom-pom shrubs lining a pebble stone walkway. Rose bushes full of radiant, sweet-smelling blooms. And music. Fun, old-timey music from the 1920s. There's a backyard party in full swing. Little hors d'oeuvres being passed around on silver trays. Guests dressed like extras in a *Great Gatsby* movie. It's the same party. It's the best party. Every single night.

There's no music now. No party. The lights are out. The shine is gone. But it's mine.

I turn off the car and rest my head against the wheel, listening to the engine tick quietly. Then, before I even register the movement, my hand is reaching for the door handle. It's like my mind and body have been on autopilot for the last two weeks. I've been like a different person, making very un-Libby-like decisions. I am not impulsive. I never step out of line. I'm the girl who sets my alarm thirty minutes early so I can lie in bed and mentally plan my day, step by step, every little detail accounted for so there are no surprises.

Steady as she goes, my dad likes to say.

"Buckle up, Dad," I mutter as I imagine just how *unsteady* everything's going to be when they find out. Dad will be furious. Mom will do that yelling-sob thing that makes my ears ache. I've seen her do it to Peter a thousand times. And Peter? He'll laugh because it'll finally be me in the doghouse and not him. Then Dad will take one of his long, bracing breaths before he stoically tells me all the reasons I'm wrong and he's right and if I'll just do as he says my life will be amazing. My teeth clench at the thought.

I step out of the car and walk back to the house. Its enormity is breathtaking, all ornate gables, eaves, cone-shaped towers, and a huge, spindled wraparound porch. Several pieces of loose siding droop crookedly above the dingy, discolored downstairs windows. Upstairs, the two front-facing windows are covered by wood planks. The roof still has the original shingles, although a few patches are missing, like bald spots. I see past all that, past the age, past the decay. I picture the house in all its glory, with Model Ts and jazz bands; shimmery dresses, hats, and gloves; all the wonderful things the big Victorian must have seen before its eyes were shut by those awful boards.

Gammy and I used to stand in front of this old picket fence, my small hand gliding reverently along the aging wood, spotted and worn, like Gammy's skin, bearing the marks of time. Little me would daydream about the house, about the lives that happened there.

Now it belongs to me. All of it. Even . . .

I look down.

. . . the green glass stone. It's oblong, like a small glass cylinder. At least the part that's visible. The rest of it is buried in the sidewalk. I've memorized this stone as thoroughly as I've memorized the house, brushed my fingers across the emerald glass a hundred times, across the numbers that are etched just beneath: *2 3 6*. It looks like they were written with a fat stick, or a slim finger. Decades of trampling feet and harsh weather have taken their toll on the inscription, fading the numbers to shallow grooves. I have no idea what the numbers mean, but every time I see them, my stomach does a slow flip. The house calls to me, but the stone makes me sad.

Something catches my eye. Movement. A chill runs down the back of my neck.

Someone is standing inside the house. A woman, staring out the window, her hand resting along the bottom of the windowsill. I lean forward to get a better look. She's youngish, I think. Her features are too hazy to make out, blurred by the sun glinting off the glass, but I can see her eyes. Deep and bright and locked directly on mine. She's staring right at me, or right through me. Right *into* me.

My cell phone rings, jolting me. I scramble for my phone and check the caller ID. It's Eleanor, my real estate agent. Good. She'll know what the hell is going on. I swipe the screen, and without preamble say, "Is there someone in my house?"

There's a long pause. Then Eleanor says, "There hasn't been anyone in that house for decades."

It was one of the conditions of the sale, Eleanor had told me. The seller, some distant relative of the previous owner, was offloading it, selling it as is, with everything still inside. *Everything,* Eleanor had said, *furniture and all.* Which, of course, had made me even more determined to have it. And when I saw the price, weirdly, freakishly, unbelievably low for an actual whole house (and nearly exactly what I had in my college fund), it felt too much like fate to pass up. I signed the papers without another thought. But now . . .

"Someone's standing in the front window, staring me down," I say into the phone, staring back at the woman. An electric tingle raises the tiny hairs on the nape of my neck.

"That's impossible, Libby," Eleanor says.

"I'm looking right at her, Eleanor. I'm not hallucinat—" I stop abruptly as a cloud moves overhead to block the sun. It casts a shade over the glass, and the young woman in the window is revealed. It's me, my long hair piled in a messy bun, holding the cell phone to my ear, nervously shifting my weight from one leg to the other.

I start laughing, relieved that I haven't totally lost it.

"What's going on?" Eleanor wants to know, her voice cutting through my chuckles.

"Nothing. I just bought a house, and I'm seeing myself in it, that's all."

There's another long pause, as if Eleanor is trying to figure out what I mean. I can almost see her shrug as she decides she doesn't care and says, "Um, okay, yeah, good. So listen. Couple of things. I just spoke with the listing agent again. I was able to talk them into leaving the utilities connected for a week or so, to give you time to get them switched over into your name. But they can't give you the key today, for liability reasons. I'm sorry. I know you're dying to get in there. As soon as the documents are recorded, it's all yours. I'll see if I can call in a favor, get the deed recorded earlier . . ."

Eleanor's still talking, but I'm not listening. I smile like an idiot as I impulsively wave at my reflection in the window. She waves back. Because she is me. I thank Eleanor profusely and hang up. Then, shoving all my worries of my empty college fund and my sudden lurch toward impulsivity to the back of my mind, I take one last look at the house—*my house!*—and grin. The little holes in the ground where the For Sale sign had been seem to wink up at me, one hole smaller than the other. I wink back and hurry to my car. I know I made the right decision, no matter how bumpy the road turns out to be.

～

On my way home, I swing by the flower shop to pick up my paycheck. It's only a part-time job, but it covers my incidentals: gas, clothes, and entertainment. It will be enough (if I cut back on the gas, clothes, and entertainment) to cover the Mulberry house necessities: insurance, electricity, and water.

A little silver Yorkie yips happily when I walk in.

"Hey, Georgia." I scoop the doggy up for a quick snug, then look around for my boss. She's standing near the flower fridge with her husband. She laughs shyly as she shoves him away and adjusts her bright yellow cardigan. It's not the first time I've caught them all kissy-face. Her husband just grins and reaches around to cradle her huge baby belly. Twin girls. It looks like she's carrying twenty pounds, sticking right out front. I say hi, grab my check from beside the register, and trot back out the door. I've got worrying to do, and I can't do it while basking in the reflected glow of their love, as beautiful as it is.

No one's home when I pull into my driveway fifteen minutes later. Dad's still at work, Peter's still at school, and Mom is probably grocery shopping.

I go straight upstairs and stop at Peter's room. I brace myself, then fling open the door. A blast of sour stench hits me in the face. Socks, sweat, testosterone. If I never again smell a pubescent boy, it will be too soon. I pull a package of Reese's Pieces from my bookbag and toss it toward Peter's bed. I learned a long time ago the best way to deal with my unruly brother is bribery. Candy, Xbox gift cards for his online gaming addiction, and occasionally, a used game or two from the clearance bin. Like a bank deposit. Treats go into the Peter account so if I ever need a favor, I can make a withdrawal.

Finally, I go into my bedroom and close the door. My soft, plush haven. Lots of beige and cream with tiny bits of pink thrown in. The strategic pops of color make the whole room look like it's blushing, like someone it really likes has just said the nicest thing. Cam calls it my princess prison, but he can stick it. I love my room. The mattress bounces as I drop onto the bed, cell phone in hand. I pull up my favorites and hit the first number: *CamCam*. Cam's been my best friend since first grade. A lot of things have changed since then, for both of us, but one thing hasn't. Cam is still the cheese to my macaroni.

He doesn't answer. That's the third time today. He was all about me doing this irrational, impulsive thing, and now he's nowhere to be found. I roll over and stare at the ceiling. Wouldn't it be my luck that the late-afternoon sun is streaming through the curtains just right, casting a shadow across the ceiling. A shadow that is all sharp angles and peaks. A shadow that looks kind of like . . . a house. It's the last thing I see before I close my eyes for a nap before dinner, and it's not long before I hear that far-off music as I'm lulled back into the dreamland of the Victorian.

I wake to a soft tapping on my door, then my mom's voice. "Libby. Dinner."

Mom is a great cook. She's a great mom. Most importantly, in my dad's opinion, she's a great *wife*. Molly Monroe is exactly the kind of woman who men like my dad love, with her styled hair, flawless makeup, and perfectly put together outfits. Tonight, the housewife extraordinaire is serving up roast lamb, glazed butternut squash, wild rice pilaf, and a fresh green salad. The meal clearly took her hours to prepare, and she flushes under Dad's silent approval.

I utter a distracted "This looks delicious, Mom." Peter nods in agreement, staring through thick vines of overgrown bangs. He's all dark eyes on a pale face under a floppy mop of brown hair. I cringe as he starts sucking his fork, those greedy eyes transfixed by the sweet, sticky squash. He looks like a hypnotized sheepdog. Any second now, he'll start drooling.

"Libby," my dad says, "didn't you have a meeting yesterday?"

What? I gulp and swallow hard. He can't possibly know. I stare down at my plate, at the shiny orange cubes of squash, but in my mind, I see the real estate office, the closing papers, Eleanor's grin, my signature in bright blue ink, right on the dotted line—

SNAP!! SNAP SNAP!!

I jerk my head back, away from Peter's grimy fingers that are snapping right in front of my nose. I look around, dazed, feeling like

I was just yanked off a merry-go-round. My whole family is staring at me, waiting for... "Huh?" I say, confused.

Dad's eyes narrow and he sits straighter, if that's possible, and says (for the second time, apparently), "You were supposed to meet with the debate team about joining up."

Oh. That other secret. I changed my major from political science to design.

Politics, even from the sidelines, takes the kind of personality I don't have. The last thing I want to do is mire myself in debate after argument after debate for the rest of my life. That's going to be another blow to dear old Dad. Now he'll have to hang his vicarious political aspirations on Peter, and if I'm honest, Peter will be lucky to get out of high school with a C average. One thing I can say for my younger brother is that he will never be in danger of overachieving. Mom keeps saying, "He's only fourteen, give him time," but seriously, how much time does it take to master basic human consideration like wiping the Cheeto dust from your fingers before using the remote?

No. There will be no politics for Peter. Or for me. I'm not C-SPAN. I'm HGTV. I want to be able to transform homes the way they do. Well, I want to be able to transform *one* home. When I close my eyes, I know exactly what the Mulberry house is supposed to look like, what it used to look like, what it will look like again.

Peter drops his chin and burps. It's low and loud. Sounds hot. He flicks his hand in front of his face, flapping at the fumes. I sigh and close my eyes, letting a few seconds pass before I open them again. When I do, Peter's already digging into another helping of dinner. He dumps a spatula full of butternut squash right on top of his rice pilaf, squishes it, mixes it all up, then swipes a piece of lamb through it and shovels it into his mouth, chewing loudly. God, he's disgusting. "Peter," Mom whispers, a soft reproach.

"Libby?" Dad says sharply.

"Yeah, sorry, um," I stammer, but all I can come up with is "They moved it to Monday."

"That's disappointing. I was looking forward to hearing about it."

My gut sinks, but then I remember *why* I'm not going to be on the debate team. Why I changed my major. Because of Mulberry Lane. Before a guilty grin can overtake my face, I pull a Peter, stuffing my mouth full of food and trying to chew around it all.

"Libby, what in the world?" my mother moans. My dad grumbles something about "raising a lady" as I chew and chew and chew.

2

TISH

I'm pretty sure I broke my ass. Literally.

Lola, the traitor, dumped me on my butt, right in front of everybody.

I should get out of bed and see just how bad it is, but I don't want to. After a few seconds, I convince myself that maybe a tiny peek won't hurt. I tentatively open one eye. The overhead light stabs my pupil, sharp and mean. *Nope no no no!* I squeeze my eye shut again.

"Why did you turn on the light?" I groan to the warm body behind me. The room has no windows, so it makes for a perfect sleep blackout. But right now, with that freaking light . . .

"Because I want you to get up. Everyone's already awake. There won't be any coffee left if we don't hurry," Bari's velvety voice whispers into my ear.

Bari. My best friend in the whole world and the one person who is always on my side.

There won't be any coffee left anyway, not after those locusts scour the kitchen. I would say it out loud, but I can't make my mouth move again so soon. I settle for a low grunt, which Bari understands because she speaks Tish like no one else. My tiny twin bed shakes as she laughs, curled against me, hogging all the covers. I guess she spent the night. Makes sense, after the fool I made of myself. She wouldn't have left me alone after a disaster like that.

"Come on," she says, nudging me with her knee, inadvertently in the exact spot where it hurts most. I suck in my breath and scoot away from her, clinging to the edge of the bed.

"Ow. Ow ow ow," I whine, keeping my eyes closed.

Today is already too much. I'm just gonna stay in bed.

"You did it to yourself," she says.

"Thanks for the sympathy, friend," I mutter.

She chuckles, a huff of laughter that tickles my ear. I don't need to be looking at her to know she's wearing a beautiful smirk on her too-damned-beautiful face. Bari is an Indian American goddess with a sheath of silky black hair and smooth, flawless skin. Walking around with her in middle school, I felt like a mutt next to a greyhound—Bari, all sleek and regal, and me with my mash of messy freckles and wild, carrot-red curls bobbing alongside her.

I've grown more into myself these last few years, though. My hair has deepened to a heavy orange-red, and most of my freckles finally faded around the ninth grade. Just a few left across my nose and cheeks. My curls stuck around, though. Shorter now, but still completely out of control. Most of the time, I'm perfectly content with my obvious Irish heritage. Mirrors don't break when I walk by, at least. But sometimes I still feel like that rangy mutt from sixth grade.

I shove a thick curl off my forehead, still not ready to open my eyes. If I open them, it means I'm really awake, and that means I can't pretend last night was just a bad dream born of beer, beer, and more beer. "It was almost brilliant," I sigh. And it was. Almost.

"Know what *would* have been brilliant?" Now I picture Bari's jet-black eyes dancing the way they do when she's teasing me.

"If I hadn't done it?" I reply.

"Oh, you do have a brain. One of these days maybe you'll use it." She chuckles.

"Who else saw?" I ask, not even close to wanting to know. When she doesn't answer, I groan again. Her silence can only mean one thing: Everybody saw. I snatch the covers away from her and pull them over my head. She yanks them back down, then nudges harder, trying to get me out of bed. Pain squeals through me.

"Why are you torturing me?!" I wail. Feels like she took a blow-torch to my butt. I try to squirm farther away from her, but she holds my hips still, her hands firm but gentle.

"Hold on, honey. Don't move," she says softly as she goes from barb-slinging bestie to mother hen in two seconds.

"I wasn't moving till you stuck your knee up my butt," I say with a pout. Yes, I'm pouting. Because yes, it hurts, and because I love it when Bari fusses over me. My mom used to fuss over me when I was little, but the older I got, the more it became obvious I wasn't going to be the darling daughter in dresses and bows. Instead, I was a scrappy mess with skinned knees and baggy jeans. Mom's affection dwindled from loving hugs to quick squeezes to awkward shoulder pats, each demotion confirming that I wasn't quite what she wanted. To make matters more amazingly *not* awesome, I'm from a one-parent household. Mom was all I had. Until Bari, who is now gently pulling down the back of my boxers. I reach back to slap her hands away. "There's nothing in there for you. You had your chance at prom, and you turned me down, so keep your peepers to yourself."

She ignores me to peer down the back of my shorts, hissing in sympathy pain. "Oh, Tish."

"I'm sure it's fine," I say, with a truckload of false bravado. She touches the skin of my upper hip, causing me to flinch instinctively.

"Is it bleeding?" I ask. Something else I really don't want to know.

"Noooo . . ." she answers carefully. Whew. I hate the sight of blood, especially my own. "But it's gonna bruise like a beast." The bed jostles a little as she gets out.

"It's fine, then. My pride took the biggest hit." I pull myself onto my knees, my eyes still firmly closed.

"Open your damn eyes." She laughs.

"I don't want to. You're looking at me all judgy. I can feel it."

Her sigh has a frustrated huff at the end, so I figure it's best to just do as she says. I open my eyes. Bari's not looking scary at all. She's looking so sweetly loving that my heart melts. She could have slept in her dorm room last night, all warm and cozy, but she squished in here with me instead. Now she's standing on the floor of my tiny, closet-size bedroom. Closet-size because it actually *is* a walk-in closet, hence the no windows.

I live with five other people in a two-bedroom apartment. I pay the least rent, so I've got the smallest "room." My student loans barely cover tuition and books.

My roommates are just as broke as I am, struggling to pay for school and books and housing and food, so we all ended up here, piled on top of each other. There's not a lot of elbow room, or privacy, to say the least. And I live with a bunch of theater majors. It's all drama all the time. I can't say I don't have fun, but there are moments when I just want to shout "Aaaaaand . . . scene!" and drop the curtain on Act One, hoping that Act Two will bring a really cool plot twist.

I take in a lungful of air, then let it whoosh out of me, wishing for the millionth time that my circumstances were different, wishing that I was one of those kids whose parents have money, whose parents love them. But I shut down those poor-me feelings right away. I don't want things I can't have. There's an underlying fear, though, that I'll never be enough, never do anything worthwhile, never be anyone worthwhile. Those feelings are harder to shut down, but I try. I'm always trying to ignore that fear. Or outrun it.

"You'd better check on Lola. She went down pretty hard, too," Bari says as she takes my hands, holding me steady as I shuffle on my knees toward the edge of the bed and stand up. I arch my back, stretching out the kinks.

"You're worried about *her*? She did this to me," I grumble.

"*You* did that to you. Lola's the love of your life; go take care of her," Bari says. She hands me a pair of soft lounge pants. Guess I'm wearing PJs to class today. I pull my boxer shorts down and turn my back to face the full-length mirror I rigged to dangle from a clothes hanger. My stomach heaves when I see the damage. It looks like my butt was used as a street sweeper, both cheeks scraped raw. Bright ruby red.

"Kinda makes me crave strawberry pancakes," Bari teases.

I hurl the lounge pants at her. She deftly snatches them out of the air and tosses them right back at me, somehow getting the legs to loop around my neck like a lasso.

"Yes! A ringer!" she shouts, her arms raised in victory.

"Asshole," I growl.

I unloop the pants from around my neck and pull them on, careful to keep them away from my burning ass. No such luck. It's like they're magnetized to stick right against my boxers, which in turn press right against my sore flesh. I tug at the seat of the pants, which only makes it worse. Finally, I give up and grab my filthy, well-worn Chucks.

"Please wear socks with those," Bari says.

I scowl at her, then pluck a pair from the little crate setup I call my dresser. A few milk crates, a laundry basket, and nine hangers hold all the clothes I have. It's easy for me to not take up much space, because I don't have much stuff.

I'm still tying my shoes, trying my best to sit without actually sitting, when Bari opens the door, ready to go. She answers my long, menacing stare with a shrug. She's not scared of me.

∼

Bari drops me off outside The Gag, our school cafeteria. The food's better than the nickname makes it sound, but it's not my usual breakfast choice. Most days, Jamal brings home leftover bagels or pastries from his part-time job at the deli. He didn't work yesterday, so there were no stale treats this morning, just an empty coffeepot and a bone-bare fridge, if you don't count the condiments. I need a protein bar and a Yoo-Hoo in the worst way. Maybe I'll splurge and have two. It's gonna be a long day in the scene shop.

The theater department is working on this year's production of *A Christmas Carol*. The play doesn't go up for a couple of months, but it's the department's biggest moneymaker, so we're already building the set. Professor Wallis, the set designer and head of the design department, wants it to be perfect.

Practicum is like lab hours for stagecraft. Students from all the theater classes have mandatory practicum hours two days a week, even the acting majors. It's an all-in department.

I'm here every day because Wallis pays me to be. I'm kind of an accidental theater major. I fell into it because I'm good with my hands. I can just look at something and figure out how to build it. Last year, on my second day as a freshman, I saw some students dragging wood and tools off a truck, and I hurried to check it out.

Wallis had waved me in and parked a drill in my hand before he realized I wasn't even in his class. I stuck around and made myself useful. There are plenty of backstage jobs that don't require performing. Wallis always says, "Someone's gotta be behind the scenes!" And since I basically have no life except Bari, he pays me a little bit to be available whenever he needs me. I help build the sets, hang lights, and noodle with electrics, running wires inside the walls for practical props like lamps or radios or doorbells or whatever. *A Christmas Carol* is full of practicals, so once the set is built, I'll be up to my eyeballs trying to get everything wired and working. Until then, I'm here to help with the other stuff, and make a little money. It's not a ton of money, but every dollar counts.

The big metal doors to the shop are open, so I hear the saws and hammers before I get inside. Everyone's already here, painting, nailing, building. I wave at them as I walk in, then grab a tool belt and load it up. I'd usually strap it around my waist, but the thought of it banging against my butt is too much, so I sling it over my shoulder.

We're making good progress on the exterior set. It looks just like a Victorian house. I know it's only plywood and foam, cut to look like the real deal, but for a second, it *does* look real. So real it gives me a heavy feeling in my belly. I feel it roll uneasily. I shouldn't have had that second Yoo-Hoo.

Sofia takes a nail gun to a door cutout, securing the flimsy pressboard frame to a thin plywood wall. She's pretty. So pretty that if I wanted to notice girls again, Sofia Olvera might be one I'd notice. Thick dark hair, a tiny round nose, and light hazel eyes that tilt up at the corners, like they're always smiling. I grimace and sigh, knowing without a doubt that she saw my stupid antics last night. I mean, I literally told her, "Come watch this!"

That makes me think of Lola. I'm still mad at her. I'm sure she's mad at me, too. Let her stew. I hope her butt hurts as much as mine does.

Sofia must feel me looking at her, because she turns and catches me staring. Then she laughs. Now I *know* she saw me eat pavement with my ass. I straighten my back and walk up to her. Someone fires up a miter saw, drowning out my attempt at a nonchalant "Hi."

Sofia and I wait. It's just about to get awkward when the saw finally stops.

"Where's Wallis?" I ask.

Wallis's wild hair and crooked bow tie are usually the first things I see when I get to the shop. No matter how early, Wallis is already here with his blueprint plans rolled out. Not today.

Thwip thwip thwip. Sofia drives three nails into the wood, her eyes twinkling. "He had that beach thing this weekend, remember? Guess he's not back yet," she says.

"What about Dr. B?" I look around for Dr. Bilwick. She's the theater professor and director of the play—of all the plays, I guess. She's not usually in the scene shop, but the last few weeks, she's been hanging around, with her flowy skirts flowing and her clinky bracelets clinking, watching us work, looking over Wallis's shoulder, reading his blueprints, telling him how much she loves his designs.

Sofia just grins and says, *"Neither* of them are here this morning."

Professor Wallis and Dr. B! Doesn't take a genius to know that she must've had a "beach thing," too, since we all saw her get into his car Friday night after rehearsal.

"About time, right?" Sofia smiles and—*thwip thwip thwip*—sends more nails into the door frame. I wouldn't know about their timing. Even after a year, I'm still the newbie. Theater kids have their roots planted deep. Some of them have known each other for years, from theater camps, community drama clubs, and summer stock. Even the out-of-staters. They all share a language that I'm still learning to speak. No wonder I tried to impress them last night.

I pull my mental armor tight around myself and give a cool shrug, like I'm not standing here thinking what a tool I am. Then Sofia gives me a quick once-over. Her eyes stop right at my butt area, brows rising dramatically, and she says, "How is your, uh, you know . . . Are you okay?"

She looks actually concerned, and my rear cheeks flare under the reminder, hot and painful, so I pat my tool belt and stammer, "I forgot— I need, um—" and hurry toward the tool room. God. This is worse than I thought, I realize as I glance around the stage. They all look *worried* about me. I'd rather them laugh at me than feel sorry for me! I suddenly feel a pang of longing for Lola, to see how she's holding up, to tell her I'm sorry for being an asshole, for getting us hurt with my stupid stunt. The fake streetlamps can wait. I need to see my girl.

∼

Lola's right where I left her last night, leaning against the cinder block wall in the alley behind the apartment. To say she's bent out of shape would be an understatement. Her backside's as torn up as mine, maybe more. Busted taillight, gnarled rear fender, muffler smashed against the rear shock, four broken spokes, and the kickstand ripped completely out. She took the brunt of the fall. Saved my ass. Literally. Note: Never attempt a wheelie when you don't actually know how to do one. The cool points aren't worth the wipeout. Stone-cold sober, too. The beer, beer, and more beer came after. I used it to wash down what was left of my pride.

"Hey, sweet girl. I'm sorry. I'm gonna get you fixed up, okay?" I promise her, stroking her shimmery blond gas tank. I need to go to Joe's, do some begging and bartering. Bari was right when she said Lola is the love of my life. This motorcycle is the only real thing of value I have—the only material thing, anyway. My scrappy little Lola. I can't take her with me to Joe's. She can't be ridden, and I can't ride. With a quick squeeze to her handlebars, I set out toward the scrapyard. It's not a bad walk. Couple of miles, maybe.

The fall air is crisp and cool. Most of the green is gone, and the leaves are turning. A few squirrels scamper up tree trunks, storing nuts for winter. This town is a perfect little postcard. Total Americana. I'm from the suburbs closer to the city, where the colors are all dull, washed out, and there's at least one boarded-up storefront or house on every block. I like it here. It feels roomier, easier to breathe. And there's a lot more green. That's the thing I dislike the most about the city. Not enough green.

Bari is the reason I'm here in this out-of-the-way town, at this small unknown school. This college has a good gerontology program, so this was the college Bari chose. She's kind of a saint, my Bari. The most beautiful girl with the biggest heart, a heart set on helping as many old people as she can. I'm just along for the ride. There are better schools with better programs she could have gone to, but this one's only a two-hour drive from where we grew up. Close enough for Bari to drive home on weekends, but far enough away that I don't have to.

When she suggested I apply, too, I thought she was joking. I never figured on college. I thought I'd end up working with my hands, mostly staying dirty. Somewhere like Joe's. But the stars must have aligned, because they let me in. And when I was approved for a small grant and a couple of student loans, Bari said that I *had* to come with her, that it was fate. I don't believe in fate, but I didn't have any other plans, so the decision was easy. Follow Bari. Try and keep up. It's what I've been doing since the sixth grade, and it's worked out so far.

The sun is directly above me now. I feel like I'm inching forward like a tortoise in a hare race, but I should still get to Joe's with plenty of time to get some good digging done before the sun goes down. I've already made it to Mulberry Lane, the street I always use as a shortcut.

The houses on this street are old. Way old. Even older than the people Bari is constantly learning about and fussing over and caring for. I've never given any of the houses more than a passing glance, though. Lola and I usually tear through here with blinders on, headed to wherever we're going as fast as we can legally get there. I'm not really paying attention today, either. I'm thinking of the things I'm going to need for Lola. I need a taillight. A fender. Muffler. I'll fish around for some grommets. It would be awesome if I could scrounge up a couple of—

An electric shock fires through the bottom of my right foot. It shoots up my leg, through my belly, and into my chest, where the air is punched out of me. I jerk my foot off the ground and look down. What the hell? Something green catches the sunlight. A piece of glass pressed into the sidewalk. I crouch down to get a closer look. Sturdy green glass. Opaque. I can't make out its real size because most of it is buried. And right underneath, numbers have been scraped into the concrete: *2 3 6*.

My heart gives one slow, heavy thump. Then another.

I tear my eyes away from the faded inscription and lean against the rickety old gate, feeling a little breathless. The wood creaks as I press my weight against it, so I straighten up, and that's when I notice the house. A big, ancient thing. It looks like a haunted dollhouse.

My heart thumps again as I study the house.

It needs a lot of work, but it could be really beautiful. I'd love to get my hands on it. I eye the boarded-up windows. That's where I'd start. I'd take down those boards. It's hard to turn around, hard to turn my back on the dreary old place. But I've got Lola to take care of. She's my most important project, and standing here staring at an old house isn't helping her.

3.

TISH

"Don't you dare let go," I warn Joe.

He's offended by the notion and lets me know it with a grunt and a huge spit of tobacco juice that fwaps wetly against the side of an old burned-out Jeep Grand Cherokee. I choke back a reflexive gag and cling to the rickety ladder. I'm perched on the top, so high I can see this whole section of the scrapyard. I'm looking for anything that resembles Lola, or a cousin of Lola's. Hell, a second or third cousin will do.

"Hurry up, Squirt. I ain't got all day," Joe grouses. *Squirt.* As if I'm a child. I guess to him, I probably am. He's got at least fifty years on me, maybe more, if his deeply creased, dusky skin is telling the truth. He's gotta be seventy-five hundred and something.

"Sure, you do. What else you got going on?" I ask.

"I might be running you to the hospital if you keep flapping that jaw," he says, then shakes the ladder, laughing as I holler in outrage. His leathery hands tighten their grip, and the swaying motion ends. I teeter at the top, holding on for dear life.

"When I get down, you are gonna be sorry," I yell.

"Well, in that case . . ." He shakes the ladder again.

"Okay, okay! I give!"

He laughs again and reaches up to pat the bottom of my foot. "Check your three o'clock."

My eyes scan clockwise over the corpses of cars and trucks, and a few husks of farming equipment. Then I see it, nestled between a couple of slumped tractors: the shell of a Honda CL350. The motor's gone, but I don't need a motor. I just need parts. Lola is a 1971 Honda CB350, but most of the parts from a CB350, a CL350, or a 350cc are interchangeable; they'll fit Lola just fine. My greedy eyes rake over the CL's skeleton. It's our lucky day. But I know this isn't just luck. Joe's always on the lookout for things I might need, and the old goat's gone and done it again. Just how long has that bike been sitting out here, hidden away in a part of the scrapyard I rarely see, waiting for me to need it?

"Joe, if I told you I love you, would you take it the wrong way?"

He snorts. "Only one way for me to take that, Squirt, and it's right to the heart."

I look down just in time to catch him chewing on a smile, trying to hide it from me. He won't ever say it back; he's too gruff for that. But he gives me a wink, then nods for me to come down off the ladder.

Growing up with very little money, I learned early how to make that little go a long way. The first thing I did when I got to town, after Bari and I set up her dorm room, was search the internet for nearby consignment shops, thrift stores, and salvage yards. That's how I met Joe.

And Joe is how I met Lola.

I found her while digging through this very scrapyard. It was a bright day, no clouds. My eyes caught a tiny twinkle on the farthest side of the yard. Something shining in the sun. I hurried over and there she was, hidden behind a dozen or so rusted-out wrecks, sunlight sparking off her golden tank. She was beat to hell, with so many parts missing. Still, she was the sassiest thing I'd seen in a while.

I didn't have any money, not the kind it would take to buy and fix up a motorcycle, so Joe told me he'd barter. He'd give me Lola, straight out give her to me, if I'd help him with a huge crate of random auto parts he had in the back. I could tell they'd been there a while, all gunky and rusted, some of them stuck together with grime and dried motor oil. They needed to be cleaned, organized, and cataloged. It took forever, but I got it done. In the meantime, Joe helped me make Lola a whole girl, a tough street bike who could run like the wind. She became sexy and sturdy and fast. God, I love her. I couldn't have done it without Joe.

After that, I started coming by to help him out when I had a few hours here and there. It takes a lot to run the scrapyard, and Joe's old. He really shouldn't be working like he does. He'd stroke out if he ever heard me say that, but it's true. Joe doesn't have any family of his own, and the yard doesn't bring in enough profit to take on a real employee, so it's kind of become our unspoken agreement that I help whenever I can, and he lets me take parts when I need them.

I step off the ladder. Joe goes to pick it up, but I grab it first. He gives me the stink eye, pretends to be offended for a few seconds, then says, "Got time for a burger?"

Oh. And Joe feeds me. Nearly every time I come by the shop, he insists on ordering an early dinner or late lunch or middle-of-the-day breakfast. He says it's because I'm "bony as a newborn foal," but I think he just likes the company. Nobody likes to eat alone, do they?

"I always have time for a burger," I say as I shoulder the ladder. Joe already has his cell phone out and is ordering delivery.

"Yeah, gimme two burgers— Huh? Say that again? . . . Ninety

minutes?! There's only seven thousand people in this whole town. You feedin' all of 'em right now?" Joe barks into the phone.

Ah. He's ordering from Hammie's. Joe shoots me a questioning look. I give him a thumbs-up. I'll be here for at least a couple of hours, and Hammie's is well worth the wait. Seven thousand people agree.

"All right then, gimme two of them bacon burgers you got, yeah? And fries . . . French fries, you goof. Who the hell's asking for zucchini?" He looks at me again and points to the phone, like *who are these crazy people?* I stifle a laugh as he hangs up.

"The hell's a zucchini fry?" he grouches.

"I think it's supposed to be a healthier take on french fries."

"What a load of puckey," he says. "Ain't nothing healthy that's got *fry* at the end."

The man's got a point. But I do love anything fried, so . . .

"I guess we're not getting any of them, then," I say with a sigh.

"Any of what?"

"Fried zucchini's probably gross anyway," I say, and glance at Joe, who's stuffing his phone back into his pocket and moving the tobacco around in his mouth, getting ready to spit again. Blech. I shift the ladder to my other shoulder and walk faster, limping oddly under the weight of the ladder and the scrub of the pants against my rear. I tuck my butt in as I walk, trying to avoid the rub of flannel. Joe snickers behind me.

"What?" I ask.

"You sit on a cactus or something?" He chuckles.

I stop and turn to glare at him, and *that's* when he decides to spit. This time I do gag.

"That stuff's gonna kill you," I croak.

"Something's gotta do it," he says, a dash of sadness flickering across his face. Then it's gone, like it never happened. He pulls his phone back out, dials, waits, then says, "Yeah, I just placed an ord— Yeah, that's me. Tack on some of them fried zucchinis, will ya?"

Good old Joe. A friend where I least expected to find one—in a junkyard in a tiny town that, these days, I call home. We're both misfits, old Joe and me. Joe probably even more so than I am. To hear him tell it, he came here from Alabama by way of carrier pigeon and was dropped off like a piece of lost mail no one bothered to claim. He likes to say, "I just nosed around till I found out where they kept the junk, and then I stayed there."

There's more to it, though. I can tell by the way his eyes go sad, like they did just now, or the way he'll suddenly go quiet in the middle of a sentence, and I wonder what he left behind in Alabama. I don't ask about it. I don't like people pushing me for my story, so I'm not about to push someone else for theirs. If he wants to tell me, he will. Until then, I'll just wait and wonder.

I stop to pull the flannel away from my butt again. It's not like it's hot outside, but I've been tramping around the scrapyard, and I've worked up a sweat. Sweat that is now stinging the hell out of my raw ass cheeks.

"You been yanking at your drawers all afternoon. You wanna talk about it?" Joe says.

"No."

Joe just shrugs. He doesn't push me for stories, either. I stop and let the ladder rest on the ground for a second. Joe snatches it from my hands. Now I'm the one giving him the stink eye. He just jerks his head in the direction of the CL350.

"Ain't gonna stay daylight forever. Best get busy stripping what you need."

He's right. I let him take the ladder while I head toward one of the dead cars. I'm gonna have to climb over a few to get to the motorbike. Joe needs to organize this whole place. His life would be so much easier. "So would mine," I mutter. I hike a foot onto the bumper of a car and heft myself up. As I make my way across the puzzle of inert vehicles toward the CL, I start thinking again about the inscription. The stone. The house. That big old house. Talk about something that could use some TLC.

∼

I close my eyes and sigh in happiness, my belly so full it's nearly bursting. Hammie's. Totally worth the wait. Although now I've been here a couple hours longer than I meant to be.

Joe and I sit at a metal worktable in the back of the big warehouse shop, a tarp spread over it like a makeshift tablecloth. The rest of the shop is crammed with shelves and inventory, but we're in the back corner where Joe keeps his thousand-year-old desk and file cabinets. It's also where he keeps the water dispenser and a soda vending machine.

Only Joe and I know this, but the soda machine stays unlocked. People put money in, but they really don't have to. Even though I know the secret, I still always wait for Joe to offer. I won't take what's not mine, no matter how many times he tells me I don't have to ask. Lucky for me, I never have to ask. Joe slaps the button on the machine, every time, and pulls out a soda for me. And every time, somehow, the machine is stocked with my favorite. Dr Pepper.

So here I sit, with an ice-cold Dr Pepper fizzing in front of me. My third one, because Joe's generous like that. His flimsy plastic chair squeaks in protest as he leans back and pats his belly. Then he burps. Loud.

"Mmmmm. Room for more," he says. It's the same joke he says after every meal.

"Rude," I answer. The same answer I always give.

He looks over what we have left. His burger is gone. So is mine. There are only the pickles I took off my burger, a handful of cold french fries, and one zucchini fry, deliciously battered and crispy. He opts for a limp french fry and chews reluctantly, but his eyes are on that last zucchini fry. I push the container toward him, the universal food-sharing sign for *you have the last one*.

He pushes the container back to me. I push it toward him again. He eyes the zucchini, then sighs and slides the container back to me. He wants it; I can tell. He'd torn through them like they were candy, but he was still careful to leave half of them for me, "since you're the one who asked for 'em and all," he'd said.

Now we're down to the last one. He wants me to have it; I want him to have it. Stalemate.

"Just take it, Joe. You bought them."

"You think that matters? I surely ain't eating it now. You eat it, or it goes in the trash."

I stare him down, silently calling his bluff. He calls mine when he grabs the container and stands up.

"Wait!" I screech as I reach out and take the last zucchini fry. "Stubborn old man," I say as I pop it into my mouth.

"Yeah? Next time I'll order yours with extra pickles, then," Joe says. I stick my tongue out at him. "And you keep saying you're not a kid." He gets up, turns on a tall industrial lamp, and flicks off the big overhead fluorescents. The shop is officially closed for the day. I stand up, too. I've got a long, slow walk back to my apartment. Joe grabs a push broom from the supply closet, like he does every day before he leaves. When I'm here, I do it for him, but when I reach for the broom this time, he shoos me away.

"Gonna be dark soon. Want me to run ya home?" he asks.

"I've still got some time," I say. I look out at the dim sky, at the sun hanging low over the horizon. I have about an hour before dark. Plenty of time to walk home.

Then I look down at the parts I gathered. A gallon bucket holds a taillight lens, a bracket, a rear fork, hex bolts, hex nuts, washers, rubber grommets. The big stuff rests on the floor beside the bucket. A muffler, a rear fender, and a rear wheel—spokes and all. Individual spokes are nearly impossible to replace, so Joe told me to just pull the whole wheel from the CL. I gratefully took him up on it.

Altogether, it's a big pile of stuff. It's not like I'm gonna be tucking all that into my bookbag, so unless Joe drives me home, it'll have to stay here for now. Lola needs them, I know she does, but I kind of want to take another walk past that big old house. Something occurs to me then. "Joe? You know that house on Mulberry Lane? The big one, needs a lot of work?"

He shrugs, sweeping dust and burger crumbs into a neat little pile.

"The Victorian, with the little chunk of green glass in the sidewalk."

Joe stops sweeping. Looks off into space, the way he does sometimes.

"You do know something," I say. "What is it? Tell me."

That house and that stone have been scratching at my mind all day. As I picked apart the CL350, I thought about the stone and its inscription, about the shock I got when I stepped on it. I thought about the house and how I immediately wanted to start fixing it, putting it back together.

"Just a smatter of gossip from a long time ago," Joe says as he pulls a small pouch from his pocket, unrolling it and pinching out a wad of tobacco. Just before he raises the nasty chunk to his mouth, his eyes catch mine. I shake my head. *Please don't.* I've been trying to get him to quit, telling him it's a dangerous habit, that it causes cancer and all-around mouth rot. So far, he hasn't listened. This time, though, his hand hesitates, and he surprises me by putting the tobacco back into the pouch.

I hide my smile, knowing he won't want to see it. It might make him turn around and stuff two wads into each cheek, just to prove that nobody tells him what to do. I also know he'll probably stick the wad of dried brown poison in his mouth as soon as I'm gone, but it's the first time he's ever given in, and that's a win. Probably not best to point that out, so I bring us back around to what I want to talk about anyway: the house.

"What kind of gossip?" I ask.

"Some sorta scandal back in the '20s."

"It's the '20s now," I say, confused.

Joe laughs, loud and long. "The 1920s, Squirt."

"Oh."

He laughs even harder at that.

"Shut up," I grumble. Joe rests the broom against the wall and pulls out a chair to sit down. My butt can't take any more sitting, so I lean against one of the stocked shelves, the tangy smell of old auto parts filling my nose. I sniff, sneeze, then move down a few feet, away from the dust and rust.

Joe's quiet as he thinks. His eyes have that glazed look people get when they're remembering, the same kind of look he gets when he goes sad. I'm impatient, though, because every second, the sun sinks a little farther down in the sky.

"Gossip?" I nudge again. His eyes shoot to me with a startled look, like he'd forgotten, for just a second, that I was even here.

"I saw her once, just once, the lady who lived there. It was a long time ago. Right before she died," he says.

"She *died*?"

"Not what you're thinking, kiddo. She was old. It woulda been her time. But it seemed like . . ." He moves his mouth around like he's gonna spit, then seems to remember there's nothing to spit. I totally get that feeling. After I got contact lenses, I spent months reaching for my glasses, wanting to push them farther up my face, to adjust them on my nose as I'd done five thousand times a day for five thousand days in a row. Habits are hard to break. And right now, Joe's habit is making his tongue search his cheek for tobacco that's not there. He sucks in his cheeks, then puffs them out, his wrinkled face wrinkling even more, like an accordion, only without the godawful noise.

"It seemed like what?" I ask, hanging on his every word now.

"Seemed to me like she was . . . Well, she seemed sad," he says.

A shiver trembles through my neck, all the way down my back. "What kind of sad?"

Joe's quiet for a long time before he finally says, "The kind of sad that never goes away."

I get the uneasy feeling that Joe's all too familiar with that particular kind of sad.

"She was an odd one," he continues. "Never left that house. Everybody was dying to get a peek inside there, because it never changed, even when the world grew up around it. But she kept it closed up tighter than a mummy's tomb. I was young, working on a road crew, repairing the sidewalk all up and down Mulberry. It was right after—" His throat makes a funny noise, catching on the words. He clears his throat, then says, "It was right after I settled here in town. Forty years ago, give or take. I was shoveling cement." His eyes narrow, like he's seeing it all in his mind. "And there she was, standing in that upstairs window like a ghost. I ain't ever forgot it, that look she had. The sadness. It was all over her, like she was wearing it. Had it wrapped around herself like a cloak. And she just stood there and stared out that window. Like she was looking for something. Waiting for something."

"Or *someone*," I mutter.

"Whaddya mean, Squirt?" he asks, a curious look on his face. I shake my head. I don't know what I meant. I don't even know why I said it.

I push away from the shelves. Joe stands up, but I wave him back down. "I'll walk. Mind if I bring Bari by tomorrow? She's gotta help me bring Lola in."

He brightens up. "I'd surely love to see Bari," he answers. Just like every other human with a heartbeat. I wonder what it must feel like to be so universally adored. Not that I can complain, since I adore her the most.

"Thanks, Joe. For everything."

He grunts and kicks back in his chair. The plastic groans again. I wait a second to see if it might finally drop him on his ass, but the chair holds. Joe, as if knowing what I was waiting for, just laughs and rocks even farther back. I shake my head at the stubborn old goat, open the door, and walk out into the fading light.

I can't get Joe's story out of my head, and when I turn down Mulberry Lane, the house looks different to me now. It looks sad. Like the lady was sad. I stop on the sidewalk and study it. It's just an old, abandoned house. Dark and quiet. I press my foot to the green glass stone. There's no shock. No jolt of pain. It's just a piece of green glass stuck in the concrete.

    I take one last look at the house, then I keep walking. But now I'm thinking about those windows again. Get the boards off, first thing. Then tackle those loose strips of siding downstairs. I bet Wallis would let me snag some wood from the shop. And the rest of the siding might be saved if someone took a sander to it. It would just take time, and some paint . . .

4

SUMMER 1985

The Victrola spun its shellac resin record. The machine still functioned like new, the singer's tinny voice filling the parlor, bright and clear, blending in odd harmony with the jazzy horns of the band. The music of an era long forgotten but not dead. Not yet.

"We're still hanging on, aren't we." Elizabeth smiled sadly at the phonograph, her aged voice rough like sand. "Though you've fared better than I have, I'd say."

The Victrola was as lovely as when her father had first brought it home. Elizabeth remembered all too well the moment the "talking machine" was rolled into the parlor. It was the morning of her eighteenth birthday. Her father's hard eyes had gauged her every reaction, from her initial glee to her hesitant curiosity to, ultimately, her suspicion. It was a bribe, she'd finally realized with a sinking heart. Such was her father's way, to give with one hand while the other took.

Young Elizabeth had wanted so badly to attend college. She hadn't even pined for a coed campus. She would have been happy at Wellesley, Bryn Mawr, Mount Holyoke, or any of the other handful of women's colleges. Her father's answer to those aspirations was to offer the Victrola. She could have music, but no higher education.

There would be no lofty pursuits for her. Marriage and children and a quiet life would have to do.

None of those, it turned out, would be her fate.

Elizabeth's gnarled knuckle swiped an errant tear, but more tears followed, falling softly from her lashes. It wasn't a breakdown; it was resignation. Weariness. Elizabeth was as alone as she'd ever been, and she could feel the hands of the past pulling at her, wanting her to stay in hiding, to reside in her happy memories, where it was safe. To live there and only there. But that place was a refuge, a dream. It wasn't real. She closed her eyes and let the tears dry on cheeks deeply creased with age. The skin around her eyes was wrinkled, her lips paper thin. She was older than old, her hair long and silver, her bones brittle and bent, knees knobby and weak.

"I will still run to you, my darling," she whispered to the room, to the air, to someone she could no longer see. "These old knees will move when I need them to."

It was a promise. Not one she made lightly.

She forced those old knees to stand as she pushed back from the small writing desk, resting her hand for a moment on an open journal. The pages bore her shaky script, as old and frail as her body. Line after line after line after line. She'd filled it full, right up to the very last page.

She picked up a small golden key, ran her thumb over the metal a few times, then slipped the key into her pocket. That was when the music stopped. Elizabeth shuffled to the phonograph. She flipped the record over, replaced the used needle with a new one, then turned the crank. As the music started again, she let her eyes roam the parlor, still her very favorite room in the house. She'd kept the parlor, and the house, much the same as it had been sixty years ago, preferring to spend her time surrounded by things that held the most vivid memories. So vivid she was sure, at times, she could reach out and touch them.

Elizabeth knew it was her imagination when the empty fireplace lit behind her, warming her back, when the front door opened and Patricia walked in, vibrant and young, her gold dress shining and snow in her hair. She knew it was only a memory when a blast of wintry air blew past the late-summer heat to chill her bones. She knew it was but a wish when Patricia's freezing fingers twined with hers, when that beautiful mouth asked, "Are you ready?"

Yes. She was ready.

She picked up the journal and made her slow, careful way to the big staircase in the foyer, and started to climb. She avoided looking at the broken step. She'd had both the post and the stair repaired several times, early on, during her first years alone in the house. But they'd always, somehow, become broken again. The last time, it was from a heavy area rug Elizabeth was dragging up the stairs. She'd lost her grip on it, and it had tumbled back down and slammed right into the weakened post. The post (and the stair) had broken again, and Elizabeth had given up and left it, open and exposed, like a wound that refused to heal. Because, in a way, it was.

She took one stair at a time, one after another after another, until she stood upon the upstairs landing. She stopped to catch her breath, but she didn't linger long; she had work to do.

She opened the first door she came to and stared sadly into the room. The afternoon sun washed over the bed. The bedclothes were rumpled, one side pulled down, pillows piled high against the headboard. A wooden tray on the end table was loaded with pill bottles, a box of tissues, a water pitcher, a cup, and a couple of books. Trashy romances. Elizabeth would never read these, although she chuckled fondly when she saw them.

Elizabeth moved to the bed, and as she gripped the comforter to pull it up, several shining threads on the pillowcase caught her eye. Hair. Elizabeth stared at them, those bright white hairs, and let out a harsh, tearful laugh. That hair would forever haunt her, but she couldn't let it be tossed away like so much nothing. She gathered the delicate strands, gently holding each one she found until she had several dozen or so, and then she turned and left the room.

Continuing down the hallway, Elizabeth entered her own bedroom, lifting up on the door as she turned the handle, years and years of habit ingrained so as to become second nature.

She let her gaze drift around the room, awash in memories. Her eyes fell on a vanity table and mirror tucked against a wall. She searched through the drawers until she found a long matchbox. She dumped the matches, tore a thread from her own sleeve, and tied the hairs together. After depositing them safely into the matchbox, she put the box in the vanity drawer and gently closed it, resting her hand there. Remembering so many moments, good and bad, reliving them all.

A noise outside drew her attention. She pushed off the vanity table and walked to the window. Outside, a small crew of workmen poured wet cement into a large section of the sidewalk. They spread the mixture, leveling it, smoothing it, until it was shiny and flat under the afternoon sun. One of the younger workmen noticed her. He shielded his eyes with one hand as he looked up at her. Elizabeth let her head rest against the glass.

The workers loaded their tools onto a truck, and then they all piled into the long crew cab. The young workman looked up at her again before he got in. After a moment, he closed the door, and they drove away. Elizabeth's eyes fixed on the glimmering surface they left behind. Her fingers massaged her chest, above her heart. Whether the ache was from old age or sadness, the effect was the same. It hurt. Badly.

5

LIBBY

I speed to campus, park, and jump out of the car. Today is the first day of my new class schedule, and it starts with "Designing for the Stage." It was the first open class with *design* in the title, so I grabbed it. I figure I have to start somewhere. But I'm late, and I hate to be late. I run across the quad, headed toward what I hope is the fine arts building.

The registrar sent my new schedule to my phone, and I stop on the stairs to open it, just to make sure this is where I'm supposed to be. It's a small school, but still big enough to be confusing at times, especially since I spent my whole first year on only one side of the campus. I look at the schedule. In addition to my sophomore basics, it's filled with humanities, arts, and design. Nothing at all to do with history, politics, or government.

I'm suddenly overwhelmed. Full of doubt. Scared to death, to be honest. Last night I lucked out, but my parents will find out eventually. I won't be able to avoid Dad's questions about the debate team forever.

The sun shines down, so bright it reflects off my phone screen and throws the light right into my face. I twist the phone to angle away from me, but the damage is done. All I see are shiny spots swimming around me . . . and one bright red dot floating through the sea of sparkles. It moves differently than the others. As my vision clears, I realize it's a girl. She's got the reddest hair I've ever seen. When the sun hits it, it strikes up like a match, like fire. I can't take my eyes off it. Her head turns toward me. Our eyes lock, and time slows . . . but only for a second before I'm literally swept off my feet by strong arms. My squeal is out of reflex, not fear, because I know exactly who has yanked me into the air. That would be Leo. Boyfriend.

"Put me down, caveman!" I slap at his hands, laughing. As soon as he sets me back on my feet, I turn to look for the girl. She's gone.

"Where've you been? I've been calling you," Leo says.

As if on cue, my cell vibrates inside my bag. I dig it out. I have four missed calls from Leo and a text from Mom, just now, asking me to stop by the market on my way home. She needs cream for the chicken Tetrazzini she's making for dinner.

"You skipping civics?" Leo asks, his dimples deep and perfect as he grins.

"It *was* intro to poli, but I, uh . . ." I hold up my phone and show him my new schedule.

Leo lets out a loud hoot, then says, "Daddy's not gonna be happy about that, is he?"

I mutter to myself, "That's not the only thing."

"Oh, the house! Did you get the key? When can I see it?"

"I can't go in until the deed's recorded, but—"

"But it's yours," he interrupts.

"It's mine." Saying it out loud sends a shiver through me, panic and excitement swirling together. Then I'm really swirling, because Leo picks me up and swings me around again. I pinch his arm until he puts me down. I glare playfully at him, then say, "Come to dinner tonight."

Leo looks like I just asked him to unclog a toilet. Or worse. "With your dad? You know I'd rather— Oh. You need a buffer."

I sigh because he's right. Leo is a great buffer. He annoys the crap out of Dad without even trying, so much so that Dad works overtime to contradict everything Leo says about anything, even when he secretly agrees. Case in point: Neapolitan ice cream. Dad has always loved it, but I literally heard him tell Leo, "Neapolitan is a flavor invented for entitled brats who think they should have it all. Strawberry, vanilla, or chocolate. Pick one!" And that was just because Leo said he thought it was cool to have all three flavors for the price of one. Suddenly, Dad hated Neapolitan, and Leo was "just being greedy."

Mom, on the other hand, adores Leo. *Adores* him. It's embarrassing. She would hand-churn a vat of Neapolitan every day if it meant she might get a smile out of Leo. "Those dimples, oh, honey, can you believe those dimples? And all that hair." And omigod does Dad grit his teeth every time she starts. If I can get Leo to the house for dinner, then I know he will preoccupy them, and that gives me one more night to figure out how to tell them that I turned my whole life upside down in a matter of weeks.

"Blow off dinner with the fam, and I'll take you out. We'll celebrate. We can go to Mariani's," he offers, dangling the carrot of my favorite restaurant.

The thought of Mariani's shrimp fra diavolo makes my mouth water. Leo grins even wider now because he knows he almost has me. But I hesitate. Leo's feelings, I think, are more serious than mine, and lately, well, he's ready to act on those feelings. We've been together a couple of months. He's a really great guy, and I like him. I'm just not ready to take the next step. When we first started hanging out, it was fun. We laughed all the time. It felt fresh and new, because it was. Now it feels kind of settled. Like it's on rails.

"I guess I should go home and face the music," I say.

"Why do you have to tell them anything yet? The semester's already paid for. It's not like they check your homework, so they won't know you've changed your major. Let it ride," he states confidently. I was thinking about the house confession, but maybe he's got a point. It's *all* already paid for, the house *and* the semester. Leo is a well-built bag of good genes who is sometimes funny and mostly sweet, but every once in a while, he surprises me by saying something smart. It's perfect, actually. I just won't tell them yet. Any of it. It's a temporary solution, I know, but I'll take what I can get.

"That's . . . I think that might work," I admit.

"Awesome. Now ditch the family dinner so we can celebrate."

"Ha! Nice try, but no." I glance at the time again. I'm officially late. I grab Leo's face, give him a quick peck. "Call you later." Then I hurry up the stairs and into the building.

The professor doesn't even notice when I walk in three minutes late. He's too busy fumbling with his computer. He's not at all what I expected. A mass of messy white hair halos his face, and he wears round, wire-rimmed glasses. His short-sleeved cerulean-blue button-up is topped with a navy bow tie, the old-fashioned kind, not a clip-on. I expected Jonathan Scott in a sleek blazer, not Albert Einstein in a bow tie.

I check the class schedule again: *Fine Arts Building, Room 202, Professor Wallis.*

I glance at the number above the door. This is it. It's a small classroom for a small class. There are only about fifteen students in here. I grab a desk, a little bit away from everyone else. They all seem to know each other and are chatting away while the professor tinkers with his computer, a deep furrow of concentration creasing his brow.

There are several framed pictures on the wall next to me. They're all of stage plays. There's a stage dressed to look like a living room. There's one that looks like the inside of a dive bar, neon beer signs, deer antlers, and everything. One of the stages is even built to look like an outdoor day by the lake. There's grass and sand and something glimmery that looks like water.

Oh! Designing for the *Stage*. Got it.

Flipping through slides on a PowerPoint presentation, the professor grunts when he accidentally opens his photos and they're suddenly projected onto the wall. Life-size, as luck would have it.

"Oh dear, hold on. That wasn't supposed to . . ." he mumbles as he tries to get back to his PowerPoint deck. In the meantime, we're all rewarded with a photo of him on the beach, in bright orange swim trunks, staring out at the ocean. The hair on his back is as white as the hair on his head, making him look like he's been rolled in cotton. Pic after embarrassing pic. Giddy, goofy grins. Smoldering looks right into the camera. I'm dying to know who's taking those pictures, who is with him at the beach, this odd, furry man.

He scrambles, tapping keys, trying to end the slideshow, when a girl limps in. She's dressed in slouchy pants and a tight-fitting Henley, her bookbag slung loosely over one shoulder. It's her hair, though, that really catches my eye. Springy red curls frame her face as she stares at the unfortunate slideshow on the wall. She's the one I saw. It's got to be her. No one else in the world has hair like that. She stares at the progression of photos, then steps up beside him.

"Lemme get that for you, Professor Centerfold," she says as she playfully elbows him out of the way. He steps aside to give her the run of his computer.

"Thanks, Tish," he says, clearing his throat.

Tish. Her blue eyes are almost as bright as her hair. She closes the professor's awkward beach-body slideshow and opens PowerPoint. He sighs gratefully. She clicks her tongue at him and grins. "Nice trunks. Not sure about the orange, though. Blue might be more your color."

"I'll keep that in mind, Wheelie," he says.

Tish drops her head and groans, "Heard about that, did ya?"

Professor Wallis gives her a quick pat on the shoulder and nods. "News spreads fast around here. How's Lola?" he asks.

"She'll live," Tish answers. She looks upset about it, though. Lola must be someone important. Girlfriend, maybe? Tish tosses her bookbag onto a desk. She gives the chair a long, baleful stare before gingerly lowering herself to sit. She looks up just in time to see me staring. My eyes shoot to her butt, and of course, she sees that, too. I feel a hot blush fill my cheeks. She just watches me with those blue, blue eyes. Then she says, simply, "I fell."

"Oh," I mutter like a moron.

I force my attention to the professor. He's flipping through his PowerPoint, showing photos of a stage in progress. The header reads *TWELFTH NIGHT, prod. 2024.* He's talking about design concepts and how to incorporate them into set design as he flips through his slideshow. I stare at the photos he's projecting onto the wall: the exterior of an English manor, being built right before my eyes.

"Every part of a production is vital to making a show work, from the actors to the director to the sound design to the lighting design, and of course, all plays start with the play itself—the writer. The idea, the vision. But bringing that story forth? From the page to the stage? Well, if you ask me, that starts with set design," Professor Wallis says.

The next photo shows students working on a set. Tish is among them, standing on a ladder, a drill in her hand. Then I realize . . . all these students are in one or more of the photos. *They're* building this set. From the ground up.

"So as set designers, it's our job to design a build that works for multiple scenes. How many of these exteriors can double as interiors? How many interiors can be redressed for other rooms? Can the library be turned into a bedroom in the twenty or so seconds you have for the scene change? It's our job to figure this out, then build it. The more creative, the better. It *is* theater, don't forget, and we're all here for the show," he says with a huge, goofy grin.

Professor Wallis's voice fades into the background as I sneak another look at Tish. I pull my attention back to him, trying to listen, but my eyes keep straying to his shirt. To that striking shade of blue. It's the exact color of Tish's eyes. I look at her again . . . and find her looking back at me. She blinks but doesn't look away. Then she shakes her head and turns toward the front, facing Professor Wallis's slideshow, and I'm left to stare at the back of those short, shining curls.

6

LIBBY

I'm still thinking of Tish when I park in the driveway behind Dad's car. Peter stands on the porch, the front door wide open behind him. He watches with a gleeful smirk as I lug my bookbag from the back seat. I reach farther in to grab the small grocery bag with Mom's cream for the Tetrazzini. I also have a surprise for Peter, but he may not get it, the way he's looking at me.

"What?" I ask. "Did I run over a puppy or something?"

He just snickers. His sloppy hair is completely in his eyes. How does he even see around that mess? The Charleston Chew I went out of my way to pick up for him is burning a hole in my bag, but he's not getting it if he keeps up that stupid laughing. The only store that sells them anymore is an old country store at the edge of town. I drove out there to get this treat for my little brother because I'm a good sister, and since the store is just around the corner from Mulberry Lane, I took a short detour to let myself gaze dreamily at my house, knowing that soon, I will open the latch on that wobbly front gate, I will unlock that faded front door, and I will walk inside the Mulberry house after all this time.

"What's going on?" I demand. Peter just stands there, grinning like a shaggy idiot. I start up the front porch steps toward him. "Move. I've got Mom's cream. She needs it to finish dinner."

I push past him to get inside. As soon as my foot crosses the threshold, he whispers, "They know about the house."

Ice shoots through my limbs. "What? How?" I squeak.

Now Peter freezes, his mouth gaping open in surprise. "Omi-GOD. It's true?"

"Peter—"

He points at my face and laughs hysterically. "The golden girl stumbles at last. Enjoy the fall, Miss Perfect. Right on your FACE!"

I'm too panicked to respond to his goading. What? How? When? I scramble to think, but my blood is pumping hard through my ears, and for a fanciful second, I imagine that each thudding heartbeat is shouting *run run run*. Peter has moved to block my way, as if he knew exactly what I'd do. I grab him, staring intently into his eyes.

"Listen, Peter, you owe me. Can you cover for me? Please? Just for a few—"

"Mom! Dad! She's here!" Peter yells into the house.

That little asshole. So much for my accumulated credit. I dig angrily into my bag until my fingers find the Charleston Chew. When I pull it out, Peter's eyes light up, but there's no way he's getting it now. I wave it angrily in his face, then twist it in both hands, smashing and smearing the bar inside the wrapper, totally ruining it. Peter yelps as I sling it as far as I can into the yard. He dashes after the candy like a dog after a bone.

"I hope all your teeth fall out!" I scream at him. "And I hope it hurts!"

"Lib. Come in here, please," my dad's low voice rumbles from inside the house. I can tell from the echo that he's standing in the kitchen.

I breathe in . . . breathe out . . . breathe in—

"Libby Monroe!"

I flinch. I'm nineteen years old. A legal adult—

"Now."

Where is Cam? He should be here, holding my hand, ready to walk this plank with me. I spent all day in a happy homeowner haze because I was counting on Leo's advice getting me through for a while. *Let it ride.* It was solid advice. Well, as solid as a lie can be. But somehow my parents found out anyway. Maybe it was divine intervention. I've never been a liar, so maybe the universe decided *why start now?*

I tighten my grip on my bookbag and walk inside. My parents are in the kitchen. Fuming. If steam coming out of ears were a real thing, the wallpaper would be wafting to the floor in ribbons. I approach Mom, holding out the grocery bag as a kind of peace offering. She doesn't take it. She won't even look at it (or at me), so I set it on the kitchen island with shaking hands.

"Sit," Dad says.

I drop my bookbag to the floor and perch my butt on one of the high barstools at the island. I don't have anywhere to put my hands, so I let them curl into my lap. It looks like Mom's chicken Tetrazzini was abandoned at the assembly stage. It sits in separate components all over the island. Diced chicken breast, shredded Parmesan cheese, chopped onions, minced garlic, herbs, chunks of butter, and a measuring cup half-full of white wine. All awaiting the cream. My eyes linger on the measuring cup, on the wine inside. I'd give anything to grab it and drink it down. But then I'd be in trouble for that, too.

Dad takes the lead. Of course. "We had an interesting visitor today. Eleanor Price."

I gulp. Blink. Gulp again, trying desperately to act like the name means nothing to me.

"Eleanor. Price," he continues. "She's a real estate agent."

I shrug stupidly. Omigod omigod omigod.

"She said she was able to get your key early. Wanted to surprise you."

He slides a silver key onto the island, sets it between the onions and the cheese.

Shiiiiiiit. What am I supposed to say? What *can* I say? Nothing. That's my best play here. Dad's trying to get me to hang myself. Peter falls for it every time. I won't do it. I refuse.

"I asked her what the key was for," he says, "and guess what her answer was."

Oh, I know what her answer was.

Dad just waits. There is no talking my way out of this one.

"I see how you're going to be," he finally says. "Open your phone. Pull up your college account."

Every ounce of blood in my body pools in my feet. I couldn't move if the kitchen was on fire. Someone would have to drag me out. Maybe I should start a fire. A distraction.

"Pull up your account balance," Dad says again, slowly. I'm terrified to do as he says. I'm terrified not to. I don't know what I should do, so my hands stay in my lap and my phone stays in my bag.

"Libby? Honey?" That's Mom, in her crying voice. Since she wouldn't look at me when I came in, I kind of feel okay not looking at her now. Because if I do, I'm going to lose it. I'm going to confess and tell them everything, and right now I'm just trying to think of anything I can say that will get me out of this moment.

"Is this something you cooked up with Cam?" she asks. When I don't answer, she begs, "Tell me someone convinced you to do this, Libby, because I just can't believe you'd do something so foolish. So careless. So . . ." And that's when her voice breaks. Here come the yelling-sobs. "What were you thinking?!" she chokes out on a sob sob sob as she grabs a kitchen towel and wets it, wiping down the already clean countertop, and then, in a pitch so high it could break glass, "Libby Monroe, I just can't believe you! How are you going to pay for college now?!" Yell yell, sob sob sob. I love a lot of things about Molly Monroe, but this isn't one of them. I look at the measuring cup and imagine it shattering, the wine spilling onto the counter, oozing toward me and my parched mouth. That would give her something to clean up.

Peter has slithered back into the house and is watching from the other side of the kitchen. I've seen him sit through many similar scoldings. I'll admit it's pretty terrible to be on the receiving end now. I might have felt sorry for the little jerk, but any sympathy I had for him dries up when I notice the Charleston Chew in his hand, a bit of squashed chocolate peeking from the torn yellow wrapper. Let him choke on his mangled candy bar, the traitor.

"Answer your mother, Libby," Dad says. "I, for one, would love to know how you intend to pay for college now. You won't be getting any help from us, that's for sure."

There it is. His calm, lethally stoic Dad voice. And here is where I cave. Here is where I nod and agree to whatever he says, whatever he decides. I feel my head wanting to bob already because it's my pattern. My habit. I'll say okay. I'll just give in. Let the house go.

Don't give up the house!

The words shoot through me from somewhere deep inside, like a mantra: *Don't give up the house, don't give up the house, don't give up the house . . .*

"Do you realize how much you've disappointed us?" he says in his I-know-what's-best-for-you voice.

The beautiful Victorian on Mulberry Lane. The house that was meant to be mine. The house that *waited* for me. He's going to take it away. He's going to make me give it up.

My house.

Words that I feel more than hear. *My house, my house, my house...*

"We're not made of money, Libby. And even if we were, I wouldn't give you a penny, not one cent, not after what you've done." This is his do-as-I-say voice.

It's time for me to agree now, time to tell him that he's right and that I've made a huge mistake. Time to ask forgiveness, to ask him to fix it for me. That's what he wants. But I remain quiet. I see his teeth grind. He's never had to be this angry with me before. It's confusing him, and it's confusing me. Why can't I just give in?

Dad takes a deep breath, as if to reset. There's a fresh hardness in his eyes. And this time, his voice carries a sharp edge that scrapes along my emotions. "What would your Gammy think?" Tears rush to my eyes. I fight them as he says, "The utter disregard you're showing for your grandmother, who loved you so much." Unrelenting for even a second. "She sold her house, gave up her home so you would have money for college, and you spent it on a run-down shack that isn't even worth tearing down."

That's the one, the voice that had me majoring in political science, resigned to a future I didn't want. The voice that has been planning my life so methodically for nineteen years.

"Your Gammy would be so disappointed by what you've done," he says then, sliding the blade all the way in.

A rogue tear breaks free to trickle down my cheek. I swiftly wipe it away, but he sees it and leans back with a triumphant sigh. He takes my hand, gentle now that he smells victory, now that he's won. I scrub my face with my free hand.

He pats my hand and says, "It's okay, Lib. I've talked to Josiah Reed over at the courthouse. He's going to pull the deed so we can get you out of it. Just let me handle everything. I'll take care of it . . ."

My mind mutes the rest of what he's saying as something clicks in my brain, like a rusty cog suddenly switching on. And when it starts to turn, slowly, painfully, so many things fall into place. Those mental lists I make every morning—they all come to me in the voice of my father. Every time a thought runs through my head, it's his voice I hear. It has always been his voice. His. Not mine.

Except for the house. Buying that house had nothing to do with him and everything to do with me. Now this new voice is urging me on, telling me to stay strong, making me either incredibly brave or unbelievably reckless. Maybe both. Before I realize it, I'm pulling my hand from his. I watch in wonder, and a little horror, as my fingers clench around the key. My hand trembles violently, the silver quivering in my grip, and I hear myself say, in a shaky voice, "I'm not giving it up."

"Libby!" Mom squelches. She lunges for the key, but my hand curls tightly around it.

Images race through my mind:

Gammy's face. This *is* what she would want me to do. I'm so very sure of it now.

The house. Empty, alone, waiting for me.

The young woman in the window. My reflection. Me, inside my house.

There's no good explanation I can give my parents that will make them understand, but I belong to that house as much as it belongs to me. So, as scared as I am, as trembly as my legs are, I find my feet and stand to face my dad. "I can't do it, Dad. I won't."

Dad just sighs and shakes his head. "Libby. Sit down."

The key gets hotter in my hand. It's my imagination, surely, but it bolsters me somehow. I take a breath and borrow the eyes from the reflection in the window yesterday, piercing and intense. I let them stare into my father the way they stared into me. Then, with a strength I've never heard come out of my own mouth, I say, "The Mulberry house is mine."

Brave. And very, very reckless.

"Ha!" Peter barks out a loud, astounded laugh. He slumps into a kitchen chair, the last of the ruined candy bar falling from his grasp, hitting the floor with a sticky plop. Mom peals out a long, high whine of disbelief. Dad's face turns purple, and the blue vein on his temple throbs, pounding as hard as my heart is right now. I feel faint, sick, but that voice inside me tells me to hold firm just a little longer.

And then Dad loses it like I've never seen him lose it before.

7

LIBBY

I thought I had my way all laid out in front of me. I thought I was so smart, so clever.

Now here I am, garbage bags piled high in my back seat, a line of black Hefty mountains in my rearview mirror. I don't even know what all I have in there. Dad was still bellowing at me to "GET OUT!" as I fumbled to grab my laundry hamper, which was only half-full. I was able to empty a few drawers into it. Underwear, socks, loungewear. Peter was *kind* enough to throw some garbage bags at me. His way of helping. I hurriedly filled them with armloads of anything I could, all while Dad followed me around, reminding me how much I was about to lose, how much he would withhold from me if I didn't "stop this insanity right this minute!"

I couldn't say anything. There were too many tears, so many it was hard to even catch my breath. I just kept packing and tried to shut out his tirade.

I stop the car in front of the Mulberry house. It radiates in the golden-hour glow; this big, beautiful thing that has cost me so much more than money. I turn into the driveway and pull all the way up under the porte cochere. In its day, it would have sheltered a horse-drawn carriage, then, after the turn of the century, some really sweet roadster that got maybe eight miles per gallon. But tonight, and every night from now on, it will house the hundred and fifty worn-out horses that labor under the hood of my ten-year-old Toyota. Dad isn't wrong about the money. We don't have a lot to spare, but there are student loans, grants, things we could have applied for. It didn't have to be the end of the world.

I reach for my bookbag, opening the side zipper for my phone. I'm hoping that Cam has called and I somehow missed it. I called him on the way over and cried my way through a rambling voicemail, telling him how my dad hates me, my mom won't stop sobbing, my brother can't stop laughing, and I'm alone, cut off.

I've always known Dad was controlling, but his fury was next level. His words echo in my mind, bouncing around in stereo. "You've never done one damn thing on your own, and this is where you want to start? With a tear-down house, no money, and no help? Because that's what you're getting from me: nothing. Don't come back here asking for help. Don't come asking for favors. Don't come asking for anything. You won't get it. Not here. Not anymore!" His words cracked like thunder over my head and were twice as loud.

Now I stand face-to-face with my newfound freedom and a whole lot of fear. For the first time in my life, there is no safety net. I have Leo and I have Cam, but neither of them can replace the support of a parent, emotionally or financially. Is this how baby birds feel when they're shoved from the nest and suddenly expected to fly? Tears well up again, but I can't let them win. I've wanted this house for years. All my life. Now here I am, the key in my pocket and the deed in my name. I rub my thumb across the skin of my right palm, where the key had felt so hot earlier. I look down, half expecting to see its little jagged outline there like a warm red tattoo. But there is no key-shaped tattoo. Just a lifeline that maybe seems a bit shorter than it was this morning. I definitely feel like I lost a few years today.

I wiggle my fingers into the front pocket of my jeans and pull out the key. The metal catches the last of the setting sun and throws its reflected light onto the doorknob, like the key knows exactly where it wants to go. The door looks dark, covered in shadows, and somehow it feels like opening that door will change everything. Permanently. Maybe if I don't open it, if I just go back home—

A light comes on.

I jerk back, startled. I didn't even see it there, mounted right over the door. A tiny lantern-looking thing with a small bulb that buzzes and flickers, like it's waking up from a deep, long sleep. A motion light, maybe? A short in the wiring? Whatever; at least it means Eleanor was right about the electricity. Its timing, though, is perfect, because now the door is lit up like a glow-in-the-dark invitation that I can't resist. The key slips easily into the lock; the door opens with a quiet snick. I step inside, holding my breath in pent-up expectation, and then . . .

. . . nothing happens. No shaft of heavenly light. No bells ringing, no angels singing. Just a dim entryway and a thick, musty smell. I shove the door open wider to let in some fresh air, and that little light above it goes out. I whirl to look at it. Cobwebs hang off the black iron frame. With shaking fingers, I reach up to touch the fixture, hoping I didn't imagine it, that light shining on the door, that very obvious invitation to come inside. I sigh and relax when I feel the warm glass. I'm still sane. Good.

I drop my bookbag onto the floor and move farther inside, fumbling my hand around the nearest wall in search of a light switch. My fingers find a panel with a small button in the middle. I press it. A light comes on under a translucent glass fixture on the ceiling. Then my eyes are caught by a wide staircase in the front room. The rosy sunset streams through the grime-streaked windows, casting the stairs in a sublime glow. It's not angels singing, but it'll do.

There's a small series of hooks on the wall near a skinny closet door. I hang the house key, and my car keys, and walk toward that staircase.

The sun has warmed the whole area, a soothing heat that surrounds me as I step into the foyer, into the fading light. Dust motes hover high in the air, reflecting the sun, making me wrinkle my nose against a sneeze as I move up the staircase. Halfway up, I turn to survey what I can see of the house. Furniture, lots of it, covered in limp sheets. Little odd-shaped ghosts. The whole place has a sort of sag to it, a kind of slope-shouldered weariness. I give the banister a soft rub, soothing the old wood as I would an old friend. "We'll get you fixed up. I don't know how yet, but we will," I promise.

I keep moving up the stairs. One of the steps has a deep crack down the center. Then I see the banister post. It's been snapped in two, the jagged pieces canted away from each other. There's something visceral about it, like looking at a fractured bone. I yank my eyes away, step over the cracked stair, and keep climbing.

The top landing opens into a hallway that leads to a darker part of the house, cut off from the light downstairs. I search the walls for a switch. Nothing . . . nothing . . . nothing . . . until my fingers come across a niche in the wall, a deep indentation built into the plaster. I feel around inside and grab something cold, something metal. A brass candlestick holder, the stub of a white candle still nestled in the well. Strings of hardened wax pool around the small base. I feel around inside the niche some more and come out with matches—

My head whips around at a sudden . . . sound? No, not a sound. A *feeling*. A feeling that I'm not alone in the house. I hurry back to the stairs and look down. I wait and wait and wait. Nothing. My reactionary goose bumps fade. I strike a match, pressing its tiny fire to the blackened wick. It pops and cracks, then settles into a steady flame. The hallway brightens just enough for me to continue my walkabout, exploring the closed doors along each side of the hall.

The first door opens into a bathroom with beautifully tiled floors and a huge claw-foot tub. I walk over to turn on the faucet. It squeaks and rattles as I hold my breath. *Come on, come on.* Finally, brown water spurts from the tap, then runs clear. Relieved, I turn it off. I make a mental note to text Eleanor tomorrow to thank her. No power would have been a problem. No water would have been a nightmare.

I leave the bathroom and move on, floorboards creaking under my feet. I open the second door. It's a bedroom. The windows are boarded up from outside. More sheeted furniture. Something about this room makes me sad, just the vibe of it, like one of those bad dreams that you can't remember, but the feelings stick around for days after.

The candle flickers as I head farther down the hallway. I come across some wall sconces, but I can't find a switch. The candle will have to do. I open the third door.

A linen closet. A few folded towels sit on the middle shelf next to a couple of washcloths. There's a box of detergent on the bottom shelf, and a glass bottle full of clear liquid. A handwritten label reads *Lamp Oil.* I pick up the detergent box. The powder has congealed into a heavy white chunk. I drop the box back onto the shelf, where it lands with a thud.

At the end of the hallway, the candle flickers again. It's almost burned down, just a tiny bit of wick left. I reach for the doorknob. It turns easily, but the door doesn't budge. I step closer and try again, but this time, as if by instinct, I lift up on the door as I turn the knob. The door swings open. I smile and hold the candle in front of me, pushing light into the room.

It feels different in here. It feels good. These windows are boarded up, too, but soft twilight filters through the slats. Not bright enough to see by, but enough to give the room a dim haze. I'm halfway across the room before I realize it, pulling draped sheets from the furniture, tossing them into a messy heap on the floor. Without looking, and with an accuracy that would have startled me had I been paying attention, I set the candle on a newly uncovered end table and turn directly toward the foot of the four-poster bed, yanking the sheet from a big, rectangular object on the floor, coughing as I wave away the sudden dust cloud.

It's an elaborately carved hope chest. Beautiful. I kneel down and pull at the latch. It doesn't budge. There's a keyhole embedded in the front closure. I trace my hands across the surface, front, back, and sides, hoping the key is taped against the wood. It's not. My hands pat the floor around the area. No key. I bend to look under the bed, but the candle's light doesn't reach all the way under here. I squint into the darkness, trying to force my eyes to see what they cannot. I could kick myself for leaving my phone (with its megawatt flashlight app) in my bag downstairs. I inch closer to the bed, about to plunge my arm into that shadowed void, when I hear it:

The soft creak of a floorboard right behind me.

And breathing.

Right . . .

. . . behind . . .

. . . me.

Suddenly I'm hyperaware of everything. I hear every molecule of air moving, see every grain of dust on the floor, feel every thump of my pounding heart, pumping cold sweat now instead of blood. The stickiness of it blooms under my arms and behind my knees and on the back of my neck, where I feel . . . a breath . . . ruffle the tiny hairs there. Oh. GOD.

Then I feel a rush of air as a whisper breathes into my ear, "What are we looking for?"

Fear spikes through me and I shoot off the floor with a shriek, launching myself directly into the body behind me. I land sharply on my hip, the thud rattling through my bones. It should hurt, but the only thing I can feel right now is panic. I roll onto my knees, about to run, when a hand darts out and grabs my ankle. That's when I totally lose it. I scream bloody murder, twisting away to scramble backward, kicking and flailing.

Someone screams in pain, then yells, "What the hell, Libs?"

It's all I can do not to pee my pants as I go limp with relief. I flop back onto the floor, arms and legs sprawled, and start to laugh. It's Cam, it's Cam, it's Cam.

He groans, gets to his feet, and kicks lightly at my legs. "What's so funny? You scared the hell out of me."

"I scared *you*? You're the one who snuck up on me like a serial killer."

"Dramatic. And no, I did not. You left the side door wide open. I was literally yelling your name, but you were so glued to whatever you were looking for, I guess you didn't hear me," he says, helping me up. "It was kinda bizarre, actually," he continues as I brush floor dust from my jeans. "The candle was making you look all weird and glowy."

"Yeah, well, everybody looks glowy in candlelight. That's kind of the point."

I throw my arms around him and hug him tightly to me, so, so happy he's here. Cam just hugs me back, rocking a little from side to side, and says, "That bad, huh?"

Tears swarm my eyes, and I nod, pulling back to look at him. His finely structured bones, at once beautiful and handsome, are like carved ebony, and those dark eyes, unfairly wide and round, have been my touchstone for as many years as I can remember.

"I'm so glad you're here. Mom and Dad—" My voice cracks.

He pulls me into his arms again, and I turn my head into his neck, wiping my wet face on the collar of his shirt. He jerks away. "Not on this shirt, not this shirt!"

Before I can ask why the shirt is so important, he's already released me and is searching the walls for a light switch. "Good old Dan and Molly Monroe," he grumbles. "Score one for the quarterback and the homecoming queen and their picture-perfect parenting skills." Then abruptly, "Where the hell are the lights in this place?"

As if on cue, the candle stub sputters, then goes out. Both Cam and I shriek in surprise, grabbing at each other in the dark. Laughing, we fumble our way out of the room.

Cam complains about my parents all the way back to the living room. ". . . They're just so *basic*." He spits the word like it's the worst insult ever. To Cam, it kind of is.

"Mom's not so bad. She's got her own way, that's all."

"If you live in 1950," Cam says, adding under his breath, "with all the other breeders."

"Well, I can't be too mad that they decided to breed."

Cam throws an arm around my shoulders. "True. They made you, I'll give them that. But they also made Peter, so maybe it's a wash."

"He really is a jerkwad," I admit.

"Finally, she comes to the dark side!" Cam exclaims. "Purge them all!" I snort. He laughs, too. "Molly makes a mean lasagna, though. We'd miss that."

"We would," I agree solemnly. "And she's always loved and supported you."

Cam knows I'm right about that. My mom immediately accepted Cam's transition, even before his own parents did. "Yeah. All right," he says, "Molly stays."

I wait, because I know it'll only take a second for him to . . .

"Fiiiine. I don't want to purge anyone. I'm just pissed they hurt you." There's my sweet Cam who couldn't hurt a soul. He grabs me up in another hug and says, "It's gonna be okay."

That's when I smell it. Cologne. His super-expensive fancy cologne. The one he keeps in his underwear drawer, in the dark, in its original box so it lasts longer. The one he only wears on special, special, very special occasions.

"Whaaaat's going on?" I ask as I take a step back to really look at him. He looks good, like he made a hell of an effort. His purple button-up shirt fits his slender frame perfectly, tucked into his favorite jeans, and paired with his gray high-tops.

He straightens under my scrutiny, as if trying to steal a couple of inches from the air. Cam's not a big person. About my height, but thinner. If he were taller, he'd be called lanky. He's not tall, though. It used to really get to him, but last year, when he finally accepted who he was meant to be, he claimed his confidence, and he's been nothing but strut ever since. But here, now, he looks unsure.

"Very handsome," I say. "Now tell me why you look and smell so good."

"I may have a date. With a guy."

"With a— What? I thought—"

"Yeah, well, it's all kinda fluid, ya know," he says shyly.

"When?" I screech.

"In about thirty minutes. But when I heard your message—"

"I mean when did this happen? Who is he? Why didn't you tell me?"

Cam mumbles out something I can't quite hear. I give him a pinch, and he says more clearly, "Instagram. My post. You know . . . the one?"

And suddenly we're right back in that moment, holed up in my room, Cam's trembling thumb hovering over the Share button. Me with a white-knuckle grip on his arm, loving him, terrified for him, my lips pressed to his shoulder as he shared the photo with the world, the one that would celebrate his true identity, his true self. Then we both squealed in glee, in terror, in astonishment that he'd actually done it.

I look at him now and see everything he was and everything he is and everything he's going to be. Standing up to my father was scary, but it was nothing compared to what Cam does every day. Cam is the brave one. He watches it all cross my face and says, "Love you, too, Libs."

I take his hand, twine our fingers. "So . . . date?" I prod him.

Cam's fingers tighten around mine as he says, "He saw the post and he DMed me and—"

"Wait. When was this? What—"

Cam starts talking quickly now, something he does when he's very, very nervous.

"Look, I know we haven't talked about it, and I wasn't expecting to meet this guy, I really wasn't, but he's just, I don't know, I like him, what I know of him, anyway, and we've been talking on the phone and chatting online, but he knows everything, okay? I told him about everything, literally *everything*, and he's cool, or he seems to be, anyway, and I just don't want to limit myself, that's all, and look, I wanted to tell you, but I also needed to figure out how *I* was feeling about it all, and omigod, Libs, it all just sort of happened—"

"I get it," I assure him. "Things are changing really fast. It's okay."

He eyes me, then motions to the house. "Things are changing fast for both of us."

He's right. And this is why I won't be upset that he didn't tell me this huge thing that's going on with him. We all need the time we need to process the things we need to process.

"Tell me his name, at least," I coax, smoothing my hands over Cam's already perfectly pressed shirt. The fabric is stiff under my fingers. He's ironed it, with starch. This date really is a big deal. Anytime Cam pulls out an iron, it's a big deal.

"Horatio," he says.

"Well, Horatio is going to fall madly in love with you. How could he not?" I say, straightening his collar, which is also already perfect. He rolls his eyes and pats my arm.

"Okay, Miss Molly," he says, laughing at my cringe as I yank my hands away from his shirt. How many times have I seen my mother do this very thing to Dad or Peter: straighten a collar, tighten a tie, adjust a sleeve?

Cam laughs. "Don't worry, Molly Monroe would never have the guts to tell Dan Monroe to shove it." Then he says proudly, "But you sure did."

My stomach coils, remembering what I'd said. What Dad had said. I block it all from my mind and try to focus on Cam's big night instead.

"So, where are you going? For your date?" I ask.

"We're meeting at Mariani's for dinner."

I nod, but don't dare mention that Leo was trying to get me to go to that very restaurant tonight. Cam doesn't understand the whole Leo thing. He thinks it's not a good fit, but I don't want to think about that right now, either.

"Get the shrimp for me? Or at least wave to it on the menu?" I pretend-beg.

"You *know* I'm getting the shrimp." Cam grins.

"You said you're meeting him in thirty?" I ask casually.

"Well, I want to get there a little early, scope it out from the car, you know, but I can spare another ten," he says. I slip my arm through his and walk him to the still-open side door.

"So . . . enough time to help me unload the car?" I ask, and now my begging isn't pretend.

Cam recoils. "Did I say ten minutes? I meant ten minutes *ago*."

"Please? Before it gets dark." I grab him before he can run away.

~

Cam honks at me as he pulls out of the driveway, then suddenly stops, rolls down the window, and sticks his head out to say, "Depending on how things go, maybe I'll see you later?"

"I sincerely hope I don't hear from you until tomorrow. Late tomorrow. I hope you're . . . sleeping in." Cam blushes and, in a moment of shyness, buries his face in his hands and screams. I laugh, already anticipating the delicious phone call I'll get tomorrow night detailing the exploits of his first date with a man. My mind is still blown.

Cam kissed me one time. Only once. We were sixteen, young and yearning for love. The kiss surprised both of us, especially when I kissed back with everything I had. We were shooting for the real thing, hoping our friendship could make the leap to something more. We ended up wiping our mouths, matching grimaces on our faces. Then Cam said, horrified, "I love you, but . . . *ew*." We'd nearly rolled off the bed in a fit of laughter, but we were a little sad, too. It would have made everything so easy if that shoe had fit.

"Be safe!" I yell to him as he drives away. He flings one hand out the window in a sign that says yes, he heard me, and yes, he'll be safe. I head back into the house, kicking garbage bags out of the way so I can close the door.

It only takes a few minutes to find the switch in the living room. A large fixture comes on overhead. It doesn't give a ton of light, but it's better than nothing. A few more minutes, and I've stripped the room of sheets. I'll come back to take a good look at all this furniture later, but right now I'm looking for a small lamp, or some more candles, anything that I can use in the bedroom upstairs. My iPhone may have to do, but I'd have to hold it the whole time, so that's not ideal. There are several lamps in this room. Two tall standing lamps and three desk lamps. They all have colored glass domes and look expensive. But not one of them has a light bulb. Then I come across a delicate glass lantern tucked into one of the built-in shelves along the wall.

An oil lamp!

It has a big round bulb at the bottom for the oil, a tall, curved globe on top, and a little glass handle for carrying. I'm immediately in love with everything about it. I hurry back up the stairs to the linen closet. A few minutes later, I'm sitting on the hallway floor with the lantern, the lamp oil, and a box of matches. There was a little oil still in the bottom of the lamp when I found it, so I'm hoping the wick is already soaked. I pour a little more oil into the base, just in case, then close it up tight.

I strike a match and cross my fingers (I literally cross my fingers) and hold the tiny fire to the wide cloth wick. My heart flutters as a corner of the cotton begins to burn, and when a large, bright flame comes alive, I release the breath I didn't know I'd been holding.

"Yes yes yes yes yeeessssss!" I squeal happily as the hallway is filled with light. I look up and around. The wallpaper is a soft yellow color, thick, like it's made of . . . *Wait.*

I settle the glass globe over the flame and pick up the gleaming lantern, careful not to slosh it too much. Holding the light in front of me, I touch the wall. It's not wallpaper exactly, but a rich, satiny cloth that shimmers when the light hits it, so different from the boring beige paint I grew up with. I let my fingers trail along the textured fabric until I reach the bedroom.

I've never used an oil lamp before, never even held one, but it feels surprisingly natural to juggle it with my left hand while my right hand pushes open the bedroom door. The warm light reveals the room more fully. Like the hallway, the walls are covered in thick fabric. These have a light creamy sheen, not quite white, but not quite ivory, shaded light orange in the places where the lamplight hits. It feels like being inside a warm cloud. I set the lantern down on the table, next to the candlestick holder, and turn toward the chest. Time to find that key.

"If I were a key, where would I be?" I whisper to myself, my eyes already scouting out the room's various hiding places. A dresser. Nightstands. Two wingback chairs. A reading nook next to the window. I stop for a moment to relish that—a reading nook!

There's a standing mirror and a vanity table, with a velvet chair tucked neatly into place. Six beautifully carved perfume bottles, in all different shapes and sizes, are deliberately arranged, with an empty space in the center. I pick one up, open the cap, and give it a sniff. My head snaps back and my eyes water. It's cloying and noxious, like four hundred church ladies packed into one tiny glass vial. Even Gammy wouldn't have worn this. I put it back, then pull out the velvet chair and sit at the vanity.

The mirror is hazy, so I wipe it with the sleeve of my shirt. I look at myself in the old mirror, the bedroom reflected behind me. The glass lantern casts the room, and me, in a sepia-toned glow, making me look like a modern girl in an antique photograph. I gather the ends of my hair in my hands and hold it up to my chin, the illusion of a bob cut. I stare at my reflection. Something about the image staring back at me makes me shiver, so I drop my hair.

If I were a key, where would I be?

I open the vanity drawers. Lots of old makeup, dried-up and cracked. Brushes, ribbons, clips, combs. An ancient curling iron with a thick cloth cord. More perfume bottles. I leave them where they are. The last drawer has only one thing inside. A long, narrow matchbox, the kind that holds those long fireplace matches. I shake it. It sounds empty, but I slide it open anyway.

It's *not* empty. Inside are a couple dozen silver-white hairs, tied together with a piece of blue thread. The hairs are so thin and there are so few of them, it's almost like they're not even there. But someone took great care to gather these hairs and bind them, so I gently put them back and close the lid. Is that what a life comes to when it's all said and done? A few hairs in a box?

I shake off the sudden melancholy and push back from the vanity.

Digging around the reading nook nets several really great finds. Some poetry books, some modernish fiction (1970s and '80s), and tons of classics. I find a dog-eared copy of Shakespeare's sonnets. Mary Shelley's *Frankenstein*. And sitting on the wide windowsill, alone, a dark blue book. The light catches the gold lettering on the spine. *Wuthering Heights*. I pick it up. It's been there so long I have to blow dust off the cover. There's no jacket, just the worn hardback. I set it gently on the nook bench and resume the hunt for the key.

The large mahogany dresser is full of clothes. Suddenly excited, I run to the closet. It's there that I hit a jackpot of vintage gold. I pull out a midnight-blue dress. It looks like it's from the 1920s, the kind you'd wear to an afternoon tea, or on a day out on the town, with a hat and gloves. It's silky and loose, with a low-slung waist and a loosely tied bow on the side. I quickly riffle through the other clothes. All beautiful. All in unbelievably perfect condition. I hold the blue dress up to myself as I eye the other garments. Then I stop myself. I'm not shopping for clothes. I'm looking for a key. I reluctantly hang the dress back up and keep searching.

There's nothing in the nightstands except some tissue, a few newspapers, and a handful of bobby pins. But no key. I can't bear to think of destroying the chest to get inside. And my brain hurts. Today has been a lot, and it's lasted so long, and the bed looks so inviting. It's early, but I'm tired. Emotionally and physically. It will all be here tomorrow. And so will I.

I leave the oil lamp burning, not ready to face the full dark just yet. It should be weird to crawl into an unknown bed, however many years old, having no idea who last slept here, but the smell of the bedding is comforting in some weird way, and when I turn down the covers, the sheets are clean and fresh. I shuck my jeans, slide in, and pull the blankets up around my shoulders. I'm immediately filled with a sense of calm. I feel safe here. I close my eyes and wait for sleep to take me.

The light of the oil lamp flickers brightly outside my closed eyelids, and I hazily wish that I'd turned it down, just a little, just enough to sleep. Without opening my eyes, I can feel the light grow dimmer, darker. I crack open one eye to glance at the oil lamp. The flame burns low.

Impossible. Either the wick isn't fully soaked, or it's too old to burn right, but I still give it a quiet thank-you as I close my eyes again and vow to change the wick tomorrow. Sleep comes fast then. It's the first night in weeks that there are no dreams of the party, the backyard shindig. No dreams of this house. Just a deep, heavy rest.

8

TISH

One good thing about this apartment is the water pressure. The bad thing is it has a tiny water heater and too many roommates. I've only been in the shower five minutes and it's already cold. I force myself to stand under the stream anyway, ignoring the chill.

I'm dragging ass this morning, even worse than yesterday. Not because I was sleeping in, but because I *couldn't* sleep. Not after the dream that woke me up at 2:00 a.m. There was snow. I was cold. Tired. No, not tired. I was *weary*. The girl from stage design class, the new girl, was there. Her eyes were wide and scared. I wanted so badly to reassure her, but reassure her about what? I turn my face into the cold water and remember the weight of her leaning over me. I try to imagine it now, but daydreams aren't like night dreams, where everything feels more real.

A loud pounding on the door shocks me out of my thoughts. Good luck getting ten minutes of privacy in this place. "I'm in the shower," I yell.

"I need my flat iron," Alisha, one of my roommates, yells back, "and Jam brought home bagels. We saved you one." At least there's that. I douse myself in the icy spray again, twist the shower knob, and grab my towel. Time to face the day.

Bari's in my closet-room when I get there. She's on my tiny bed, scrolling through her phone. She sighs as I walk in, as if she's been waiting ten years, not ten minutes. I roll my eyes. I'm not in the mood today. Spending a Saturday with my mother never puts me in a good mental space, but doing it on no sleep? That cranks the suckage right up to twelve. I go to my crates and start digging through my clothes.

"How's the tailbone?" Bari asks, still looking at her phone.

"Worse."

She looks up. "What do you mean? Lemme see."

Bari and I have been changing in front of each other since before either of us had anything to look at. We could pick out each other's naked parts in a lineup. So it's easy now to just drop my towel and turn my bare ass to face her.

"Omigod! Tish!"

I know exactly why she's freaking out. The strawberry pancakes have morphed into blueberry cobbler.

"I've never seen a bruise that big. Does it hurt?" she asks.

"Is the sky blue?" I grab a pair of boxers, pull them on. "Sitting down is a freaking nightmare," I grumble while wrangling into my sports bra. I find a black Henley on the floor. Smells clean enough. I pull it on and look around for pants.

"Gonna be a long ride home, then," Bari says. "I'll try to avoid any potholes."

"Trust me, I know how bad it's going to be."

Lola is still at Joe's, half put back together, but my ass isn't anywhere close to ride-ready anyway, so I'm riding with Bari. I dig around for anything that might be soft enough to wear. Joggers? Meh. Jeans and flannel? Maybe. The black coveralls I wear when I'm working tech at the theater? That might be an option. All black. Feels like a funeral anyway. Decisions, decisions.

"The later we are, the more pissed she'll be," Bari sings, her nose back in her phone.

"I don't give a shit," I say as I reach for my jeans. Bari's head snaps up. I don't usually talk about my mother that way. My go-to is to be as nice as possible and pretend that I don't care if she loves me or not. That's pathetic. I'm pathetic.

"Will Bill be there?" she asks.

"Is Bill ever *not* there?" I answer.

I fling the jeans back into the crate and grab my blacks instead. They're looser, less chance of rubbing against tender skin. I glance at Bari in the mirror. She's still staring at me.

Finally, I snap at her, "Do you mind?"

She eyeballs me for a few more seconds, then stands and heads toward the door with a curt "Hurry up," and with that, she leaves. She does close the closet door behind her, which I appreciate. Even when I'm making her crazy, she's still good to me. Or so I think, until I walk into the kitchen a few minutes later to find her eating my bagel. Blueberry. With strawberry cream cheese. My favorite.

"I hate you," I tell her, grabbing a soda from the fridge. No Dr Pepper here. That's a treat I buy for myself never. I scrounge for the first thing I can get my hands on that's cold, caffeinated, and fizzy. I finally find a lame-ass diet soda. It'll do.

"That's Hannah's," Bari says around a mouthful of *my* bagel.

"She ate my string cheese. She owes me," I reply as I pop open the tab. The crack and hiss make me groan happily.

"You should at least leave her a note," Bari mumbles.

"Says the girl eating a stolen bagel," I snark. I glare at her as she smirks, slathers on more cream cheese, and takes another bite. I stare at the disappearing bagel. God, I'm hungry. I'm thinking about begging her to share when she slides a small bag across the table. Her finger crooks, beckoning me to the table.

"Come on, now. Here's a sweet treat for my grumpster," she teases, lifting the corner of the paper to reveal another blueberry bagel. Things are looking up.

9

TISH

"You got *married*?" I hear myself ask, feeling like I've been shanked.

"We just thought it was time," Bill says.

"Oh, did you, Bill?" I say, not hiding my snark, because screw this guy.

"Tish," Mom warns.

They "just thought it was time" to get married. I would have appreciated a heads-up. I move my lunch around on my plate. Dry meatloaf with a blop of ketchup on top. Mom eats tiny bites of hers, while Bill shovels meat into his mouth. He has no worries, clearly.

Bill's daughter, Ava, stares down at her plate. She's just a kid, twelve-ish, but she's more like the daughter my mom always wanted, and it's so obvious it stings. Ava's pretty hair is pulled back in a French braid, exactly the kind of braid Mom used to put in my hair before I chopped it all off in a fit of defiance. Mom never forgave me for that.

Sixth-grade picture day. Until that morning, my red hair had always been long and curly. Too long and too curly. It would have been beautiful on some other girl. It was beautiful on my mother, just not on me. I hated it. So that morning, I hacked it all to hell. My curls, wouldn't you know it, became springier than ever, uneven coils sprouting from my head. Total backfire.

Mom had stared and stared. Tears welled up in her eyes. I couldn't figure out why *she* was crying when it was *my* hair. Then she said, "Why did you— *Why*, Tish?"

She stared for another horrified minute, then walked out. She didn't look at me the whole drive to school. Even when we pulled up to the curb, she never took her eyes off the windshield. I picked at my loose-fitting cargo shorts, waiting for her to say something. Anything. Even her yelling would have been better than her silence. But she didn't make a sound. I got out of the car. She just sat there, staring out the windshield. Behind me, the school bell rang. Finally, I left her there and walked into the school building, looking like something the vacuum cleaner spit out.

That awful haircut was how I first met Bari. I was in the bathroom, hating my reflection, when she walked in. I knew who she was. Everyone knew Bari Khatri. And of course, she had to walk into this very bathroom, on this very day, when I looked like a jagged, janky jack-in-the-box clown. Mom was right not to look at me. I wasn't worth looking at. But beautiful Bari Khatri, whose hair was always sleek and shiny and perfect, eyed my haphazard haircut, crossed her arms, arched one brow, and said, "Rock star."

I sat with Bari at lunch that day. And every day after that.

If Bari were here now, like she's supposed to be, this would be much easier, but when we got to Bari's house, Paps was having a hard time. She didn't want to leave him. I totally understand, and I'm not mad about it, but still, I really wish she were here. That was the plan. The only reason I agreed to come. I could so use her sanity right now, because I just want to scream.

Bill and Mom are talking about how Mom's giving up the house that she's rented forever. Our house. "You're in college, and you almost never come home anymore," Mom is saying, "but there's a guest room at Bill's, so if you ever want to visit . . ."

A guest room. From now on, I'll be a guest. If I ever want to *visit*. Not my home. Not my house. No room for me there. I want to ask her, why can't the guest room just be *my* room? What if I came home more often? Could it be my room then? I'm afraid to ask that, though, because I'm afraid of the answer. I don't want things I can't have.

"It's fine. I can stay at Bari's," I say instead.

I don't want to hear any more. I push my plate away and stand up.

"You don't have to leave right now," my mother sighs, like she's so sick of all this. Well, so am I, and I am ready to leave. Right now. I text Bari on my way to what used to be my room, asking her to please come get me, then I stop in the doorway and stare at the empty room. The furniture is gone. Everything's gone.

"I'm sorry, Tish," Ava's tiny voice says behind me.

I turn and force myself to smile at her. The tears in her eyes surprise me. I guess she gets what's going on, too. I'm being replaced—by her. She can't help it that she's exactly what my mother wants. Ava can't help who she is any more than I can.

"No worries, kiddo," I say, thinking how much I sound like Joe. Thinking how lucky I am to have him. And Bari. They are my real family. Before I get all emotional, I ask, "Do you know where my stuff is?"

Ava points to the closet. "She put a box in there."

"Okay, thanks. You mind giving me a minute?"

She nods and leaves. I close the door and slide down the wall to the floor. I lie back for a few minutes and stare at the ceiling, trying to remember a time when I felt like I belonged here, because I can't figure out why this hurts so much if there's nothing left for me anyway.

I think of my favorite time here, my favorite memory of this room. I was four or five. A storm was whipping outside. The way the wind hit my window made it sound like the howl of some terrible animal. I was sure it was coming to get me. Mom climbed into my bed, curled up with me and stroked my hair, my bright red hair that was just like hers. I pulled one of her long red curls to mine and twined them together until I couldn't tell whose hair was whose. Another howl let loose outside the window, but I didn't hear it. I was looking at our hair.

"Look," I whispered, my small voice sneaking in between the windy shrieks outside.

"We're the same," she whispered back, and kissed my head.

But we weren't the same. I wasn't like her. We would discover that soon enough.

I hold the memory close for a few seconds, and then I let it go. I'll leave it here, where it belongs. I stand up and go to the closet. There's the box, just like Ava said. The rest of my clothes are in it, clean and folded. I don't know what Mom did with my other things, my books and posters and other shit, and I don't care. I pick up the box and leave the room.

Mom tries to talk to me as I walk out of the house, but I'm not having it. I slam the door and sit on the porch to wait for Bari, my box of clothes on my lap. I'm stuck. No Lola to carry me away from Mom's and Bill's voices inside the house. The conversation is about me. I know this because Bill isn't trying to be quiet at all. I wonder why he's upset, considering he's getting exactly what he wants. Me. Gone.

I stand up, ready to start walking, when Bari's car turns the corner. I hurry to her car, get in, and slam the door. Mom's standing on the porch as we pull away, but I ignore her, asking Bari to just drive faster, please.

~

"They're getting married?!" Bari shrieks a few minutes later, scrubbing her feet along the dirt, pushing herself a little in the swing, her hands wrapped around the squeaky chain links.

"Already *got* married," I mutter, my own feet in the dirt.

We're at the city playground, where we've been a million times since we were kids to sit on the swings to talk about big things. My first fight with a bully at school that ended in a black eye—not for me. Bari's first and only heartbreak. My first heartbreak, Sasha. My second heartbreak, Charisse. My third heartbreak, Emily. My vow to never touch another straight girl. To never let myself be used as a try-on outfit they can stuff in the donation bin when they end up not liking it. Lots and lots of talks about my mom. I'm definitely the messier part of this duo.

Now here we are again, and it's about my mom. Again.

"They went to the courthouse or some shit because, you know, they're so in love," I say.

"Tragic," Bari says.

Bari takes love very seriously. She's the only person I know who literally, absolutely, and forever believes in true love. I think true love is a crazy fairy tale wish, something that happens to almost no one, almost never. Most people "love" the way Mom and Bill do. For companionship. For convenience. Because it checks off one of the big boxes on life's grown-up to-do list. But my Bari? She believes in the love-at-first-sight, till-death-do-us-part, happily-ever-after, forever-and-ever-and-then-some kind of love. Because Bari has proof that puts the *almost* in the almost never. Bari grew up in the middle of the greatest love story ever.

Bari's parents died in a plane crash when she was three, one of those single-engine ones, so she was raised by her grandparents, and there is no love like the love between Paps and Hasina.

Paps was a serviceman in the army when he met Hasina. She'd just moved to America from India with her family. True love, according to Bari. They'd only known each other a few days, but still, they got married before he left for the war. Their different backgrounds, cultures, and beliefs all took second place to the wholeness they felt when they were together. *Love at first sight.* While he was fighting, Hasina wrote to him every day. And he wrote her back. Every day. They fell even deeper in love through their letters. Paps memorized every one of them, every single word Hasina wrote to him. When Paps was captured, a prisoner of war, those words kept him going. He refused to die in captivity; he refused to let them break him. He would get back to Hasina, no matter what it took. *Till death do us part.* The war finally ended, and when he came home to her, they had a couple of kids and . . . *happily ever after.*

Then, a few years ago, Paps lost Hasina. His Alzheimer's stole her from him.

He still loves her. He still looks for her. He's still trying to get back to her. Every day.

He calls her name when he can't find her, and he falls asleep reaching for her hand. She's right there beside him, every day, every time he calls her name, her hands wrapped tightly around his, waiting for those rare moments when the fog clears and he can see her, if only for a few seconds. He will always search for her, and she will never leave his side.

Forever-and-ever-and-then-some.

That's the kind of love Bari believes in. A love to end all love. The kind of love that has her studying gerontology because she's so sure there is some key, some secret chemical code that will unlock the brains of Alzheimer's victims, and she's determined to find it.

I've seen them together, Paps and Hasina. I've been in their home more times than I can count, eaten more dinners there than I ever ate at my own house. They are legendary when it comes to the true-love thing. Epic. But that's like lightning striking in the right place at the right time under the right circumstances with the right two people standing right where they need to be. It just never happens. Well, almost never. To almost no one.

It's definitely not the case for Mom and Bill.

I shove my feet against the ground and start to swing. Higher and higher, like when I was a kid, trying to run from the emotions I didn't want to feel. It works less and less as I get older.

~

Late that night, Bari sleeps beside me. Her high school bedroom hasn't changed at all. That's the most comforting thing about this whole day, that as weird as everything else was, this is still the same. The same tartan plaid comforter. The same corkboard with a million notes and ticket stubs. The same photo of Bari and me at the senior day picnic, fully loaded hot dogs stuffed into our mouths. Then there's Bari herself, curled on her side of the bed, head tucked down like a bird. The same way she always sleeps.

And finally, the same murmurs coming from down the hall. Hushed whispers. One voice urgent, fearful. The other voice patient and soothing. Paps is looking for her again. I hear Hasina say, "I'm here, sweetheart. I'm right here."

I go to sleep hoping Hasina's voice leads him home.

10

LIBBY

My knuckles ache from gripping the sponge, dragging it back and forth across the wet floor. I hadn't intended to dive into a full house cleanup, but that's one trait I did inherit from Molly Monroe: the compulsive need to clean when something's bothering me. It's lunchtime. I can tell because I'm hungry and grumpy and tired. I woke up before the sun this morning, tossing and turning. The bed's really comfortable, and most nights, I sleep like the dead. But some nights, it's just hard to sleep. Too much on my mind.

I should stop, take a break, but the Monroe cleaning gene keeps me scrubbing at this wide black streak on the parlor floor. It's long, runs half the length of the room. It looks like a scorch mark, like the floor was set on fire. All the other dust and grime in the house came up easily enough, but this mark isn't budging.

Neither are my thoughts about Dad. I've worked myself to death on the house already, and no matter how tired I get, no matter how late it is when I fall into bed, I'm still thinking about him. Still waiting for him to call or text or even drive by to check on me, to see if I'm alive. But there have been no calls or texts from Mom or Dad. Just the silent treatment.

Peter sent me a text, the little turd. A picture of himself in my room, lounging on my pristine comforter in his dirty Vans, holding an open bag of Doritos, his garbage head resting on my decorative pillows. It took me a year to get that room just the way I wanted it, and now that smelly skulker is in there, rolling all over my things. I've never wanted to cause a person actual bodily harm before, but when I saw that picture, I wanted to skewer Peter on a spit and roast him. I snort a little as I scrub, imagining his screams of agony.

I put more pressure behind the sponge, bearing down on the mark.

Leo offered to do this last night. I should have let him try. As strong and independent as I am, there's no denying Leo's muscles are bigger than mine. But because I am strong and independent, I refused to let him do it for me. It was weird, anyway, having him in the house. Leo is as sure-footed as an athlete, but he tripped coming in the door, then whacked his head opening a kitchen cabinet, then cracked his elbow on the wall while using the bathroom. After that, he was ready to go, and the scorch mark was left right where it was.

Maybe I'll let Horatio have a go at it. He and Cam are supposed to come over this week. Their date was a wild success, and as soon as I met Horatio, I knew he was going to be a part of our little forever family. Loud, funny, furry as a hibernating grizzly, he's the exact opposite of my sleek, elegant Cam, but their insides are a perfect match. Sweet and smushy and generous and kind. I've been hiding just how stressed/scared/exhausted I am. If Cam thought I needed him, he'd be here in a second. But he's taking such a chance with this relationship; I want him thinking about Horatio, not me.

I dip my sponge back into the soapy water and scrub harder. I'm a big girl. I got myself into this, and I can handle it, even if it means scrubbing this floor all by myself. The house is finally starting to look less like a museum and more like a home. I've been exploring as I go, searching every room in the house for the key to the hope chest, and doing some tiny repairs using DIY vids.

In the sad room, I went straight to the windows, opened them, and knocked off the boards with a hammer. They fell to the ground below with a satisfying clatter. But even then, with the sunlight shining in, the room still clung to its sorrowful vibe. I felt my heart twist a little bit. When I really looked around, I figured out why. It looked like it had been someone's sickroom. All the furniture was antique, like the rest of the house, except the bed was one of those adjustable ones. The kind you find in hospitals. There were lots of plain white hand towels in the nightstand, and a stack of those blue bed pads. The whole thing made me remember Gammy, when she was dying, and I was heartbroken all over again at losing her.

The window in there had some breaks in the panes, some glass cracked, and some completely missing. I was able to use a small handsaw to cut some board into small squares, then I used them to cover a few individual panes. It looks like crap, a real hack job, but at least they're covered.

That same thick, satiny fabric wallpaper is all over the house, different colors for every room. In the downstairs hallway, the fabric has a design. A pale sage background with green trees, like a forest motif.

I found two more small bedrooms (the only rooms with no wallpaper) down here at the very back of the house, right off the kitchen. Each room has a plain wardrobe cabinet, a plain table with a plain ceramic washbasin, and two skinny twin beds. Dorm-style. Servants, maybe? So glad those days are over.

There were also two more bathrooms, a couple of closets, and a parlor with a huge fireplace. The fireplace took up almost the entire wall, massive and open. This room had the most furniture. It looked the most lived-in, like it was home base for whoever lived here before.

The first thing I uncovered in the parlor was a real Victrola phonograph, with a crank handle and everything. I chose a record at random, put it on the green cloth disk, and flipped the switch, amazed when the record started to turn. I put the needle on, and crackly music came from the speaker. I recognized it immediately. That New Year's Eve song. "Should old acquaintance be forgot . . ." and that's as far as it got before the record started skipping like crazy.

I switched the record out for another one. This one played perfectly. Upbeat with lots of horns and men singing in high, whiny voices. The old music made the perfect soundtrack for my exploration of the house and my search for the key.

I went through every room, pulling off sheets and searching cabinets, drawers, and cubbies. I didn't find a key, but I found literally everything else. Eleanor wasn't kidding when she said the house hadn't been touched. There were old phone books and balls of yarn impaled by knitting needles and little handwritten notes, jots of thoughts that didn't make much sense, written by someone old and frail. Just touching the notes had given me a shiver, but I collected them all and put them away with some of the other odds and ends and personal things. I'd never realized that handwriting could look weak until Gammy had gotten old. Her fingers had trouble managing the pen, so the letters came out all faint and scratchy. Just like these little notes.

I wish Gammy could see me now, on my hands and knees, wondering why there is a burn mark on this otherwise perfect parquet floor. My hand is starting to throb. I force my fingers to unclench and drop the sponge into the bucket, then try to rub some feeling back into my hands. I wonder if Mom ever felt better for having cleaned her fingers raw. I sure don't.

I stand up and reach for the ceiling, stretching out my shoulders and back.

That's when I hear the front door open.

I whirl around. The door's closed. I can see it from here. And it's locked. All the doors are locked; I learned my lesson after Cam ambushed me that first night. But I know I heard a door open. I hurry to the kitchen. The side door is still closed, too.

One of the downstairs bedroom doors is open a crack, though. One of the maids' rooms. I feel clammy all of a sudden. Not scared, but alert. I move slowly to the room and push the door open, standing way back. There's nothing in there. Just the furniture. I pull the door closed and look around the kitchen again. Nothing's here.

Feeling a little weird, a little electrified, I look back at that closed bedroom door.

The tiny hairs on my arms are standing up like I've just walked past one of those bright blue balls, the ones with the lightning inside. I hurry over to the door and sling it open again, like there's something in there I might catch if I'm fast enough. But it's just a plain, quiet, nothing-special room. A room in an old house that has lots of history.

I'm letting all this house stuff get to me, with its vintage clothes and museum furniture.

I rub my hands over my arms and go back into the parlor. It's broad daylight and the sun beams through the big front windows. Outside, I see a garbage truck's grabby arm raise a big black container, clicking and squeaking as it dumps the trash into the back of the truck. I guess that could pass as the sound of a door opening?

I look back down at the scorch mark. That's not coming up today. I'm going to need stronger detergent or something. Mom would know, but she's not talking to me. I stretch again. My back sounds like a cracking watermelon. I move toward the stairs, easily sidestepping the broken banister as I make my way up. I stop to look down at the messy, off-color seam where I (kind of) repaired the deep crack in the stair. It looks terrible, but I can step on it now.

I get to the bedroom I've been staying in. My bedroom, since it's my house. I lift the door as I twist the doorknob, second nature now, and walk inside. As I'm passing the bed, my arm lifts over my head and I rise to my tiptoes, all in one motion, my body moving on its own. I pluck something from the top of the bedpost. Something small. Something metal . . .

. . . and I stop . . .

I open my hand. There, in my palm, is a key. A tiny golden key.

A flutter starts in my stomach. No. Freaking. WAY!

I hurry to the hope chest and shove the key into the lock. It fits!

The latch flips, and the lid of the chest bounces open a tiny bit, like it's relieved, like it's been holding its breath. I open it and find myself gazing at more stacks of perfectly folded clothes, but it's the two flapper-style dresses, one silver and one gold, that I'm most excited by. I pull out the first one, silver and beaded and, omigod, I think it's real silk. Holding the dress up to myself, I hurry to the standing mirror and do a little twirl. I love this dress. Love, love, love it. Grinning, I lay it across the bed and go back to the chest.

I reach for the other dress. The gold one.

As soon as my fingers brush the fabric, my heart swells. It suddenly feels too big for my rib cage. I swallow hard and pull the dress from the chest and draw it close to me. I want to hug it. I want to push my face into the fabric. I can almost, *almost* feel the body that's supposed to be wearing it. Solid. Warm. It feels so, so good. Like I've found something I didn't know I'd lost.

The dress is stunning. A simple cut made extravagant by hand-sewn gold beads that move across the silk in a spiral pattern, like the dress itself is a whirlwind.

My eyes are drawn back to the chest, and I see a couple of books tucked into one corner. I pick them up. A thin book of poetry, and what looks like a journal. The poetry book is old and worn, like it's been read over and over a thousand times. The journal, though, looks new.

I forget the poetry and go for the journal. Its leather cover is in perfect condition, not a crease, not a scratch. Embossed in gold on the front are the numbers *2 3 6*. The same numbers that are etched into the sidewalk under the green glass stone. The room dims around me, the edges of my vision wavering until all I can see are those numbers:

2 3 6

I put the gold dress on the bed, carefully laying it out next to its silver mate, then sink to my knees with the journal. It's heavy, and when I open it, I see the same handwriting I found on the little notes downstairs. Old, frail, weak.

I pull the journal onto my lap, turn to the first page with shaking hands, and begin to read:

My name is Elizabeth Post.
I was born on the morning of March 3rd in the year 1906. I was born to wealth. I was born to privilege. I would have renounced them both had I known what they would cost me.
This story, our story, began on May 31st. The year was 1925.

Sarah, my lady's maid, had taken on a strange melancholy, so unlike the cheerful Sarah I had known for years. I suspected her shift in disposition might involve a certain clerk's apprentice for the Sawyer house, but I would never allow such an utterance to pass my lips. I left that more salacious gossip to the Harper girls.

Delilah, their mother, was my mother's closest friend. I use the word _friend_ strategically. Mother kept her at arm's length, as was wise with a woman such as Delilah Harper.

"A creeping, climbing cat," Mother frequently hissed in private.

In public, however, they were to each other as blooms were to bees. You couldn't very well have one without the other. Thus was the nature of friendship, I suppose, in society, anyway . . .

11

MAY 31, 1925

Elizabeth sat at her vanity table, studying her reflection. She gathered her wavy, shoulder-length brown hair in her hands, raised it to her chin, then leaned over to compare her look to the button-faced model in the magazine that lay open beside her. Elizabeth sighed. Oh, how she would love to take a pair of shears to her woefully unfashionable locks.

Brisk footsteps outside her closed bedroom door launched her into motion. One hand reached for a wide silk ribbon, and the other hurried to stuff the magazine into the vanity drawer. She shoved the drawer shut and quickly tied the ribbon into her hair to hold it away from her face, leaving the lengths free around her shoulders. How she hated it. Hated, hated, hated it.

She pasted a smile on her face as her bedroom door swung open. At the sight of her intruder, she relaxed her arrow-straight posture, letting her smile ease into a natural grin, relieved to see it was only Sarah barging into her room like a battering ram.

"Cripes, Sarah, you scared the life out of me. I thought you were Mother."

Sarah pulled Elizabeth from her chair and began undressing her. Elizabeth automatically held her arms up and out, a move made habit from all her years of having a lady's maid. Other girls might think it pleasing to have someone dress them, brush and style their hair, but Elizabeth found it invasive. She loved Sarah dearly, but this she could do without.

Elizabeth had been looking forward to a quiet day alone in her room, perusing her fashion magazines and dreaming of life as a modern woman, a life she would never get to experience. Her moralistic father would see to that. But a girl could dream, couldn't she? To have Sarah unceremoniously interrupt her daydreams was more than a dash of cold water. It was a geyser.

"Is everything all right, Sarah?" Elizabeth asked carefully.

Sarah's hands faltered for a moment before she forced a smile of her own. "Everything is fine. But the new kitchen girl comes today, and Caroline"—then she murmured so low that Elizabeth had to strain to hear—"is nowhere to be found."

"Caroline? Again?" whispered Elizabeth, which earned her a stern look. "I won't say anything. You know I won't."

"No. I know you won't," Sarah replied as she pulled the dressing gown from Elizabeth's shoulders and tossed it over a wingback chair. Elizabeth's fingers went for the buttons of her silk sleep shirt, intending to help, but Sarah swatted her hands away.

Sarah was only a year older than Elizabeth, but lately, she seemed a decade beyond her, in years and in life. A permanent crease marred the smooth skin between Sarah's brows, and her once meticulously trimmed fingernails were now chewed to the quick.

"And the hens will be here soon," Sarah said as she began unfastening the tiny pearl buttons of Elizabeth's shirt.

"What? Why? When was this decided?" squawked Elizabeth.

"You'll have to ask your mother. I'm not privy to her schedule until after she makes it," Sarah answered absently, urging Elizabeth to step out of her silk pajama pants.

"You know, Sarah, I can do this myself, if there are other things you need to attend to."

"Don't tempt me." Sarah chuckled. Elizabeth brightened at the quip, happy to see some humor return to her friend's face.

She covered Sarah's hands. "I'll do this. I'll even do a good job. Mother will never know I dressed myself." They laughed at their long-running joke. Society was changing. Women were becoming more liberated, doing things for themselves. None of this mattered to Elizabeth's parents.

"Next thing you know, you'll be smoking cigarettes," Sarah said.

"Don't tempt me," Elizabeth teased in return.

They laughed again. Then Sarah gave Elizabeth a long, questioning look.

"Go," Elizabeth said.

Sarah nodded her thanks and hurried toward the door. She was gone only a moment before she popped back in, saying quickly, "Your mother wants you in the green."

The green. Elizabeth groaned. Her newest dress was slightly more in keeping with current trends, but still far too conservative to be considered modern. The dress could have graced the pages of her magazines three or four years ago, far too long ago for Elizabeth's liking.

Fashions were evolving at breakneck speeds, and social mores had become as loose as unstrung bootlaces. Women were wresting control of their lives from the iron grip of history. They were becoming more independent by the day: drinking, smoking, driving, moving to cities and working, living in apartments alone or with friends, living their lives out from under their fathers' watchful eyes. And finally, at long last, women were voting. Voting! In elections! Women had voices, and they were using them.

That's not to say every woman was as enamored of this newfound freedom as Elizabeth was. Her mother, Lillian, had joined the movement *against* women's suffrage, much to Elizabeth's dismay, although she suspected her mother's choice had more to do with Elizabeth's father's wishes than her mother's own. Nathaniel Post was a staunch authoritarian, and he spared no pity for the new progressive ideals that were sweeping the nation.

"Tarts and harlots"—and these were her father's exact words, precisely—"have no place in decent society. My house will not cater to the whims of a culture in decline."

And so, the revolution was passing Elizabeth by as she watched, nose pressed against the window of the world, wanting so badly to participate, but shackled to a life of propriety.

She tried to shake her suddenly blue mood, but she was having a hard time of it.

The Harpers were coming to tea. Delilah and her daughters, Honey and Rose, were always in step with the latest trends, and Elizabeth would be greeting them in this dowdy green thing. She swallowed her frustration and took a seat at the vanity to make herself presentable. It was a fine dress, if a bit matronly. She would wear it proudly and present herself as the young lady she was brought up to be.

Cripes. Honey Harper. All thoughts of a pleasant afternoon evaporated in the heat of knowing that hell was on her way in the form of a blond-haired, blue-eyed viper named Honey.

Elizabeth descended the stairs half an hour later, wearing the green, just in time to catch a death glare from her mother.

"What took you so long? Don't tell me you were up there with your nose in those pages again," Lillian complained as she brushed imaginary lint from Elizabeth's shoulders.

Elizabeth avoided the question by giving her mother a sweet smile and a slow turn, modeling the dress. "I . . . I like it. Do you?" she asked.

"It suits you," Lillian said, and placed a firm hand between her daughter's shoulder blades, an entreaty to stand up straight.

Elizabeth blinked back a stab of hurt before she twisted her hands together, turned, and walked into the parlor, saying quietly, "I'll get the cribbage board."

"You might have worn the dark shoes, though," Lillian called after her.

~

Honey Harper. Never had a name been less suited to its owner.

Honey had a face like a razor blade and a new haircut to match, bleached platinum and cut into a sleek bob, with arrow-straight bangs and angled ends that slashed sharply along her high cheekbones. Elizabeth had never seen such hair on a woman before, even in her magazines. Earlier, she'd considered herself bold for just contemplating a shorter style, but this . . . this was spectacular, and from the glint in her hard eyes, Honey knew it. Honey always knew.

Those eyes raked over Elizabeth now, not attempting to hide her smirk as Elizabeth touched her own hair, then self-consciously smoothed her hands down the front of her modest green frock.

Cribbage is a two- or three-person affair, four if played in pairs. Never five. So, Elizabeth watched as Honey and Rose paired off against Lillian and Delilah. Of course they'd pestered her, half-heartedly, to play, but Elizabeth (as the daughter of the house) had graciously declined in favor of simply observing the game. It was the same song and dance every time. Lillian would feign dismay at having one too many players, they would pretend to coax and cajole and offer to sit out, and Elizabeth would find herself on the settee, sipping her tea and daydreaming.

The one time she had let herself be convinced to play, she'd been partnered with Honey (because Honey never sat out), and it had been one of the most dismal afternoons of her young life. It was the only time, after years of needling, that Honey had succeeded in making Elizabeth cry. She'd been unable to hide the tears, so she'd faked a sneeze, blamed her wet eyes on an attack of pollen, and had withdrawn to her bedroom for the rest of the day.

Honey Harper. Viper.

". . . and just what did she expect would be said about her when they were found crouched behind the shrubbery? That she was giving the poor man a lesson in *dic*tion?" Honey half laughed, half snarled. The words were poisonous on their own, but Honey's targeted delivery made them deadly. No one could spin innuendo and rumor into truth as deftly as the Harper girls. And Honey? Honey was a master. It was a game to her, and like cribbage, Honey never sat out.

Lillian's lip curled in displeasure. "The stupid girl should have known better."

"Or at least known how to hide it." Rose snickered. Rose was a hand-me-down version of her older sister—less lethal, but it wasn't from lack of trying. *She has a few years yet to sharpen her fangs*, Elizabeth thought, then blinked guiltily as she caught Honey's eyes on her, those piercing, all-knowing eyes boring into her as if she knew exactly what Elizabeth was thinking.

Honey swept a dainty hand across her new bangs and laughed delightedly, drawing everyone's attention to her hair. "Can you believe it? I had my doubts the color would work, but I decided to be bold, throw caution to the wind, do something daring."

"It is daring, certainly," Lillian replied, the tiniest bit of disapproval coloring her tone.

"Lillian, I'll tell you, when Honey came home with that hair, I thought I might die," Delilah said, "but she swears to me it's the newest thing, and who am I to stop progress?"

"Who indeed?" Lillian muttered, then smiled at Honey. "It's lovely, Honey, dear."

Delilah patted Lillian's hand soothingly. "We aren't all lucky enough to have such a good girl as your Elizabeth, Lil. My little chickens never let me off my toes. It's one surprise after another with these two. Count yourself blessed, darling."

"*Such* a good girl," Honey agreed. Then to Elizabeth directly, she said, "Be glad you don't have to suffer the excitement of being wild, Elizabeth. It's overwhelming, really. Sometimes I can't even sleep. Try as I might, I just can't find it in myself to be meek, and yet you pull it off with such grace. How do you do it?"

Elizabeth's throat worked as she tried to swallow. The words landed like blows, just as Honey had intended.

"See, darling?" Lillian turned to her to say. "Virtue is nothing to be ashamed of."

Honey smiled her sweetest smile at Elizabeth, as if daring her to disagree.

Elizabeth's spine wilted under the silent assault. "No, Mother,

I'm sure it's not," she managed as she got to her feet. "Excuse me. I'm going to check on the refreshments."

She could hear Lillian sputtering for her to "just ring the bell, darling," but Elizabeth was already leaving the room. She couldn't take one more minute of Honey Harper and her vile, vicious . . . She was just such a nasty . . . Elizabeth sighed. She wasn't one to employ bad language, but if she were, she would have some rather pointed things to say about Miss Honey Harper.

She found Sarah in the kitchen. A refreshments tray was on the table, partially loaded, but Sarah was staring out the window, brow furrowed, like she was thinking unpleasant thoughts.

"Sarah?" Elizabeth said softly. Sarah whirled, then quickly went back to loading the tray. Tiny sandwich triangles, baby gherkins, warmed olives with rosemary, mini puff pastries, and a pitcher of lemonade. Elizabeth's stomach rumbled in anticipation. Sarah, having heard the low gurgle, smirked and gave her one of the little sandwiches. Elizabeth ate it as she watched Sarah add plates, goblets, and cocktail napkins to the tray.

The chime on the kitchen service door rang just as Lillian's handbell clanged loudly in the sitting room, followed by her annoyed voice, calling, "Sarah?"

Sarah looked to the service door, then toward the front room, torn.

"You take the tray. I'll answer the door," Elizabeth offered.

"No," Sarah said. Then, under her breath, "Damn Caroline. If she were here . . ."

"But she's not here," Elizabeth said. "See to Mother, or you know how she'll be. I'll answer the door. It's the new kitchen girl?"

"Her name is Patricia," Sarah sighed. "Just . . . just let her in and tell her I'll be right with her." She picked up the tray and hurried from the room, the sound of Lillian's obnoxious handbell clang-clang-clanging.

Elizabeth smoothed her green dress again, touched her hair, and moved to answer the door. When she opened it, time slowed, then seemed to stand still as Elizabeth stared.

Here was wild. *Here* was bold. *Here* was . . .

"Patricia," Elizabeth whispered.

The young woman on the steps was glancing past her into the room, taking in what she could see of the kitchen. Elizabeth stammered, then caught a breath.

"Um . . . I'm Elizabeth." She recovered as her manners, stamped into her since birth, took over, and she moved aside, inviting Patricia in. Patricia nodded slightly as she stepped past her and into the house.

Elizabeth tried to tear her eyes away (it was impolite to stare), but she failed miserably. Patricia had hair that looked and moved like fire. Gloriously red, cascading in riotous, coiled waves around her face.

Then Patricia's crystalline eyes landed on Elizabeth, and Elizabeth felt as though she were being swallowed whole. She'd thought Honey with her new haircut was exciting, but this . . . *this*. Elizabeth had no frame of reference for this breathless feeling, for the thready beat of her heart. Her fingers twitched unconsciously at her side, searching, perhaps, for something to hold on to as her whole world shifted beneath her feet.

Patricia's eyes followed the movement, then traced Elizabeth's green dress, her softly styled hair, and returned to look into Elizabeth's eyes. The blue calmed, became gentler.

"Hello, miss."

Her accent circled around Elizabeth like a warm breeze. Scottish? Irish? Elizabeth couldn't tell, but it had the sound of mist-drawn mornings, rocky cliffs, and fields full of heather. She wanted to hear more of it, wanted to hear many more words from that mouth, the mouth that was now so adorably quirked in a shy smile.

12

JUNE 19, 1925

"These are lovely, miss," Patricia said, touching a pale finger to one of the several perfume bottles displayed on the vanity.

Elizabeth allowed herself a self-deprecating chuckle, then opened one of the vanity drawers, revealing myriad bottles, atomizers, and vials, all filled with perfumes.

"I'm a bit of a collector," Elizabeth admitted as she plucked an atomizer from the drawer and gave the air around them a liberal spray.

Patricia leaned forward and drew deeply through her nose, breathing in the scent. She was so close that Elizabeth could see each individual eyelash, thick and brown. They made Patricia's eyes look all the more blue. She could see, up close, several heavy red curls that had escaped the braid Patricia wore under her maid's cap. She could count the (exactly twelve) freckles that marked Patricia's narrow, slightly arched nose.

Patricia's presence in the house had thoroughly upended Elizabeth's daily ho-hum humdrum. Instead of spending her days in her books and magazines, Elizabeth now spent her time wondering about Patricia. Where, exactly, did she come from? How was her life before America? Was she happy here, in Elizabeth's house? Had her hair always been that red, or had it grown redder as she got older? Did she like Elizabeth? Did she know that Elizabeth very much wanted Patricia to like her, wanted it so badly that she thought about it even in her sleep?

For Elizabeth, the nearness of Patricia was like having rich red wine when she was accustomed to simple cider. It was a heady rush, one that threw her off-balance.

Patricia closed her eyes and sniffed again, her face still inches from Elizabeth's.

"It smells like you. On Saturdays. Before you go to the park," Patricia lilted, then exhaled on a long sigh, her warm breath brushing over Elizabeth's cheek.

An unfamiliar heat bloomed in Elizabeth's belly, and her fingers reflexively clenched the atomizer bulb, sending a douse of fragrance directly into Patricia's face. Patricia sputtered and coughed. Elizabeth leapt from her chair to clumsily wave at the air, hoping to disperse the overwhelming scent of Gardenia Summer, more than a little humiliated that she'd reacted so foolishly.

She needed to get control of herself. Having Patricia in her room was no different from having Sarah. The atomizer clinked loudly against the other bottles as she returned it to its drawer, then shoved the drawer closed.

"It's silly, I think, to have a collection of anything, really," Elizabeth said, still embarrassed. "What can one do with pretty bottles, except make clutter of a vanity table?"

Patricia, seemingly recovered from Elizabeth's atomizer mishap, pressed her fingers to her nose one last time and turned her thoughtful gaze to the vanity, then to Elizabeth. "You should do what makes you happy, miss. If it's collecting bottles, then collect them all."

"Patricia, please call me Elizabeth."

"Thank you, miss," Patricia said.

Since her arrival, Patricia had been diligent in her work. A bit rough around the edges and quick to temper, but it was clear the young woman appreciated her position in the household, and even clearer that she would not risk breaking protocol for fear of being turned out. That left it to Elizabeth, then. She would have to work harder to hear her name from Patricia's lips, to enjoy with Patricia the friendly banter she so easily shared with Sarah.

Patricia, however, was more wary than Sarah had ever been. Of course, that was understandable. Patricia was Irish, and the Irish were, for all intents and purposes, a serf class in America. Though their plight had improved some in the last decade, it wasn't uncommon to still see placards proclaiming IRISH NEED NOT APPLY. Not for employment. Not for housing. Not for help. The Irish barely scraped by, their lives meager and hard.

The only reason, Elizabeth knew, that Patricia had been allowed to remain on staff was that word had gotten around of Lillian's "good deed" in hiring one of the poor unfortunates. She'd been so highly and publicly praised by her congregation that she was seen as something of a saint to several of the younger pew-sitters, a kind and generous matron after whom to model themselves. That was a position Lillian was loath to lose.

The cap of it was, of course, that Delilah Harper would never have allowed "an Irish" in her house, not for any reason, not even to scrub the fireplace flue. Therefore, Lillian currently sat one rung higher on the ladder of moral superiority, something she lorded over her dearest friend with all the self-righteous humility she could muster.

So, Elizabeth didn't begrudge Patricia's reticence. She could not say she understood the life Patricia must have known, but she could sympathize. Elizabeth was so lost in her thoughts that the gentle touch on her shoulder surprised her. Patricia stood behind her, a freshly pressed frock in her arms. Elizabeth swallowed hard and turned to face her.

Patricia let the dress fall over one arm while she went to work on the buttons of Elizabeth's sleep shirt. Elizabeth didn't know if the heat she was feeling inside would show on her face, so she kept her eyes trained on the floor. A tremor passed through her as Patricia slid the shirt from her shoulders. The garment dropped to the floor and Elizabeth shivered again.

"Cold, miss?" Patricia asked. There was a hoarse quality to her voice that Elizabeth hadn't heard before, but Patricia just cleared her throat and reached for Elizabeth's silk bottoms.

"No. No, I'm just . . . Yes. No. Yes," Elizabeth stammered.

Patricia cleared her throat again, focused on her task.

Elizabeth watched Patricia's face now, as those clear blue eyes looked everywhere but her exposed body. She dropped the ivory dress over Elizabeth's head, then yanked it down over her shoulders, a little too roughly.

"Sorry, miss," Patricia said quietly.

"It's all right," Elizabeth answered, her own voice quiet and low.

No. Having Patricia in her room was nothing like having Sarah. Nothing at all.

13

LIBBY

My finger runs along each page, following the shaky handwriting, as if touching the words will somehow make them real. I'm totally absorbed, totally lost in Elizabeth's world. I turn the page, my eyes flying across the words:

> . . . and though I knew my staring to be inappropriate, my eyes would not heed my silent command to look away. I could not, for the life of me, stop gazing at her.
> She was wild as the wind, her cobalt eyes flashing like twin suns. I had to resist the urge to touch her, to discover for myself if her skin was as smooth as the ivory it resembled, if those untamed curls were as hot as their fiery hue promised.
> Would she burn if I touched her? Would I?

I raise my eyes from the diary. My heart's pounding, and there's a light sheen of sweat on my hairline. I should stop reading. These journals aren't mine. I'm invading Elizabeth's privacy. But I can hear her voice so clearly in my mind, almost as if she's talking directly to me, whispering her secrets right into my ear. So I read until I'm bleary with it, until the words creep down the page with each gritty blink of my eyes.

Finally, I crawl into bed, the journal hugged close, precious to me now.

As soon as my eyes drift shut and everything goes black, images of Elizabeth and Patricia play out like a movie on a screen. I hope they get together. My gut tells me that's unlikely, especially back in their day, but a girl can dream, can't she?

14

TISH

"Watch it, Sof," I say as I barely dodge the wood that swings wildly at my face.

Sofia turns around and the plywood plank she's carrying on her shoulder swings again. I duck and grab it to keep it from beaning me.

"The hell is wrong with you?" I ask. It's harsh, but she's almost knocked me out twice with the same stupid piece of plywood.

"Well, someone took my nail gun, so now I'm on construction crew."

"Being the nail gun mistress *is* part of construction crew, but okay," I answer glibly.

"We were totally right about Wallis and Dr. B," she says, nodding toward the smitten couple.

Wallis's fuzzy head is leaned over his blueprints. Dr. B's long, mostly frizzy hair lies across his back as she stands on tiptoes to see what he's showing her.

"So dang adorable. Gotta love love, right?" Sofia says.

I hear a loud *THWIP* from nearby, and a pained "Ow. Damn it."

"That's *my* nail gun. She doesn't even know how to use it," Sofia grumbles, then makes off with her plywood, taking one more accidental swipe at me before she's gone.

I turn to see who would dare the wrath of Sofia. It's the new girl. Libby Monroe.

Not a theater major. Definitely not a nail gun mistress. She squats on the floor, trying to load the nail gun, her hand shaky. That's not good. Especially with a pneumatic instrument that can send tiny daggers flying through the air at fourteen hundred feet per second. Nobody's dodging that shit.

"Hold up. Let me help you with that," I say, and jog over to her.

I haven't really paid much attention to her since she joined class, but there's something about the way she looks now, crouched in front of the huge foam fireplace we just built for the parlor/library/Christmas Past interior set, that tugs at my ribs in a weird, weird way.

Libby looks up at me, her eyes big and round. They're deep brown with a wine-red kind of undertone, making them look almost liquid. I've never seen eyes like that. I stare a little too long, then kneel down and take the nail gun from her. I load it, but I don't give it right back. She slumps heavily and leans her head against the fake brick hearth, closes her eyes, and lets out a long sigh. There goes that tug again.

"I'm not inept, you know," she says. "I'm just tired."

"I can see that," I say, but it must not come out right, because she opens one eye and narrows it at me, so I sputter, "I can see that you're *tired*, I mean. Not inept. I'm sure you're perfectly— That you're very— Anyway. Here. Don't shoot anyone."

Just shoot *me*, right in the eye. A nice, quick lobotomy so I don't have to think about how stupid I am. I hand her the nail gun. Her fingers are still shaking, but she takes it.

"You really are tired. Maybe just . . . go home? Get some sleep?"

"I want to learn how to do this. I *need* to learn how," she says, her eyes closed again, "but I stayed up all night reading . . ."

"Oh, you like to read?" I say. Literally the most idiotic thing I can say, because I *don't* like to read. If she answers *yes*, I have zero follow-up for my lame attempt at a conversation starter. I can't even remember the last book I read. Maybe I should just use the nail gun on myself. But then Libby smiles up at me. My stomach does a little flip. I ignore it.

"You sure I won't get in trouble? For not doing my hours?" she asks hopefully.

"I'll cover for you. Give it here."

I need for her to give me that nail gun and get the hell out of here before I forget she's off-limits. Totally and completely and absolutely off-limits.

～

"We've already talked about this. No more straight girls for me," I mutter to Lola, lining up the rear fender I filched from the ruined CL350. I push the bolts through their mounting holes, attach the washers and nuts, then tighten them with a socket wrench.

After practicum, I came straight to Joe's to finish up the work on Lola. He helped me do the big stuff: changing out the tire, replacing the shocks, resetting the chains and gears. Only finishing touches left now, and those I can handle by myself. Being with Lola is usually the best way for me to get out of my own head, whether it's a long ride or just working on her. Not this time, though. She won't let me.

"Yeah, and look how well that turned out. My ass hurt for two weeks. Yours did, too, so just drop it," I say as I torque the wrench a little too hard. The bolt squeals. I quickly back off and rub my thumb across it. "Sorry. You okay?"

I hear Joe laugh behind me. He spits—yes, the tobacco's back— and says, "What're you two fighting about now?"

"Nothing, you dirty eavesdropper," I answer. I carefully run the electrical wire to Lola's new rear brake light, then I click the red lens into place. I reach up to the handlebars and give the brakes a squeeze. The light comes on.

"Good job, Squirt. Couldn'ta done it better myself."

Sure, he could. He could build a Ferrari from the wheels up, but I appreciate the praise. Joe's opinion means a lot.

"Gotcher eye on somebody, then?" he asks.

"Nope."

"Bring her round to see me anyway, huh?" he says with another laugh.

He puts an ice-cold Dr Pepper on the floor beside me and goes back to tinkering with whatever he's tinkering with. I love that old guy. But that doesn't mean I'm about to spill my guts, since there is absolutely no one I have my eye on. Especially not super-femme Libby Monroe with her uber-buff boyfriend. She's got a few pics of him on Instagram—not that I was looking—and they don't come more hetero than those two. I shove away the mental images of his arms around her, stuff the Dr Pepper into my bag, and hop on Lola. I give her blond gas tank a loving pat, then jump on the kick-starter. She comes to life with a low, purry growl.

Joe looks up from his work, his hands oily from a dissected crankcase. He gives me a huge grin and a thumbs-up. I wink at him as I pull my helmet onto my head and drop the visor. Then I slowly guide Lola out of the workshop. Time to ride.

The chilly air whips by us as Lola and I roar up the curvy road to the overlook. The view from there makes the town look like one of those paintings on the old calendars Joe's got hanging all over the walls of the shop. He has so many, it's like wallpaper.

This is our favorite ride, Lola's and mine, this long, twisty road that winds its way up to the overlook, where I'll sit on the edge and stare out over the town and daydream about a time when the world was all so much greener. Beautiful, lush green, fading into fall.

The colorful autumn trees on either side of the road become a blur of red . . . yellow . . . brown. It's heaven. Lola thinks so, too. I can feel it in the way she pulls beneath me, vibrating with excitement, wanting to go faster. It's a clear afternoon and the roads are dry, so I decide to risk it. I twist the throttle and Lola practically shouts in joy. She digs her wheels into the asphalt and takes off like a rocket.

Red   yellow   brown   red   yellowbrown   redyellowbrown *redyellowbrownredyellowbrown* . . .

15

LIBBY

Tish is still on my mind as I collect Elizabeth's books and move them from the window seat/reading nook. How sweet she was to cover for me in practicum. How I should probably take her advice and get some sleep. How she stared at me for a long, long time, and how I didn't mind it, not at all. How when anyone says her name, it's never just *her* name but *Tish and Lola*, like they're one person. How I don't feel anything close to that for Leo, and is there something wrong with me for that? He's literally the perfect guy. I should feel more. But I don't.

The late-afternoon sun is the ideal light to read by, but I keep the oil lamp close, just in case. The sun is setting earlier and earlier these days, and though I'm completely comfortable in this room now, I don't want to have to fumble around for a light once the sun goes down.

I tuck myself into a corner of the nook, silently thanking Elizabeth for the warm throw that I pull over my lap. I've figured out, from the journal, that this was definitely her room. Her reading nook. Her vanity table. Her bed. Her things. I've basically just stepped into her life.

I wonder how many times Elizabeth sat right here, just like this, back braced against the wall, right side leaning against the window.

If I look down, I can see the green glass stone glimmering in the sunlight. So pretty. So strange. Did she look at it, too?

I run my fingers over the gold numbers on the front of the journal. *2 3 6.*

Curled up and cozy, I open the journal to the next entry. My heart leaps at the sight of Elizabeth's frail, faint cursive:

> *The summer season was turning out to be a dramatic one.*
>
> *Caroline's absences had become more common, and Sarah was run ragged as a result. She refused to tell Mother, choosing instead to shoulder the additional duties herself, with the help of Patricia, whom she'd quickly promoted from kitchen help to housemaid. And when necessary, lady's maid.*
>
> *My own silence on the Caroline matter wasn't a hardship, as it reaped for me such personal rewards. While I did miss spending time with Sarah, sharing gossip and general chatter, I cannot deny that I looked forward to the mornings when Patricia would knock gently on my bedroom door.*
>
> *Patricia, with a brush for my hair. Patricia, with my frock for the day. Patricia, with her quick, cool fingers buttoning or unbuttoning my garments. Those were the days I lived for, the days wherein bloomed the hope that I might coax from her a few words more than "Yes, miss," or "Thank you."*
>
> *The wildness that was in her at our first meeting was still there. I caught it on occasion, roiling in her eyes as Mother ran her white gloves over every surface in search of dust, or when she was scolded for a corner of toast that was a bit too brown.*
>
> *That was the Patricia I longed to see, the one whose energy could collide with the sun and send sparks to fly. That was the Patricia I was determined to know.*

16

JULY 1, 1925

Elizabeth darted out of the way as a clutch of children ran down the sidewalk, freshly scooped ice cream cones gripped in their sticky little hands. The youngsters weaved in and out of the thick pedestrian traffic, careful to keep their treats intact and their feet under them. Elizabeth grinned at their antics. It wasn't so long ago that she'd have been one of those kids. Lillian would have never let her run in public, though. That would have been too scandalous.

The town square was more populated than usual on this Wednesday, bustling with shoppers preparing for their Independence Day festivities. For Elizabeth, this meant a trip to town with her mother, and today, as Elizabeth's good luck would have it, with Patricia.

Caroline had finally been permanently dismissed from the house. "Sent packing" was how Sarah had put it, a strange terseness in her tone. But Caroline's dismissal meant Sarah had to remain at the house to set everything right for the coming celebration. There would be additional hired help for the event itself, as Elizabeth's parents wouldn't dare host a gathering with less than adequate service on hand. It fell upon Sarah to quickly instruct these temporary hires on the ways and rules of the house.

Nathaniel and Lillian Post were known for their extravagant parties, and this one was not to be outdone. Nathaniel had gotten his hands on a carton of genuine fireworks, crowing that the Post house would be the only house in the entire county to celebrate in true American style. "Come sundown, this town will witness the rockets' red glare with their own eyes, by God!"

Lillian had preened at the thought, clacking on and on about how envious Delilah Harper would be and how every other party would pale in comparison, her eyes aflame with the fire of catty competition. This year's turnout would be the grandest yet, Lillian was just sure of it.

"In fact," Lillian had boasted, "it wouldn't surprise me one bit if the Turners cancel their barbecue altogether. They will be welcome here, of course."

Of course, Elizabeth had thought. Her mother was on a tear and there was no talking her down, not that Elizabeth would have tried. If this was to be the grandest party, then Lillian's daughter must be the grandest daughter. That meant shopping for new frocks.

So, Elizabeth accepted her mother's societal ambition for what it was and, in turn, happily accepted the benefit to her own wardrobe—allowing that she not be burdened by yet another dowdy, dull thing. That thought stole some of the wind from her sails, and she slowed on the sidewalk, imagining herself at the *grandest* party wearing a limp brown burlap sack, cinched tightly at the neck and ankles. A prisoner of bad fashion, found guilty on all counts. She sighed.

"Is everything all right, miss?" Patricia asked quietly. She had been silently keeping pace beside her all day, and every few seconds, Elizabeth's eyes had peeked toward Patricia to watch her take in all the shops swathed in stars and stripes and every manner of red, white, and blue.

Elizabeth slowed, putting more distance between the girls and Lillian.

Patricia shot a look toward Lillian, who strode blithely ahead of them, greeting neighbors with officious glee: "Martha! So good to see you, dear . . ." and "Oh, Bonnie, you will never believe who I ran into . . ." and "My word, Celia, it has been ages. Hasn't it just been ages . . . ?"

Elizabeth put a tentative hand on Patricia's arm. "Patricia. Please stop calling me *miss*."

Patricia turned her gaze to Elizabeth and said, "Your mother made it clear—"

"I don't care what Mother said," Elizabeth countered smartly, her tone rising.

Patricia stopped walking now, one brow arched in surprise. Elizabeth checked to make sure Lillian hadn't heard her. She hadn't. She was still strolling merrily along the sidewalk, marching in her own one-woman brag brigade.

"You don't like the way I say *miss*?" Patricia asked. Elizabeth heard the melody of the accent first. The actual words registered a moment later. Elizabeth very much liked the way Patricia said *miss*, but . . .

"I would like it better if you said Elizabeth."

Patricia's eyes narrowed, the blue reflecting the intense heat of the summer sky. A hush passed between them. A thousand words flooded Elizabeth's throat, yet not one of them made its way out. They were stuck there, an anchor on her tongue. Elizabeth could neither force them out nor swallow them down.

Just as she began to fidget nervously, Patricia smirked and said, "Yes, miss."

"Stop that."

"No, miss. I cannot."

"You most certainly can," Elizabeth huffed. She very nearly stamped one of her feet.

Patricia fought off a grin, as if she were having a lark at Elizabeth's expense.

"Are you laughing at me?" Elizabeth asked.

"No," Patricia said solemnly, "I would never laugh at you, miss. You're not funny."

"I *am* funny!" Elizabeth sputtered, outraged. Now she did stamp her foot.

"I'm sorry to tell you, but no." And this time Patricia's smirk broke into a full grin, a grin she promptly squelched as Lillian whirled to see what Elizabeth's (rather loud) fuss was about.

"Elizabeth Mary Louise Post, control yourself," Lillian tutted sharply.

Elizabeth burned with embarrassment, then turned playfully hostile eyes on Patricia.

"You're to blame for that. You goaded me," she accused. Her tone suggested displeasure, but her cheeks were happily pink from their interaction. Elizabeth didn't mind being goaded by Patricia. Not if it came with that burst of a smile.

Patricia admitted as much with a short nod, then answered, "I do apologize, *Miss* . . ." and just as Elizabeth grew disappointed, continued in a lower tone, "Elizabeth Mary Louise Post."

Hearing her name issued like that, from Patricia, with the accent and the inflection and the warmth, made the hairs on Elizabeth's arms tingle. She watched Patricia's lips for a long moment, hoping for more. Then her gaze found Patricia's, who stared intently back at her.

Patricia's eyes jerked away. "Tell me more about this Independence Day you have here," she said brusquely, her eyes roving the town square with exaggerated interest, the thick ribbons, the fluffy bunting. "I've never seen anything quite like it."

The sudden shift made Elizabeth's head spin. She struggled to snag the thread of conversation. "Um, oh. Oh, yes. It is a uniquely American holiday, that is true. Father loves it because it represents our freedom from tyranny," Elizabeth explained.

"Are you? Free?" Patricia asked.

The simple question stumped Elizabeth. Was she free? What did that even mean, freedom?

Before she could answer, Patricia said, "Your mother has gotten too far ahead of us." She walked quickly toward Lillian, leaving Elizabeth standing in front of a small shopfront. A new perfumery! She was drawn immediately to the window display, an arrangement of glass bottles, all shapes and sizes and colors. They were beautiful.

She turned to look for Patricia, who had caught up with Lillian. Elizabeth replayed the last few moments in her mind. Had she said something to make Patricia walk away? Elizabeth's body still pulsed with the residual buzz from their shared gaze, and she was left to wonder about these odd, unusual, utterly foreign feelings.

"What is this world coming to?" a smooth voice intoned.

Elizabeth tensed. Standing right behind her was Honey Harper. Elizabeth could see her reflected in the perfumery window. All her muscles encouraged her to flee, but she steeled herself as much as she could, and turned to face the viper.

Honey was wearing a thin silk dress that clung to her willowy frame, sleeveless, her alabaster arms shaded by a shockingly colorful parasol. Red, white, and blue. Of course. And perched on her flaxen head, on that thoroughly modern haircut, sat a hat of pure perfection. She looked like summer personified.

Her hawkish eyes were on Patricia, though, whose hair had surrendered to the heat and humidity, errant curls sprouting from her braid like weeds in a garden.

"Darling, that hair . . ." Honey tut-tutted. "You should make her cut it," she said, giving a pointed look to Elizabeth's own hair.

The barb stung, as Honey had undoubtedly intended. Elizabeth's hand twitched. She was just able to keep herself from reaching up to self-consciously smooth her own too-long locks, and although Honey's dart had hit its mark, Elizabeth forced her face to remain passive, unbothered.

So, Honey looked back toward Patricia and sneered, "For the love of fashion, at least hide her under a hat. Or a sack."

Elizabeth watched Patricia take a shopping bag from Lillian and hook it over her own arm, leaving Lillian's hands free. Her ire rose at Honey's insult, but she heard herself say, "She's . . . Irish."

"As we are all too aware," Honey said, looking at Patricia as if she were a diseased stray. "Well, you can wash that off her, I suppose, if there is enough soap at hand."

Elizabeth flinched. Honey was quite possibly the worst person she'd ever known. Patricia's fortunate position in the Post house did not change the fact that she, so new to this country and still imbued with her natural wildness, wasn't seen as much more than white trash. *White trash.* Elizabeth hated the term. No person was trash. Not one. Not in her eyes.

But that wasn't what she'd said to Honey, was it?

She's . . . Irish.

As if it were an excuse. Or an apology.

Shame on you, Elizabeth, she thought, cringing at her own cowardice. She loved Patricia's untamed hair. She loved the earthiness of her. Never stopped thinking about it, in truth.

So why couldn't she simply tell Honey Harper to shove her opinion where the sun didn't shine? Why couldn't she defend her,

her . . . her . . . what? Her servant? Patricia did serve in her house, but Elizabeth had never thought of her as "the help," as her mother would say. She never thought of Sarah that way, either. Or Henry, who tended the yard, or Richard, who tended her father. They were people. Sarah was her friend, and Patricia was— What was she to Elizabeth?

"Your mouth is hanging open. Are you catching flies, dear?" Honey drawled.

Elizabeth snapped her lips shut. Honey was studying her with those frightening, all-seeing eyes of hers. Elizabeth's stomach twisted.

"Are you— Will we see you at the barbecue?" Elizabeth asked, trying to recover.

Honey allowed the change of subject with a nonchalant sigh and said, "I'm afraid I'll be missing the festivities this year. Chess Pennington has insisted I join his family for brunch."

Chess Pennington. The town's most eligible bachelor.

The Penningtons were wealthy beyond belief, too wealthy to even acknowledge Independence Day. They considered it a gauche affair, a celebration of American bluster and brawn. They didn't fly the flag or bend the knee the way Elizabeth's father did. Still, they were the most respected family in town, if only for their ability to make money. Nathaniel Post envied Skip Pennington as much as he despised him.

It didn't surprise Elizabeth, then, that Honey would choose a Pennington brunch over any other party. Honey knew how to keep her bread buttered, and when best to eat it. She would be the ideal complement to Chess Pennington. It was something Honey herself thought, too, if her simpering smile was any indication.

Elizabeth's gaze shot to the patriotic parasol in Honey's grip, and she smirked. Parasols had gone out of fashion several years ago; even Elizabeth knew that. The smirk just slipped out, really, it did. But Honey caught it. Her eyes turned to icy slits.

"Obviously, this *dreadful* thing"—she waved the parasol as if it were a repugnant afterthought—"belongs to Rose." When Elizabeth again failed to rise to the bait, Honey bared her teeth in a feral grin and continued, "But you, dear, without a shade at all on this midsummer afternoon. You'll soon be like a grape left too long in the sun. Only common folk allow themselves to wither on the vine." Her gaze swept across Elizabeth's face. "In your case, I suppose it doesn't really matter."

That one landed.

Elizabeth was considered plain by modern standards. She was self-conscious of that fact with every breath she took, a fact that Honey used time and again as her dagger of choice. Elizabeth didn't even wear cosmetics, as did the other young women of her class. She did not use rouge or kohl or even lipstick. She wasn't allowed.

A hand on her arm stopped Elizabeth's hurt gasp. She knew the feel of that hand, of those fingers. They lent her a steady calm that she didn't deserve, not after what she'd said. Patricia stepped closer to Elizabeth, as if shielding her. Another kindness Elizabeth did not deserve. "Your mother sent me to fetch you, miss."

"Like a bone, then." Honey snickered. "Elizabeth, your mongrel has come to fetch you."

Elizabeth felt the tension snap in Patricia, saw the eruption in those stormy blue eyes, but Patricia visibly took hold of herself and turned to face Honey.

"My *name* is Patricia."

Honey cocked her head and gave Patricia a withering once-over, then she jutted her pointed chin and murmured, "Woof."

With that, she twirled the parasol, turned on her dainty heel, and walked away.

Both Elizabeth and Patricia were silent, until Patricia said, "I don't like her."

Elizabeth laughed, an almost unladylike snort. "I don't particularly care for her, either," she agreed. Then Elizabeth's conscience surged up to remind her of her spineless capitulation in the face of Honey's nastiness. She suddenly grasped Patricia's hand tightly. "Patricia. I'm so sorry," she said, her voice almost agonized.

"'Twas her forked tongue doin' the talking. You've nothing to apologize for, Elizabeth," Patricia said softly, with that accent that hit Elizabeth squarely in the knees.

Elizabeth hated herself because she *did* have something to apologize for, but she knew in that moment that she would never confess it. Patricia had called her *Elizabeth*, without prompting. Any confession now might lead to a regress, and Elizabeth, for reasons she could not yet name, refused to cede any ground. So, she smiled at her . . . her . . . *friend*—yes, her friend—and she promised herself that she would never again allow anyone to abuse Patricia in any way, not even with words.

Patricia peered into the perfumery window and gazed at all those colored glass bottles.

"Look at all of 'em," she said quietly. "They make quite a show."

Elizabeth could only nod. She traced a finger across the glass, outlining the bottles. She saw, in the window, Patricia gaze softly at her, and her heart tripled its beat. The fingers of Patricia's hand laced with hers, and for a brief, spectacular moment, they held hands. Then Patricia let go and nudged Elizabeth away from the display and toward her mother, who was waiting, exasperated from the look of her, at the far end of the block.

Elizabeth hurried toward Lillian, feeling Patricia behind her the whole way.

17

LIBBY

The sun is almost down, leaving the room so dim that I can barely see the words I'm reading. My eyes are glued to the journal as I reach blindly for the oil lamp . . .

> *It is clear, in hindsight, that the arrival of Patricia in my life was the beginning of our end, but it was an end that I would chase, as fast as my legs would carry me.*

. . . strike a match, and hold it to the cloth wick like a pro. A soft yellow glow rises in the room, casting light over the journal, and Elizabeth's words are once again visible.

I'm just about to turn another page when the oil lamp brightens. I turn to look at it. The wick is where I left it, but it's definitely brighter. Or maybe my eyes are still adjusting to the fading light. I'm about to turn down the wick when a sound from downstairs stops me. Knocking. Someone's knocking at the door. I close the journal and grab the oil lamp. My knees are stiff from having my legs curled under me for so long. I stretch them as I hurry out of the room. The knocking is coming from the front door.

I take the stairs quickly, thinking maybe it's Cam. He and Horatio canceled on me tonight (they were, um, busy), but maybe there was a change of plans? Unlikely. But even so, Cam would come to the side door.

It takes less than thirty seconds for me to reach the front door, but I've already gone through a hundred different scenarios in my head. It's Cam; something happened with Horatio. It's Leo; he's found out I'm alone tonight and has come to try and take advantage of the privacy. It's Peter, coming to throw more empty garbage bags at me and laugh in my face again. It's Mom, bringing her delicious Tetrazzini as a housewarming meal—weeks late, but I would accept it gladly. Dad, coming to say he was wrong, that he's proud of the decision I made.

I laugh out loud at the last one. Yeah, right. It would literally be Patricia, straight from the pages of Elizabeth's diary, before it would be my dad. I walk a little faster, in a hurry to get rid of whoever's at the door so I can get back to Elizabeth's journal. A dart of exhilaration zings me, and I swear that the overhead light flickers just a little brighter as I smooth my hair over my shoulder, wipe my damp palm against my jeans, and open the door.

And then I get a jolt that buzzes straight through me, from head to toe. I can imagine exactly what Elizabeth must have felt when she first saw Patricia standing on her steps . . .

. . . because Tish is on my porch. Flame-haired, cerulean-eyed Tish.

18

TISH

It's Libby. Beautiful, doe-eyed, so-tired-she-looks-like-she's-about-to-fall-over Libby.

"Tish," she says, standing in the open doorway, the door I just knocked on for who knows what reason.

"Didn't get any sleep, huh?" I say, without preamble. I don't know what I meant to say, but it wasn't that. It's not like I'm the sleep police, handing out tickets to all insomniacs.

"How did you know I live here?" she asks.

"I didn't. I was just riding, and . . ." I let it trail off, because what answer could I possibly give her that would make any sense? I feel a little stalkery. Unintentional, obviously.

Lola and I spent the whole afternoon together, making up for lost time, riding the roads. We stopped for ice cream for me, and gas for her. We made a day of it and were on our way back to my sardine-can apartment when I decided to cruise down Mulberry Lane on the way home. No good reason except I just felt the urge to see the big house again. And the green glass stone.

It was the light that made me stop. A dim flicker in the upstairs window. Barely there, but I couldn't take my eyes off it. Then that tug looped around my ribs again. Like a finger. Pulling. It wasn't until I felt the sting of the wood against my knuckles that I realized

I'd actually knocked on the door. Knocking on a strange door. After dark. At a dead lady's house. Where's that nail gun when I need it?

And then *she* opened it. After I spent the whole damn day thinking about her. I don't believe in fate. That's Bari's thing. I do believe in coincidence, though. At least I do tonight.

She's still looking at me. Then she looks to the street, where Lola waits in the moonlight.

She says quietly, "But . . . what are you doing here?"

"I don't— I saw the light and—I don't know . . ."

I'm confused as hell about it, but when she opens the door wider and makes room for me to come inside, instinct carries me across the threshold and into her house.

The first thing that hits me is the smell. Sharp and tangy. Like bleach. She's been cleaning. Makes sense. The place, and everything in it, looks old as hell, but it's all clean. The too-shiny Victrola in the corner of the parlor has a weird vibe, though. The lid is open, and I feel like it's one big eye, staring at me. I don't love it.

Underneath the clean smell is another smell. Wet. Musty. Old.

I wonder if Libby knows about the lady who lived here before. I probably shouldn't bring that up. I don't want to spook her. Not saying the place is haunted, but if that creepy Victrola is any indication . . .

"This whole place looks like—" I'm about to say the *Christmas Carol* set when Libby beats me to it with "The set! I know, right?"

After a few more breaths, the smell isn't as strong as it was. Maybe I'm getting used to it. Or maybe I'm just distracted by the way the flickering oil lamp in Libby's hand makes her look like she's a character in one of those old movies Bari watches with Paps. Like she's from another time. Another place. Not from Small-Town-Wherever, population not-enough.

Suddenly, Libby looks at the glass lamp as if she's just realized she's holding it. She shrugs, explaining, "I needed it. For light."

Light? My eyes shoot to the light overhead. It's on. Seems to be working fine.

"Oh. Not down here. Something's wrong with the lights upstairs," she says.

"The lights upstairs don't work?" I ask, literally repeating what she literally just said.

Nail gun. Now.

"Yeah, well, we haven't covered that in class yet, so . . ." She trails off.

"I can look at the lights for you. If you want?"

Libby looks as relieved as I've ever seen anyone look, and says, "I do want. Very much."

My throat is suddenly itchy, so I clear it and ask, "You know where the fuse box is?"

She smiles, damn it, and says, "I'm sure we can find it," and walks toward the kitchen.

"You coming?" she asks, looking over her shoulder at me.

The soft glow of the flame hits her just right, highlighting everything that's beautiful about her face. I should get the hell out of here. But I don't. I just follow her deeper into the house, her oil lamp leading the way.

Damn damn damn damn damn.

19

LIBBY

We walk out the side door, under the porte cochere.

Tish steps around me, looking for the fuse box. She's so close I can feel her shadow. I take a deep breath and open the flashlight app on my cell. The glass lantern, traded for my iPhone, still burns softly in the kitchen. The phone's not as elegant, but it's much more convenient. And brighter. I shine it over the side of the house until it lands on the fuse box, then trail behind Tish as she moves toward it.

"It's a big house. You got roommates?" she asks as she pries open the old fuse box, and before I can answer, she says, "Whoa. Holy shit."

"What?" I hurry over to see what she's seeing.

She stares into the open fuse box with a look of wonder. "I think this is the original fuse box. Like, the *original* original," she says as she runs her hand back and forth over her short curls, making a cute little clicking noise as she studies the tubes and wires.

I lean in closer to get a better look.

The only time I've ever had a reason to look inside a fuse box was the one time my parents left me to babysit Peter and his friends. In less than an hour, I was fed up with their antics. Running, shouting, jumping all over the furniture. They were uncontrollable hell-hounds. I tried bribing them with unlimited Xbox time, endless candy bars, soda till they popped, but nothing would dissuade them from their maniacal *Lord of the Flies* reenactment. It made me want to bash them all in the head and scream "I got the conch!"

I didn't hit them, because I'm not a savage. I didn't even yell. Instead, I went to my room, slammed the door, and left them to do whatever ten-year-old boys do, which turned out to be a massive, messy water gun fight. In the house. Like the savages *they* were. Peter's Super Soaker flooded one of the outlets, there was a loud *POP*, and the whole house went dark. I had to call Dad to figure out what to do.

"Open that little metal door on the basement wall and flip the breaker."

It was so easy. So easy that I feel like a doofus now, not having tried this myself. All these weeks, and all I had to do was (maybe) flip the breaker. A real electrician was out of the question, because money. It also didn't really rank that high on my list of priorities. Even if Tish does get the upstairs lights working, I'll probably just keep using the oil lamp. It feels right in the house, in my hand.

But the last thing I want to look like in front of Tish is a helpless girl, so I straighten up and lean in even closer, pretending to be interested in getting the lights fixed. It'll make midnight bathroom trips easier, anyway. And . . . I want to watch Tish fix something.

The electronics inside this fuse box, though, are definitely older than the ones at home.

Correction: the ones at my *other* home. My previous home. The place where my parents and brother now live without me. I've gotten to where I don't think about them all day every day. It's only at times like this, when something reminds me of them or makes me remember. The weight of my decision bears down for a second and

I place my hand against the wood of the house, letting it calm me. My house. My home. Mine.

Works every time.

I breathe a little easier and peer into the fuse box. There are four murky glass fuses, each one screwed into the electrical panel, and cloth wires are attached to each of those, moving from the fuses into the house like veins or arteries.

Tish reaches out to touch one, but I grab her hand. Her fingers are warm. Almost hot.

"Wait. Don't . . ." But I'm not sure what I'm trying to say. I look at the fuse box, its hatch hanging open, and I suddenly feel like we're about to do surgery on the little heart that keeps the whole house alive. "Can we just leave it?" I ask. My fingers are still touching hers.

I pull my hand back. She stuffs hers into the pockets of her jacket.

"Um, yeah. If you want. Not sure if you'll have lights upstairs, though," she says.

"It's okay. I've kind of become one with the lantern, so . . ." I shrug.

"Well, it works for you—I mean, for the house. It works for the house. You know, the aesthetic. It . . . fits," she finishes awkwardly. She inches toward the driveway, like she's getting ready to bolt, but I'm not ready for her to leave. I want her to stay. Just a little while longer.

"You want to come in? I have some lemonade in the fridge. It's out of a packet, but it's not too gross. And, um, some ramen, maybe? I haven't eaten yet, but, um, you wanna join me?"

She looks to the street, to where her motorcycle is parked.

"You should probably get some sleep," she says. The rejection hurts. I nod stiffly, about to tell her she's right, when she adds, "But I almost never turn down food. If it's Top Ramen, I'm in."

I can feel the grin split my face, like she just told me I won a million dollars.

Her eyes drop to my mouth, for the splittest of a split second, then she claps her hands together and says, "Ramen! Let's do it."

I hurry to open the side door, excited about my dinner company.

Before she goes in, Tish stops and gives me a long look. She says quietly, "And then you'll get some sleep, okay?"

The look she gives me is warm and sincere, like her toughie mask has slipped just enough for me to see a tiny bit of squish beneath. It makes me want to hug her.

But instead, I just say, "Okay."

"Okay?" she says more firmly.

"Okay!" I promise.

She walks past me into the house, and something clicks deep inside me, something that hasn't really settled since I left home. It feels familiar and good. I feel *happy*.

I close the hatch on the fuse box, letting my hand rest there for a second, letting my fingers *thump-thump, thump-thump, thump-thump* lightly on the metal, giving it a heartbeat.

That outside light snaps on above me.

It hasn't come on since that first night, when I hesitated to open the door. This time, even though it startles me, I grin. It must be a short in the wiring, and my tapping triggered it, but then a whimsical part of me thinks that maybe, just maybe, the house is starting to feel happy, too.

20

LIBBY

The morning sun wakes me bright and early. Ugh. Why didn't I close the drapes?

I slap blindly around the bed for my phone, finally finding it under my pillow. One sleep-deprived eye opens to check the time: 6:30 a.m. Way too early, especially for a Saturday morning. I wrap my arms around my pillow and snuggle back in, intent on sleeping at least four more hours. I don't know what time I finally went to bed, but I was so tired that Tish practically carried me upstairs to my room—

I bolt upright.

Tish!

Maybe she's still here. We'd been having such a good time, so I kept us up later and later, until we were both so tired we could barely see. I told her to just crash in one of the other bedrooms, so, maybe . . . ? I hurry out of bed and start for the door, then catch sight of myself in the mirror. I'm wearing the same clothes I wore to practicum yesterday, the clothes I then lounged around in on the parlor floor last night. I sniff the sleeve. No way. I can't go down there like this.

I grab some fresh clothes and slip into the bathroom. The pipes clang when I turn on the water. If Tish is still here, and if she's not already awake, this stupid plumbing will do the trick.

I scrub my teeth, a dribble of foamy toothpaste sliding onto my chin as I smile. My sides ache from all the laughing we did last night, like I did a hundred crunches, then added two hundred more for good measure.

"So *that's* what was wrong with your butt!" I'd choked out when I was finally able to breathe. I was facedown on the parlor rug, gasping, tears rolling down my cheeks.

Tish was laughing, too, even though her face was red with embarrassment.

"I didn't walk right for a week," she said. Then she got up and hobbled around the room, holding her pants away from her butt, imitating herself. "It was a low point, trust me."

"So you . . . hit bottom," I joked, still laughing. Tish glared at me, then she laughed, too. "Are you okay now? Did it scar?" I asked, wiping my eyes with the back of my sleeve.

Tish's face froze, her blue eyes wide and comical.

"You haven't looked?"

"Do you make a habit of looking at your own ass?" she asked.

I shrugged. "I mean . . ."

She jumped up and ran to the hallway bathroom. I heard her clothes rustle, then some grunts, as I imagined her twisting around to look over her shoulder. The mirror in the bathroom isn't much help if you're needing a full-body view, but I guess she saw enough, because she strolled out a few seconds later, cocky as could be, waggling her brows.

"No scars?" I guessed.

"Smooth as a baby's backside," she said. Which, for some reason, made me laugh again.

I spit, rinse, then yank a brush through my hair. It's been a long time since I made a new friend, and Tish had notched into place like a puzzle piece. A foundational piece. Like a corner. Like Cam. I can't wait to introduce her to Cam. They are going to crush on each other so hard.

I change my clothes, then hurry out of the bathroom. I stop first at the sad room and listen at the door. Silence. I scratch lightly, then quietly open the door. She's not in there.

In the kitchen, I find our dishes in the sink, carefully stacked, because the only dishes in the house are Elizabeth's, and it's the good stuff. Bone china, with little (I'm sure) hand-painted flowers on them. If Tish had any thoughts about us eating fifty-nine-cent ramen out of antique china bowls, then she kept them to herself. We had carried our noodles into the parlor and sat on the floor to eat, using the fireplace hearth as a kind of table. It was just chilly enough that Tish decided to make a fire. I watched her check the flue, arrange a small stack of wood, then light it easily, as if she'd done it a thousand times before.

"Is there anything you can't do?" I asked her.

She just laughed and curled up on the big oval wool rug and started eating, telling me about her love for building things, for making things work, about Joe and his shop and all the time she spent there, about Paps and Hasina and Bari and how they became her family, about Professor Wallis and all the time she spent at the scene shop. She was always building something. Anything she could get her hands on.

Then it was like the floodgates opened, and suddenly, it no longer felt like we were getting to know each other. It felt like we were *catching up*. On everything. Our whole lives.

I told her about the house, about my lifelong dream of owning it, of living here. I told her about the meltdown it had caused, the literal scorched-earth tirade that my father had gone on. I told her about my wonderful, wonderful Gammy, about subhuman Peter, about Molly-Holly-Homemaker, and about the perfection that is Cam. I didn't talk about Leo. I started to, but then . . . I left him out. Because I was talking about things that mattered most to me.

Whoa. I file that feeling away to think about later.

Some of Tish's stories were hilarious, like her broken butt; some were bittersweet, like how she and Bari became besties; and some had me holding back tears. Her mother. Everything about her mother.

Dan and Molly are far from perfect, but I never felt invisible to them. I never felt like they were embarrassed by me. I know, even when they're angry with me, even now, even with everything about this house, I know they love me. They're just not acting like it.

"No, no, none of that," Tish had said when she caught me sniffling. "No crying."

I waved it off. "I'm just tired. I always cry when I'm tired."

"Bedtime for you, then."

I hurry from the kitchen into the parlor. The blankets we'd been curled up on are folded and stacked on the sofa. The fire is out; the hearth is cold.

She didn't stay.

I swallow a twinge of disappointment and head back to the kitchen to wash the few dishes we used. I'm rinsing the first dish when I think I hear a quiet click and squeak. I shut off the water and listen. I turn the water back on, but something inside nudges me. *Check the maid's room.* Not quite loud enough to hear, but strong enough to *feel*. When I turn around, the door to one of the servants' bedrooms is slightly open.

She's here!

I move toward the door and listen. It's quiet, so I push it open and peek inside.

She's *not* here. But one of the twin beds is rumpled, like it had been slept in and hastily made up. I can't stop the smile that breaks across my face. She may not be here now, but she definitely spent the night, and that makes me happier than I could have imagined.

I walk over to the bed and smooth the blankets. A bright red hair clings to the pillowcase. I reach for it, and just as I pick it up, a wave of dizziness swirls through me. It's Tish's hair. It has to be. But this was *Patricia's* bed. I'm as certain of it as I am of my own name.

I sink down to sit on the bed, pick up the pillow, and hug it to my suddenly aching chest.

It's not that I didn't know the journal entries were true, but I have never felt time the way I'm feeling it now. Time feels alive, like the house feels alive. It's all suddenly very, very real. Elizabeth's journals, they're real. This pillow I'm holding is real. It's from another time, another era, and yet here it is. Patricia slept here. Right here. She lay in this bed, every night, and thought about . . . what? Did she think about Elizabeth? Did she have any idea that Elizabeth was upstairs, thinking about her, too? Every night?

21

AUGUST 1, 1925

Elizabeth had always cherished her Saturdays, but in the last few weeks they had become especially precious, because, coincidentally, Saturday afternoons just happened to be Patricia's afternoons off. That coincidence had nothing, Elizabeth would insist, to do with the fact that she had convinced Sarah to swap her day off (Saturday) for Patricia's (Sunday).

Sundays for Elizabeth were church, church, church, from sunup to sundown. Early service, followed by Sunday school, followed by a ladies' luncheon, then charitable duties, whether it be visiting the infirm or feeding the indigent, then evening service, and finally, home for a late dinner. When it came to religious dedication, the Post family would not be found wanting. But the rigorous Sunday schedule left no time for Elizabeth to simply *be*.

Elizabeth's Saturdays, though, were free, and she aimed to spend that time, or as much of it as she could, with Patricia.

But Sarah had capitulated to the trade too easily, and though Elizabeth was getting exactly what she wanted (Sarah's usual day off exchanged with Patricia's), she couldn't let go of the issue without pressing her friend for more information.

"Sarah. We are friends, aren't we? You and I?"

"Of course we are."

"Then tell me what's the matter? I never see you anymore. You stay too busy, or you stay in your room. Are you all right?"

Sarah hesitated. Then she said, "Timothy has . . . He has gotten married. Not to me, obviously." And after a long hesitation, she finally admitted, "To Caroline."

Elizabeth gasped. Timothy, the clerk's apprentice for the Sawyer house, and Caroline, the wayward maid. Everything suddenly clicked into place. Caroline's absences, her subsequent dismissal, Sarah's withdrawal from . . . everything.

"That snake!" Elizabeth hissed. "That worm! And that dirty, rotten, little—"

"Yes," Sarah said sadly, "all those things."

"Why didn't you tell me?"

"What was there to tell, except a silly little story of heartbreak and stupidity? I didn't even see it. I knew that something was wrong, that Timothy had been distant, but it would never have occurred to me that Caroline would . . . Oh, well. I'd really rather forget it, if you don't mind."

So, that was the end of it. Sarah worked on mending her broken (and humiliated) heart, while Elizabeth found her own heart blossoming like a flower under the sun of Patricia's shy, but devoted, attention.

During their new Saturday hours together, she'd learned that Patricia was nineteen years old, and that she'd made the harrowing voyage to America only a year prior, on a ship crowded with economic and political refugees. She'd learned that Patricia had been born into hardship, had been faced with the harsh realities of life at far too young an age. Patricia had never been sheltered, as Elizabeth was, which, along with her natural willfulness, had only served to make her doubly resilient. Patricia was strong where others might be weak.

And Elizabeth had learned, perhaps most importantly, that Patricia was perfectly content to spend all her free afternoons with Elizabeth, telling her everything she wanted to know.

This particular Saturday saw the afternoon warm, the leaves still green on the trees, and the air thick with humidity. Their only reprieve was the constant breeze provided by the elevation as the girls lounged on the modest overlook that peaked above the town, the remnants of a picnic lunch spread before them. Elizabeth nibbled at the corner of a tea cake as she watched Patricia take in the view. Her wild red hair, untethered (upon Elizabeth's insistence), was swept back by the wind. It billowed behind Patricia's strong profile, making her look like art in motion.

"If we were in Ireland, all that you see there would be green. So many miles of green you wouldn't believe your eyes," Patricia said, "and above you would be the biggest blue sky you'd ever seen. With clouds, sheer like lace." She stretched out her arm over the east area of the town. "Right over there would be the potato fields. You'd be happy enough to never again see another potato, Elizabeth, if you'd grown up eating those and only those. We starved on 'em, we did, but oh, what a view we had. The most beautiful land that ever graced the earth."

Patricia painted a picture of her homeland that was both beautiful and tragic.

Elizabeth put a comforting hand on Patricia's arm. Elizabeth had never known hunger; she couldn't fathom it, but just as her eyes filled with sympathetic tears, Patricia's hand covered hers, warm and sure, and she said quietly, "No, no. There'll be none of that."

Elizabeth pulled Patricia's hand to her face, touched it quickly to her cheek, then let it go. Patricia's gaze lingered on Elizabeth's cheek, on that very spot she'd touched, for long moments. Then she swept her arm to the other side of the imaginary view.

"Over there would be a few homesteads, with stacked stone borders for those lucky enough to have a sheep or two. We did not." She pointed off in the far distance. "And out there, way out yonder, would be a sea of such purple that you'd swear you'd died and gone to heaven."

"Heather," Elizabeth whispered.

"Lots and lots of it." Patricia nodded with a smile.

"Do you miss it terribly?"

"I do, sometimes. But . . . there are things here I would miss more." She cleared her throat and pointed to an area near the center of town. "Right down there would be the vicar's house."

Elizabeth jokingly sneered, "Catholic, of course."

Patricia whispered back, "What would you know about it, you filthy Protestant?"

They both laughed, Elizabeth using the opportunity to move just a little closer, until she was shoulder to shoulder with Patricia, nearly touching.

"What a scandalous pair we make," Patricia said, still chuckling. "Oh, the trouble you'd see if you were caught cavorting with the riffraff."

Elizabeth sobered immediately. She didn't find that funny, not one bit.

"You're not— Look at me. You're not riffraff, Patricia," she said as she looked into those vivid blue eyes. For a moment, she was caught by their color, unable to breathe or even blink.

"We should go," Patricia said abruptly. She stood up to gather their things.

Confused, and more than a little flustered, Elizabeth got to her feet and started folding the blanket. "I've upset you. I'm sorry."

When Patricia didn't answer, Elizabeth grew concerned that

she really had upset her friend. She dropped the blanket and her hands twisted themselves together, her fingers so rigidly locked the knuckles turned white. She watched Patricia toss their lunch scraps off the overlook, then quickly pack their soiled plates and utensils into the picnic basket.

"Patricia?" Elizabeth tried again. "I don't know what I did . . ."

"No. I know you don't."

The words were harsh. Unintentionally so, given the way Patricia immediately pulled her bottom lip between her teeth, as though that might withdraw the sting.

She put down the basket and took Elizabeth's clenched hands into her own, gently separating the twisted fingers, rubbing them, restoring the blood flow, restoring the feeling. Elizabeth's eyes followed the movement of Patricia's fingers over hers. Her thumb moved to stroke Patricia's skin, as if the wayward digit were not under her control.

"I don't want you to be angry with me," Elizabeth said.

"Oh, Elizabeth. It's not anger, my love." The endearment startled them both, Elizabeth blushing to the roots of her hair, and Patricia stammering as she grabbed the picnic basket. "I'll see you at home—I mean, at the house."

She hustled toward the long, winding path that led down the overlook, leaving Elizabeth to stare after her, her heart pounding right out of her chest. She wiped her sweaty palms on her dress, then picked up the blanket and set out toward the path, keeping several lengths behind Patricia, watching those fiery red curls bounce in the sun.

22

LIBBY

The flower shop is slow this morning, so Cam and Horatio make themselves at home behind the counter as I pick through a pile of soft-colored flowers. Someone emailed the store this morning and ordered an arrangement for a midnight picnic. Since *picnic*, to me, has always meant *date*, I'm loading up the arrangement with romantic flowers. Scattered on the counter are lisianthus, sweet peas, ranunculus, and roses, all in mild pinks, creams, and whites.

I arrange the roses first, turning the vase as I go, until they're all nestled in their green foam home. When I pick up the sweet peas, Cam shoves his phone at my face. "Holy hell, is this her?"

He's found Tish's timeline.

"That hair," he says. "That can't be real. She colors it, right?"

"Nope. It's real." I know it's true. I have no reason to be so sure, except I just know it.

"Gorgeous," he sighs. I nod because I wholeheartedly agree. Tish's hair is electric. From the corner of my eye, I see Cam scroll through the pics. I chuckle as I layer in the flowers.

"Doing a little sleuthing?"

"Oh, please. You trying to tell me you haven't had your nose all up in these?"

Horatio belts out a huge, honking guffaw. I shoot him a stink eye. He pretends to zip his lips, then flips a page in the catalog. Cam knows me too well. Of course I've snooped through all of Tish's socials. It took me less than three seconds to find her. Tish O'Connell. Her profile pic is a selfie in the sun, her hair shining, sitting on a ragged-looking motorcycle.

She hadn't captioned any of her posts, but there were dozens. Photos of theater shows, Tish backstage, working on sets, laughing with the costumed cast. Professor Wallis standing close to Dr. B, who, Tish told me the other night, was the one who took all those beach photos of Wallis. Very sweet. There was a series of pics of a motorcycle and parts. A selfie with a grizzled old man, his arm around Tish's shoulder, both of them covered in oil and dirt.

The rest were pics of Tish with a girl. Long black hair. Jet-black eyes. Too pretty to be real. In every picture, she either had her arms around Tish, or was leaning against her. There was even one of her holding Tish by the face and biting her jaw, her straight white teeth lightly clenched on the skin close to Tish's mouth. At first, I thought that must be Bari, based on Tish's description, but if that was Bari, then where was Lola? No pictures of Lola online, but she talks about her all the time? *Lola and I went riding. Sunset is Lola's favorite time of day. Lola hates cold weather; she's so pissed that it's about to be winter...*

I never ask the obvious follow-up questions: Where did you meet her? How long have you been together? What does she look like? Why is she never with you?

I never ask because I don't really want to know.

I've noticed that Tish never asks about Leo, either.

"Can I help it that I'm curious about someone who regularly *spends the night at your house*?!" Cam sings with glee, bringing me back to the present.

"Omigod, don't say *regularly*, and it's not like she sleeps in my bed."

It is true, though, that in the last few weeks I have spent more time with Tish than I have with anyone else. Mainly because after that first night, she dove headfirst into my house project. She's almost as passionate about it as I am, but unlike me, Tish can actually make things happen.

The first thing she did was remove the hacked-up wood squares I used to cover the broken windowpanes and replace the glass. She *found* the glass, something about knowing how to scavenge. She helped me strip, sand down, and re-stain the stair I fixed (my woodglue patch job has been holding just fine!). Then she got someone in the scene shop to make a new spindle for the banister. It's an exact match of the others. Except for the tiniest color difference in the repaired crack, the staircase looks like it was never broken.

She rewired a couple of the downstairs outlets, so the lamps work now. The upstairs, as it turns out, was never wired for electric power. Apparently, back then, they really only had electricity in the main areas. That's why there are only four glass fuses in the fuse box. She also discovered, with just a glance, why the upstairs lights don't work. They were gas lights. She pointed to a skinny metal pipe (artfully painted to match the wall fabric) that runs from one of the sconces. There's a tiny valve on the side that controlled the flow of gas, like a light switch. "Woulda been typical for a house this age," she said. A double check on Google proved her right, of course. Then she blushed and looked away because I was staring, way too impressed with everything she seemed to just *know*, off the top of her head, like a genius.

We patched a tiny hole in the back wall of the kitchen so the little mouse who gnawed his way through several packs of my Top Ramen can't get in anymore. She found some gorgeous antique sconces and wired them up on either side of the front door; now the front porch isn't dark on the nights when I get home late. And she spent two whole days on the roof, filling in those bald spots with new shingles she picked up somewhere. They aren't a perfect match, but they're so close it doesn't matter. Not to me, anyway. The house is starting to look the way I always envisioned it, like those dreams I had before I moved in.

A few of those nights, Tish slept over, when we worked really late on some house thing, or when we just stayed up by the fire talking too long. Each time she stayed, she chose to sleep in Patricia's room. I couldn't blame her for not wanting to go home. I wouldn't want to walk through a bedroom where two other people were sleeping to get to my closet-bed, either. I hate that she sleeps in a walk-in closet. I hate it, hate it, hate it. I wish—

"Are you thinking about her now? Because you're literally a million miles away," Cam says, snatching me back to the present.

"Don't be stupid," I mutter. *And stop reading my mind. Please and thank you.*

He comes over to watch me work, resting his chin against my shoulder. "Just asking because it's only eleven thirty and you've already mentioned her about five times," he says.

"Make that ten," Horatio adds.

"You shut up," I say, and throw a rose at him. It hits his chest and falls to the counter.

He picks it up and offers it to Cam—"For you"—with a gallant bow. I yank the rose away from them both and stuff it into the arrangement.

"That's thirteen. Is that unlucky? Thirteen roses?" Cam asks.

I quickly count the roses. Thirteen. Then I smile. How very apropos. For us, anyway.

"What?" he asks, catching my look. "What does thirteen roses mean?"

"Friends forever," I tell him with a wink.

"You just made that up," Horatio says.

"I did not. It means friends forever," I say, and smile at Cam.

"Damn right, honey," he says, and kisses my cheek.

"How do you know all the meanings?" Horatio asks.

"Part of the job. Especially here. The owner is a stickler about it."

I'm about to remove the surplus rose from the arrangement, to move the friend zone back into romance, when the front door opens, the little bell tinging lightly. As if I summoned her just by talking about her, my boss walks in. She struggles to get through the door, her hands full.

"You're not supposed to be here today," I say, surprised to see her.

She wears a dark yellow peacoat over a pale yellow dress. Her little Georgia, wiggling and happy, is tucked under her arm, and she pulls a small utility cart behind her. Cam hurries to hold the door. When she smiles sweetly at him, his eyes go all soft and gooey. She does that to people. Even Horatio is staring at her, instantly smitten.

"I went to town, downtown, to look for some things for the nursery." She lets go of the cart to pat her massive belly. "I stopped at the flower mart, and look what they had!" she exclaims happily. Her little cart is filled with stargazer lilies, bright pink and white. Stargazer lilies were instrumental in her own love story. For a romantic second, I wonder what it must be like to find one's perfect match. To have a literal dream come true. I glance at Cam and Horatio.

No magical fairy tale there, just a perfectly modern he-slid-into-his-DMs story. But it works for them. It's perfect.

And my story with Leo? We're not even at chapter three, and I'm already bored.

~

The shrimp aren't as good as they usually are. Or maybe it's just me. Probably it's me. I pick at them, moving them around my plate. Leo reaches across the table, touches my hand.

"Still nothing from your parents?" he asks.

The question surprises me. Not because he wouldn't ask, but because I haven't thought about my parents in a week, maybe more. I've been so focused on the house, having so much fun, loving school for the first time, and just being myself, more than ever before, that I'd kind of forgotten all the bad stuff. So, no, it's not my parents' complete lack of communication that has me out of sorts, unable to enjoy my very favorite meal on the planet.

Leo nudges his carbonara toward me. "Want mine?"

I give him a small smile and grab a noodle with my fork. Carbonara isn't my favorite, but it's sweet of him to offer it. After one bite, I'm done.

Leo watches me for a few seconds, then stands up. "Bathroom. Be right back."

There's a live band somewhere nearby. I can hear it off in the distance. A muffled guitar and muted drums. I snag another noodle from Leo's plate and roll it around in my fra diavolo sauce. Not bad. Creamy and spicy. I spear one of my devil-flavored shrimp and swipe it through a little pool of carbonara sauce on Leo's plate. Mmmm. Even better.

By the time Leo gets back, I've got a whole cream-spice-shrimp-noodle blend going on. He sits down and gives it a long, curious look.

"Try it," I say, and stab another spicy shrimp. I sweep it through the carbonara, wrap a couple of noodles around it, then hold my fork out to him. He leans in to take it. His eyes open wide in surprise. "It's good, right?"

"It *is*," he mumbles around the food, almost dribbling. Then he laughs, trying to keep from spitting food, which makes him laugh harder. And that makes me laugh.

When did we stop having fun? The house has taken up all the space in my life, and where I used to see Leo four or five times a week (sometimes more), I now see him three, or two. I blow him off more than I make time for him. And when I am with him, my mind is always somewhere else. Maybe I'm not bored by Leo. Maybe I just haven't been present enough.

I watch him put together another bite, but this time he swipes his noodles through my fra diavolo sauce. He eats it, nods, gets another bite, then grins at me over the table. He really does have great dimples. And that hair. Look at all that hair. It's average brown, but not everyone can be raging red.

Someone comes into the restaurant, holds the door open for his friends, and a guitar riff follows them in from the street, until the heavy door shuts and dampens the sound again.

"Wanna get out of here?" I ask.

Leo looks up, wipes his mouth with his napkin. "Sure, lemme just . . ."

He pulls out his wallet and flags down the waiter as I gather my purse and coat.

Outside, Leo heads for the car, but I grab his hand and pull him toward the music. It's coming from a little bar with a wide-open door. We can see the band inside the bar, playing their hearts out.

"Dance with me," I say to Leo.

"Here?" He looks around. There are quite a few people out tonight, at the bar, at restaurants, strolling along Main Street, heedless of the frigid air. It's the weekend. Everyone's free. Everyone's having fun.

"Yes. Here."

Leo's head tilts, and he looks toward the bar, toward the band, toward the people milling around us. He's not going to do it. I sigh. But as soon as I turn away, I'm swept off my feet.

Leo swings me around. I laugh and hold on tight.

"You wanna dance, huh?" he says, those dimples deep and sweet.

He sets me on my feet, takes my hand, and twirls me around, like they do in old-fashioned movies. Like Fred and Ginger, but not at all like them, because neither Leo nor I know anything much about dancing, especially that kind of dancing. But we try.

A few people stop to watch. This would normally be where I would stop, where I would get embarrassed for being so silly in public. But I just hold Leo's hand and dance harder, ignoring the grins and grimaces of the growing crowd.

23

LIBBY

Leo's kisses are hot and urgent. I fumble to get the key in the door, twisting it in the lock and letting him shuffle us inside. We stumble through the house in the dark, bumping hard against the kitchen table, overturning a chair, elbow-checking a half-open door.

He feels solid under my hands. He feels good. It's not perfect. But it's definitely not bad.

Leo stops and pulls away. I reach for him again and he says, "Wait. Wait. Libby. Wait."

I can feel the dampness of his chest under his shirt, the thudding of his heart.

"Are you sure?" he asks, breathing hard.

I'm mostly sure. My body is sure. My head is on board. My heart? I really don't know.

I kiss him again anyway and move us toward the staircase. Our feet tangle on the way, so he wraps his arms around my waist and carries me up the stairs. My legs dangle in front of him, the tips of my shoes brushing each step as we ascend. I just hold on and keep kissing.

Then I hear it. A low groan. It's barely there. Under Leo's heavy breathing. Under the sound of our kisses. Under the clomp of each step Leo takes, trying to keep us both upright.

There it is again. A *groan*. Not like a person. More like the sound a boat makes when it hits a large swell. Or like a house makes when the wood shifts, when the ground is too soft.

I open my eyes. The house is dark around us. The only light is from the moon shining through the big front windows. And outside those windows, buried in the sidewalk, the green glass stone gleams brightly. Then it dims. Then it shines again. I stare at it, over Leo's shoulder, that green glowing dot, pulsing in long, slow pulses ... light ... dark ... light ... dark ... like it's breathing, and for a split second I see snowfall, thick in the night air. I see my own breath puffing, heavy, frantic little clouds. I see pale lips. Long red hair. Blue eyes.

I let go of Leo, start to push him away just as he takes another step up ...

... right onto that wood-glued, barely repaired cracked step.

It breaks beneath our weight.

He yelps as his foot goes through.

I land hard on my butt, watching helplessly as Leo tries to keep his balance. He can't. He teeters back. His other hand shoots out and grips the spindle, the very spindle Tish replaced. It snaps in two and Leo slides backward down the staircase. His butt thuds rapidly as he rumbles to the bottom. *BRRRRRRRT.*

"Leo?! Are you okay?"

For two seconds too long, it's totally silent. Just as I start to panic, he moves.

"Ow," he croaks. I hurry down the stairs to check on him. I run my hands over his arms and legs. Nothing seems broken. He flops back on the floor, feet still propped up on the stairs, and starts laughing. "I don't think this house likes me very much."

"I think you might be right," I say as I lean against the bottom of the banister. I can see the green glass stone outside. But now I can tell that it was just the moonlight, peeking in and out of the clouds, that made it look like it was breathing, like it was alive.

Leo sits up and reaches for my hand. I let him take it, but even as he runs his thumb sensuously across my palm, we both know the evening's over. He sighs and sits up. "Welp. I guess that was a mood killer."

"I'm sorr—"

"Nah. Not your fault. Don't worry about it, Lib."

The way he says *Lib*, just like my dad, makes me curl up inside. I grab his hand tighter and yank him to his feet. He laughs again and uses the momentum to loop his arms around me.

Strong. Warm. Wrong. Oh, shit. Shit shit shit.

∼

I reach over to hold the hand of the man in my bed.

"Thanks for coming over," I say into the quiet room.

"I'm here. Anytime you need me. Thirteen roses," Cam says softly. He leans his head against mine. I turn and bury my face in his neck. He's wearing his special cologne again.

"Oh no. I took you away from a date night."

"Every night's a date night with Horatio." He smirks. I squeal happily and wrap my arms around him. He squeals, too, and suddenly we're kids again. Sharing a bed. Sharing secrets. He runs a hand over my hair as our limbs twine together and we get comfortable.

"I don't want to be one of those girls who ends up with a guy just like her dad."

"Uh-huh. And . . . ?" he prompts me.

"I don't want Leo."

Cam nods like he already knew. Which, of course, he did. I

watch the shadows play across the ceiling while I gather my thoughts.

"Cam?"

"Hmm."

"Do you believe in ghosts?"

He goes very, very quiet. Then he slowly turns his eyes to mine. "I'm sorry, what?"

"Never mind."

"Too late. Spill it."

So I tell him about the weird moment on the stairs with Leo, the green glass stone shining in the moonlight, how I saw those pale lips and that red hair. And then, although it feels so private, like I'm about to air someone else's deepest secrets, I tell him about the journal. I tell him about Elizabeth and Patricia and how I'm sure, how I'm so very sure that they're in love and just haven't realized it yet—in the past, of course, but it feels so, so like it's happening *now*. Today, instead of 1925.

"That could be because you're just now reading it, hon," Cam says wisely. "Here's a thought. Is Patricia the only redhead you know? I mean, there's a certain solar flare you haven't stopped talking about for days. Maybe it wasn't Patricia on your mind, but another redhead."

Cam might be hitting a little too close to the truth with that one, so I roll over to face the window, my back to him. He doesn't let me go far. He curls up right behind me, his arm around my waist, his legs tucked up behind mine. I grab his arm and hold on tight.

"Why don't you come stay with me for a few days? Give this house a break. Give yourself a break," he offers.

I don't even have to think about it to know the answer: "No. I'll stay here."

"Omigod, please don't go all Havisham on me." He chuckles.

I just laugh and snuggle closer. "I can't. I don't even have a wedding dress."

We lie still for a minute. Breathing. Thinking. Finally, I ask, "What's it like, to *like* a girl? Like that."

I can feel Cam's grin against the skin of my shoulder. "Exactly the same as liking a boy. But totally and completely different. In every way."

"Very helpful. Thank you." I yawn until I feel my jaw pop. Then after a couple of seconds, I whisper, "Kinda fluid, indeed." Cam laughs, and I feel him settle in behind me. I close my eyes, wrapped in the arms of my best friend, and fall asleep. Safe and sound.

24

SEPTEMBER 6, 1925

Summer had decided to linger this year. The heat was unbearable. Elizabeth sweltered under a shade tree, her hair heavy and hot, her skin slick in more than a few uncomfortable places. Her misery was only amplified by Honey Harper, who fluttered around like a butterfly in a breeze, and Rose, trailing along in her sister's perfumed wake. If Elizabeth squinted her eyes, the girls looked like marionettes bobbing on invisible strings, underscored by the music of the small jazz band playing nearby.

Honey was home for the weekend. She had spent half an hour peppering Elizabeth with stories of her first two weeks at Vassar. Honey was "having more fun than should be legal," she said, and said, and said again to Elizabeth, who swallowed the acrid jealousy threatening to choke her. Honey knew very well what she was doing, knew how badly Elizabeth had wanted college, had wanted that freedom for herself.

"And you, still here in this senseless town, beating back time with a stick," Honey drawled as she gave Elizabeth's two-years-out-of-fashion frock a scathing look. "How very dutiful you are, dear. Always so reliable. The apple of your father's dearest eye."

Elizabeth gritted her teeth. God, how she hated hated hated Honey Harper.

The band suddenly lit into an upbeat song, a real swinger.

"Oh, my favorite!" Honey exclaimed loudly as she peeled away from Elizabeth. She grabbed Rose's hand, and to the guests' delight, they began to dance the Charleston. As was the general way of things, Honey made herself the center of everyone's attention.

Save one.

Patricia could be seen through the open back door, working in the kitchen. Her eyes caught Elizabeth's, and the warmth in that gaze melted all of Honey's ice-tipped barbs, rendering them harmless. Elizabeth smiled back at her, then turned her focus to the party, careful, among so many watchers, to keep her affection for the young woman off her face.

Their time together had increased as of late, had moved beyond their Saturday afternoons. Patricia would linger now in Elizabeth's bedroom to lounge and talk after dressing her for the morning. No topic was found lacking, from their giddy dreams of visiting a real live speakeasy in the city, to the scent of the new detergent used to launder Elizabeth's garments. They could, and often did, talk for hours.

At least three nights a week, when Elizabeth was unable to sleep, she would sit by the fireplace in the hope that Patricia would sense her presence and come out of her room to join her at the hearth. She was never, not once, disappointed. She had only to wait a few minutes to hear the swing of Patricia's bedroom door, then her soft tread as she rounded the corner from the kitchen into the parlor, as if she, like Elizabeth, had been hoping for the encounter.

Some of those nights, Patricia would even build a tiny fire in the fireplace, heedless of the persistently warm weather, because Elizabeth loved to read by firelight. Then, to Elizabeth's immense pleasure, Patricia would listen raptly as she read aloud from her favorite works: *Wuthering Heights*, because Emily Brontë was nothing short of brilliant; Shakespeare's sonnets, because no one could turn a phrase quite like the Bard; and *Frankenstein*, by Mary Shelley, because, as she told Patricia, "Who doesn't fancy a fright now and then?"

This was how Sarah had found them, just a few nights ago.

It was long past midnight. They were in the parlor, lying on the big wool rug in front of the fireplace, both keeping an ear tuned to any sound from upstairs that meant Elizabeth's parents might be awake. Patricia was curled on her side, her eyes half-closed as Elizabeth read from a sublime collection of poetry by Kahlil Gibran called *The Prophet*.

"'Yet the timeless in you is aware of life's timelessness, / And knows that yesterday is but today's memory and tomorrow is today's dream . . .'" Elizabeth read reverently.

They were so enthralled by the elegant phrasing, the depth of meaning, that they had forgotten all else. Until Sarah walked in and scolded them fiercely.

She sent Patricia to her room and then accompanied Elizabeth up the stairs.

"We were just reading," Elizabeth protested as Sarah opened the door to Elizabeth's bedroom. Sarah pinned Elizabeth with a look of such disbelief that Elizabeth could not hold her gaze. She slumped past Sarah and sat on the edge of her bed.

"And yesterday, were you just *walking*?" Sarah asked.

Elizabeth flushed. They had been on their way home from the park, and she'd reached out and slipped her hand into Patricia's. Only for a moment. Only long enough to let the thrill of touching her skitter up her spine. She hadn't been aware of Sarah watching, of anyone watching.

"You're playing a dangerous game, Elizabeth," Sarah said.

"It's not a game. Patricia and I are friends."

"*You* and *I* are friends," Sarah said. "What you're doing with Patricia—"

"I'm not doing anything with her!"

Sarah stared at her for a long moment, then perched beside her on the bed. "I know that you are not stupid, Elizabeth. You have read enough"—she looked to the piles of books in Elizabeth's window nook—"to know that what you are feeling is not friendship."

Elizabeth picked at her coverlet, keeping her eyes away from Sarah's knowing gaze.

"This cannot be, my dearest. It simply cannot be," Sarah continued. Elizabeth opened her mouth to argue, again, that her feelings for Patricia were completely innocent, but Sarah stopped her with a hand on hers. She squeezed Elizabeth's fingers.

"Is this how you feel when Patricia holds your hand?" Sarah asked quietly.

Elizabeth swallowed and shook her head.

"There is no place in this world where this . . . friendship . . . would be accepted. Not one. When it is discovered, and *it will be* discovered, you will be ruined."

A tear broke from Elizabeth's lashes and made its way down her cheek. Sarah wiped it with gentle fingers, but she did not relent.

"*You* will be ruined, but you will still be Elizabeth Post, and there will at least be something in that for you. But Patricia . . . Elizabeth, there will be no protection for her. She has neither a name nor a family to defend her. She will be destroyed." Sarah stood then. She stopped at the small table and lowered the wick of Elizabeth's oil lamp, reducing the light in the room to a dim glow. "Now, get some sleep. And stop this *friendship* before it goes any further."

She gave Elizabeth a kind smile and a curt nod, then left Elizabeth to her thoughts.

But those warnings, as much as they tormented her that night, as much as they frightened her (for herself *and* for Patricia), were wiped away by the bright morning sun. Elizabeth could not harbor any fear of punishment or destruction, not when Patricia's fingers trembled against her bare back as she worked the buttons on her dress, the dowdy green one. It was Patricia's favorite, a fact that Elizabeth would have never believed were it not for the look in those blue eyes when they drifted over her. Patricia loved the dress, loved to see her in it, without a doubt.

Elizabeth's reverie was rudely interrupted by a buzzing fly. She swatted at the insect, until she realized she must look crazed, waving her hand wildly in the air. She dropped her arm and moved a few inches farther under the big oak tree to avoid the shifting sun. Having found more shade, she surveyed her backyard and its milling guests.

She saw Lillian holding court with Delilah and a few other ladies. Lillian was clearly trying to walk the line between paragon and partygoer, as if she were unsure which persona to wear. What would the Sunday school ladies think if she were to (gasp!) cut loose and have a dance? Elizabeth chuckled; she had never seen her mother so torn. Delilah Harper wasn't torn at all. She grabbed Dale, her lanky husband, and dragged him into the yard to dance alongside their daughters. Soon, other guests joined in.

This impromptu hootenanny was Elizabeth's father's idea. He'd even hired a band. A jazz band. A jazz band that was currently playing "The Charleston." A song written especially for dancing. *Dancing.* On a Sunday, of all things hallowed and holy. This whole affair was so beyond Nathaniel Post's strict sensibilities that Elizabeth was at a loss as to its motive.

He stood off to the side of the yard, near the house, his expression more grimace than smile. His teeth were showing, but his lips turned down, as if sucking a lemon. No, no, this was not her father's mode at all. Not that Elizabeth was complaining; this was the most fun this big house had ever seen. But what was the fun all about? What was it for?

Then she heard Honey issue a gleeful gasp and turned to see Skip Pennington walk into the party with his wife, Judith, on his arm, their son, Chess, not far behind.

Elizabeth's father had always derided the Pennington clan as "the perennial rich."

Nathaniel had done well enough for his family. They were firmly upper-class. They had a big house, their own automobile, servants. But the Penningtons were so monied that neither Skip, nor Chess, nor his children, grandchildren, or great-grandchildren would ever need contemplate working, and yet, somehow, Skip Pennington was always making more, creating more, accumulating more. Every venture he touched, it seemed, turned into piles of gold. So, as well as Nathaniel Post did on his own, he was no Skip Pennington.

Elizabeth choked back a surprised laugh. *Money.* It was money her father was after.

Nathaniel had spent the last few weeks expressing interest in a new automobile plant that had opened upstate. Elizabeth would bet her eyeteeth that Skip Pennington had a stake in that plant, and that this little shindig was her father's way of proving himself a man of the times. Skip Pennington reviled traditional values, traditional mores, traditional manners. Nathaniel would have to suppress his own nature, then, if he wanted someone like Skip to see him as a partner.

So, Elizabeth realized, standing under that shade tree in the hot

September sun, that Nathaniel Post, for all his righteous posturing, was replacing God with gold.

Elizabeth burned with anger for every time he had refused progress for the sake of his *tradition*, every time Elizabeth had been made to feel like a possession, like property, because of his *religion*. Every time he had held her back from living a real life, a life like the ones other young women were living—a life like Honey Harper's.

Today, Nathaniel's stiff, high-minded morals had taken a back seat to greed.

One nation, under Money.

"You are a false man, Father mine," Elizabeth whispered, repulsed by his very being.

Honey rushed to greet the arriving royalty, clutching Chess's arm possessively. Chess laughed lazily and let himself be dragged to what had become the dance area.

They made quite the modern pair, Honey and Chess, she with her sparkling air and willowy frame, and Chess, who was a little too tall, a bit too lean, and moved with the casual slouch of a young person of immense privilege. He had slim shoulders and a triangular chin, topped by a head of fine amber hair, slicked flat with pomade and parted on the side. His eyes were his most unbecoming feature. Flat black, reminiscent of the sharks Elizabeth had seen at the aquarium on their seaside vacation last summer.

Honey didn't seem to mind that Chess was not a particularly handsome man. He was rich, an advantage that seeped from his every pore. He swung Honey around as they danced, not a care in the world. Honey squealed in delight, her smile as bright as the too-hot sun.

Elizabeth wanted to dance like that. She wanted to fling herself around with no regard for decorum. She wanted to laugh too loudly and speak too brazenly. She wanted to *suffer the excitement of being wild.*

Honey's platinum bob bounced with every dance step. Her silk dress had a hemline so much higher than Elizabeth's that when Honey kicked her foot to the music, the cut of the dress revealed her legs all the way to the knee. No one screamed in shock. No one fainted dead away. This was the new world, and Elizabeth decided that if Nathaniel could lower himself to live in it, then Elizabeth should be afforded the same right. What could he say to her now that his feet (and his wallet) were firmly planted in the present-day soil of 1925?

Elizabeth used the thick ribbon in the front of her hair to pull the whole mass up into a messy, dangling, accidentally lovely style. Tendrils fell around her face, escaping the ribbon, as she turned once again toward the open kitchen door. Patricia was watching her, eyes blazing with pride, a grin on her face. Elizabeth grinned back and stepped into the sun. She walked right into the dance area and joined the party.

25

TISH

Poor girl doesn't know how to be broke.

"You want me to go dumpster diving?" Libby screeches, her eyes narrowed dangerously.

"Not for garbage, you nutter. I passed a build site up the road. A remodel. They throw away so much good stuff, but we've got to hit it fast, before someone else does."

"Someone *else*? This is, like, a *thing*?"

Absolutely no idea how to be broke.

"When you don't have money, you gotta improvise," I tell her. "I scoped it out earlier. Looks like it's a full remodel, so it'll be a gold mine. Lumber, tile, spools of wiring. Oooh, maybe there'll be some copper pipe. We might be needing that soon. I'm kinda scared of what we're gonna find in here."

We're in one of the downstairs bathrooms, and I'm getting ready to take a sledgehammer to the bottom wall, where the bathtub backs into the corner. I'm a nervous wreck, actually, so I make sure one more time: "You ready? Speak now or forever hold your peace."

"Do it," she insists.

"If I screw it up—"

"You're not going to screw it up," she says with confidence. Like she has faith in me.

I still hesitate, so she comes over, grabs the sledgehammer, and swings it—underhanded, like she's swinging a really heavy mini-golf putter—into the wall. The wall cracks. Before she can swing it again, I grab it away from her and nudge her out of the room.

"You don't have any safety equipment on. Get out of here."

She laughs and backs up to the door.

That musty smell in the air has been bothering me for a while. It should have faded by now. Libby swore it was just "old-house smell," but old-house smell goes away once someone new moves in, once a house has life in it again. That meant this smell was something different, and after following the sniff trail, we finally found the source: this old bathroom.

It's either the bathtub, or the tile, or the wall, or, as I suspect, something *behind* the wall.

I push my dust mask up over my nose, pull my work goggles down over my eyes, and swing the hammer. The wall breaks off in thick, heavy chunks. Shit. It's plaster. I hadn't thought of that; I'd just assumed it would be drywall, like every other house. It totally didn't occur to me that this house is more than a hundred years old. Plaster is a real pain in the ass to repair, at least in a way that doesn't look like an amateur did it. But I *am* an amateur. Great.

"What is it?" she asks. "You tensed up."

I can't believe she saw that. Nobody, and I mean not even Bari, would have picked up on that. But Libby did. I turn to look at her through my thick plastic goggles, a literal cloud of plaster dust floating between us.

Libby stands just outside the doorway, looking in at me. It feels like I'm looking at her through a scrim. The pale green wall behind her, with its tree designs on the wallpaper fabric, makes it look like she's outside. Her loose green pants and tight T-shirt look like . . . a dress. And her hair is all bundled up on her head, tied up in a thick green ribbon, messy but beautiful.

An image hits me, a flash so intense my knees almost buckle. A hot kitchen. Little tarts loaded on a silver catering tray. Music. Something really old and dancey. Then it's gone.

I stare at Libby as the dust clears from the air, my eyes locked on the ribbon in her hair.

"You okay?" she asks.

I have no idea, so I just nod and say, "Yep. Just fine." I rip my eyes away and start to swing the sledgehammer, but something makes me stop and ask, "That ribbon, in your hair . . ."

Libby reaches up and touches the ribbon. She smiles softly, fondly, and says, "Oh. I found it in the vanity upstairs. Do you like it?"

My heart thuds one time, hard, then it feels like it leaps right into my throat because I'm barely able to choke out, "Yeah. Yeah. I like it."

Then I go to town on that wall, swinging the sledgehammer like I'm a lumberjack.

~

Watching Libby dig through the dumpster might be the most fun I've had all year. The light on her iPhone bounces around inside the huge bin, and she huffs and puffs every time she shifts a big piece of material. Then I hear her grumble, "I really hate this." She hears me laughing, and her "Shut up!" echoes off the metal dumpster walls.

When we exposed the pipes in the bathroom wall, we immediately found the source of the smell. The pipes are old and corroded, and they've been leaking for who knows how long. The whole area behind the tub is wet and squishy and covered in mold. It's all got to come out.

"Good thing I can only use one bathroom at a time," Libby had joked. I'd seriously expected her to freak out or something, but she just grinned and asked, "So what's the plan?"

Her head pops out of the dumpster, some kind of packing peanuts in her hair. She's adorable, damn it. She blows a bit of hair out of her face and says, "I'm tired and I'm cold. We've been working all day. Can't we come back tomorrow morning?"

The temptation to say *yes* is overwhelming, but scavenging isn't done in the daylight, not if you want to get away with it. I glance at my phone. It's midnight. We've only been at it for an hour or so, but it *is* getting cold. It's even colder hunched down inside these big metal boxes.

"Okay, let's hurry up. Just look for anything copper," I tell her, "or some PEX, um, thick plastic tubing. It'll be blue or white. And the copper will be—"

"Kind of orangey gold, looks like metal?"

I just grin from the dumpster next to hers and dive back in.

So far, I've got a pretty impressive pile of keepers. Several unbroken pieces of tile; it's got an antique look that I think will be nice in the bathroom we just tore up. The workers, for some crazy reason, tossed away a bunch of brand-new caulk guns and buckets of plaster; we will definitely take those. Three gallons of unopened paint. It's plain white, but we'll be able to use it. Tons of clean wood, a couple dozen strips of quarter-round, some two-by-fours, four-by-sixes, and several long, flat pieces that are sure to come in handy.

I toss stuff around, hoping to find something that can be used for *another* new banister spindle, since her idiot boyfriend broke the last one. And this time, I'm just going to replace the whole stair—no more of that patch-job shit. That stair is dangerous, and I don't want Libby hurting herself on it.

Something shiny catches my eye. I reach down and grab a plastic bag full of cabinet hardware, brushed silver knobs and handles. They're not new, but they're in great shape.

"Hey! Look at this!" Libby says.

She holds up a dented metal box. In her other hand, she's got some kind of little something. I squint at it, but I can't see it, not in the dark. I clamber out of my dumpster. She hops out just as I get to her. I shine my light on her hand and see a small tin toy, a motorcycle with two riders, hand-painted, with a tiny plastic wheel underneath for rolling it around. Like an antique Matchbox toy.

"Reminds me of you," Libby says.

"Oh, man, Lola is going to love this," I say, staring at the toy.

"Well. Yeah. You and Lola," Libby mutters, touching the second rider on the bike. I look up at her strange tone, but she's already climbing back into her dumpster.

It's not long before we load up Libby's car with our finds—copper pipe included—and head back to her house. The ride is quiet, almost uncomfortable. I've had a lot of feelings about Libby Monroe since I met her, but *uncomfortable* was never one of them. Maybe she's quiet because she's concentrating on driving slowly and carefully. We had to open both back doors and slide the wood through, so now it looks like the Camry has skinny wings, like some weird car that wanted to be an airplane but didn't quite get there.

I've got the tin toy motorcycle in my hand, my fingers tracing the second rider. I'm trying not to think about Libby on the back of Lola, of Libby holding on tight to my waist as I twist the throttle, of Libby laughing in delight as we roar down the road. I glance over at her. Her focus is on the road; she looks like she's concentrating hard. Of course, she's not thinking of riding on the back of my bike. Of course, she's not thinking any of those thoughts.

We turn onto Mulberry and the first thing I see, way down the street, is the tiny sparkle of the green glass stone in the sidewalk. Freaking full moon is lighting it up like a tiny beacon.

"Do you know what that is?" I ask Libby, breaking the silence. Her eyes are on the stone, too. The closer we get, the brighter it shines. After a few seconds, she sighs and shakes her head.

"It's been there as long as I can remember. Far as I know, *no one* knows what it is."

The green stone flickers as Libby's headlights hit it dead-on. It gives me a queasy feeling, but it could be I'm just tired. It's been a long day. Libby pulls to the curb, unable to park under the porte cochere with the wood sticking out of the back.

I get out and notice something else glowing. My sweet Lola's golden gas tank. She's parked by the gate. Her headlight catches the full moon, reflecting it like a prism. "Hey, sweet girl," I say, and walk over to her, holding out the little tin toy. "Look what Libby found for you."

"Who are you talking to?" Libby asks as she gets out of the car.

"Lola," I say in a tone that makes the unspoken *duh* loud and clear. "Hey, we should weld this onto Lola's front fender, make her look fancy, like a Rolls Roy— What?" I ask as Libby just stares at me. Then she stares at Lola. Then she grins. Then laughs.

"Come help me with this wood," she says, and starts pulling planks from the back seat.

"Wanna leave it till the morning? I can swing by first thing."

"You're not staying? Just sleep here, Tish."

I should say no. I'm getting too comfortable in that house, in that room. It feels too much like it's where I'm meant to be, and I was never meant to be anywhere. Not in my mother's house. Not shoved into a closet-room, either. I've never had a place where I really felt like I belonged, except Bari's, but even that isn't really *my* place. It's a place where I'm loved, but it isn't a place that's mine. But the more time I spend here, in the Mulberry house, in that room, the more at home I feel, and the more I want to stay. I should say no, mainly because of how badly I want to say yes.

"I'd love to, but I just remembered Wallis needs me at the ass crack, so let's unload this now, and maybe I'll see you tomorrow." I'm actually not expected at practicum tomorrow at all. But I stick to the tiny fib and haul lumber from the car faster than I've ever hauled lumber.

26

TISH

My stupid closet-room feels more like a closet than it ever has. I can feel the walls closing in. I look at my phone. 3:15. I flip over onto my stomach. Now not only do I feel claustrophobic, but I literally can't breathe because my face is smushed into the pillow. I'm tired, frustrated, and crammed into a tiny room that I don't fit in anymore. I grab my phone to text Libby, to see if I can still sleep there, but now it's 3:17. In the freaking morning.

I sit up. I have a key! With all the work we've been doing, and all the coming and going, she finally just handed me a key and said, "Use it anytime."

I think about that key now. In my satchel. Waiting to be used.

~

"Shhhh," I whisper to Lola as we get closer to the house. I kill the engine and coast to the curb. There's a light on downstairs. Libby leaves a small lamp on in the foyer at night, so that's to be expected. The rest of the house looks dark, except for the light in Libby's room.

Libby is standing in her bedroom window, her oil lamp gleaming in one hand, and the other hand pressed against the glass of the window, like she's trying to touch something. The oil lamp glows a soft orange, and for a long moment I can't look away. Then I pull my eyes from the light of the oil lamp and look to Libby. I wave at her, but she just stands there, staring out.

I hop off Lola and hook my helmet over her handlebars.

As I move toward the gate, the moonlight hits the green glass stone again, lighting it up like a jewel. A big jewel buried in concrete. I look back up to Libby's window. She's still there, but now she's looking right at me. I wave again, swinging both arms high and wide, but she doesn't wave back. She just slides her hand down the window.

There is something very not right about this. I grab my satchel and hurry toward the door.

Inside, I take the stairs two at a time, hopping the broken step altogether. I go straight to Libby's room. The door is open, and her oil lamp burns dimly, the wick turned almost all the way down. She's still at the window, her back to me.

"Libby?"

I take a slow step into the room.

"Libby? Hey."

She still doesn't move.

I saw her like this one time before. I came out of the downstairs bedroom I was sleeping in to use the bathroom. Libby was sitting on the rug in the parlor, the oil lamp flickering on the hearth. She had a book open in front of her, but she wasn't reading. She was staring into the fireplace, even though there was no fire. I didn't bother her because, well, it's her house and she can sit by a cold fireplace in the middle of the night if she wants to. But now that it's happening again, I think she must be a sleepwalker.

And if I've seen her sleepwalking twice, then how many times has she actually done it? How many times has she roamed this huge house asleep? How many times has she gone down those freaking stairs, with that gaping cracked step and that stabby broken banister that could kill her if she fell on it? Just the thought of it makes me ill.

I walk up behind her, careful not to spook her. She must sense me, though, because right as I get to her, she turns around and smiles. Then she says quietly, "There you are," like she expected me to walk in, like she was waiting for me. But she's looking *through* me, her eyes staring into mine, but glassy. Like she's half here and half somewhere else.

"Here I am," I whisper.

I wait to see if she's going to say anything else, but she just looks at me, smiling. I don't even let myself think about how beautiful she is, here in the dark with the lamplight glowing around her. I just take her hand and guide her to the bed. She crawls in and snuggles into her pillow, no questions. I pull the covers over her.

As I'm turning to go, her hand shoots out and grabs mine. Her eyes are closed, but she whispers, "Don't leave me." It sounds so broken and sad that my throat tightens up. I touch her shoulder, give it a comforting stroke, hoping whatever this is will pass. Then she says it again, her eyes open now, wide and scared, staring right at me. "Please don't leave me," she whimpers.

What kind of dream is she having?

"I won't," I tell her. I'm just trying to reassure her, but saying it out loud wakes up that old fear in me, the one that says she's not talking to *me*, so don't get my hopes up.

She whimpers again, louder this time. I sit down on the edge of the bed and pull her hand into my lap. I want to stroke her hair. I want to rub my thumb across her brow, to smooth out the worry lines there. But I just gently hold her fingers until she calms down, until her hand goes limp in mine, and she's asleep again.

27

LIBBY

Who knew making a pie crust from scratch would be this complicated?

I glance over at Mom, who can do this blindfolded with both hands tied behind her back. She's humming, smiling, and she looks so at home in my kitchen that tears spring to my eyes. I wonder, for a second, if I'm not dreaming. Mom would look at home in any kitchen, but I definitely know it's not a dream when she turns and says, for the fiftieth time, "I can't believe you let him go."

Breaking up with Leo was easier than I thought it would be. I think he knew, like I did, that it wasn't quite right. He asked if I was sure; he said he would really like to give it a little more time, that he could be more present, more available, more . . .

Then he'd stopped. Because he knew that he'd already been all those things. I was the one who wasn't present. I was the one who wasn't available. And I was the one who was asking to end it. Here's the part I didn't tell Mom: Being with Leo, as great as he was, would have been a one-way ticket to Molly Monroe's housewife life. An ideal life for Mom, but the more I settle into this house, the more I feel I'm settling into myself. And Leo? He fit into my old life, my life before Mulberry.

There are parts of that life, though, that I've really missed, Mom being the biggest one.

I sent a few texts to her, in the beginning. She'd waited days before putting a little heart on one, and a thumbs-up on another. But she hadn't answered, not with words. She's apologized for that a dozen times already, but I know how Dad is. Apparently, he's still so pissed he won't let her mention my name. And Peter, from what she's said, is loving being an only child, the shithead. But she's here now, with me, even if we do have to keep it a secret.

"If you would think about . . . Honey, I know you love this house, but if you sold it—"

"No, Mom. No. Don't even go there."

She backs off with a nod, then starts scooping the fruit filling into the pie crusts.

"I'd love for you to be back home, that's all."

"This is my home now, Mom."

"I know," she says quietly.

"And I love it. I really, really love it," I tell her.

Dad won't budge, and neither will I. It's a stalemate. Mom cracks a small smile. "I'm so proud of you, though," she whispers, like she's afraid he might hear her.

Running into Mom at the grocery store this morning was a bit awkward. It's a small town, so it was only a matter of time. My mind was still on Leo, on our surprisingly amicable breakup convo, so she had to say my name three times before I even heard her.

The real shocker was when she didn't turn and run the other way. Instead, she ran right up to me and wrapped her arms around me and hugged me tight. I tried not to cry, but I couldn't help it. I didn't know how much I missed her until I smelled her. Underneath her perfume, she smelled like our house, like her kitchen, like Mom. And when she asked, a little bit shyly, if she could come see the Mulberry house, come see what I'm doing now, I cried just a little bit harder.

She got here, took one look in the pantry and the fridge, and we went right back out again. Now we're making homemade pies in my fully stocked (thank you, Mom) kitchen. Cherry and apple. Mom questioned the cherry, since apple has always been my favorite, but I just shrugged and told her, "My tastes are changing," which wasn't a lie. My tastes are changing in a lot of ways lately. I open the oven, and Mom slides the pies in.

We're in the parlor, drinking fresh lemonade (Mom threw out all my cheap packets), when I suddenly wish Tish were here to start a fire. I could do it, but Tish makes them better. Smaller, hotter, and more compact. Kinda like Tish herself.

"It's a nice house, honey. Big," Mom says.

I gave her the grand tour, took her all around the house, hoping that maybe she would see why I love it so much. I proudly showed her some of the repairs that Tish and I had done. She loved the kitchen cabinets, freshly painted white, with the reclaimed silver hardware. She praised the new stair that Tish had built and installed. It still needs to be stained and varnished, but it fits like it's always been there. But she hummed and grumbled about the open hole in the bathroom wall, the pipes capped to stop the leak, the sledgehammer still leaning against the toilet.

"How do you know how to do all this?" she asked.

Earlier, when I'd finally confessed to Mom about my change of major, her lips had pursed the way they do when she's thinking hard about something. Then she'd nodded and kept shopping. So it was easy then for me to say, "We're building a set in design class, for a stage play. I learned a lot of it there. But it's mostly Tish. She can do anything, really."

"Except plumbing?" Mom asked, still looking at the big hole behind the tub.

"Well. She said that's above her pay grade, but I think she could do it if she just tried. I know she could." That's when I realized how it all must sound, Tish this and Tish that. So I closed the bathroom door and said, "And that's why we don't use this one." But I said *we* again, a word I'd been saying all day. Mom just gave me a look and followed me into the parlor.

"I like this room the most," Mom says, the ice clinking in her glass as she finishes her lemonade. I smile and look around.

"It's my favorite, too," I reply, my voice softening a little.

"Does that work?" she asks, tilting her head toward the Victrola.

I nod and hop up excitedly.

A record is still on the green felt, ready to play. I've played it constantly since I found it in the attic, in a box of Elizabeth's stuff. I quickly swap out the old needle for a new one, then I crank the handle. When the music starts (a jazzy rendition of "The Charleston"), I'm filled up inside with so much *something*. Potential. Promise. Power. I don't know what it is, but it makes me feel reckless and brave, like the feeling I had when I signed the contract to buy the house, the same feeling I had when I told my dad, right to his face, that I would never give it up.

Mom's watching me, tapping her foot, and then I just can't keep still. I dance around the room a little, something I never used to do at home. I do a little twirl, then a horrible version of what I think the Charleston is supposed to look like, and I glance up to see Mom all teary-eyed, with a sad but sweet look on her face.

"What's wrong?" I ask her, breathing a little hard.

She just shakes her head. I stop the record. She stands up and walks over to me, looking at me like she's studying me. Then she puts her hands on my cheeks and says, "I just looked at you, and I didn't see my baby anymore. You're growing up. You're really doing it, honey."

I'm quiet for a moment before I admit, "I wish Dad could see it."

"I'll work on him," she says.

She reluctantly looks at her watch, a gold bracelet-watch that goes perfectly with her wool trousers, her blazer, and her mid-heeled leather boots.

"Do you have to go already?" I ask.

She nods, but kisses my cheek and promises, "I'll be back." She gives the house another sweeping look, then says, "I'm glad you're not doing all this alone."

"No," I say, "I'm not doing this alone."

I have Tish, who's teaching me how to do it all, who's teaching me how to do it cheaply, how to dumpster dive for materials. Tish, who, a couple of days ago, was in my room when I woke up. She was sitting in a chair beside the bed, her head resting on the edge of the mattress, her hand holding mine. The sun washed over her back and hair, lighting it up, just the way I love to see it. I wasn't sure how she even got there, in my bedroom, almost in my bed. My thumb had instinctively moved across hers. She sat straight up and stared at me with bleary, but alert, eyes.

"Hey. You okay?" she asked, her voice hoarse from sleep but concerned.

She told me I'd had a nightmare, that I was . . .

"Mom?" I say as I walk her to the door, "did I ever sleepwalk? When I was a kid?"

Mom looks confused by the question, as confused as I was when Tish told me she'd caught me sleepwalking. It didn't make sense.

"No, honey. Never," Mom says.

Something about it, though, must have hit Tish the wrong way, because she fixed that stair the very next day. Then she slept over that night, and almost every night since. I always offer her the second bedroom upstairs. It's bigger and better furnished, but she always chooses Patricia's room. It twinges a little inside me, every time she goes in there and closes the door behind her. But it also feels right, Tish sleeping in that room.

I kiss Mom again before she leaves and make her promise—again—that she'll come back soon. She stops on the porch and turns, giving me a long, loving look. Then she says, "I've had a lot of time to think about . . . all this . . . and I'm sorry, honey, for my part in making you think you couldn't do it, or shouldn't, or . . . Well, I did a lot of thinking about you, and a lot of missing you. I am really proud of you, Libby. Gammy would be proud of you, too. She would be so proud."

"Then you don't think . . . ? I mean, when Dad said . . . ?"

"Don't you listen to what your father said. I should know; she was *my* mother. This is something"—she snorts—"this is *exactly* something your Gammy would have done."

I grab Mom and hug her so tight I think her ribs might crack. There's nothing in the world she could have said to me that would have been more healing, more inspiring.

"I love you," I tell her.

"Oh. Oh, honey. I love you, too."

As soon as she's gone, the timer on my phone quacks. I hurry to the kitchen, grab the new silicone pot holders Mom bought for me, and take the pies from the oven. Lightly browned crusts, with fruit filling bubbling up through the sugared lattices.

One apple and one cherry. They're perfect.

28

OCTOBER 8, 1925

Autumn had firmly settled in. The air had cooled, the trees had turned, and winter was around the corner. Elizabeth loved winter weather best. Most people despised the cold, with its ice and snow, but Elizabeth thought winter made the whole world look magical: snow-covered trees and ice-covered lakes, little dots of frozen white rain falling, falling, falling for days on end, and fires in the fireplace that burned from morning to night.

That firelight would warm their toes as she read to Patricia; that snow would swirl around them, would catch in Patricia's curls; that icy world would be their wonderland.

Elizabeth could not wait, for it seemed this winter might be the best winter yet.

Her father's partnership with Skip Pennington had already yielded positive results, the most tangible being that the downstairs part of the house had recently been suited for electricity, with sockets and bulbs and bright, steady lights. The works. All the old wall coverings had been replaced with pristine new fabric, erasing the smudgy heat marks left behind from the gas lights. Then there was the shiny new roadster under their porte cochere, a ruby-red gem that rode like the wind. The convertible leather top was the color of heavy cream and could be removed, folded flat into a tiny accordion, and stored in the trunk.

Lillian was simply giddy over it all. She floated from room to room on her money-lined cloud, pressing switches and watching the lights come on and go off. She giggled like a schoolgirl each time, a sound Elizabeth found too unbecoming for words.

The house was a flurry of activity tonight (under the newly installed electric lights) as Nathaniel and Lillian prepared themselves for an extended business trip. Skip Pennington somehow saw fit to send Elizabeth's father to Brazil to secure a trade relationship with one of the rubber merchants there. The mere thought of three months away from Patricia made Elizabeth's stomach twist, so she had declined her father's invitation to join them. When he insisted, rather forcefully, Elizabeth stated, with a vehemence she'd never before shown to her father, *"No!"*

She turned and walked into the parlor, leaving him to follow, bellowing, "Don't you walk away from me when I'm talking to you, daughter!"

Lillian hurried after them both, sputtering, "I daresay she would be more trouble than she's worth, Nathaniel. After taking such a posture with you here, in your own house, imagine what she will be like once she's there. Insufferable, I should think."

It was clear from Elizabeth's face that her intention was, indeed, to be as insufferable as possible. Nathaniel eyed his daughter for a long moment, then, with a clenched fist and a growl, he turned and went up the stairs.

"Was that wise?" her mother asked her.

"Probably not, but I cannot seem to care," Elizabeth said, and turned toward the fireplace.

"Elizabeth Mary Louise Post, what has gotten into you?"

Elizabeth gave the question real thought, and the answers were many.

She was growing up. She was finding herself. She was shedding her meek skin in favor of a new boldness. And she was in love. She knew it as surely as the sun and stars shone in the heavens. Her heart beat with it; her lungs gasped for it; her mouth longed to taste it; her eyes looked upon it each morning when Patricia entered her room, and they followed it each night when she left. Elizabeth could deny it no longer. She could deny *herself* no longer. She was, for better or worse, madly, irrevocably, in love.

So she answered her mother's question as simply as she could: "Life, Mother. Life has gotten into me."

29

TISH

It's lunchtime, so The Gag is packed. Bari and I finally find a little table, crammed into a corner near the soda machines. I scarf down my cafeteria pizza while Bari spools spaghetti around her fork. She watches the tomatoey noodles go round and round and round, then finally says, "So what you're telling me is you're basically rebuilding a house for her, but you're *not* into her. *At all.*" She rolls her eyes, throwing my own emphasis back at me.

The ice machine whirs as someone fills their cup. I wait until they're done, then say, "I'm not *rebuilding* a house; I'm just helping her fix some things."

Bari stares at me, not buying it for a second. And why would she? I'm a terrible liar.

She knows something's up, because the last three times she's gone home for the weekend, I've stayed behind. I told her that *A Christmas Carol* was getting close to tech week, that I was working at the scene shop all hours. So, on her way out of town, Bari, being Bari, went by the scene shop to drop off dinner for me and doughnuts for everyone else. But the scene shop was closed, and I was busted.

"And now she's asked you to move in," she says, zero tone in her voice, so I can't tell at all what she's thinking.

"She just said I should think about it, since I'm there so much anyway..."

I trail off as Bari smirks, and I replay in my mind what I just said. *Since I'm there so much anyway...*

"Look. It's a real bedroom in a big house. Better than a stupid closet that costs me most of my money every stupid month—"

"You should do it," Bari interrupts.

I stop babbling and brace myself for the other shoe. Bari just smiles, giving me nothing.

"Good. Great. End of conversation, then," I say, hoping she'll just let it go. But—

"Oh, no, Tishy-poo. We're just getting started."

"Why are you so bent out of shape? Because I didn't tell you?" I say, stuffing pizza into my mouth, chewing fast. I have about one minute left in me of this conversation, then I'm out. Bari knows this, obviously, so she cuts straight to the point.

"Because you've been lying about it, and I know the only reasons you ever lie are, one, to keep from hurting someone's feelings, or, two, to keep from hurting *your own* feelings."

Damn. I keep my mouth shut. I will admit nothing.

Bari grabs my tray and hers.

"What are you doing?" I say, turning to watch her dump our lunches into the garbage. She grins wickedly and jingles her car keys.

"Let's go move you into your new house."

~

Sweat prickles under my arms. I try to focus on setting up my crates, but I can feel Libby watching me. And I can feel Bari watching Libby. Then Bari says, "Tish says you have a boyfriend."

I choke, then try to mask it by coughing. Bari laughs, the brat.

She's been quizzing Libby all afternoon, about buying the house, about her family, about herself. If it were me, and some girl I'd just met was asking me all about my life, I'd tell her to shove her questions up her own butt. But Libby's been answering them all. The boyfriend question, though. *Damn you, Bari.* The last thing I want to hear is Libby talking about—

"No," Libby says, "no boyfriend."

I whirl around before I can stop myself.

"Oh. I thought . . . Leo . . ." I stammer.

"I broke up with him," Libby says as she walks over to me and slowly starts undoing my crate setup. I only kind of half notice because I'm more focused on the *no boyfriend* news.

"When?" I ask, feeling like the floor is literally shifting under my feet as I try to clamp down on my suddenly racing heart.

Libby shrugs. "Not long ago. But long enough that I know it was the right thing to do."

"Why?" Bari asks, sticking her nose in exactly where I need her to this time, because I wouldn't have had the guts, and I desperately want to know.

"I . . . He just didn't feel right," Libby says quietly, pulling my last crate to the floor.

Bari's eyes shoot to mine. She grins excitedly, but I shake my head. Not gonna happen. Boyfriend or not, I cannot have Libby Monroe. I feel it in my bones. It's too much to ask for. Too much to even think about. I don't want things I can't have.

That's when I realize Libby has undone all my crates, and I'm standing there holding a pile of clothes. "I need those," I say.

"No, you don't," Libby says. "Use the wardrobe." She points to the huge cedar cabinet in the corner of the room.

"There are a couple more things in the car," Bari says, then leaves. Libby picks up the crates and heads for the door, following Bari out.

I look at the wardrobe. A real place to hang my clothes, not some makeshift rack I cobbled together from old pieces of junk. I didn't realize something so small might mean so much to me. A bedroom that's mine. In a whole house. A house with a kitchen that's been filled with food ever since Libby's mom has been making regular visits. A house with a bathroom just for me, where I can shower without setting a timer, without being interrupted every single time for every stupid thing under the sun. A huge parlor where I can hang out and do homework, or just sit and listen to Libby read her books. I do love that, maybe a little too much.

We decided to pool our money, each putting in half of what we make—Libby at the flower shop and me at the odd jobs I scrape together, doing things for Wallis or Joe or both. The money will go to house stuff and electricity and bills like that. Libby won't even let me try to pay rent, so the compromise is the split. Like a 50 percent tithe, but to a church we both love. The church of Mulberry Lane. Because I love this house now. I feel like, in a way, it really is my home.

We still have a long way to go on fixing it up, but I'm glad to give Libby in sweat equity what she refuses to take in cash. I will, as Bari put it, rebuild the house for her. As best I can.

I open the wardrobe doors, and a chill runs through me, from the roots of my hair to the tips of my toenails. Clothes. Perfectly pressed and hanging. Not many, just a few things. Two plain dresses, a cotton nightdress-looking thing, a winter coat, and a maid's uniform, the apron and bonnet hanging separately. On the bottom shelf of the cabinet are two pairs of basic leather lace-up shoes, and a pair of ratty, thin bedtime slippers.

It's like seeing a ghost. Or seeing inside a ghost's closet.

Right at that moment, the Victrola in the parlor comes on, playing some old song that Libby's been listening to for days. Bari squeals excitedly, and I hear Libby laugh. She's showing off her toys. The old thing gives me the creeps. Just looking at it makes me nervous, but I brush it off because it's just a freaking record player.

I stare into the wardrobe, at the clothes hanging there. I wonder if these belonged to the lady who lived here before, the one Joe said stood in the window, staring out, looking for something. Not likely. These are a servant's clothes. Someone who didn't have much to her name. Someone lower-class. Someone like me.

Libby's been wearing a lot of old-fashioned-looking clothes lately. Ribbons in her hair, blouses and skirts and things. It's like she's got her own personal vintage collection. But I'm not about to pull a Libby and wear hundred-year-old clothes, vintage or not. As much as these old-ass things might match my class, they're definitely not my style. I lean inside the cabinet and reach for the dresses, intending to stuff them into a box and put them in the attic. There's tons of old shit up there, plenty to keep these clothes company.

As soon as my fingers brush the fabric, the green glass stone flashes in my mind, buried in the sidewalk, the numbers *2 3 6*, and Libby's frantic voice, "Don't leave me."

My head whips toward the open bedroom door, but Libby's still laughing, with Bari, in the parlor. I pull my hand away and stare at the clothes. The music goes quiet. The house is silent for a long moment, and then another happy, upbeat song plays.

I hear Bari say, "Ohhhh, my Paps loves this song."

I look back at the dresses. The shoes. That maid's apron and bonnet.

Forget it. I close the wardrobe doors with a heavy thump. Those clothes can stay right where they are. My crates will have to do.

30

LIBBY

That evening turned into a best-friends bonanza.

After Tish got her stuff moved in, I called Cam and Horatio to see if they wanted to come over for dinner. Mom had dropped off a Tetrazzini earlier that morning, before Tish and Bari arrived, on her way to do her weekly errands. Dad wasn't giving an inch, according to Mom.

She said, "Hang in there, baby. You're the only daughter he has. He'll come around." I wish she'd really have a go at him, tell him how dumb and stubborn he's being, how wrong he is for cutting me out like he never knew me. I must have the worst poker face ever, because she sighed. "I can only be who I am, Libby. You have your way; I have mine."

I couldn't argue with that, and I can't blame her. *My way* wasn't my way, either, until the Mulberry house. Until everything changed in the blink of a winking For Sale sign.

Mom had set about the kitchen, making coffee (plucked from one of the several bags of groceries she brought with her), putting the Tetrazzini in the fridge, and jotting a little note on how to warm it up. Then she said, "I know that lasagna is Cam's favorite, but the Tetrazzini . . . I just felt like it was overdue."

Overdue, for sure. I could stay low-key angry, let it flare up whenever anything (like a Tetrazzini) reminds me of what happened. But life is too short to stay pissed off. People screw up. Mom was here. By my side. *On* my side. So I just smiled and said, "Thanks, Mom. I love it."

"Tell Cam I said hi," Mom said as she kissed me on her way out the door. I promised that I would, and that I was going to tell him she would make him a lasagna soon.

Mom just laughed and nodded. "That's right. Put me to work."

At first, when he found out dinner was Tetrazzini and not lasagna, Cam declined the invite. He and Horatio had "at-home" plans. But all I had to say was "Okay, well, Tish will be here, so . . ." and then I could hear him scrambling, knocking things over, as he yelled at Horatio, "Hurry up! We're gonna meet the cherry bomb!"

Bari stayed, too, and after chicken Tetrazzini and salad and wine (thank you, Horatio), we all moved to the parlor. Cam and Bari are obsessed with the Victrola. They pushed some of the furniture out of the way, and now Cam is spinning Bari around to an old, fast-paced song.

I move to sit beside Tish on the sofa, tucking my feet under me, watching Bari and Cam dance. They've got YouTube open, copying the old-time dance moves. So far, they've tried (very poorly) the foxtrot, the turkey trot, the raccoon, the bunny hug . . .

"What's with all the animals? Y'all starting a farm?" Tish snickered, but Bari just glared at her, grabbed Cam's hand, and they started high kicking.

Horatio helped me lug a few boxes down from the attic, and he's been digging through them, picking song after song. This song is the fastest one yet. Cam and Bari are barely keeping up, glancing between YouTube and their own feet. Finally, Cam just stops. He bends over, clutching his ribs. "Have they ever heard of a freaking waltz? I'm exhausted."

Bari's huffing, but not nearly as hard as Cam is. "Am I wearing you out?" she teases him.

Cam straightens up and controls his breathing. "No chance. I could go all night, honey."

We all squeal in scandalous delight as Horatio buries his head back in the box, pretending a little too hard to be rummaging, his face beet red.

"Prove it," Bari says to Cam, and holds out her arms.

Tish drops her head and groans, "Oh, they're a dangerous pair."

"Like dynamite and a fuse," I agree with a chuckle.

"Let's hope nobody lights it," she says.

I laugh, and at that exact moment, Cam bumps into a small table near the fireplace. My oil lamp, burning low, jostles precariously. It teeters . . .

. . . we all scream . . .

. . . both Tish and I lunge for it . . .

. . . it rocks two more times, back and forth, the oil inside sloshing . . .

Tish's fingers are ready to grab it when it stops rocking on its own. It just settles down.

Tish sighs, "That was close."

I sink to my knees in relief, then realize I'm sitting right on top of one end of the scorch mark. I look up at the oil lamp. It's still burning, the flame smooth and steady. I stand up and push it farther back onto the table, right to the middle. I'm not taking any chances.

"Why is that damned thing down here, anyway?" Cam barks.

He's right. The electric lights work fine down here, and with the fire, it's plenty bright. But the oil lamp . . . I can't explain it, really. I'm so used to having it in my hand upstairs that I feel strange without it downstairs. So, after sundown, I carry it with me all over the house, electric lights be damned. And Tish likes to see me with it. She'll look at the lamp, glimmering softly, then at me, and she'll smile. Just a little tiny smile. I don't even know if she's aware of it, but I really like it. I'm not giving up the lamp. Not for anything.

"Holy shit," Horatio says to no one in particular, "look at this."

He pulls an antique photograph from the box. It's a grainy old black and white. Crumbly around the edges. It's of the house. This house. There's a date on the back, written in black ink, so faded that it looks almost gray: *Mulberry Lane, Dec. 1925.*

I grab it from him. This is exactly what I always imagined, exactly how I always knew the house would look. The whole yard is a puffy white blanket, with pom-pom shrubbery lining the walkway to the front door, like icing-topped cupcakes. In the corner of the yard, just on the edge of the photograph, is a snowman. Scarf, hat, and a stubby carrot nose. It gives me the sweetest pang in my chest. I'm such a sucker for nostalgia.

There's a gleaming convertible parked under the porte cochere. I wonder what color it—

Red. It was red.

My mind immediately conjures the image of a ruby-red roadster with a cream leather top.

"Wow. Beautiful," Tish whispers from over my shoulder, her nose almost in my ear, her words alive against my skin. I take a moment to let myself really feel her so close to me, so warm behind me. I think of Bari and Cam dancing those fun dances, and I wonder what it would be like to dance with Tish. Not the wild, fast dances, though. The slow dances. The dances where arms are around waists and shoulders, and knees and thighs brush with every step.

I shiver hard enough that she puts a gentle hand on the small of my back.

"You cold?" she asks quietly.

"No," I say with a rueful laugh. "No. I'm not cold."

How could I be cold with the fire crackling beside us? With the fire crackling inside me?

Would she burn if I touched her? Would I?

My face feels hot. My stomach tightens. My fingers tingle.

I get the image of a quick blinding light, like the flash of a camera. Elizabeth and Patricia race into my mind, their faces nebulous collections of imagined features, Patricia's hair and eyes the only things that pop, bright and vivid. I pull the box from Horatio and drag it toward me. It's heavy, loaded with all sorts of stuff. Record albums, trinkets, books, and a few more photos. I paw through them, but they're all of the house, and one of the snowman solo, a big smile made from tiny pebbles on his frozen face. Another pang hits me.

I riffle through the other two boxes. No more photos there, either. These are the only ones.

"What are you looking for?" Tish asks, settling down beside me.

"I thought, maybe . . ." I glance up, then find myself staring at her hair, backlit by the firelight. The short, thick curls look like flames. Patricia's hair must have looked much the same, but longer. Wilder. Untamed. Not that anyone would ever call Tish tame. I softly mutter, "Wild as the wind."

"What?"

"Nothing. Just something I read." I shove the box away from me and say with a sigh, "I was hoping for more pictures." I look again at the photo of the Mulberry house.

"Nice car," Tish says, pointing to the roadster.

It is a nice car, but I'm looking at the house, and I'm filled with a sudden sad realization. "It's never going to look like this again, is it?"

Tish takes the photo from my hand and studies it. "It's a lot of work, yeah," she admits, "but we can do it. Little by little."

"And when we're eighty, we still won't be done."

I just said *we*, talking as if we'd still be here, together, when we're eighty.

Then I realize how quiet it is in the room. I had totally and completely forgotten about the others. For a few minutes, Tish and I had been the only two people on earth. Definitely the only two people in my parlor. But there's Bari, Cam, and Horatio, on the sofa, the three of them lined up like birds on a wire, watching the show unfold in front of them. Watching Tish and me.

"What?" I demand, but they all just smile.

Their smiles are each a little different. Horatio's is all gooey-eyed and dreamy. Cam's is oh-so-knowing. And Bari's is— I can't read Bari yet, but whatever those narrowed eyes and that tiny smirk mean, Tish doesn't like it, because she growls, "Zip it, or you can go home right now."

Bari hadn't said a word. Then again, I know too well how besties can mind-meld. Cam's trying to do it to me right now, so I slash my hand across my throat. *Stop it!* He just waggles his eyebrows. Horatio throws his arm around Cam's shoulder and waggles his, too. I'm outnumbered.

Tish rolls her eyes and looks again at the photo of the Mulberry house in all its glory. She runs her hand back and forth over her curls, making that adorable clicking noise she makes.

~

It's another two hours before everyone finally goes home.

Tish tamps down the fire until it's just embers. She starts to move the fireplace screen across the opening, but after what almost happened with the oil lamp, I run to the kitchen and come back with a pitcher of water. Tish doesn't laugh at me. She doesn't roll her eyes or tease me. She just nods and pulls the screen away, and I douse the embers. They hiss and steam before finally turning into a sodden pile of blackened mash. I feel much better now.

It's weird, this first night with Tish in the house as a roommate, as someone who lives here now, not just crashing because she's too tired to ride home. There's an awkward moment as we both head to our rooms, Tish turning to say, "I guess I'll, um—"

"See you in the morning," I finish for her.

The lights in the house are all turned off, except the little lamp I leave on in the foyer every night. Otherwise, the only light is the glow of my trusty oil lamp. We both stand in the soft light, each waiting for the other to say something else.

I finally say, "If you need anything, just, you know . . ."

Tish suddenly laughs. "We're acting stupid."

Then I laugh, too, and nod. "Yeah, this doesn't have to be weird."

"Oh," Tish says quietly, a note of uncertainty in her voice, "is this weird? For you?"

"No! I didn't mean it like that. I'm glad you're here," I say urgently. I reach out with my free hand to grasp hers. "I mean it, Tish. I'm so glad you're here."

Of their own accord, my fingers twine with hers. I feel the tension in her hand. Then she squeezes my fingers and pulls away.

"Well, it's an upgrade, for sure. I really appreciate it, Libby."

"My pleasure," I reply, and I realize as soon as I say it that it really *is* my pleasure. I'm so happy she's here that I'm a little dizzy with it. I force myself to move, to turn and head for the stairs. As I reach the staircase, I look back. She's standing in the doorway of her room, watching me. Then she retreats and shuts the door. I wait, half expecting the door to open again. When it doesn't, I make my way up the stairs to my own room, the oil lamp lighting my way, as it's done every night since I moved in.

I've put some personal touches in the room: throw pillows on the bed, a big beanbag chair under the window reading nook (it's just more comfortable), and some of my makeup and hair products on top of the vanity. One thing I haven't touched are the perfume bottles. They're so deliberately arranged, even the space for the missing one, that I would feel wrong moving them. My clothes share space with Elizabeth's in her closet. Most of her pieces are adorable. They fit me perfectly, so I've been borrowing a blouse here, a pair of wide-legged flowy pants there. For some reason, I feel very strongly that Elizabeth wouldn't mind at all. I even feel like maybe she would love to know I'm wearing her clothes.

I've gotten to know her pretty well, I think. I've been savoring the journal, reading it slowly, because I want it to go on forever. But I know it ends, if only because she's not here. All stories end, I suppose. I glance to the hope chest, drawn to it more strongly tonight than usual.

In my hand, the oil lamp flares up brightly, with a little pop, then dims again. I look at the wick, where a little burned spot is still brighter than the rest. I put the lamp on the side table and move to the chest. I brush my hands across the silver dress, then the gold dress, as I do each time, almost like a ritual, then I pick up the journal.

I run my thumb across the numbers. The gold embossed *2 3 6*.

Then I curl up in the beanbag chair and start to read, the frail handwriting as familiar to me now as my own:

Each day we grew closer, she and I.

Incrementally, minute by minute, second by second. The anticipation of every encounter, no matter how insignificant, threatened to drown me. The brush of her sleeve against my arm as she laid my silverware; the glance of her eyes as we passed in the hallway; our private afternoons on the overlook, where we were free to simply be two young women, not lady and servant; and always, always, her hands in my hair, on my clothes, dressing and undressing me—a task on which I'd fought Sarah for years, now welcome beyond measure from another's hands.

Patricia's mere proximity in the house was a weight looped around my heart, an anchor that pulled me down, down, down. Wherever she was—in her room, in the kitchen, in the bath—I would imagine myself there with her. I had never considered myself the type to obsess, but I found that day and night, in waking and in sleep, I was thinking of her. All my other pursuits fell by the wayside; all my other interests paled in the shade of the dreams I dreamed of her. She was my sole purpose; she was my light.

I can only pray that I was not her darkness . . .

31

NOVEMBER 12, 1925

Elizabeth watched from her upstairs window as the elder Posts were whisked away from the house in a taxi. Nathaniel had sent Henry and Richard ahead to set and secure their living quarters on the big ship that would carry them all to Brazil. Sarah would also be accompanying them, for Lillian's sake. It had been Nathaniel's intention to take Patricia, too. It was clear that his desire was to punish Elizabeth for her willfulness.

"If it is a big, empty house you desire, daughter, then it is a big, empty house you shall have," he'd leveled at her over the dinner table the night before.

"Nathaniel, I trust your judgment, dear, I do," Lillian had countered carefully, "only, how will it look, our leaving a young woman alone for three months? Our daughter, no less."

Not *How will our daughter cope on her own for months on end?*; rather, *How will it look?*

Elizabeth had also heard the implicit meaning in what her mother had *not* said: *What would Skip Pennington think?* She could see her father's wheels spinning, see him weighing his options, considering all tacks before deciding to "leave her with the other one, then."

The other one. He hadn't even used Patricia's name.

It had infuriated Elizabeth, but she'd soothed herself with

the knowledge (and the breathless anticipation) that he, and her mother, and the rest of the household staff would (very soon) be gone for three months. Twelve glorious weeks, just Patricia and herself, alone, to do as they wished. The thought had sent tingles searing across her entire body as she dipped a piece of bread into her broth, trying to hide the smile that threatened to give her away.

Sarah had spied the gleam in her eye, however, and had pulled her aside at the first opportunity. "This is a terrible idea. I'm staying. I'll tell them—"

"Sarah, no. Everything will be all right, I assure you."

"You have talked with Patricia, then? Told her that . . . told her . . . well . . ." Sarah stuttered.

"I have told her that we are no more than friends," Elizabeth promised.

She had told Patricia no such thing. What she had said, as Patricia brushed her hair that morning, was "I can't stop thinking about you."

Patricia's eyes had smoldered, but her hands had never strayed from their course as the brush glided through Elizabeth's thick strands. Patricia's breathing, however, had become shaky and shallow, evidence that she was likely burning in the same fire that had been consuming Elizabeth for weeks.

"You're being overly cautious, Sarah, and I do love you for it," Elizabeth reassured her friend, "but you need this trip. You need to be far away from here, somewhere warm and tropical. Even if it is with Mother, who will surely drive you mad."

"Don't I know it," Sarah said with a short laugh. "Heaven preserve me, that bell alone . . ."

With Sarah's fears calmed, Elizabeth was once again free to think only of Patricia. Three months was a long time, and she intended to live each of those days to the fullest.

32

NOVEMBER 14, 1925

Pinning down Patricia was starting to frustrate Elizabeth.

She had barely seen her. When she'd finally tracked Patricia to the kitchen, "too much work" had been the excuse. Elizabeth knew that was untrue. There were no pairs of Henry's boots to clean after he came in from working the yard, no shirts to press for Richard before he served Nathaniel, no Sarah issuing gentle orders, and no Lillian prowling the rooms with her white handkerchief, swiping furniture, looking for any trace of dust.

The only *work* Patricia had, now that everyone else was gone, was to see to Elizabeth, yet she hadn't come to Elizabeth's room yesterday morning, nor yesterday evening, nor had she shown up this morning. Patricia had taken her meals in her own room and left Elizabeth to fend for herself in the kitchen. There was only one explanation: Patricia was avoiding her.

Today was Saturday, however, and Elizabeth was determined to spend it with Patricia. She dressed herself as quickly as possible and rushed downstairs. The door to the room Patricia shared with Sarah was closed. Good. That meant she had time.

Elizabeth trotted quietly to the kitchen.

She opened the larder to peruse the contents. Dry goods and staples.

In the coolest corner, she found the fresh foods. Cured meats, fruits, vegetables, some hard cheeses, and half a loaf of bread. She unfolded the cloth wrapping from the bread. The outside crackled when she squeezed the loaf between her fingers, and she could feel the softness beneath the crunch. A grin played on her lips as she started pulling items from the shelves.

Half an hour later, Elizabeth stood outside Patricia's door. She'd prepared a lovely charcuterie-style picnic for the two of them, even going so far as filching a bottle of cider from the cellar. It was one of Lillian's favorites, rich and sweet, and would pair perfectly with the cheeses and dried fruits Elizabeth had chosen.

She wanted this Saturday, today, to be special for Patricia, who'd had precious little specialness in her life. So she'd taken her time preparing the food, carefully assembling their lunch. She'd been with Sarah in the kitchen enough to know how to put together a meal, but it had taken her longer than she would have liked to shave the meats and carve the cheeses. The morning was nearly gone already.

She rapped her knuckles lightly against Patricia's door. Hearing no sounds from inside, she turned the handle and let the door swing open. Patricia wasn't there. Her bed was made. The washbasin was clean and dry. Elizabeth sighed. She roamed back to the parlor, where the stuffed picnic basket waited at the foot of the staircase. She hefted it onto her arm.

She had a good notion as to where Patricia might be. It was a long walk, mostly uphill, to the overlook. She thought of the heavy basket, laden with delicious treats, and dreaded the long, lonely hike. It was a different experience when Patricia was making the trek with her, sharing the burden of the basket, trading turns carrying it up the hill. Then again, every experience was different with Patricia. Reading, walking, sitting quietly together in the park or at the edge of the overlook. Everything was magic for Elizabeth when they were together; every color was heightened, every light brightened.

Having decided that the labor was worth the reward of Patricia's company, Elizabeth moved to the coat closet to retrieve her wrap. As she reached for the garment, something caught her eye. A series of keys dangled from a row of tiny hooks beside the closet door. Several door keys, a cellar key, and one brand-new shiny key. The shiniest of them all.

Elizabeth's fingers tingled with temptation. She couldn't. Could she? Then that willful rebel asserted herself again, and before she had time to talk herself out of the idea, Elizabeth had flung her wrap around her shoulders and was headed out the side door to the porte cochere.

The ruby-red roadster was waiting, its caged power still and silent under its gleaming hood. Elizabeth looked at the key in her hand. She'd only ever driven Henry's truck, and that was when she was much younger. Henry had been teaching Sarah to use the clutch so she could go to town on the off times that he or Richard might be unavailable. He'd taken pity on the boss's daughter and let her grind the gears, too. It had been awful, Henry cringing and gritting his teeth with every crunch of the gears, Elizabeth's dainty hand wrapped around the gearshift, yanking and pulling while she stomped on the clutch.

She stared at the car. This was a bad idea. She should let it go the way of bad ideas, out of her head and into the void where it could only damage the nothingness of nothing. But . . .

Elizabeth felt the weight of the picnic basket on her arm, felt the morning slipping into afternoon, felt the seconds she could be spending with Patricia sliding through her fingers like so much sand. She opened the car door and plopped the basket onto the passenger seat.

"In for a penny . . ." she muttered as she slid into the driver's seat.

What would Honey Harper think, to see Elizabeth driving such an automobile? What would she think to see Elizabeth driving at all? That thought alone was spur enough to have Elizabeth shove her foot against the clutch and turn the key. The roadster growled to life.

". . . in for a pound," she finished with a tremulous breath.

It turned out to be a bit harrowing, her ride to the top of the overlook. The roadster lunged and lurched and careened as Elizabeth fought to control the mighty motor. She was a hazard on the clutch, and a nightmare around the curves of the smooth packed-dirt roads. Blessedly, she didn't encounter many other drivers, and since the overlook was nearby, there was no need for her to drive through town, no need to chance the paved streets that would surely have seen more traffic than this quiet, winding road up to the overlook.

She certainly hoped she would find Patricia there, or this whole calamity wouldn't have been worth the undertaking. Luckily, as she crested the top of the hill (the roadster complaining the entire way), she saw Patricia standing at the edge. The redhead was turned toward her approach, clearly having heard the car rampaging its way up the road.

Elizabeth juddered the car to a stop and turned off the engine. She had broken out in a light sweat along her hairline and under her palms. She took a moment to gather herself, to thank her lucky stars that she and the automobile were still intact, and to inhale the striking picture Patricia made, standing on the side of that peak, her hair full of life, long and loose around her shoulders, just the way Elizabeth liked it. Now her hands shook for another reason entirely.

She took a bracing breath and opened the door, dragging the

heavy basket out of the roadster. Patricia didn't speak. She showed no encouragement, nor did she approach the car. Instead, she stood rooted on her spot. It made Elizabeth nervous. Perhaps she'd misread things. Perhaps Patricia was avoiding her because, well, perhaps Elizabeth was alone in this, after all. Alone in her feelings, alone in her longings. She had felt, all this time, that Patricia was just as taken in her emotions as Elizabeth, but what if she'd been wrong? What if she had projected her own feelings, her own desires, onto Patricia?

Elizabeth was suddenly very aware of their stations—in the house and in life—very aware that Patricia was required to do her bidding, required to like her (the daughter of the house, the boss's only child) because it kept a roof over her head and food in her mouth. Had Elizabeth's attentions been uncomfortable to Patricia? Worse, had they been *unwanted*? Dear Lord, had Elizabeth been such a terror? Why else would the young servant have spent the last two days avoiding any contact with her? *Oh God. Oh God. Oh God.*

Elizabeth's shoulders slumped as she turned in on herself. She was a fool. When she could manage it without dissolving into tears, she would apologize to Patricia, beg her forgiveness for any untoward behavior, for any actions that may have made Patricia ill at ease. Every insecurity Elizabeth had ever harbored, from the superficial dislike of her daily attire to her deepest fears about herself and her worthiness to be loved, crept up like a strangling vine meant to suffocate her.

She whirled back to the car, overwhelmed with the need to run from this place, from Patricia, from herself. The heel of her shoe caught on the hem of her wrap, and she lost her footing. She pitched forward hard. The basket landed with a thud against the shiny red car, then tumbled to the dirt. Elizabeth was headed for the same fate, but just before her chin made contact with cold metal, her own tumble was stopped short as reedy (but surprisingly strong) arms wrapped around her.

"S'okay. I've got you," Patricia whispered into her ear.

Patricia's arms were gentle but tight, steadying her, keeping her upright. Warm fingers cradled Elizabeth's face, wedged between her skin and the open car door, where Elizabeth's chin would surely have struck had Patricia not rescued her.

When Patricia bent to unloop the shawl from around Elizabeth's ankle, her fingers took a moment to stroke the soft skin she found, almost as if she couldn't help herself. Then Elizabeth heard Patricia sigh, the sound so full of longing that she nearly cried. She had not been wrong. The heat of Patricia's hands, the tremor in her fingers, and her shallow breathing gave her away.

Patricia straightened, but stayed close, her body still pressed against Elizabeth's back.

She heard Patricia swallow, heard her voice quaver as she said, "You were thinking heavy thoughts, my love. They weren't of me, were they?"

Patricia was close enough that Elizabeth could feel the words ruffle her hair.

Again, Patricia had called her *my love*, and this time, Elizabeth melted under the heat of it. She turned and pressed herself fully against Patricia's body, molded her form to Patricia's, buried her face in Patricia's neck. She trembled with the power of it, with the sensation of being this close, of feeling Patricia's skin against her face. Patricia's arms pulled her even closer.

It wasn't the chill of the outside air that had them shaking.

"I was afraid for a moment that you weren't . . . that you didn't feel . . . about me . . ." Elizabeth stammered, unable to coherently string together her words.

"I do feel it," Patricia husked. "I feel it so much, I cannot feel anything else."

Elizabeth's fingers clutched at Patricia's back, her lips pressing themselves, swiftly and of their own volition, to the soft skin of Patricia's throat. She felt Patricia shudder. Elizabeth hurried to kiss that spot again, but Patricia stepped back, out of Elizabeth's embrace.

"What?" Elizabeth gasped, disoriented. "What's the matter?"

Patricia seemed to struggle to pull her thoughts together, blinking several times before returning her eyes to Elizabeth, their color deeper and richer than Elizabeth had ever seen them.

"I do feel so much for you, love. And I want so much from you . . ."

Elizabeth was elated! That was what she wanted, too! She wanted to *have* so much and she wanted to *give* so much, that same *so much* that Patricia wanted, but when she moved to reclaim her territory, grasping at Patricia's waist, Patricia held up a hand, a silent plea for distance. Elizabeth stopped, uncertain now of what to do or what to say.

Patricia soon solved the silence for them both. "Wanting, but not having, is the most miserable ache to bear. I . . . cannot have you, Elizabeth, so I shall not want you. Don't you see?"

The yearning on Patricia's face broke Elizabeth's heart, even as her whole being swelled with such love that she could scarce contain it. She let the wave of feeling flood her, let it pool and settle right in the middle of her soul. She smiled softly and leaned in, touching her forehead to Patricia's, and whispered, quite deliberately, so Patricia could in no way mistake her meaning, "You can have me. Have me, Patricia."

Patricia's eyes closed on the words, as if savoring them. Or perhaps she was simply afraid to believe them, because to Elizabeth's disappointment, Patricia again stepped away.

Upon Elizabeth's huff and pout and the stamp of her foot into the dirt, Patricia chuckled. "No, miss. I won't be taking advantage of you outside on a hilltop for God and sundry to see. So . . . what have you got in your pail, there? What have you brought me?" she finished, nodding at the picnic basket. Elizabeth picked it up, allowing the subject change. For now.

"Every good thing I could find," she said, and handed the burden over to Patricia, who, after one last long, heated look, settled on the grass and opened the large woven container. Elizabeth watched Patricia unwrap the cheeses, the bread, the meats, but her attention was on those long fingers, not the food.

33

TISH

I feel like a creepy stalker, always listening for her, watching for her. Last night, I heard the floorboards creaking above my bed. I hurried from my room and crept up the stairs. When I peeked around the top banister, I saw she was just going to the bathroom.

She stopped and whirled, as if she sensed me there, so I stepped fully onto the landing. I must have scared the shit out of her, because she froze, stood perfectly still, her mouth open, eyes staring, like she was seeing a ghost.

I moved into the circle of light made by her oil lamp and said, "Libby. It's me."

Her hand shot to her chest, but then she relaxed and said, "What are you . . . Oh, you thought I was sleepwalking again."

"No! No. I just— Okay, yeah. That's what I thought," I admitted, and I went back to bed feeling like a super-paranoid dumbass.

Tonight, though . . . tonight, she *is* sleepwalking. I woke up to the sound of movement outside my door. It freaked me the hell out at first, but then I heard a soft knock. The handle turned, the door swung open, and there was Libby.

She has that glazed look in her eyes, like she's seeing *through* everything. And she's standing at my door with an ancient-looking picnic basket hooked over her arm. The basket is dusty, so old the wicker is cracked in places.

I slip from the bed as quietly as I can and whisper, "Okay, Libby. You're okay." I lift the basket off her arm. Her hand drops to her side like it's weighted. She just stands there, all trancey, barely breathing, not blinking. I take a second to open the basket and glance inside. It's empty. I put it on the floor and gently stroke Libby's arm. "Let's get you to bed," I say quietly, trying not to startle her.

I googled *sleepwalking* after I found her outside last week, kneeling on the sidewalk, her hand covering the green glass stone. She was pushing down on it, like she was trying to press it farther into the concrete. There were tear tracks on her cheeks. She'd been crying, and the sight of it made me sick inside, like I should have been able to do something to make her *not* cry. But I couldn't do anything except lead her up the stairs and back to her bed. That's what all the internet experts say to do, anyway.

That's my plan tonight, too, since it always seems to work, but halfway up the stairs, she runs her fingers down my arm, then slides her hand into mine. My heart thumps as her fingers tangle with my own, and even though I try not to let it mean anything, I can't help twisting my fingers around hers and holding on tight.

I'll let myself have this one moment. This one moment of her hand in mine, like we're more than just roommates, more than one friend leading another friend to bed after a sleepwalking dream. I let myself hold her hand like it means everything. She won't remember any of this tomorrow. Only I will remember it, and I can live with having just this.

I open the door to her room and usher her inside. She moves straight to the bed, but she doesn't let go of my hand. She pulls me with her. Even as she climbs under the blankets, she holds on tight.

I've got no choice but to sit on the side of the bed as she settles onto her pillow with a happy-sounding sigh.

I'm jealous of that sigh. I haven't been sleeping very well. When I'm not forcing myself to stay awake, in protective mode, I'm dreaming. Dreams that, once I do wake up, keep me awake thinking about them. They're always dreams of the Mulberry house. Of Libby.

Two nights ago, I had one that felt so real I got up and went into the parlor to make sure I wasn't crazy, skipping time or something. In my dream, the Victrola was playing a Christmas song. The fireplace was burning bright. And the whole house was decorated for the holiday.

We were in the parlor, and Libby was dressed in those old clothes she likes to wear now, standing on a chair, hanging a garland across the hearth. I could feel the heat from the fire, toasty on my belly, almost too hot, as I held the chair so it wouldn't wobble beneath her. She attached the garland to the last hook, then smiled down at me, her eyes happy, reflecting the firelight.

I stared at her eyes as her hand reached down to softly stroke my cheek. They were lighter than I've ever seen them. Not the deep liquid brown I know them to be, but a bright mossy green. *That's not right,* I thought, just before I woke up, a little shaky.

I shoved the covers off and hurried into the parlor. It was a mess, just like we'd left it after our spaghetti-dinner, homework-in-front-of-the-fire session the night before. We'd taken our dishes to the sink, but our textbooks, laptops, and Libby's backpack were still on the hearth.

It took me a few minutes to convince myself that it was just a dream, because it had felt more real than any dream I'd ever had. It left me tired. And a tad off-balance.

That must be my problem now, because Libby's wine-brown

eyes are staring up at me, and my heart starts to pump a little too fast. She smiles the softest, sweetest smile I think I've ever seen. As much as I'd love for that look to be for me, I know it's not. It's for whoever she's dreaming about. She blinks and just stares up at me, still with that look, and I suddenly have the need to get the hell out of this room before I do something stupid. Like kiss her.

I pull my hand from hers. She mumbles, yawns, and closes her eyes with a long sigh.

I take my chance and hurry from the room, practically running down the stairs, and burst through the front door. The cold night air hits me like a million ice needles, but I don't care. I just need to breathe. I need to get control of my stupid, stupid heart.

I'm going to get hurt badly by all this. I just know it.

I walk through the front gate and look up at the sky. The clouds are heavy and white against the dark sky, like they forgot that they're not supposed to look like daylight clouds this late at night. They're supposed to be dark. They're supposed to blend, the way the naked tree limbs blend. I can't see them, but I know they're there.

There's barely any moon tonight, but the green glass stone still shines brighter than it should. I can see it from the corner of my eye, down there on the sidewalk, right next to my foot. I finally give in and look down at it. It's so green, even at night.

I see Libby's face, her tear-stained cheeks, as she sat out here, her hand pressing the stone.

After a few seconds of staring at it, I kneel down and reach out my hand. I want to touch it, but I don't want to touch it. I breathe once, twice, then I shove my hand down on the stone, all tensed up like I'm expecting a lightning strike. But I get nothing. It was only that first time that I felt the shock, in my foot. Since then, it's just been a pretty chunk of green glass. It makes me squirm like I have worms squiggling around in my guts, but it's just glass.

I let my fingers trace it, get used to the smooth feel of it, what I can see of it, anyway. I know, absolutely for sure, that it's not a stone. It's something else. I can almost picture it, long and narrow, but round, like a tube. A shudder creeps up my back, and I pull my hand away.

My running instincts are kicking in. The need to breathe, the need to feel the wind on my face. I should grab Lola and go. But I don't. I just stand up and look at the house. At Libby's room. There's something here that just won't let me leave.

34

TISH

I have to stop riding with Bari. Lola is at Joe's having her carburetor flushed because she was coughing and spitting like crazy, and now I'm stuck in this car for the next two hours, and Bari won't shut up. She bounces in her seat as she drives and says, "I just love her."

Again. For the ten thousandth time. About Libby.

"You're supposed to love *me*," I reply.

"I love you both."

"Hmmph," I grumble.

Bari and Libby bonded quicker than paper and glue. Every Tuesday and Thursday, Bari's light-load class days, I wake to find Bari in the kitchen, laughing it up with Libby. Having both of them there is like a gift I never thought to wish for. And at least once a week, we have Cam and Horatio over for dinner. Most of the time, Bari joins us for that. It's starting to feel like a little family, and I don't want anything to screw that up. Especially me.

Bari turns onto the highway that will take us to her house. It's Paps's birthday this weekend. Hasina makes a big deal of it every year, whether he remembers it or not. Last year, he surfaced from his Alzheimer's fog for about an hour, which was a long time for him. Halfway through the cake, he suddenly looked up and said, "Well, happy birthday to me."

Hasina grabbed his cheeks and kissed him so hard it was almost embarrassing. Then she buried her face in his chest and held on tight while he whispered words we couldn't hear, snuggling his face into her hair. It was the sweetest and the saddest thing I'd ever seen.

After a few minutes, he stood up and told Bari to put on some music. Bari played an old song, like the ones Libby plays all the time now, and Paps and Hasina slow danced while they laughed and talked and just held each other.

For that hour, he was just like the Paps I remember from when I was a kid, hanging around his garage while he tinkered with some old something he was trying to fix. Paps was my first introduction to DIY. We worked on clocks and bikes and radios. We built things. Shelves for Hasina's pantry, a folding shoe rack for Bari's must-have-every-color-Converse phase in ninth grade. We even wired special overhead lights in Hasina's little workshop, where she still makes her gorgeous glazed pottery.

First Paps. Then Joe. My mentors. The dads I never had.

But after that hour, Paps disappeared again, in a blink. He was there . . . then he wasn't. I remember Hasina saying, "Sixty minutes, sixty seconds. It doesn't matter. What matters is that he was here. That he was free, even for a little while." Then her eyes filled with tears, and she went inside before anyone could see her cry.

God, I hope this birthday is good. For Paps's sake. For Hasina's.

I've thought so many times that Hasina has the worst part of this deal. Paps disappears into his fog, but Hasina is the one who waits, hoping he'll come back. She's the one who has to wonder, every time, if it's the last time she'll see *him*, her Paps—the soul, not just the shell.

"This whole thing with you and Libby . . ." Bari is saying. I missed half of it, but it isn't hard to catch up. She's still talking about true love, the same thing she's been talking about ever since she met Libby. "I think you should give it a shot. What's the worst that can happen?" she finishes hopefully.

What's the worst that can happen? Yeah, right.

I could lose my new room, in a house where I finally feel like a person, not just someone who's shunted into a closet, out of the way. I could lose this new family that has sprung up around me like flowers, when I didn't even know there were any seeds growing. And I finally feel like I have something to *do*, a purpose. I want to fix up the Mulberry house. I want to see it as close to finished as I can get it. I want to see Libby's face when she sees it—

I stop myself there. It can't be about Libby. But even as I tell myself that, I already know that of course it's about her. Everything I think and do these days is about Libby.

"I've got a good thing going. I don't want to screw it up," I say to Bari, hedging.

"I don't think Libby will ever kick you out of that house, no matter what happens between you. You seriously need to pay attention to the way she glows when she's around you."

"That's her oil lamp."

"That's her *heart*, dummy. Stop being so stubborn," Bari says.

"It won't work out," I say firmly. "Nothing good has ever worked out for me."

"Excuse me?!" Bari exclaims, offended.

"You know what I mean."

Clearly, she doesn't, because she's still glaring at the road in front of us.

"Sasha? Charisse? Emily?" I remind her.

"Them?! Come on, Tish. They weren't good because they weren't *the one!*"

"Oh my GOD, shut up!" I snap, ready to jump from the car, moving or not. I'll take a broken bone and some stitches over Bari's true love hammer. It hits too hard. At least stitches will only leave a scar.

I plug in my phone and find a playlist that Bari will like, something that will keep her mouth shut and her attention off me. Then I lean against the window. I haven't gotten much sleep lately, what with listening and watching for Libby and the dreams I've been having. Bari's car is warm and cozy, and the drive is long. It feels too good to keep my eyes open any longer.

When I wake up, we're parked in Bari's driveway and the car is off. She's looking at me in a strange way, and it feels like she's been looking at me for a while.

"What?" I ask.

She just shakes her head, still giving me that look, like she wants to say something.

"What?" I ask again.

"Nothing," she says, then opens the door and gets out.

I get out and stretch, groaning as my back pops. I didn't pick the best position to fall asleep in, all slumped up against the door, the seat belt pressed into my shoulder and neck. I rub the skin there, then reach into the back seat and grab my satchel.

Hasina opens the front door and calls out, "Get up here and hug this old lady."

I laugh and trot to the porch, up the four steps, and into Hasina's arms. Bari's right behind me. When she hugs Hasina, I hear her whisper, "How is he?"

"We'll see, sweetheart . . ." Hasina whispers back. "We'll see."

~

Turns out it wasn't a good day for Paps. Not a good day at all. He was disoriented and confused and agitated. He didn't know who anyone was, and he yelled at everyone at least once. The few friends Hasina had invited left early, all with hugs and sweet words for her on their way out. No one was angry with Paps. They were all just sad for the man they used to know, and for the woman who would never stop loving him. I was sad for them, too.

It was too much to even watch, so I went into Bari's room, stuffed my earbuds into my ears, and listened to a podcast. I don't know when I fell asleep, but the dream came in flashes, little spurts of images.

Colored confetti falling in a hot, crowded room.

Thick snowflakes falling through the air.

Scared. So scared.

Old-timey music and lots of hoots and hollers.

A countdown. A flock of voices.

"Eight!"

"Seven!"

A voice close to me whispers into my ear, "Two, three, six." It's Libby's voice. I'd know it anywhere.

Horns blow loud, and there's a drumroll. Then a crowd yells, "Happy New Year!"

"Give me this," Libby's voice says. Then her mouth is on mine. Kissing me.

I can feel her. I can hear her. I can taste her.

All I see, though, is green.

Bright green glass.

And the snow.

"Don't leave me!"

I jerk awake to find Bari's eyes open and watching me. I'm jittery from the dream, from Libby's voice, again, begging me not to leave her. Bari's eyes locked on mine aren't helping.

"Quit staring at me, weirdo," I mutter.

"What were you dreaming about?"

"Not sure," I say. And it's kinda true. I don't know what the dream was *about*; I only remember the images. The sounds. The feelings. And Libby. No, not Libby. Libby doesn't have short hair. But I do remember Libby's voice.

"Who is Elizabeth?" Bari asks.

My mouth goes dry.

"You said her name just now, in your sleep," Bari says. "You said it in the car, too."

"I don't know," I say. She just stares at me. But I really don't know anyone with that name. "Elizabeth," I murmur. The name, when I hear my own voice say it, sends heat through me, my neck prickling.

Then a loud, anguished cry carries down the hallway. Paps. Calling for Hasina.

"He's been that way for the last few minutes," Bari says, tears in her voice. I move closer to her, and she squeezes right up next to me. "I hate that I can't help them. I mean, brilliant minds are working on it. More brilliant than mine. What if I do all this school, and I still can't . . ."

I wrap my arms around her and hold her tight. We can hear Hasina trying to calm him, shushing him gently and cooing, "My dearest. It's all right. Shhhhhh . . ."

It makes me want to close my ears forever. "If that's true love, Bari, I don't want any part of it. It's too much," I admit.

"Oh, Tish," Bari says with a little laugh, through her tears, like

I'm the stupidest person on the planet. Then she says, sniffling, "You don't know anything, do you?"

I guess I don't, because the sounds from down the hall don't make the prospect of true love seem all that tempting. That kiss still tingles on my lips, though.

Libby Monroe kissed me, and dream or not, it was the realest thing I've ever felt.

35

LIBBY

With Tish gone to Bari's this weekend, I have the house to myself. I've gotten so used to her being here that I miss her. I miss hearing her clunking around in the kitchen or hearing the bathroom pipes squeak when she's in the shower. Hearing her try to tiptoe around at night to check on me, peeking into my room to see if I'm in my bed or if I'm blindly roaming the house in one of my sleepwalking fugues.

I didn't really believe Tish about the sleepwalking. I thought she was just exaggerating, seeing me up in the kitchen or something, or going to the bathroom, like the other night. But I believe it now, because I just woke up standing in front of my window.

I thought I was dreaming. It had certainly felt like a dream. Or, it felt like I was *inside* a dream. It was daylight, and everything was hazy except my window and the view outside, almost like tunnel vision, fuzzy around the edges. A group of men were working on the sidewalk. One of the men, the youngest one, looked up at me. I only saw him because he was right in my sight line. He raised a tiny wave, but I couldn't make myself wave back. I was on autopilot, like someone else was in control. My eyes pulled from his to stare at the sidewalk, all that fresh concrete, wet and shiny in the sun.

I could feel something in my hand, something I was holding tight. Like a small cylinder. I couldn't make myself look down at it. But I didn't have to look. I knew what it was. My eyes were still glued to the spot where I would soon press it into the sidewalk. I could feel the idea happen as it came into my head, could feel my fingers tighten around the object.

Then my hand lifted to the window, but it wasn't *my* hand. This hand was wrinkled, with age spots and knobby fingers. Old. So old. I tried to jerk it back. Instead, I woke up, and here I am. Standing at the window. Just like in the dream. So . . . sleepwalking, I guess.

The room is dark and chilly, the only light coming from the oil lamp, turned down low. I can see its reflection in the glass, flickering behind me, on the side table. My hand is against the window, just where it was in the dream, but it's *my* hand this time. Young.

Still young.

The voice! I'd almost forgotten about it. Whispering in my head, giving me those impulsive nudges that made me do crazy things, like buy a house, defy my father, figure out my own way. And because of those things, I broke up with my boyfriend, invited a girl to live with me, fell in love with her—

In love?

Yes.

No.

Well . . .

I pull my hand from the window and stand there in the dark, still staring down at the sidewalk, only now the green glass stone is there, where it's always been. The dream/sleepwalk/whatever fades (as everything does) when my mind turns to Tish.

Yes, I like Tish. A lot. More than a lot. More than I've ever liked anyone. Definitely yes, I find her so irresistibly attractive that sometimes I can barely stop myself from reaching out to touch her, just to see if she feels as good as she looks. But . . . love?

Yes. Love.

The feeling sits so deeply in me that it can't be anything but true.

Omigod. I love her.

When, exactly, did that happen? When she hobbled into design class, her ass on fire? When she covered for me in practicum so I could go home and rest? When she showed up that same night, and so many times after, to help me, or just to hang out?

So many images of Tish flash through my mind, so many moments they pile on top of each other. Tish, so excited about the cherry pie. Tish, her head popping out of a dumpster with a silly grin. Tish, backlit by the fire, her red curls ignited around her face. Tish. Tish. Tish.

I can't pinpoint the exact moment because now I can't remember a time when I *didn't* love her. I feel like I've loved her all my life, that I was just waiting to meet her, waiting for her to show up on my doorstep, waiting for her to take my hand and smile that smile. A shudder runs through my whole body, shaking me so strongly that my knees tremble. I sink down onto the reading nook and lean against the glass. Holy shit. I'm in love.

I look to the bed, my sleepwalking completely forgotten as my eyes catch Elizabeth's journal lying open on the pillow next to mine. I fell asleep reading it. I can't help the smile that comes over my face when I think of the journal, of Elizabeth and Patricia on the overlook, Elizabeth staring at Patricia's hands.

"Oh, girl," I say to Elizabeth, wherever she is, "I know exactly how you feel."

I get up, move back to the bed, and pick up the journal. When

Tish left with Bari, I gave myself permission to sink completely into Elizabeth's story, to finally finish it, to bask in her words, in her house, in her life, in her forbidden love. I lean over and turn up the wick on the lamp, loving the way the flame grows and brightens the room. I pile my pillows against the headboard and lean back, tucking the covers around my legs. Then I turn the page . . .

36

NOVEMBER 18, 1925

Elizabeth wondered whether it was possible to be happier than she was right now, lying in her bed, her elbow propped on Patricia's naked back. The oil lamp glimmered from its spot on the bedside table, casting a burnished glow across Patricia's ivory skin. From her vantage, Elizabeth had an ideal view of the book she was reading (*Wuthering Heights*), the rounded globes of Patricia's bare bottom, and the long, long legs that extended beneath.

"You are glorious," Elizabeth whispered.

Patricia chuckled, and murmured into the pillow, "And you are cracked, my love."

"I suppose I am. But are you not crazy for me, too?" she asked quietly. She already knew the answer. Patricia's eyes, mouth, and hands told her how much she was loved.

Patricia let loose a soft sigh, then said, "A fair doin' you've done to me, miss. You've turned me inside out, you have."

Elizabeth bent to place a reverent kiss upon one smooth shoulder, then turned the page, reading quietly of Heathcliff and Catherine and their doomed romance:

"'And—did she ever mention me?' he asked, hesitating, as if he dreaded the answer to his question would introduce details that he could not bear to hear.

"*'Her senses never returned: she recognized nobody from the time you left her,' I said. 'She lies with a sweet smile on her face; and her latest ideas wandered back to pleasant early days. Her life closed in a gentle dream—may she wake as kindly in the other world!'*"
Elizabeth read, her voice rising with the passion of the words.

Patricia shifted as she turned her head toward Elizabeth, causing the novel to slip to the mattress. Elizabeth kissed her shoulder again, retrieved the book, then continued, in a ragged whisper:

"*'May she wake in torment!' he cried, with frightful vehemence, stamping his foot, and groaning in a sudden paroxysm of ungovernable passion. 'Why, she's a liar to the end! Where is she? Not* there—*not in heaven—not perished—where? Oh! you said you cared nothing for my sufferings! And I pray one prayer—I repeat it till my tongue stiffens—Catherine Earnshaw, may you not rest as long as I am living; you said I killed you—haunt me, then! The murdered* do *haunt their murderers, I believe. I know that ghosts* have *wandered on earth. Be with me always—take any form—drive me mad!'*"

A tiny sound burst from Patricia's throat. Elizabeth looked at her, found those blue eyes wide and tearful. They held hers for a long moment, then Elizabeth returned, shakily, to the page:

"*'. . . only* do *not leave me in this abyss, where I cannot find you! Oh, God! it is unutterable! I* cannot *live without my life! I* cannot *live without my soul!'*"

Patricia turned her head away. Her shoulders heaved one time. Then another.

Oh God. She was crying.

Elizabeth shoved the book away and laid her bare body across Patricia's back, rubbing her hands up and down Patricia's arms, warming her, comforting her.

"What is it?" Elizabeth asked. "What is the matter?" To have this woman, so strong in every way, weep in her arms was more than Elizabeth could bear. She held tight, stroking Patricia's shoulders, her arms, her back. She pushed aside that wealth of hair to murmur into the skin of her neck. "Patricia, please tell me. Please."

After a lengthy silence, Patricia whispered, her voice thick, "I know why Heathcliff aches so. He knew he could never have her, yet still, he hoped. Hope is a fool's folly. He deserves his broken heart"—and her next words were mumbled into the pillow, hushed, in that accent that killed Elizabeth every time—"just as I will deserve mine."

"No . . ." Elizabeth whimpered. "Oh, no no no."

Sarah's warning came back to her. *She will be destroyed.*

Yet here Patricia was, in her bed, in her arms, risking it all.

Elizabeth shoved the thoughts away. They meant nothing to her, because she knew something Sarah did not. Elizabeth knew that she belonged to Patricia. Heart and soul. Now and forever. She could no more hurt Patricia than she could hurt herself. She tugged at Patricia's shoulders until her lover faced her, then she wrapped arms and legs around her, clinging like a vine, and said, "I am not going to break your heart. I swear it."

"I've nothing to offer you, Elizabeth. I've got nothing."

I cannot have you, so I shall not want you.

Now Elizabeth understood. It wasn't fear of danger, or abuse, or exile that haunted Patricia. She was afraid because she believed that, at some point, Elizabeth would find her lacking in some material way. Patricia did not believe that she, just the woman, was enough.

For Elizabeth, Patricia was more than enough. She was everything. If their love was found out and Patricia was expelled from the house and thrown onto the streets, Elizabeth would go with her, taking nothing save the clothes on her back. Did Patricia not know how dearly she was loved? She took Patricia's face in her hands, rubbed her thumbs over wet cheeks. Patricia shut her eyes, hiding, it seemed, in any way she could. Elizabeth would have none of it.

"Look at me," she said, never ceasing the gentle movement of her thumbs over Patricia's face. They moved over her cheeks, over her brow, down to her lips, and back again, but those eyes, which she so loved, remained shut. She brushed her lips along Patricia's nose, her cheeks, then each eyelid. She said, more firmly this time, "Look at me . . . *my love. My love, my love.*"

Patricia's lips quirked at Elizabeth's terrible attempt at an Irish lilt. She chuckled in spite of herself, and finally opened her eyes. Tears still clung to her lashes. Elizabeth wiped them gently away, one by one. She waited until Patricia's eyes had calmed, until they gazed directly into her own, until she knew she had her complete and undivided attention.

Then Elizabeth said, most sincerely, most earnestly, most passionately, "You've got the one thing I want most in the world. The only thing I need." She moved her hand to rest over Patricia's rapidly beating heart. "This, my darling."

Patricia held her eyes and took a long, deep breath. Then she seemed to relax. Seemed to surrender. She squeezed Elizabeth's fingers, where they still rested above her own beating heart, and said, "Oh. That's not mine, love. It's not been mine for a long, long while."

Elizabeth fisted a gentle hand in those fiery locks and pulled Patricia's mouth to hers.

∼

"Will you always love me?" Elizabeth asked. They were entwined, her head on Patricia's shoulder, their legs tangled beneath the blankets.

"Till my very last breath, and ever after that. Will you always love *me*?" Patricia asked.

"Till the end of time," Elizabeth said. "I want us never to be apart."

"Then we won't be," Patricia said.

"Promise?" Elizabeth whispered.

"I promise."

Elizabeth stretched to reach the oil lamp. She turned up the wick as far as it would go, the flame flapping and flickering wildly. She needed to see Patricia's face, her every expression, every color of blue in those blue, blue eyes. She hovered over her, their noses mere inches apart.

"Swear it," Elizabeth insisted.

Patricia stared up at her, traced a finger along her cheek, and smiled softly.

"I swear, Elizabeth Mary Louise Post, that I will love you forever, and should we ever be separated, I shall not rest until we are together again. I am yours, my love," Patricia vowed.

"And I am yours," Elizabeth returned. Patricia kissed her then, a kiss so deep and full of emotion that Elizabeth thought she might never breathe again.

The wick of the oil lamp popped loudly as the room brightened with the sudden flare. Both girls jumped and turned to look at the lamp. A tiny spot on the wick still burned brighter than the rest, but otherwise, the flame was steady.

Elizabeth nestled herself against Patricia's side.

"What will we do when they return?" Patricia asked, tracing lazy fingers along Elizabeth's spine. Elizabeth curled closer, slid her arm over Patricia's stomach, and sighed.

"I suppose we will do what we always do. You will undress me in the morning and undress me at night . . ." she said with a coy glance.

"Well, then. Why bother getting dressed at all? It would save my poor fingers having to navigate button after button after—" She squealed as Elizabeth's fingers dug into the soft flesh of her side, tickling her mercilessly until she gasped for breath. "Surrender! I surrender!"

Elizabeth relented, chuckling. She sat up and pulled the coverlet over them, then turned down the wick on the oil lamp, leaving just enough flame to see by. She watched Patricia close her eyes, memorizing the sight of her, the feel of her. As Patricia's breathing deepened, Elizabeth yawned and settled down next to her, skin on skin, and fell asleep.

37

DECEMBER 24, 1925

Elizabeth had received a telegram from her parents a week prior. They had wished her a happy Christmas season, blessings for the New Year, and explained that they would be remaining in Brazil through spring, to establish their business ties more permanently. Elizabeth did not care, she did not care, she did not care! Let them stay forever! The days since their leaving had been the best she had ever known.

She and Patricia had settled into a domestic tranquility that saw them always together.

They took their meals at the small table in the kitchen, leaving the formal dining room table to gather dust. They played records and danced away the mornings in the parlor. At night they lit the Christmas tree. They bundled themselves into blankets in the parlor and watched the tiny candles burn, whispering their deepest secrets and sharing their wildest dreams. They both knew this freedom was temporary, but they ignored reality in lieu of their pure, unfettered joy.

They bathed together in the afternoons and slept together at night and loved together during it all. And, just as Elizabeth had predicted, the winter landscape had become their very own polar paradise. Walks through the park, ice glinting on the naked tree limbs, the frozen pond twinkling in the sun. Frigid picnics on the overlook, braving the cold to hold hands and watch the town below—tiny cars and even tinier people, bustling here and there.

The first heavy snowfall had come upon them the night before, and that morning, Elizabeth dragged Patricia outside to play in the snow.

They built a snowman, a first for Patricia, who'd never seen so much snow all in one place. Elizabeth handed her a carrot and watched as Patricia planted the vegetable right in the middle of the snowman's face. Patricia then removed her wool cap and plunked it atop their snowman's head. Freed from its captivity, all her hair tumbled down around her shoulders. Her expression was so wondrous that Elizabeth could clearly picture what she must have looked like as a child: eyes wide, mouth agape, hair wild and woolly, and those twelve precious freckles dotting her nose.

Elizabeth lifted a hand to her chest and rubbed the skin there, so moved by the image of little-girl Patricia that her heart twinged painfully. Patricia, of course, caught her staring, and Elizabeth, of course, blushed, her cheeks bright pink against the snowy background.

They'd been playing a game since the night they'd made their vow, each of them posing scenarios, each proposition more outlandish than the last.

"If I were to be lost in the woods . . ." Elizabeth prompted.

And Patricia answered, "Then I shall lead a pack of horses and hounds to track you down, my love."

From Patricia, "If the world were to go dark, and there was no light for me to find you . . ."

To which Elizabeth replied, "I would light my oil lamp and let its flame lead you home."

"And if a cloud carries me away?" Elizabeth asked.

"I shall loop a string to your foot and fly you like a kite."

For her impertinence, Patricia received a swift pinch to her bottom.

"And if the moon steals me from you?" Elizabeth posed.

"I shall steal you back, and take a hefty chunk of cheese for myself in the bargain."

"Would you share it with me?"

"No."

That earned her a snowball to the face, but Patricia was quicker than Elizabeth had anticipated. She ducked, and the packed ice whizzed over her head and whacked the snowman, knocking the carrot to the ground. It landed like a bright orange dagger in the snow.

"Oh, you. Look what you've gone and done to his sniffer," Patricia said.

The next snowball hit Patricia squarely in the face, leaving Elizabeth to giggle and snort as Patricia spit snow from her mouth, and wiped the fluffy powder from her coat.

The rest of the day, and night, went on to be the best Christmas Eve of Elizabeth's life.

38

DECEMBER 25, 1925

Christmas Day, however, was a miserable affair.

It had started as wonderfully as last night had ended. They'd spent a decadent morning lying in bed, finally rising when their bellies grumbled loudly for attention. They'd had oatmeal by the fire, toasty and warm, as they eyed the gifts under the tree. Two with which Elizabeth was familiar; she'd purchased and wrapped them herself. The other one was for her.

Elizabeth hadn't expected anything, and Patricia had scowled at her when she'd asked where it had come from, why it was there. "It is Christmas. That's why," Patricia had said. "Besides, what makes you think it's from me? Does not Saint Nicholas visit America, too?"

It was decided they would wait until evening to open their gifts, to prolong their Christmas, to savor the anticipation. Then, as they sat down for a small lunch in the kitchen, the front doorbell chimed. Patricia startled, her fork halfway to her mouth. "Are you expecting—?"

"No. No one," Elizabeth said, and dropped her own fork. They hurried to the parlor and peeked around the staircase into the foyer. Through the long, narrow glass beside the door, they could see, standing on the front porch, Delilah Harper. And Rose. "The hens!"

Elizabeth's heart pounded as she thought of everything they

would see. The house wasn't in order! The dining room was dusty. *All* the rooms were dusty. She and Patricia had been living exclusively in her bedroom and in the parlor. Patricia wasn't in her maid's uniform, and she herself was still in her sleep clothes and dressing gown.

"Oh God," Elizabeth moaned.

"Oh, *shite*," Patricia corrected. Then she called out loudly, "Just a moment!"

She darted into her room and slammed the door. Elizabeth realized quickly that Patricia was right to run. While it was one thing to find the daughter of the house still in her loungewear on a lazy Christmas afternoon, it was quite another to discover the maid in her morning slippers.

Elizabeth tied the sash on her dressing gown and bolted into motion. She snatched the blankets from the parlor floor, where they'd been piled and waiting, night after night, and shoved them into the coat closet. She slid the dining room doors closed to hide the room, then rushed to the nearest mirror to check her appearance. Cripes, she looked a mess. She ran her fingers through her hair, then nicked a ribbon from the Christmas tree and tied back the front.

She heard Patricia come out of her room, and they both rushed into the foyer at the same time, Patricia tying her apron behind her as she reached the front door. When she spotted Elizabeth beside her, she hissed, "No!" as she straightened her maid's cap over her hastily braided hair. "You go to the parlor. Be reading."

Elizabeth ran back to the parlor. She stopped at the closet to retrieve one of the blankets she'd only just stuffed in there a moment ago. She heard the front door open, and Patricia say politely, "Mrs. Harper. Miss Harper. A fine merry Christmas to you."

She heard Delilah reply, "Merry Christmas, Patricia."

There was a long silence, time that Elizabeth used to scramble onto the sofa. Then she remembered that the book they were currently reading, *A Christmas Carol* (in deference to the holiday), was upstairs, lying open on their bed. Cripes!

Delilah cleared her throat and said sharply, "Patricia. Invite us inside."

Rose's nasty giggle carried all the way into the parlor.

Elizabeth suddenly recalled a passage from Bram Stoker's *Dracula*, about invitations to enter, and she considered shouting, "Do not invite them inside! They are vampires!" But she did no such thing. Instead, she looked swiftly to the Christmas tree, to the gifts, and made a lunge for one of them. She knew it was a book because she'd wrapped it herself.

She tore off the paper, stuffed the shreds behind a sofa pillow, and tucked the blanket around her legs just as Patricia said, "My apologies. Please, come in. Miss Post is in the parlor." *Miss Post.* It felt odd to have Patricia refer to her so formally. She did not like it. She did not like it at all. She remained quiet, though, pretending to read as Patricia said, "She's just in here." Her accent sounded thick, even to Elizabeth's ears. Nerves, Elizabeth thought.

"We know where the parlor is, Patricia," Rose said, as if she were talking to a simpleton.

Elizabeth could only imagine what storms were raging in those beloved blue eyes. She opened the book just as the hens strutted into the room. They were dressed as they were always dressed: to perfection. But Elizabeth couldn't let that bother her. Not now.

She looked up and feigned surprise. "Oh!" she said as she closed the book. "I was so engrossed, I didn't even hear the door. How awful of me."

She pushed aside the blanket and made to rise, but Delilah simply kissed the air in her direction, then waved at her to remain seated. "We only wanted to stop by and wish you a merry Christmas and, of course, to check up on your well-being. We haven't seen you at any of the parties, and we know you've been invited."

Elizabeth had been "cordially invited" to several gatherings. She'd declined every one of them, choosing instead to spend those hours here, with Patricia, but that was something that she could never confess. So she lied. "I took a chill and it lingered, I'm sorry to say, but it was fine by me. You know I don't do as well at those gatherings as do Honey or Rose . . ."

Rose's chest puffed and Elizabeth fought not to roll her eyes.

". . . so I was content to remain here with my nose in my pages, as Mother would say."

"Well, darling, not everyone can be the belle of the ball," Delilah said with great and absolute insincere sympathy. Elizabeth knew to whom Delilah was referring, and it wasn't Rose.

"Where *is* Honey? Did she not make it home for the holidays?" Elizabeth asked, caring not a whit for the answer, but desperately wanting a change of subject.

"She's spending this afternoon at the Penningtons'. She will be with them for the New Year, as well. Chess has taken quite a liking to our little chicken, hasn't he, Rose?"

Elizabeth had never been happier to see Honey get exactly what she wanted, as it meant she was not here with her mother and sister, ruining her Christmas Day.

The next two hours passed as though they were twelve, with Rose imitating (but never rising to) her sister's bladed wit. Several times, Delilah hushed her youngest, clearly embarrassed by the display. For the entirety of the visit, Patricia stood in the corner of the room, eyes on the floor, waiting to serve these undeserving women. Watching her now, the memory of that night together, their first, welled up in Elizabeth. *"I've nothing to offer you, Elizabeth. I've got nothing."*

Indignation flared in her gullet, and Elizabeth sat up straighter, her eyes as fierce as Honey's had ever been. She had no idea what Rose was prattling on about, but she didn't want to hear one more word of it. So she interrupted her. It's what Honey would have done, and this was *her* house, not Rose Harper's.

"I was reading *Wuthering Heights* recently . . ." She paused, sensing Patricia's sudden alertness. "And I was struck with wonder over why the most enduring love stories always seem to be the most tragic. Why does love not triumph, when it should?"

Delilah clearly had no idea where Elizabeth was taking the conversation, but as manners dictated, she inclined her head for Elizabeth to continue.

Rose, on the other hand, remarked snidely, "I'm sure I have no idea."

Elizabeth smiled and continued, "So I bought a new book for Christmas. Love poems. I've just opened it and was reading one when you came in. Would you like to hear some of it?"

Delilah's "Of course" was only minimally louder than Rose's aggrieved sigh.

Elizabeth lifted the book and read: *"'You and I have floated here on the stream that brings from the fount. / At the heart of time, love of one for another. / We have played alongside millions of lovers, shared in the same / shy sweetness of meeting'—"* This time, Rose's bored moan was downright rude. Elizabeth put down the book and, daring a quick glance at Patricia, said, "It is called 'Unending Love.' By Rabindranath Tagore."

"By *who*?" exclaimed Rose, before Delilah gave her a solid pinch.

Elizabeth's teeth ground together in her bid to restrain her thoughts about that stupid, stupid Rose Harper. The dolt! The clod! The wretched ingrate! She wanted both Delilah and her insipid brat out of her house! She hated hated hated them!

Fifteen minutes later, she got her wish. As Patricia closed the door behind them, Elizabeth snarled, "'*By* who?' How dare she? She walks around this town with her nose in the air, a *lady*, yet she's as uncultured as an old billy goat."

"In a fancy dress," Patricia said as she pulled off her maid's cap, untied her apron and let it drop to the floor, and loosened her braid, allowing her hair to flow free.

"It was a nice dress," Elizabeth sighed. Many things inside her had settled since this newfound love. Since Patricia. Her envy of the Harper girls' wardrobe had not. "Tagore is only the most brilliant poet who ever lived," Elizabeth grumbled, still offended on the poet's behalf.

"I thought that was Shakespeare," Patricia said.

"Well, I think they would have been good friends," Elizabeth replied with a reluctant grin. She lifted the book again and said, "It was your Christmas present. I'm sorry I had to open it. I had no other books down here."

After they'd opened the remaining gifts, Patricia wadded the spent wrapping paper, tossed it into the fire, and laid herself down on the sofa, resting her head in Elizabeth's lap. She pulled her brand-new overcoat across her legs (a gift from Elizabeth) and picked up the Tagore book. She held it out to Elizabeth with a quiet request: "Read it again?"

Elizabeth sank her fingers into Patricia's hair. The Harpers were gone, a healthy fire burned in the fireplace, and Patricia was here, with her. She found the poem and read quietly, in a soft voice she reserved only for Patricia: *"'I seem to have loved you in numberless forms, numberless times . . . / In life after life, in age after age, forever. / My spellbound heart has made and remade the necklace of songs, / That you take as a gift, wear round your neck in your many forms, / In life after life, in age after age, forever.'"*

"Much better than poor old Heathcliff," Patricia muttered, her eyes closing.

There they stayed, poem after poem, hour after hour, until darkness fell outside and the only light in the room was the fire, burning low. Elizabeth stared into the embers, red-hot coals beneath dying flames. The house was quiet. Elizabeth's thoughts were not. The visit from Delilah and Rose had jarred her. They hadn't been prepared. They had almost, almost been caught. It was fortunate that Honey had not been with her mother. Honey, with her all-seeing eyes, would have known immediately. She would have seen right through them. She would have seen *everything*. The thought sent a shudder through Elizabeth.

"We're okay, love," Patricia said, rubbing her cheek against Elizabeth's belly. "They don't know."

One of the coals popped. It cracked right down the middle, bright red and glowing. Elizabeth stared at it, uneasy. It looked like every illustrated image of brimstone she'd ever seen.

"And if we were lost in the pits of hell . . ." Elizabeth whispered.

There was a long silence before Patricia reached up to tug at a lock of Elizabeth's hair. "I shall find you. The Devil himself cannot keep me away."

"How will I know it's you?"

A quiet foreboding had crept in now and was gnawing at the

corners of Elizabeth's happiness. She felt Patricia's eyes on her, but she could not look away from the fire, from those burning, blistering coals.

"I don't rightly know. Let's see . . ." Patricia said in a low, grumbly voice.

She sat up and gave the question ponderous thought, her lips pursed, fingers stroking her chin, as would an ancient Greek philosopher. Elizabeth laughed at the silly gesture and squeezed Patricia's hand, silently thanking her for rescuing them from her suddenly solemn mood.

"My brothers used to have a code. They would talk in numbers," Patricia suddenly said.

"Numbers?" Elizabeth asked, wondering how that could possibly work.

"I didn't understand it then, either, for I was but a wee girl and I couldn't yet read, but I understand it now. We will take their trick for ourselves, you and I, and we will use it to the Devil's disadvantage."

"Tell me how," Elizabeth whispered, excited now, back in the game.

"The number of letters in the word is the number you speak."

"Wha— I don't— *What?*"

Patricia went on to explain, "For example, *I love you* would be one . . . four . . . three."

"I— Ohhhhh. Clever boys," Elizabeth said. She leaned in to drop a sweet kiss on Patricia's lips and whispered, "One . . . ," and with another kiss, "four . . . ," then another, "three."

"I love you, too. But that one is so easy even Rose Harper could guess it."

Elizabeth squawked, her laughter ringing through the parlor. "She is not on par with her sister, that is true," she admitted.

"So, our secret code, when I find you, will be . . ." Patricia nuzzled into her ear and whispered something low.

Elizabeth smiled and worked out the code: "Two . . . three . . . six."

"Two . . . three . . . six," Patricia confirmed.

Elizabeth stood and removed the screen from the fireplace. She poured water over the embers, then held out her hand. "Let's go to bed." She tugged Patricia to her feet, and as they reached the staircase, she asked, "What would your brothers say to your mother, that had to be said in code?"

"Oh." Patricia laughed. "Only the rudest words you could imagine."

Elizabeth snorted and led the way up the stairs. She held tight to Patricia's fingers, and stopped midway up, turning to whisper down at her, "Merry Christmas, Patricia."

"Merry Christmas to you, my love."

39

TISH

I jerk awake with a heavy tingle in my belly and thighs. It's been a long time since I've had one of *those* dreams, and now I'm sweaty and frustrated. Like the other dreams, I only remember flashes, quick moments, like one of Wallis's accidental slideshows, except this slideshow makes me feel a million things.

Libby's mouth, her hair, her skin, soft and warm. Sunlight streaming through the window and across the bed, making her look like an angel, all lit up from behind. The parlor, decorated. A real Christmas tree, with bows on the branches. Bits of torn wrapping paper, the plain brown kind. Ribbons. A small box in Libby's hands. A glimmer of something green. Libby, smiling through tears, asking how I was able to afford it.

I saw a tiny cloth pouch at the bottom of the wardrobe, the wardrobe in my room.

I saw my hand open the pouch. Inside were a few coins.

I saw my gloved hand give those coins to a girl in a shop. A girl dressed in old-fashioned clothes, the kind Libby's been wearing lately. She took the money and gave me a small box.

Libby. Unfolding a small piece of paper. Bursting into tears. Launching herself at me.

Back to Libby's bed. Her hands on me, all over me. Everywhere.

Me, staring into those pretty green eyes . . .

. . . when I know Libby's eyes are brown . . .

. . . then those green eyes closed and she was touching me again, her lips on mine, hands moving . . .

And I woke up. In Bari's room. Two hours away from the Mulberry house, where Libby was in her own bed, sleeping. I hope. I lie there, trying to be still, to remember every single detail, but that's all I'm able to catch. Just those flashes. But they're enough. Especially those last ones. Libby's hands. Her kisses. I'm all wound up, and it was only a dream.

Bari is still asleep beside me, thank God—how embarrassing would that be?—so I slide out of the bed. The bathroom is down the hall, right across from Paps and Hasina's room. Their door is open. It's silent. I creep down the hallway, trying to make as little noise as possible. I hurry into the bathroom, do my business, then hurry back out—

—and nearly ram right into Hasina in the hallway. She's got a cup of water in her hand that sloshes on us both before she steadies it.

"Hi, sweetie. We . . . didn't keep you up, did we?" she says.

"No. No, I just, um . . ." I point to the bathroom. Hasina nods, then reaches for my hand. I let her take it, feeling the fragile bones underneath her skin. When did Hasina get so old?

"I was just headed to have myself a slice of that birthday cake. You want some?"

Hasina knows me well enough that she doesn't even wait for my answer; she just walks toward the kitchen, totally expecting me to follow. Which I do, obviously. It's cake. Hasina cuts two big slices and sets them on the table, then pours two glasses of milk. My fork clinks on the plate as I scoop a big bite, still thinking about Libby. And that dream.

Hasina sighs and I look up. She's not eating her cake. She's just dragging her fork through it, making little trails in the icing. Usually, I would not stop eating for anything, but something makes me put my fork down and just sit quietly. To just . . . be with her. Hasina fed me when I needed it, hugged me when I needed it, and has loved me since the first time Bari brought me home like the stray I was. I can ignore this cake and be there for Hasina now, assuming she wants to confide in a nineteen-year-old. Weirder things have happened, I guess.

All that thinking, and I missed that Hasina has put her fork down, too, and is looking at me over the kitchen table, a sad kind of smile on her face.

"He doesn't have a lot of time left," she says. She doesn't have to explain who she's talking about. "I'm not sure how to tell Bari. She lost her parents so young, and now this." Before I can say anything, she asks, "How is she? My Bari? Is she having fun at school?"

"Yeah. Yeah, we have fun. It's fun. She studies a lot, but she comes over all the time."

"Oh, yes. Congratulations on the new roomie. Bari just loves her," Hasina says, and now she's got that same dreamy look Bari gets when she's talking about Libby. About Libby and *me*.

"I know she does," I sigh.

Hasina just laughs and finally takes a bite of her cake. Now I'm the one who doesn't want to eat. Now I'm thinking about love, and Libby, and those dreams, and Paps and Hasina, about how their love is about to end.

"Hasina?"

"Hmm?"

"Is it . . . Well, I mean . . . What are you going to do . . . when . . ."

"When Tom dies?"

It sounds so matter-of-fact, the way she says it, but there are tears in her eyes.

"I've been lucky to have him for so long. There aren't many people anymore who love like that. We were so, so lucky. For so long..."

"But everything ends?" I say.

Stupid. What a stupid freaking thing to say to her while she's talking about her husband and how he's dying and how much she loves him. I hate myself right now. But she just smiles.

"No, sweetie. It never ends. I don't believe so, anyway. I grew up learning that every life is a cycle. Time after time, again and again. Each time around, we grow, we evolve, we get new chances to... do things better. To do things right. I believe that. I believe it with everything that's in me. It's how Tom and I... I think that's how we knew, how we just *knew*, the moment we met, that we were meant for each other. Because we always were. We always will be."

I'm not sure I believe in that, but it sounds nice, so I take a bite of cake and nod.

"I only hope that we're able to be together again the next time around. Because if we're not, then... then I *will* miss him, and then... then I just don't know what I'll do," she says as her voice cracks. "I'm sorry. I'm sorry, sweetheart."

She gets up from the table and heads for the hallway. I stand up quickly, wanting to say something, anything, even though I know the only thing that would make her feel better would be to have Paps back. Her Paps. The way he was. And suddenly, I really understand, I *feel*, why Bari is so dead set on gerontology and finding a cure for Alzheimer's. She has to do *something*, she has to *try*, because that's the only thing she can do.

"Hasina, I'm sorry—"

Hasina stops, turns, and comes over to hug me tight. She says, "It's all right. Don't you worry about me. But, Tish, sweetie, please don't tell Bari about this. She worries about us enough already, and I want her to be young, to do young, fun things, not constantly worry about her old grandparents all the time. Okay? Please?"

"Okay," I say.

And I know I shouldn't lie to Hasina, but I just did.

Bari would never forgive herself if she found out too late that Paps was dying and she could have been here, if she found out that Hasina needed her and she was at school, or at breakfast with me and Libby, or having dinner and a dance party at the Mulberry house with Cam and Horatio, or doing anything that's even close to having fun. I will tell Bari because I have to, even though it will hurt her. Because it will hurt her more if I don't.

Hasina kisses my cheek and pats it, the way she's always done, that old lady pat on the cheek that makes me think of powdery perfume and Kleenex. Then she leaves me alone in the kitchen with two huge pieces of cake, but I don't want it now. I put the pieces, plates and all, back in the fridge and go to Bari's room. Bari's still curled up and sleeping hard. I want to wake her up and tell her what Hasina said, but I should let her rest. It might be her last good sleep for a while.

I look at where I had been lying, at my smushed pillow and the rumpled covers. It makes me think of the dream, of Libby, and my body goes hot. Shit. I can't sleep there.

A few minutes later, I've got on my coat and I'm sneaking out the back door. I hurry to the old garage and go in through the side. There they are—our old Huffy bikes. Bari's is a beach cruiser, pale green with a little white basket. Mine is a mean-looking black thing with knobby wheels and racing stripes. Paps and Hasina got them for us when we were fourteen, for Christmas. We rode everywhere on those bikes, until Bari got her car. Then we parked the bikes in the garage and forgot all about them. I walk up to the black Huffy. My pre-Lola Lola.

The Huffy doesn't feel alive like Lola does, but I talk to it anyway. "Wanna take a ride?"

It's cold as glaciers outside, but the fresh air feels good. I can breathe. It's exactly what I need right now. My Huffy and I coast down the neighborhood streets until we get to the playground. It's probably not the safest place to be in the middle of the night, but I give the area a good look. I'm alone. Just me and the squeaky swings. I park my little black beast against the side of the jungle gym, grab a swing, and start pumping my legs. Higher and higher.

The dream sneaks up on me again. Heated kisses. Legs wrapped around mine. Then images of dreams and memories flash like a collage as I soar back and forth, until I can't tell what's a dream and what's a memory, until it's all just a jumble of thoughts about Libby.

Libby hanging a Christmas garland on the mantel. Libby sleepwalking, kneeling on the sidewalk with her hand on the green glass stone. Libby staring up at the little light above the side door. Libby, with a sleek haircut, confetti falling around us. Libby standing outside, her hair all tied up in a ribbon and that defiant smile on her face.

I focus my eyes on what's in front of me instead of the images in my mind. I see the lights of the city, some of the buildings tall enough that I can count each window on each floor. I wonder who's in there, awake like I am, and what are they doing? I swing higher, the cold air burning my cheeks. The clouds are white again, standing out against the dark sky. Snow clouds, I hope. The snow is late this year, and I'm ready for it.

A Christmas Carol opens next weekend. I love to see the audience appreciate all the work we've done, Wallis and Dr. B, the actors, the techies. I can't wait for Libby to see it all.

Libby.

Maybe we can get that siding sanded down and weatherproofed before real winter hits. It'll be much harder after it gets all icy outside.

The house.

Thanksgiving is coming up. Then winter break. I wonder if Libby will want to decorate the house. *Of course she will.* Then I wonder if she will want to spend the holidays with me. Or will she try to make nice with her family? What will Bari's holiday be like this year? And Hasina's? And . . . will Paps even have a holiday?

Paps. Hasina. Bari.

I swing faster. The temperature is dropping the longer I swing. Even my sweat is cold. I should go back to Bari's and sleep on the sofa, but I keep swinging, the cold air getting colder, my lungs aching, my frozen fingers clenching the chains, my tired legs pumping, pumping.

I grab any random thought I can find, but they all keep coming back to the one thing I'm trying *not* to think about: love. How scary it is. How painful it is. And most of all, how unavoidable it is. I bear down and swing harder, until I'm swinging so fast the city lights are a blur. But I can't outrun the feeling that my running days are over, whether I like it or not.

40

TISH

From Bari's bedroom window, I see Joe's rusty work truck rumble up outside. I grab my satchel and rush for the hallway. I was supposed to stay till the end of the weekend, with Bari, but as soon as I told her about Paps, the shit hit the fan. Now Bari and Hasina are in the living room arguing, and I'm seeing my way out. I hit the hallway and stop.

The door to Paps and Hasina's bedroom is open.

A million moments scatter through my mind. Paps giving us "play money," $20 each, and making us promise to spend it all on candy. Picking us up at school when we got busted skipping to go to the arcade with the older kids; he never told a soul. Sitting on the bleachers with me and Hasina for all of Bari's lacrosse matches. Sitting by his bedroom window with a blank stare, having no idea where he is, or who we are.

I look at that open bedroom door. I know he's in there. Probably sitting by that window right now. I can't leave without saying something. Without seeing him, maybe one last time. Without . . . saying goodbye.

I walk into the room. He's right where I thought he'd be. By the window. Staring out. I drop my satchel on the bed, kneel beside his chair, and touch his arm. "Paps?"

He doesn't move. Doesn't even blink. I take his hand and hold it tight.

"Paps, it's me. Tish. I just wanted—" Too many things rush in. Too many feelings, too many images, too many thoughts, too many words. And if I'm feeling all this, I can't imagine what Hasina and Bari are feeling. I finally end up saying, "Thank you. For everything. For . . . everything."

I hope he hears me. I especially hope he hears all the things I can't figure out how to say. All the things that are just jumbled-up feelings about how much I'm going to miss him and how much I love him and how he and Hasina and Bari changed my life. How they saved me.

So I just tell him, "I love you, Paps." Because it's the most true thing I can say.

His fingers tighten on mine, and maybe I'm just wishing, just hoping, but I think he knows. I hope he knows. I kiss his cheek, let my head rest against his for a second. I'm not ready to let go, but I squeeze his hand, grab my bag from the bed, and get the hell out of there before I lose it. I hurry through the living room, with a hug and kiss for both Hasina and Bari.

I say, "I'm sorry," to each of them, each for different reasons.

To Hasina because I ratted on her, because she asked me to keep a secret and I didn't.

To Bari because, well, because she's about to be hurting really bad.

This is not me running. I would stay—for either of them—if I thought I could help. But I can't. I'm family, but they're *family*. They need to do this together. They know it, too. That's why they don't try to stop me. That's why they let me go. I close the front door behind me as I walk to Joe's truck. My other surrogate dad. He's old, too. When will I lose him? God, I can't even think about it. I climb into the old work truck and slam the door.

We've been on the road about fifteen minutes before Joe says, "You okay, Squirt?"

I'm not. Not really. But I nod. Joe is Joe, though, and he knows I'm lying.

"What happened that you yanked this old tail outta bed to come and get you?"

The heater is suddenly too hot, so I roll down the window. The truck is so old that it's got one of those crank windows that you have to roll and roll and roll as it squeaks the whole time. The window shudders down until the outside air finally blows across my face.

Joe's got a fat wad of tobacco in his cheek. He moves it around, then spits into a red disposable cup he plucks from the cup holder. It's lined with blue paper towels from the shop, splattered brown from all the tobacco juice. It's wet and gross and I turn my eyes away. I can't watch him do that to himself anymore. I just can't.

"You and Bari have a fight? I thought you two was thick as pine needles in a tornado."

I shake my head, about to cry. I do not want to cry.

Joe must see it, because he just pats my shoulder and says, "All right. I ain't gonna bother you about it. But roll that damn window up before you freeze my eyelids off."

He's right. It is too cold. I roll up the window, crank by squeaky crank. I look over at him, at his weathered hands and his wrinkled eyes and his almost-gone hair. I don't know exactly how old he is, but I know I don't want him to get any older, not by one second.

"You're not . . . you're not sick or anything? Are you?" I ask, staring at the road.

"The hell?"

"You would tell me, right? You'd tell me if you were?"

He looks at me, then at the road, then back at me. He starts to slow down—

"No! No. Don't pull over. Just tell me," I insist. I don't want this to be a big thing. I just want to know that he's not dying, like, next week. I need lots and lots of time to prepare.

"I won't pull over if you tell me what the hell's going on," he says. And I can tell he means it this time. We don't force info from each other, but his eyes are worried now.

"Paps isn't doing so well."

That's all I have to say, and Joe gets it. He squeezes my arm and nods. "Okay. All right." Then after a few seconds of only road sounds and my short breathing—still trying not to cry—he says, "I'm fine, kiddo. Ain't nothing wrong with me a good night's sleep can't fix." When that doesn't convince me, he sighs and admits, "I even got me one of them ladders with the training wheels you been harping about."

A laugh bursts out of me. I'd found the safety ladder in one of the catalogs Wallis uses to buy stuff for the practicum shop. The ladder is a big sturdy thing that you'd have to *try* to fall off of. Much safer to use alone than the flimsy one Joe's been using, but when I suggest stuff like that, stuff he calls *feeble old man shit*, he just laughs and leans too far back in that damn chair, trying to scare me.

But he bought the ladder, that *old man* ladder, and it calms me down some to know he's trying, that he's listening when I ask him to be careful. I can feel him giving me another side-eye. Still watching me. Still worried. Then he mutters, "Ah, hell screamin' hell."

He reaches down and digs through the deep pocket on the driver's side door and pulls out a handful of fast-food napkins. He moves the tobacco in his cheek again, but this time, he spits the whole wad into the napkins, then stuffs those napkins into the dirty red cup. I just watch him, because I'm not exactly sure if he's doing this for *now*, or for *good*. Not until he pulls the tobacco pouch from his shirt pocket and rolls down his squeaky window. Freezing air rushes in, but Joe ignores it. He opens the pouch and flicks it into the wind. I whip my head around to watch the little bits of tobacco shoot away from the car. I stare at him, a stare he clearly misunderstands, because he says, "What? It's biodegradable, ain't it?"

When I just keep staring, he shoves the empty pouch into the red cup, opens the tiny back window, and drops it all into the truck bed. "There. Happy now?" he says, all gruff and grumbly. I twist around to look. The cup is lying against the wheel well, the wind holding it in place. "It'll stay there. Don't even wanna know what you'd do to me for littering."

"I'd break your fingers," I say, snappy and quick.

"I bet you would." He chuckles. "But who'd help you with Lola?"

"Hmm. Shit," I say.

He laughs and laughs, and I just love it. I love that we're being normal, giving each other hell, when everything this morning hurt so much. And it still hurts, it does. But Joe makes it better. Knowing he's here. Then I think about that tobacco cup. Joe's grand gesture. Wondering if it means what I hope it means.

So I ask him, "Really? You quit? You mean it?"

"I'll throw out every shred of it when we get to the shop," he promises. "Save me a ton of money, too. Maybe then we'll look at getting some more of that safety crap you love so much."

"That sounds really good," I say in a quiet voice. Because if I talk any louder, he'll hear that I'm having trouble holding in all my feelings.

He pats the middle of the long bench seat and says, "Scoot on over here, where it's warmer." He doesn't take his eyes off the road as I unbuckle my seat belt and move to the middle. There's a lap belt there—it's a *really* old truck—so I strap myself in, where I'm just a little bit closer to Joe, and move the vents to blow on me, letting the warm air dry my not-quite-tears.

After a few minutes of just us and the road, I say, "Joe?"

"Yuh?"

"Thanks for coming to get me. I know it's early, and it's a long way."

His own voice sounds thick when he says, "I'd drive to the moon for ya, Squirt."

And then I do cry.

Joe grunts, like he didn't just break my heart with happiness, but his eyes are watery, too, so he cracks his window and says, "It *is* damn stuffy in here, ain't it?"

I laugh as I nod and wipe my eyes with my sleeve. I turn on the radio. Some old country song warbles out, something about beer and a back porch. Joe starts singing along. The sun shines on the road ahead of us, and even as sad as I am, it's just about perfect.

41

LIBBY

A beam of sun hits the window and the light scatters in a huge rainbow across the journal, open on my lap. I don't even know when the sun came up. Sometime last night, I moved to the beanbag chair, and I've been so caught up in Elizabeth's story that when I look outside now, I fully expect to see the ground covered in a blanket of snow. It's not. Just hard, dry grass. The snow is on its way, though. I can feel it in the damp air and see it in the heavy clouds.

I wonder if Tish likes the snow. If she would ever build a snowman.

When I first met her, I would have said no way. The badass girl who rides a motorcycle and can build anything? No. But when I picture it now, us rolling huge balls of snow around, piling them on top of each other, Tish laughing, her hair piled up under a big wool cap, face full of powdery ice, it feels right. Now I can't wait for the snow.

I run my thumb along the remaining journal pages. There are only a few entries left. I stayed up all night reading (again), but this time I'm not tired. I'm *wired*. Like, electrified. Good thing, because when I check the time, I realize I'm going to be late for work.

I fly off the beanbag, grab the first clothes I see, and race for the door, mentally brushing my hair and teeth as I go. But as I pass the standing mirror, the sun hits it just right and bounces into my eyes. I glance at the mirror, do a double take, then freeze.

That's not me. It looks like me. It looks just like me. But it is *not* me. There's something different. Something I can't quite put my finger on. The sun shifts again, and I see it, so clearly I can't believe I didn't see it immediately. The eyes in the mirror are green. My eyes are deep reddish brown. *Wine-brown*, Tish said one time, one of the times she was so close to my face that I was breathless, trying not to lean in and brush my lips against hers.

The green eyes in the mirror pick up the sunlight and seem to glow from within. I step closer, needing to see if I am finally actually really truly losing my marbles. I'm not. There I am, in the mirror, with green eyes. In my hand is a green dress. I look down and realize I'm holding the *green thing* that Elizabeth so hated, but Patricia so adored.

The oil lamp still flickers on the bedside table, and when the sun moves again, a beam hits the lamp and the flame flares up so high I think it might explode. I whip around to look. The sun shines on the glass globe and casts a rainbow across the room, covering the walls, the bed, the door. The green color stands out the brightest, growing brighter, and I suddenly have a desperate need to see the green glass stone. To hold it. To feel it in my hand.

I drop the green frock and run out of the room.

Downstairs, I hurry into the bad bathroom (as we now call it) and grab the sledgehammer that's been resting against the open wall for weeks. I march out the front door, heedless of the cold, and walk to the little gate in the fence. I fling it open and head straight for the green glass stone. The sun's shining on it, making it sparkle up at me, like it's daring me to dig it up.

I take two steps back, aiming a little bit away from the stone. I don't want to break it. I just want—I *need*—to know what it is. I bring the sledgehammer down hard. Gray dust and concrete chips spray into the air. But the stone is still there, still staring up at me, defiant.

I bring the sledgehammer crashing down again. This time, the sidewalk shatters, breaking up all the concrete around the green glass stone. Then . . . there it is. There's still too much powder in the air to really see it, but it's there. Naked. Exposed. Hidden only by a thick gray cloud. I reach down, push my hand through the floating silt . . .

. . . and wake up gasping.

I'm in bed. The room is sunny and bright. The journal lies open on my chest, and the oil lamp burns low. My heart is pounding. I sit up, swing my legs over the side of the bed, and take a few deep breaths. Then, just to make sure, I get up and go to the window. The green glass stone is still in the sidewalk. On the floor are my clothes, a long skirt and a chunky cable-knit sweater. No green frock. And in the mirror is just me. Plain old me with wine-brown eyes.

Just a dream.

I check the time. I do have to work today, but thankfully, I'm not late. Saturdays at the shop are pretty busy, so I need to be on time. I pick up the journal and close it. I'm almost finished with it. I could blaze through it now, but I don't want to rush it. This is the end. The big finish. I'm going to need time and space to absorb it all, and that's not right now.

I grab my clothes and head to the bathroom for a quick shower. Fifteen minutes later, I'm trotting down the stairs. I stop when I see

Tish sitting at the kitchen table. She's holding the little metal motorcycle toy I found in the dumpster, turning it over and over in her hand. She stares at it, touches the two riders once, twice. The soft look on her face makes my knees weak. I can't imagine how I'd feel if she looked at me the way she's looking at that toy.

"Hey," I say quietly, not wanting to startle her. She looks up at me like she already knew I was there. "Are you— I thought you were with Bari . . . I mean, what are you doing home?" I ask, and when I say *home*, her mouth smiles a little and the butterflies I always feel when I'm around her wake up and start dancing in my belly. But now I know why. I love her. I love her, and I have no idea what to do with it.

"I'll, um, I'll tell you later," she says, and turns the toy over in her hand again, and she looks so deep in thought that I wonder if she's forgotten me standing there.

"Are you okay?"

She nods, still staring at those two riders.

"What are you thinking about?" I ask her.

At first, I don't think she's going to answer me, and I start to think that maybe she just wants to be left alone, maybe she doesn't want me bothering her. Then she shrugs and says, "I'm thinking about people, and when they get so old that there's more life behind them than there is in front of them, and how that's gonna be us someday."

I have no idea what she's saying, so I just nod.

"And how maybe I've been wasting time I shouldn't be wasting."

Oh. She's talking about wasting her time *here*. Working on my house. With *me*.

"Okay. I see. I understand," I stammer as I grab my keys off the little hook by the coat closet and hurry toward the side door, wanting to get out of the house before she sees me totally break into a million pieces.

"I'm thinking," she says, a little louder, right as I reach for the door, "that if everybody I trust is saying the same thing, then maybe I should listen."

"Right. Well, I'll let you, um . . ." I mutter. I turn the knob and yank open the door—

"Libby."

Something in her voice makes me pause. It sounds different. It sounds serious.

"I don't want to waste any more time, but I don't know if . . ."

I turn to look at her. The motorcycle toy is on the table, and she's rubbing her hands up and down her pants. Like she's nervous.

"You don't know if what?" I ask. The butterflies go crazy now because there's something in the air, some kind of tension zinging between us, and every time it ricochets my way, my heart trips a few beats, like it's being shocked. Over and over and over.

Tish rubs her hand back and forth across her hair, making that clicking noise I love, right before she says, "This is a chickenshit way to ask, but . . . if I wanted . . . I don't even know if you're open to it, to, um, same-, uh . . ." She kind of vaguely waves her hand between us. "I know there was . . . Leo . . . but . . . if I asked you to, I don't know, go to dinner or something . . ."

My heart leaps, but I wait to hear the rest of it because I *need* to hear it. I need to know I'm not misreading the situation. I need to know that she is asking what I hope she's asking.

But she's having a lot of trouble doing it.

"Tish, just say it," I quietly urge.

"Would you want to go to dinner or something, if I asked?" she finally chokes out.

I stand there, her eyes on mine, those big blue eyes wide and terrified, and I love her so much that I'm spinning in it. But I'm still so scared she might not be saying what I think she's saying, so I have to ask, "You mean . . . just us? Not friends?"

"We're friends . . . aren't we?" she asks.

"Oh. So you mean, go to dinner as friends, you and me—"

"No! I mean, we go to dinner, you and me, but we don't bring any . . . Damn it . . ."

"We don't bring any friends?" I ask hopefully.

"Yes. That one," she sighs.

"Like . . . a date?"

"I mean, if you want to be all boomer about it," she says with a shrug, her shoulders slumping, like she's so sure the conversation is already over.

"Molly Monroe is my mother, so . . . boomer is what I know."

She looks up when she hears the tease in my voice. I'm standing half inside, half outside, and I hear a loud *bzzzt* as that light over the door comes on, that freaky little light with a mind of its own. I try to keep from smiling too big when I slowly step back inside and close the door.

"Tish. Stand up," I say to her. She looks confused, but she stands up.

"That *was* a chickenshit way to ask me," I say, and I can see that she already knows my answer, that I'm going to say yes, so she grins and takes the criticism like a champ.

She rubs her hand across her curls again, stands straighter, and says, "Libby. I want to go to dinner. Just you and me. And . . . I'd really like to see what happens from there." She's so confident that my toes tingle. Then she adds, "I mean, if you want to."

That tiny bit of sweet uncertainty destroys me, and I grip the doorknob tight to keep from throwing myself at her. When I can breathe again, I just say, "Yes. I do want to."

She tucks her chin and rubs her hair again, smiling happily, and I could just about die.

42

LIBBY

I float into the flower shop on a cloud of happiness. I flip a switch inside the door and a bunch of tiny neon cherry blossoms appear across the top of the display window. I take a deep breath. I love being here, with all the smells and colors.

My boss was here last night. I know it because the window display has been changed to a winter scene, and she's the only one (in this flower shop, anyway) who could create something so magical out of flowers.

Hundreds of white rose petals cover the bottom of the display, making it look like snowy ground. In the middle, a frosted mirror creates a frozen pond. A few tiny plastic ducks sit on the ice, and near the edge are those adorable ceramic figurines with the big eyes, a pastel-painted boy and girl, in mittens and ice skates, holding hands. A snowman is in one corner nearest the glass, made of small white hydrangea puffs. He has a tiny black felt hat and a little orange pipe-cleaner nose. And hundreds of baby's breath buds have been strung from the ceiling by threads of fishing line, individually, so they look like falling snow. I blow air toward the display and the snow-buds move. It must have taken her forever. It's beautiful.

I look at the snowman again and think of Tish. I think of her sticking a carrot into the snowman's face. I think of her pulling off her wool cap and all that hair tumbling down—

I stop myself.

That's Patricia. I realize that I did it earlier, too, when I wondered if Tish even liked the snow, when I imagined her in a wool cap. I've never seen Tish wear any kind of hat, except the helmet she wears when she's riding Lola. It's just the red hair and blue eyes, I suppose, that have me comparing them. But we are definitely going to build a snowman, right in the middle of the front yard, as soon as the first snows come. I'm going to make sure of it.

My phone makes a trilling sound. It's a calendar alert, and before I even open it, I suddenly remember it's Mom and Dad's anniversary today.

I've always been the one to arrange Mom's gifts and flowers and cakes. Dad was always "so busy" he would hand over the credit card with a "Buy your mother something she'll like," and Peter only ever cared about the cake, so he would always try to get me to order vanilla when Mom's favorite is red velvet. I have the most sinking feeling, and I'm sure I'm right, that without me there, Mom won't have a gift at all. And when Dad finally remembers (if he ever does), she'll just smile and pretend it doesn't matter. But it does matter.

Molly Monroe is all about occasions. She never misses one, and she never fails to go full-out. Every year, she makes our birthday cakes by hand, never using a box mix, and they're always elaborately decorated. Gifts are wrapped with perfectly matched ribbons and bows. Every holiday starts a month early when she decorates the house from top to bottom. Last year we had three Christmas trees! The only occasions Molly doesn't plan for are her own birthday, her anniversary, and her own Christmas. She'd let those pass without a word if I didn't shop for her and sign all our names to the cards. I don't want that for her. Mom deserves to be appreciated.

I just saw her yesterday. We spent the afternoon trying to get that scorch mark off the parlor floor. When even Molly couldn't budge it, I finally gave it up as a lost cause. The scorch mark reigns supreme! But basically, my mom came to my house to provide an afternoon full of tedious labor, and I didn't even bother to remember her anniversary was coming up.

I grab my phone, and as much as I don't want to do it, I pull up my dad's number.

I don't want to be the one who breaks first, who calls first, who caves first, and when he sees me calling him, that's exactly what he's going to think. But this isn't about me. It's about Mom. So I tap his number and brace myself. It rings until it goes to voicemail. I hang up and call again. This time, it rings one and a half times, then goes straight to voicemail, just like it does when someone pushes the Decline button. He sent me to voicemail. He ignored me.

It's like a slap. I can almost feel the sting on my skin. I do feel the sting in my heart. I sit there for a minute, thinking *screw him*, then I think about Mom. Fine. I can be a grown-up, even if he can't. I shoot off a quick text to let him know that today is their anniversary, that I'm going to send flowers to her, from him, then I give him the number of the bakery where I always order her cakes, in case he wants to go above and beyond. I figure worst-case, at least she gets flowers, because I'll do that myself.

Then I call Mom, to wish her happy anniversary, and tell her how happy I was to spend yesterday with her. We make plans for lunch this week, and I hang up, smiling as I head toward the cooler to pull Mom's favorite flowers, all purples and blues. Then I put together the most beautiful arrangement I've ever made. I sign the card *You make my life complete. Love, Dan*, and call the courier.

After the courier is gone, I pick up my phone again and send another text to Dad: **Mom's flowers are on the way. I signed the card from you.**

I wait, and wait, and wait, but he never texts back. Not even a thumbs-up to acknowledge he got them. That he read them. That he even gives a shit. At all.

Now I'm mad at him, and mad at myself for taking so long to realize that Dan Monroe is just being who he's always been. The only difference is now I'm *not* being who Libby has always been. Now I'm being *this* Libby, the Libby I was always supposed to be.

I think of what Cam said last week, when I was nervous about the upcoming holidays and wondering if Dad was ever actually going to talk to me again, when I wondered if Dan Monroe would ever be someone who supports me just being me, and Cam, of course, said exactly the right thing. He said, "Libby can only be Libby. Libby *should* only be Libby."

My best friend Cam. How I love him. I grab my phone and call him, because I don't want to sit here at the flower shop all day stewing about what an asshole Dad is, when I should be thinking about this morning, about Tish's face when she asked me out, and her surprised, proud smile when I said yes. I need to share the news, so when Cam answers, I don't even give him a chance to say hello. I just start with "So . . . Tish and I are going to Mariani's tonight. Together." There's a long beat of silence, just his breathing, then I say, "*Together*, together."

And then I jerk the phone away from my ear because when Cam screams, it nearly breaks every vase in the shop, even through the puny cell phone speaker. I'm laughing and talking over him, blabbing about the morning, and how sweet she was, and how nervous she was about asking me, when my phone dings again.

I tell Cam to hold on and open my messages. It's from Dad. It says: **Thank you.**

My eyes fill with tears. Hopeful tears. Because that *Thank you* means there's a chance that at some point, at some time, no matter how long it takes, we might all be a family again.

∼

I'm excited and a little breathless as I pull up to Mariani's. Tish is beside me, and she's barely said two words since I got home. I would almost think she was changing her mind, if she didn't keep smiling. We're both being ridiculous, so I finally say, "Why are we being weird? We're still just us."

Tish seems to relax a bit then, slumping into her seat the way she normally would.

"Yeah. We're just us," she agrees. Then we both grin like idiots.

I get out of the car. I turn to see her right behind me, her breath making fuzzy clouds in the freezing air, her short red curls bouncing as she joins me on the sidewalk. I reach for the door, but she gets there first, opens it, and ushers me inside. The warmth hits me immediately, then the luscious smells of pasta and garlic bread.

We wait for service at the reception stand, and for half a second, I remember the last time I was here, with Leo. But then I feel Tish touch the small of my back, and all thoughts of anyone else vanish. Right this second, we're the only two people in the world. I'm staring at the tip of her nose, still rosy from the cold outside, thinking about what it might feel like to kiss her, when she says, "You look beautiful. I meant to tell you earlier."

I took my time getting ready. Flat-ironing my hair took an hour!

I'm wearing a long, loose pair of pants I found in Elizabeth's things, one of my own shirts, and one of Elizabeth's scarves, a green silky thing that I've tied into my hair.

And Tish noticed. She noticed and she said something.

Now I really want to kiss her. It doesn't matter that we've never kissed before. It doesn't matter that we're in a crowded restaurant on a Saturday night. The only thing that matters is Tish, with her bright blue eyes and raging red hair and that tiny spatter of freckles across her nose. My eyes lock on those freckles, and for some reason, I'm compelled to count them.

One two three four five six . . .

We're so close I can feel her breath on my face.

. . . seven . . . eight . . . nine . . .

Her fingers tangle with mine. The tip of her pink tongue shoots out to touch her top lip. An impulse swells inside me, one that screams *kiss her!* But I'm still counting.

. . . ten . . . . . . eleven . . . . twelve.

Exactly twelve freckles.

The world pauses around me as Patricia's face, or how I imagine she looked, looms in front of me. A coincidence. A weird one, for sure, but that's the only explanation. The butterflies take flight again, spiraling like a tornado in my stomach, as I stare at Tish's freckles, wondering why I never paid attention to them before, why I never noticed there were twelve.

Tish's fingers squeeze mine, bringing me back to her, to us, and I want so badly to give in. Just one small kiss, just a little taste of her, then maybe the butterflies will calm down.

Maybe I'll do it. Maybe I'll kiss her right here in front of everyone in this place. Maybe I'll reach out, touch those freckles, one by one, and run my finger down her cheek to her lips. Maybe I'll rest my thumb against her chin and lean forward, pull her gently toward me—

"Your table is ready."

Like an anvil hitting the ground. I turn to give the stink eye to the hostess, who came out of nowhere and is now standing right beside us, a knowing smirk on her face.

Tish is flushed like she knows exactly what I was thinking, what I wanted to do. Then I grin. We have the whole night ahead of us. I'll get my chance.

The hostess winks at me as she grabs two menus, motions for us to follow her, and says, "Not sure if you know, but our shrimp fra diavolo is the best around."

"Yeah," I say, and hook my index finger around one of Tish's. "I know."

43

TISH

I keep wanting to pinch myself to make sure this is all really happening.

We're on Lola. Libby is behind me, her arms wrapped around my waist. I can feel her breasts pressed against my back. It's definitely not the cold air that's making my teeth clench. It *is* cold out, though. Freezing, actually. The air is heavy and thick, and there are thin patches of ice on the road. Winter's early this year.

"I hope it snows tonight," Libby said earlier, gazing up at the dense clouds, just before we'd hurried inside the house to grab our gloves and the smaller helmet I keep for Bari on the off chance that she rides with me. I have no idea if it will snow tonight, but if that's what Libby wants, then I hope she gets it. Anything to see her smile.

Libby's wearing my helmet. I insisted. It's bigger and warmer and much, much safer. The spare is good enough for me. There's no face visor on this one, so the wind is cutting right through the front of me, but Libby's heating up my back, so I'm just fine. Libby squeezes, holding me tighter, and I hold on tighter to Lola.

Lola purrs beneath us, gliding us through town until we reach the darkened, narrow road that leads to the overlook, my favorite place to go with Lola. I'm ready, now, to go there with Libby. Dinner was amazing. Libby was amazing. The entire freaking night was amazing. And when we got home and Libby leaned against Lola and asked for a ride, saying she wasn't ready for the night to end, I literally had zero choice.

As I make the turn that will take us up to the overlook, that old fear suddenly sneaks in, telling me this is all too good to be true. It's a stupid move, to want what I can't have. I'm just a girl with nothing, who's always gonna have nothing, so what the hell am I doing shooting for the moon? Then Libby's hands slip down, low across my belly, her fingers digging into my hip bones, and I ignore my better instincts and give a little twist to Lola's throttle.

Lola launches forward like a jet eating up a runway. I can almost hear her chuckle, ready for more, ready to really show Libby what she's made of. So I let her loose. She vibrates heavily under us, roars like the queen she is, then takes off. Behind me, Libby shrieks happily and grips me even tighter.

"There you go, girl," I whisper to Lola as she flies us up the winding road.

A few minutes later, I guide Lola to the edge of the overlook. Our little town below is all lit up. It's still two weeks until Thanksgiving, but they've already put up a huge Christmas tree in the square on Main Street, like a beacon of holiday cheer.

We're sitting on Lola, my feet braced against the ground, holding us centered. Behind me, I feel Libby take off the helmet. She leans forward, tendrils of her hair brushing my cheek, and says, "I love this place. I'm so glad you brought me here."

"You come here?"

"I used to. Something about it just makes me feel *so much*. Like the house, but sadder. But the kind of sad that you love, the kind you hold on to, because it feels like something you don't want to lose," she says, sounding just like Joe when he talked about the lady who used to live in Libby's house, the lady whose clothes Libby wears, whose clothes I'm pretty sure she's wearing now, looking so beautiful that I've had a lump in my throat all night.

I think about mentioning her to Libby, asking her why she wears the other woman's clothes, why she plays the woman's records on the Victrola, why she sits on the sofa and stares into the fireplace, even when she's *not* sleepwalking . . . but then she slides her arms back around me, and I can't think of anything but the feel of Libby's hands resting lightly on the sides of my hips. She leans her forehead against my cheek and gives me the tiniest kiss, so light I barely feel it. But I *do* feel it. I grip the throttle too tightly and Lola roars. Thankfully, she's not in gear, or we'd be headed right over the edge.

Libby laughs and says, "Turn her off."

My hand shakes as I shut off Lola's engine. Now the only sound around us is the wind in the trees and our own breathing. Libby peels herself off my back, then pulls at my shoulders.

"Now turn around."

Again, that fear spikes, that awful reminder that, no matter how brave I was this morning, nothing, absolutely nothing is going to change the fact that it always ends up bad for me. I always end up being not enough. But Libby tugs again, and I just can't resist her anymore. I exhale hard, swing my leg over Lola's seat, and turn until I'm facing her.

The moon is shining through the naked trees. It hits her face just right, making her skin look so soft, making the scarf in her hair look so green, making her lips so pink. In reflex, I lick my own lips and watch her eyes shoot to my mouth. This is it, the moment from the restaurant, when I could see so clearly on her face that she wanted to kiss me. Now we're here again, but no busy restaurant, no hostess to interrupt us, and I feel like I've just swallowed a bowling ball.

I've kissed before, and I've been kissed, but something inside me is screaming that this will not be the same, that this kiss will change me forever. I think of how stupid that sounds, like one of my theater roommates on a poetic rant about romance. But it's not stupid. And I'm not being dramatic. Because it's exactly what I'm feeling right this second.

If this girl kisses me, I will never be the same.

And then . . .

. . . snow.

The first flake lands on the green scarf in Libby's hair. Bright white against deep green. It melts just as another lands in Libby's hair. I smile.

"What?" Libby asks.

I touch her chin and gently nudge it, prodding her to look up. She does, and gasps. I follow her gaze. More snow is falling now, a light flurry. If this night wasn't perfect before . . .

When I lower my head to look at Libby, she's staring at my freckles again. As the snow falls around us, she takes off one of her gloves and touches the bridge of my nose, her lips moving as she silently counts them. I close my eyes at the feeling of her fingertip on my skin.

The softest touch to my nose.

"Five . . ."

My cheek, right under my eye.

"Four . . ."

My mind flashes back to the dream. The horns. The confetti. The crowd, all shouting:

"Three!"

She traces her fingers lower, closer to my mouth, in a barely there touch.

"Two..."

2...3...6...

The warmth of her breath as she leans in, closer, closer.

An icy chill sears me. So cold it burns.

Snow. Blood. Pain. Fear.

"Wait! Wait," I say, pulling away from her.

My eyes pop open. Libby's right there, her mouth less than a centimeter from mine, our foggy breaths mingling as we both gasp, and I can't do it. I can't kiss her. I can't let her kiss me.

"What is it?" she asks, her hand cupping my cold cheek. "What's wrong?"

I don't know what's wrong. I get off Lola and walk to the edge of the overlook. I watch the snow, heavier now, falling on the twinkling town below, as I stand there wondering why I'm letting some stupid dream stop me from having this moment. Libby wants me. She wants to kiss me, she wants to be with me, she wants *me*.

"Tish..." she starts as she walks up beside me, but I stop her.

"It's not you, I swear. I'm just..."

Scared. I'm scared to death. And this isn't my normal, everyday fear of being unwanted or unlovable. This fear is different. This is deeper. This feels like... the source fear. The big fear. The one that all the other fears get their marching orders from. Only I don't know what this fear *is*. It can't just be about a freaking dream!

The ride home isn't nearly as wonderful as the ride up. Libby's arms are around me again, but there's a different tension in them now. I park Lola, and Libby gets off. She pulls off my helmet and hands it to me, her head down, the green scarf in her hair squished and rumpled. That's how I feel, too. Beaten down. It's not even nine o'clock and the night's already done.

The snow falls silently around us for a long moment before she says, "Thanks for tonight, Tish," her eyes still on the helmet I'm holding. Then she turns to go inside.

"Libby, wait." I jump up to run after her, catching up with her at the side door, under the porte cochere. It's dark under here tonight. I thump the light above the door, but the little bastard refuses to come on. I've rewired this damn thing three times already. I give the side of the casing a firm slap. Libby grabs my hand, pulls it away from the light.

"Stop that," she says, then unlocks the door and goes inside.

She's mad. She must be mad. She's not looking at me. I hate myself so much for screwing this up. "Libby . . . I . . . Listen . . ."

She stops at the staircase, her hand on the banister, her thumb stroking the wood, almost like she's soothing it, the way she'd soothe a person. "Tish. I need to say something . . ."

My stomach plummets as everything good I've known for the last few months flashes before my eyes, like a part of me is dying, and I can only stand there and watch. Images of Libby, and the house, and me. Libby standing in her window, her oil lamp shining. Libby in front of the cold, dark fireplace, an open book on her lap. Me leading a sleepwalking Libby to her room. Libby in the kitchen, laughing with Bari over breakfast before school. Libby, Bari, Cam, and Horatio dancing in the parlor. Libby Libby Libby . . .

She's going to ask me to leave. A room of my own, a place where I belong—it's ending, right before my eyes. I won't see her every morning. Or every night. And it's my own fault.

"Libby, I'm sorry—"

She walks toward me, and I just can't make my throat work

anymore. I don't know what to say to fix this, except I'm so fucking scared of something that I can't name, something that haunts me in my dreams, something that ruined our wonderful evening, just like it's ruining everything right now.

"No, Tish. *I'm* sorry."

She stands in front of me and sighs. This is it. It's over. It's all over.

She takes my hands and holds them tight, trembling when she says, "I know you're not sure about me, because of the whole Leo thing, and I don't blame you. I've only ever been with guys, that's true, but Tish, that's because I hadn't met *you*. The way I feel about you..."

That's not at all what I expected her to say, and now all I can think is *it's not over, it's not over, it's not over.* It's just beginning.

I'm shaking, on the verge of tears, for a whole different reason now. I shove all my fear aside and finally do what I've wanted to do since the moment I saw her sitting on the floor in practicum, fighting with the nail gun, her eyes droopy with exhaustion. I slide closer to her and wrap my arms around her waist and pull her in tight to me, so close that her body is flush against mine, and nothing in my life, nothing, has ever felt so right. No one has ever fit so well.

"I feel it, too, Libby. I feel it so much," I confess.

She whimpers and tucks her face into my neck. I feel her lips moving against my skin when she says, "I knew it. I knew you did." They're almost kisses, her lips moving right against my skin, each word sending earthquakes through me. "We'll take it slow. We don't have to rush anything," her lips whisper into my neck. She trails her words up my jaw. "But... I just want..." she murmurs as she comes closer and closer to my mouth, "this one thing. Just... give me this..."

Give me this.

The fear spikes again, a desperate thing chewing me up from the inside, but this time I shove it down, and I give Libby what she's asking for, what she wants. What we both want.

I slip my hands into her hair and catch her mouth with mine.

I've never had a first kiss like this. It's like our lips know exactly how to move, exactly how to tangle and pull, all heat and fire, like we've been kissing forever. The fear tries to inch in, but I ignore it and kiss her harder. Libby melts against me, her arms around my neck, her thighs pressing into mine.

We pull away from each other, breathing hard; then all the lights in the house flicker.

After a long, quiet moment, I say, "Can I *please* get someone to look at that fuse box?"

Libby laughs and nods.

I kiss her again, lightly this time. "Tonight was . . ."

"Yeah," she says, "it was." She steps back. I'm reluctant to let her go. Our fingers catch just before she sidles back toward the staircase. "See you in the morning?"

"I'll be here," I tell her. I watch her walk up the stairs. She stops halfway up the staircase and turns to look out the big front window, watching the snow come down.

"Tish?" she says, her eyes still on the window.

"Yeah?"

"Do you like . . . snowmen?"

Standing there on the stairs, the light reflecting off the snowfall, with the vintage clothes and the scarf in her hair, she looks like someone from another time. I stare at her until my eyes water, and I say, "I love them."

I love *you*.

Libby turns, like she heard me. Like she knows exactly what I just said in my mind but didn't have the nerve to say out loud.

Then she says, "Me too."

And I hear her. I hear her loud and clear. Before I scream with a happiness I never thought I'd feel, I go into my room and shut the door behind me.

44

LIBBY

My bedroom door clicks closed behind me. My whole body is singing. The creamy, satiny walls are awash in warm light, and it takes me a few seconds to realize that the oil lamp is flickering softly on the bedside table. I don't remember lighting it before we left. That was stupid. And dangerous. But the oil lamp just burns quietly, its flame steady and strong.

"Thank you for not burning down the house," I say with a chuckle—this house that feels so full of love that I'm about to burst. My love for Tish. Elizabeth's love for Patricia. Patricia's love for Elizabeth. Tish's love for me. Because I know she loves me. It was there, in her eyes, in the flush of her skin, in the way she kissed me. My soul is filled up with it. Brimming. Spilling over like the happy tears I brush from my cheeks.

I love, and I am loved.

The hope chest at the end of the bed is still cracked open, unlatched. I'm drawn to it now, drawn to Elizabeth and Patricia. To their story. To their love. I pick up the oil lamp and carry it to the chest. I lift the lid. The light immediately catches the dresses, silver and gold, throwing shimmery spots on the inside of the wooden chest, like a party. Like a celebration.

A twinge flitters through me as I look at the dresses, at the other clothes folded neatly, at the small book tucked in the corner of the chest where I found Elizabeth's journal, the journal that now rests in the window nook. Waiting for me.

45

DECEMBER 31, 1925

Elizabeth peacocked proudly into the house, a stack of garment bags flung over one arm and a fistful of shopping bags in her hand. She removed her hat, coat, and gloves, and dropped them onto the sofa in the parlor. She laid the garments and shopping bags over one of the highbacked chairs near the fireplace, still coasting on the feeling of independence from a day spent in town alone, with no one following her or catering to her or carrying things, not even Patricia, whom she loved more than breath. She had meandered from store to store freely, answering to no one except herself and, eventually, the increasingly snowy weather.

Home now and warming herself in front of the fire, she called Patricia's name, her foot tapping impatiently until she heard the accent she so adored. Patricia rounded the corner, chirping brightly, "So, you're home, then. You were gone all . . . afternoon . . . Christ Almighty on the cross." Elizabeth giggled as Patricia stopped in her tracks, mouth moving, hopelessly searching for words. She finally sputtered, "Where has my Elizabeth lass gone, and who is this magnificent creature before me?"

Elizabeth gave a slow spin, showing off her new look.

The hairdresser had taken Elizabeth's desires to heart and had given her a smooth, chin-length bob that cradled her soft bone structure. The woman had then convinced Elizabeth to go one step further with a dark rinse that gave her hair a richer hue, a deep, glossy sable that flaunted the green of her eyes, all set off by expertly applied makeup. Right down to a little red Cupid's bow mouth.

Her new dress could have been plucked from the pages of any one of her magazines. A silky midnight blue with a dropped waist and a loosely hanging side bow. Her new shoes, with their kitten heels, clicked on the parquet floor, just like Delilah's, or Rose's, or Honey's, and her fingernails were varnished blood red, in a moon manicure, as was all the rage.

She twirled once more, then awaited Patricia's verdict.

"You are the very image of a modern woman, my love. As beautiful a woman as I've ever been blessed to lay eyes on," Patricia said, her eyes roving this new and current incarnation of Elizabeth. She looked flustered, much to Elizabeth's delight.

"I have some things for you, too," Elizabeth said.

"Oh, do you now?"

"And I have some . . . ideas, for you, for tonight. If you trust me?"

"I am yours to do with as you please," Patricia said.

Elizabeth trotted over to Patricia, planted a quick, firm kiss on her mouth, then gleefully hurried to the dining room, her grand plan blooming like fireworks in her mind.

She returned, grunting under the weight of a solid oak dining chair. It was heavy in her arms, unwieldy. When Patricia moved to help her, Elizabeth guided her to place the chair beside one of the lamp tables. Elizabeth then disconnected the fancy new electric lamp from the fancy new electric socket that was stationed midway up the wall.

"Whatever are you doing?" Patricia asked.

Elizabeth winked and retrieved one of her various shopping

bags. She upturned it, depositing its contents on the little table. Small jars and compacts and application brushes clattered out. Elizabeth let her gaze lovingly caress the makeup before she reached for an odd-looking contraption. A long black ceramic handle that tapered into a narrow metal cylinder. Elizabeth pressed on the handle, and a thin, curved plate opened.

"A curling iron," Patricia said, a skeptical tone creeping into her voice.

"An electric curling iron," Elizabeth corrected. "Father would never let me have one."

"What do you need with it now?" Patricia asked, eyeing Elizabeth's newly shorn locks.

"It's not for me."

She plugged the adapter into the wall socket with a grin. Patricia reached for one of her own natural curls, twirling it nervously around her finger as she studied the ominous device.

"I may be having second thoughts about this adventure of yours, love."

Elizabeth pulled Patricia's hand away from her hair. She led her to the dining chair and urged her to sit, pressing on her shoulders until Patricia surrendered.

"I thought you were mine to do with as I please," Elizabeth joked.

"Just don't go breaking your favorite things, miss."

Elizabeth bent down to steal a soft kiss, whispering against Patricia's lips, "Never."

Two thoroughly entertaining hours later, they were upstairs in Elizabeth's bedroom. The sun was quickly setting outside the window. Inside, the oil lamp burned brightly on the vanity table, its light bouncing off the mirrors, illuminating the room.

Patricia was seated at the vanity, her back to the mirror. Elizabeth put down the utensil she was holding, a fine-bristled makeup brush, and stepped back to admire her work.

"Oh, Patricia," she said reverently, "you are a wonder to behold."

Patricia asked, "Can I look now?"

"Almost."

Elizabeth moved to the bed, where two garment bags were laid out, side by side. She opened the first to reveal a silver dress, elegantly beautiful. The second garment bag revealed a gold dress, shiny and beaded and perfect. Elizabeth carried it to Patricia and smiled.

Still on the bed, waiting, were matching cloaks and gloves. Silver and gold.

Elizabeth knew of the illicit gin joint downtown only because her mother, some months prior, had led the church's Temperance League in their efforts to have it shut down. The speakeasy had miraculously relocated, time and again, mere hours before the police raids were set to occur. It had incensed Lillian to no end, and eventually, she'd found some other narrow-minded cause to champion, "leaving the gin-soaked sinners to their wicked deeds."

Now her mother wasn't here, nor was her father, and it was time, Elizabeth had decided, to see what these sins were all about. New Year's Eve seemed the perfect occasion.

This particular joint was notorious for its *proclivities*. Elizabeth had no idea what proclivities those might be, but she'd heard the word whispered so often that she knew she had to see it for herself. With Patricia on her arm. And oh, what a sight Patricia made.

Elizabeth had ignored every dictate of current fashion and had taken Patricia's already wild hair and made it wilder, thousands of tumultuous curls that multiplied exponentially. Her eyelids were lightly shaded in a shimmery powder, with a rich blue kohl along her lash line. Her lips were painted red. Not in a tiny cupid's bow, as was the standard. Instead, Elizabeth had followed the natural lines of Patricia's full lips, now as luscious and ripe as red cherries. As red as the varnish on Elizabeth's fingernails. And the gold dress fit Patricia to perfection, as if it had been made for her and only her. The overall effect was breathtaking. Patricia looked like a fire goddess descended from the heavens, and Elizabeth was her awestruck disciple.

"Can I look *now*?" Patricia asked again when Elizabeth had finally fixed her into the dress, fluffed her hair, and fastened her shoes.

Elizabeth turned her toward the standing mirror and said, "Yes. You can look now."

Patricia gazed into the mirror in wonder, struck with the sight of herself.

"Is that me?"

"Every glorious inch of you, my darling," Elizabeth answered.

∼

They approached a seedy little building on the wrong side of town, the lights of the city looming tall over them. Several of Lillian's "gin-soaked sinners" stood on the outside stoop in their party clothes and overcoats, bundled up with their cigarettes and cigars, glimmering, glittery people mismatched against the backdrop of the dingy alley. A hint, perhaps, of what they might find inside.

Elizabeth fairly skipped with excitement, her silver cloak catching the ambient city light. Each and every eye was glued to them as they walked toward the door. They made a striking pair: Elizabeth, with her sleek new haircut, was beautifully chic, and Patricia was as wild as wild would allow. Ice and fire. They were exquisite.

The burly bouncer tipped his hat as they approached. He pulled open the thick, solid wood door, ushering the girls inside . . .

. . . and into another world.

The room was dark and humid, scented of liquor and cigarettes and perfumed bodies. A thin layer of smoke curled against the low ceiling, swirling in circles above the gathered crowd like malignant halos, one for each "sinner." A scantily clad cigarette girl, her skin dewy with perspiration, took their cloaks and gloves. Elizabeth handed hers over blindly, her eyes glued to the scene in front of her.

People of all races and creeds, dressed to the nines in sequins, tuxedos, and top hats, danced to the steamiest music Elizabeth had ever heard: a wailing trumpet, a hot piano, the low silk of a woman's soulful alto. Elizabeth could see the chanteuse across the room on a makeshift stage, swaying as she sang, a highball glass in one hand and a long cigarette holder in the other, smoke twirling toward the ceiling.

And the dancing . . .

It was a kind of dancing Elizabeth had never seen, limbs entwined, bodies pressed against bodies. She blushed as it occurred to her that this was how she and Patricia moved when they were *together*. She felt it then, that familiar tickling along her nerves. Desire. The desire to touch and be touched. She shot a look to Patricia, torn between embarrassment and exhilaration.

Patricia did not blush, as Elizabeth did, and nothing about her body language suggested she was the slightest bit embarrassed. She merely arched one perfectly drawn brow and said, "So this is what your mother was all worked up about."

Elizabeth laughed, delighted. "Proclivities," she sang as she took in the scandalous scene.

"I'll say," murmured Patricia. Her eyes found the bar. "Shall we gin it up?"

Elizabeth nodded and took Patricia's hand. They maneuvered their way through the throng, inching slowly toward the bar as Elizabeth took it all in with wide, amazed eyes.

Men and women were dancing and drinking and kissing and—

Elizabeth blinked several times as she gave a closer look to a couple tucked into a corner table. The slightly built man, in tails and top hat, slid his narrow hand up the leg of a woman in a short (obscenely short) flapper dress. Elizabeth could see his fingers splayed on her thigh, naked under the beaded tassels of the dress. The woman's head dropped back as her arms slipped around the neck of her suitor and pulled him closer.

Elizabeth felt dampness prickle the small of her back as she watched the woman lean in to kiss the man. But . . . just as the woman kissed him . . . his hat tipped, toppled to the floor . . . and Elizabeth's world tilted so sharply and severely on its axis that her head swam, and everything she thought she knew of the world slid precariously sideways.

That was no *man.*

It was a woman. Short hair in finger waves against her face. Delicate bones, slender hips, and small breasts straining against the tightly fitted tuxedo shirt. The flapper-dressed woman lunged forward and kissed her partner, and Elizabeth nearly swooned.

"*Proclivities . . .*" Elizabeth whispered to herself, suddenly realizing . . . "Patricia, look," she urged as she turned to reevaluate the room and all the things she had missed upon her first dazed intake. This time, she let herself see past the clothes and the costumes, past the hats and hairpieces and makeup, past the facades, to the humans underneath.

Men with women.

Women with men.

Men with men.

Women with women.

All here, together in this one room, hidden away from the world. Their one safe place.

Elizabeth's heart broke for them, herself included, even as she was buoyed by the hope that someday, perhaps far in the future, people would need no longer hide, that the world in its entirety would be a safe place for everyone. For herself. For Patricia. For all of them.

"Have we stepped into Wonderland, then?" Patricia asked breathlessly as she took in the same view, both girls astounded at how they came to be at this place, on this night, where, even if only in the shadows, their love was celebrated.

"I think we have," Elizabeth answered. "Indeed, I think we have."

The barkeep, a sweaty bald man in a suit and tie, was slinging martinis and gin rickeys. Elizabeth made her way to the counter. He smiled up at her, a bit harried, then his eyes caught Patricia and he stopped moving altogether. He looked at her, a slow study from head to toe.

"I've never before seen the likes of you," he said to her.

"No one has," Elizabeth agreed, unable, *unwilling*, to keep the love from her voice. Not here, in this place, where they were free, where they belonged. The barkeep looked between them, at their joined hands, then winked.

"Something special for the lovers," he said, and pulled a bottle of champagne from a tin tub of ice under the bar. "They delivered two cases this afternoon, just for tonight. You can have the first pour," he stated, and popped the cork. He dashed a shot of gin into two champagne coupes, dropped a sugar cube into each, then topped them off with the chilled bubbly. "Seventy-fives for the ladies." He pushed the drinks their way. Elizabeth reached for the silver (to match her dress, of course), diamond-shaped pochette on her wrist, but he waved her away. "On the house. For the angels of the New Year."

Elizabeth touched the rim of her glass, so happy. So incredibly happy. She thanked the barkeep, as did Patricia, and they found a relatively quiet corner from which to enjoy this brief liberty from their real lives.

The music was loud. Not so loud they couldn't talk, but everything they wanted to say could be said with their eyes. Elizabeth took a sip of her 75, the bright bubbles fizzing in her mouth, and leaned her head against Patricia's shoulder. Patricia brushed a soft kiss across her forehead, then laughed at the rouged smudge left behind. She gently wiped it away and turned to watch the people dance. Elizabeth nodded toward the dancers. "Do you want to . . . ?"

Patricia considered the dancers, packed tightly together. "I'm happy right here."

Elizabeth sighed in blissful agreement. One dance, perhaps, before midnight, but right now she was content to simply *be*. She sipped her drink again.

As midnight neared, the revelers grew more manic, their drinks sloshing, their laughter broad and raucous, obnoxiously so, but Elizabeth absorbed every sweat-tinged, liquor-fueled moment. This night felt like a gift from the luck gods. Or perhaps it was from the love gods, from Aphrodite herself, she mused as she ran her fingers up and down Patricia's arm. Perhaps she and Patricia had truly been anointed the angels of the New Year. She felt very, very blessed.

The trumpet walloped out a high note, catching everyone's attention, as the singer raised her eighth or tenth drink, which was swiped from her hand and replaced by a coupe full of champagne. Elizabeth and Patricia had stopped at two each, over an hour ago, neither of them accustomed to the effects of strong liquor, or even something as mild as champagne. As delicious as tonight was, this was no time to tempt full inebriation. Elizabeth wanted to experience every moment, to remember every moment. She wanted to relive this night over and over and over in her mind. She did not want her head dizzied in a champagne haze.

The chanteuse clearly had no such compunctions, and the swaying she did now, as she slurred into the microphone, "Three minutes, you marvelous beings! Three minutes to midnight!" turned into a clumsy stumble.

Her bandmate swooped his arm around her waist, catching her so easily the pose almost looked practiced. He took advantage of her reclined position to plant a big sloppy kiss on her open mouth. The crowd went wild as the singer, her arms flung around the man and her lips clinging to his, straightened them both, wrenched her mouth away, then slapped him so hard the crack reverberated around the room.

"That'll teach ya to put your mouth where it doesn't belong, sailor," she crowed as the partygoers cheered her on. The musician, taking his punishment with good-natured aplomb, lifted his trombone to whine out a pathetic, four-note *womp womp womp woooommmp.*

Elizabeth snorted and leaned into Patricia. "Do you think that was planned?"

"No idea, love, but it does appear they know each other quite well."

The band took up their instruments. The singer downed her champagne in one vulgar gulp and started a slow, haunting rendition of "Auld Lang Syne."

Elizabeth stood up and reached for Patricia.

"I do not want this night to pass without one dance. Come," she commanded in that gentle, soft voice that was reserved for her Irish love.

Patricia canted her eyes up, that blue so blue that Elizabeth would have seen it in the dark, would have seen it blind, and said, "I am yours . . ." as she stood and slipped an arm around Elizabeth's waist.

Elizabeth closed her eyes and touched her forehead to Patricia's. "You do know I love you."

"As I do love you, miss."

Elizabeth grinned, remembering the months-long campaign she had waged to excise that particular word from Patricia's vocabulary, only to have Patricia use it now as an endearment, one that Elizabeth could die to hear and hear and hear again, forever.

The singer's voice, gone as she was in her boozy haze, was more suited for this song than any other. The lyrics were mournful, and hopeful. Elizabeth and Patricia wrapped their arms around each other, as did every other couple (the ones who could still stand), and they danced. Slowly. Sweetly. Each lingering on the other's beat, moving as one—because they were.

The last notes faded. There was a moment of hushed silence before the countdown began.

Then the voices rose . . .

"Ten!"

Elizabeth and Patricia remained altogether lost in each other as the count continued.

"Nine!"

"Eight!"

"Seven!"

Elizabeth leaned closer to Patricia, her lips brushing the shell of her ear as she said . . .

"Two . . . three . . ."

"Six!"

She leaned back, slipping her fingers into that mane, still as curly and rebellious as when they'd left the house in the ruby-red roadster, headed for the city . . .

"Five!"

"Four!"

"Three!"

Patricia bent to whisper, "Two . . . three . . . six . . ."

The trumpeter blew another high note as the drummer rolled his sticks, filling the gin joint with the sounds of celebration, and the crowd yelled, "Happy New Year!"

Confetti and balloons fell from all corners of the ceiling, champagne corks popped loudly, and the revelers hooted their joy to the sky. Elizabeth looked at them all, these people who were her people, but would never know it. Couples paired off. Everyone was kissing. Him and him. Her and her. Him and her. Even the chanteuse and her trombonist had gone in for a second go. Even the barkeep, who was caught up with the cigarette girl.

Elizabeth pulled Patricia's face to hers. Patricia offered only the mildest resistance, until Elizabeth said, "This one moment, my darling. This one moment when we are just like everyone else, where there is nothing to hide. Give me this . . ."

So Patricia did. She swooped in to capture her mouth in a kiss that stole Elizabeth's breath and threatened to steal the next hundred more. Right there. For God and sundry to see.

Elizabeth clung to her, having just been kissed senseless, until the room righted and the world resumed its spin. She pulled back, trailing a tender finger from Patricia's twelve freckles to her smeared lipstick. She opened her mouth to tell Patricia, once again, how much she was adored, when her gaze landed on a familiar figure across the room.

Ice-blue eyes bore into hers. All-knowing eyes that pierced right through her heart to cleave her soul in two.

Honey Harper.

The viper blinked once, twice, observing her prey, then, with a nasty smirk, turned to whisper something into her tall companion's ear. Chess Pennington's head whipped around. Those flat black eyes found Elizabeth's, hers wide and fearful—

46

LIBBY

My head snaps up, and I feel as if I've just been yanked from the gin joint and its smoky haze, from the revelers and their sweaty kisses, from that horrible Honey Harper and her evil prying eyes. That didn't feel like I was reading. It felt like I was *watching*. No. That's not right, either. It felt like I was *there*. Like . . . a memory. A weird tingling sensation sweeps over me, then goose bumps break over my whole body.

The oil lamp sputters. It pops a little inside the globe, like the tiniest firework. I turn it down, until the flame is steady again. From the corner of my eye, I glimpse my reflection in the window. I look, stare, study that reflection. It's got that see-through quality a glass reflection has, like I'm a transparent copy of myself. Like I'm here, but also there. I shake off the strange feeling.

The journal demands my attention, but dread rises in my throat, thinking of those next entries. I don't want to read any more. It doesn't matter that I remind myself it's just a story, long over. A story about two women who are long dead. It doesn't matter that I *know* this is true. I don't want to read it. But the page stares up at me, waiting . . .

Honey Harper, I know now, was always bound to deliver my defeat.

Everything Sarah said, every warning she impressed on me, I had ignored. For weeks, for months, I had fancied myself so grown, so experienced, so mature. I was bold! I was brave! The world would bend its knee to me, to us, to our love! In truth, I was but a child tempting Fate, and I had swiftly found myself outclassed, outmatched, outmaneuvered.

Fate was a fierce competitor; she would deal the final blow, and this wild, beautiful creature beside me would pay the price. Of that I was certain. No matter that it was my desire that brought us here, that it was I who set us upon this path. I knew then that Sarah's words had not been warnings; they had been prophecy. Fate is a cruel mistress, and life does not play fair.

"Life doesn't always play fair, my love," she says in a voice as shaky as I've ever heard. She is afraid. My strong, brave Patricia. Afraid.

I can hear her. I can feel her. Her voice in my head. Her hand squeezing mine. I am no longer reading the journal. I am remembering it.

"I just want to love you. Is that too much to ask?" I say, terrified and heartbroken.

We are terribly cold, the thin convertible leather top offering scant protection from the weather. I'd kept the key to the roadster in my pochette, which had stayed round my wrist all night, but our cloaks and gloves were left behind in our haste.

The roadster hits a patch of ice, and we slide momentarily. Patricia's hand releases mine to grip the wheel. She is a much better driver than I. My eyes are on her hands. Beautiful hands. The most beautiful hands I've ever seen. Her nails are short. I'd polished them a deep, dark purple. Why, suddenly, can I only think that I should have chosen a lighter color? Something with more gold, to pick up the shades of her dress. Or perhaps a russet, to complement her hair. A child's thoughts, immaterial to anything real, when we've just been discovered by the one person who will stop at nothing to destroy us for the simple pleasure of doing so—

I shove the journal away from me, turning my eyes back to the window, to that half-there reflection, to that pale, translucent image of who I am. Who . . . I . . . was . . .

My stomach clenches so tightly it feels like I'm going to be sick. Like I might vomit. Like that shrimp fra diavolo that Tish and I shared might soon end up all over Elizabeth's pretty window nook. I swallow one time, two times, three times, pulling my eyes around the room to look at anything except that open journal, anything other than the words on those pages, but everywhere I look, I see Patricia. Draping a garment over the chair. Lying on the bed, her head propped on one hand, smiling at me. Standing in front of the mirror in that gold dress, with her explosion of hair, wondering if that was always how I saw her.

"Every glorious inch of you, my darling."

The oil lamp flickers, its flame slapping at the glass globe, frantic, almost desperate. I stare at that flame, that raging little fire, and I hear . . . I feel . . . I remember . . .

I stretch to reach the oil lamp, turning up the wick as far as it will go. I need to see her face, her eyes. I need to know that the promise she's making is true, that she feels this thing between us as much as I do. I need to know that she is mine, that I am hers.

"Swear it," I insist.

"I swear, Elizabeth Mary Louise Post, that I will love you forever,

and should we ever be separated, I shall not rest until we are together again. I am yours, my love."

"And I am yours," I promise. I swear it, swear it, swear it.

She kisses me then, a kiss so exquisite I could die right now and know that I have lived. On the table, the oil lamp sizzles, then pops. The room brightens with the sudden flare. We both jump and turn to look. There's a tiny spot on the wick that burns brighter than the rest, but the flame is steady again. As steady as our heartbeats, our two as one.

Another violent wave of nausea rolls through my gut as the butterflies wake up, as they churn and twist and swirl. I look at the journal lying on the floor, pages askew.

Memories. All of them. Every single journal entry. *My* memories.

The Victrola plays softly as I sit down at the little writing table in the parlor and open the brand-new leather-bound journal. My long silver hair falls over my shoulder. My fingers ache, knobby and swollen at the joints. I move the pen carefully and deliberately across the page. Each word precious. Each line a journey. Time is fleeting now, and I must use mine wisely.

My name is Elizabeth Post.
I was born on the morning of March 3rd in the year 1906.
I was born to wealth. I was born to privilege. I would have
renounced them both had I known what they would cost me.

I vow at that moment to relive it all on these pages, hoping, praying, that the promise we made will bring us back together, will bring her back to me. I light the oil lamp, turn up its wick. It pops and sizzles, then burns steadily.

"Two . . . three . . . six, my darling," I whisper as I begin to write in earnest:

This story, our story, began on May 31st. The year was 1925.

I slump against the bed, gulping breath after breath. This is crazy. I'm crazy. I've finally flown right off the cuckoo cliff, headed toward a padded room. Maybe Tish will visit me there.

Tish. I see her adorable, adored face. Her cheeks flushed and freezing under her spare helmet. Blushing in the light of the moon. Standing on the edge of the overlook, so scared of what we were feeling. My sweet, fierce, bravehearted Tish. My darling.

My darling.

I see Patricia gazing up at me from the pillow. Her excited, childlike smile as she raises her tongue to the snow. Her nervous glance as she reaches under the tree to retrieve a small gift wrapped in plain brown paper with a bow made from holly leaves . . .

"It's not much . . ." she says, the words sounding like a song, the way all her words sound.

I don't need to unwrap the gift to know: "It's everything."

She smiles and nods to the gift. "Well, go on. Open it, then."

I rip the paper and open the box. On top is a small piece of folded paper. I pull it out and unfold it to read, in Patricia's handwriting: *Forever, my love. I swear it.*

Tears fill my eyes as I launch myself at her, kissing her soundly. "I love you," I whisper against her laughing mouth. I have never meant any words more than I mean those three. I reach for the small book of Tagore's poetry, then I refold her note and tuck it reverently inside the book, right inside the poem I read to her earlier. "Unending Love."

The note! The book! The chest!

My body is moving before my brain catches up, and I find myself at the hope chest. I yank open the lid and reach for that small book that has been tucked there in the corner, all this time, just waiting for me to see it. That slim book of poetry. Rabindranath Tagore.

My fingers are clumsy opening the book, but I turn right to the poem. "Unending Love." Between the pages, between the words, is a slip of a letter. Folded. A few tearstains mar the paper. I cried those tears. I remember them. I open the note. There is Patricia's handwriting. As real as the gold dress. As real as—

"There's more," she says as she nudges me to look inside the box. With trembling fingers, I push aside the velvet cloth and stare. The firelight catches the green glass.

"It matches your eyes," she says quietly, "so I knew you had to have it."

I drop the book and race to the window. The snow is coming down so hard all I see is a curtain of white—and that tiny, persistent spot of green, shining on the sidewalk.

The green glass stone.

I know what it is. I know what it is because I put it there.

The slight weight in my pocket shifts as I walk slowly and carefully down the stairs, my old knees aching with each step. Outside, I make my way to the sidewalk. The moon is full and bright, guiding my way. I test the soft concrete. It's still wet enough, so I kneel, slowly, so slowly, and look at the glimmering green object in my hand. I hold it tight and say a prayer that she finds it, wherever she is. That she sees it and knows that she is home. I press it down until it's almost buried. With my finger, I scratch my message in the concrete: 2 3 6.

A trail of heat races from the top of my neck to the bottom of my spine, like someone poured a thin strip of alcohol straight down my back, then lit it.

"So, our secret code, when I find you, will be . . ." Patricia says.

"Two . . . three . . . six," I mutter.

The dam breaks, and I'm filled with memories of the life I lived before this one. I remember *everything*. Every look, every word, every sigh. Every kiss, every touch, every tear. Every moment. I push away from the window, ready to scream in horror or shout hallelujah, I'm not sure which, when I catch my reflection in the glass. It's me. But it's also *her*. Elizabeth.

She stares right at me, right through me, her face so similar to mine. But her eyes are her own. Green eyes. As green as the glass of that stone buried in the sidewalk outside. I remember the first time I saw her, in the downstairs window when I was talking to Eleanor. I saw her in my house because she is me: Libby Monroe. I am her: Elizabeth Mary Louise Post.

The house creaks around me, and the oil lamp sputters brightly, as if rejoicing. The house is mine. The oil lamp is mine. The green glass stone is mine. They were always mine.

"I am yours, my love," Patricia promises, staring up at me, and pulls me in for a kiss.

"I am yours to do with as you please," she says, eyeing the curling iron suspiciously.

"I am yours . . ." as she slips her arm around my waist, leading me to the dance floor.

"And I am yours," I say.

The oil lamp flares again, and the whole room goes bright.

Tish's face swims before me, in all her expressions. Past and present. Yesterday and today. One hundred years ago. One hundred days ago. One hundred minutes ago.

Then I check myself. This is . . . It's just . . . I mean . . . This can't be true. Can it?

That voice intrudes again. Her voice. *My* voice. It's been my voice the whole time:

There's one way to find out.

47

TISH

My face is numb. My arms are numb. The rest of me is slowly going that way, inch by inch. It must be the cold. I'm freezing. I force myself to open one eye. A sharp pain slices through my temple, like an ice pick. I see white. All white.

My other eye struggles, and finally opens. More pain. A deep throbbing pulse, like my heart is beating right inside my eyeball. From this eye, everything is red, like I'm looking through one of the lens gels Wallis uses in the lighting rig to color the stage lights when he wants the set to look hellish, like a nightmare.

My vision swims a little more into focus. I'm on my back, looking up at the sky. Glittery red confetti falls toward my face. It hits my skin in tiny cold drops. Not confetti. It's snow. Blood-red snow. I want to wipe my eyes. I want to see the snow how it's supposed to look, beautiful and soft and clean. I don't want this red snow on me. My lungs clench, and I cough. Pain sears through my temple, and I suddenly see shadows move around me. A young man talks frantically, angrily. A young woman yells at him.

Then . . .

. . . a scream.

A howl. The most dreadful wail of agony I've ever heard in my life. It makes me try to move, makes me try to sit up. I can't.

"Nooooo!"

I'd know that voice anywhere. It's Libby.

Feet scramble. I hear someone running away, and someone running toward me. Libby drops to her knees beside me. I stare at her, as much as I can see of her through the haze of red and snow. What is she doing outside in that dress? That beautiful silver dress? I open my mouth to tell her to go back inside, where it's warm, but all that comes out is a faint croak. She leans over me, her hands hot against my face, her tears hotter.

"Don't leave me," she cries, her voice breaking. "Please don't leave me."

My eyes clear just enough to see that her hair is shorter and darker, cupping her chin. Her eyes are green. Not my Libby's eyes. But that *is* Libby leaning over me. My Libby, crying, afraid that I'm leaving her. I shake my head as much as I can, as much as the pain will allow. Doesn't she know that I would never leave her?

I want to tell her that I love her. Why didn't I tell her that when I had the chance? And why did I ever think I could get away with wanting something I knew I couldn't have?

She sobs, sucking, gulping, broken breaths, and lies down beside me on the cold ground.

Don't do that, I try to say. *Get yourself inside before you catch your death of cold . . .*

". . . my love . . ." That part I do say, on a cloudy breath, barely there. But she hears it.

She moves closer, presses her warm lips right against my cold ones, then against my cheek, then my ear, and says, in a voice so tormented I can't bear it, "Two . . . three . . . six. You promised."

I wake in a pool of sweat, gasping, my heart thundering like I just ran a mile in a full-out sprint. My hands fly to my head. I feel around for blood, any kind of wound, but I'm fine. The covers are twisted around my legs, like I was trying to run in my sleep. I sit up, try to shake it off, this awful feeling, the dregs of whatever nightmare I just clawed my way out of.

Icy snow slaps against the window. It's coming down hard. I kick the covers away and move to look out the window. Even through the thick snowfall, past Libby's car and past Lola, parked under the porte cochere, I can see the spark of that stone in the front sidewalk, green and glowing in the night. So much snow, but that green stone is shining like someone put a bulb in it.

I hear a door slam upstairs. Then footsteps, thudding down the stairs. Fast. Like running.

Libby. Sleepwalking again.

She's going to fall, moving that fast. My legs are still quivery, but I race out the door, my only thought a horrible vision of Libby tumbling down those stairs. I skid through the kitchen and run to the staircase. The stairs are dark. The parlor is dark. The whole house is dark. Not even Libby's little foyer lamp is on. I don't like it. It reminds me of the nightmare. Of the dark sky and the red snow.

Then I see an orange glow in the downstairs hallway. Libby's oil lamp! I get to the parlor just in time to see her come out of the bad bathroom, her oil lamp in one hand and the sledgehammer in the other. The look on her face is intense, determined. She walks right past me, still moving fast, the sledgehammer raised a little bit, like she might swing it at any second.

I follow her until I realize she's headed outside. Outside. In this weather.

"Libby," I say, forgetting that I'm not supposed to wake her, just lead her quietly back to bed. But this feels different, and her name popped out of my mouth before I could stop it. She freezes, the oil lamp perfectly still, the flame steady. Then she turns. Seems to relax, her shoulders softening, her eyes blinking, her smile so sweet and full of love. So happy.

"There you are," she says.

She's glowing. Like she's lit from the inside, too, just like the stone. I know it's just the illusion of the oil lamp, the warm light it throws, but still. She's beautiful.

"Here I am," I answer, feeling so much déjà vu that I wobble. I don't even have time to focus on the feeling before I notice that Libby's dressed for outside, wearing her coat and boots. I look at the sledgehammer. The oil lamp. She's watching me. Not like the hazy look she usually has when I find her like this, that look where she stares past me, through me. This time she's looking right at me.

I hold out my hand slowly, trying not to startle her.

"Libby? Are you . . . sleepwalking?"

"No," she says. "Not anymore."

She lets the head of the sledgehammer thud to the floor, then leans the handle against the staircase banister. She puts the oil lamp on the stairs and walks toward me, moving with a purpose. I barely have time to catch a breath before she's got my face in her hands, her thumbs stroking my cheeks as she looks at me, searching my eyes hopefully, almost frantically.

"Is it you?" she asks.

"I, uh, *what*?"

I've seen her sleepwalking, I've seen her zoned out, lost in thought, staring at the oil lamp or the fireplace or a book, but this manic look in her eyes is different, and it has me a little bit worried. Her eyes dart over my face, from my eyes to my lips to my freckles.

She touches my hair, buries her fingers deep. Now she's killing me. I can't be worried about her *and* focus on how she's making me feel, like I'm going to melt, like I'm a candle burning too hot and I'm about to be nothing but a waxy puddle right here on the floor.

"Is it you? Have you found me?" she whispers, her lips brushing mine.

A *THRUM* vibrates through me at her words, like a deep cord humming, like someone pulled the world's biggest guitar string and it's attached to me, to my heart, to my soul.

Have you found me?

The vibrations get stronger, almost shaking my whole body from the inside out. She pulls my attention back to her with her thumbs on my cheeks, still gently stroking.

"Two . . . three . . . six . . ." she says.

My heart screams like it's been poked with a cattle prod, and then it starts pounding, starts punching against the inside of my ribs, trying to break free. It wants so badly to get to her.

"Two . . . three . . . six . . ." she says again.

"There you are," she says as I slip into her warm bed, her green eyes shining.

"Here I am."

My brain stutters as I stare into Libby's eyes, into that dark wine color I love so much.

"Tell me what it means," she says, insistent now, pushing for the answer.

"I don't . . . I don't know."

"You *do* know."

She lets me go, grabs the sledgehammer, and stalks into the kitchen. It takes a second for my mind to catch up to the fact that I'm alone in the foyer, until the oil lamp flickers brightly from the stairs, drawing me back to myself. I hurry to follow her. She's already at the side door. She opens it. That little light over the door comes on, buzzing, brighter than it's ever been.

Snow and ice whip into the kitchen, freezing, blowing all over the floor. The cold slices through my tank top and lounge pants. I run to my room and stuff my feet into my cheap knockoff Uggs. Where the hell is my coat? It feels like my world just barreled out that door and if I don't follow her, if I don't catch up with her, I'll be left behind forever.

Before I even know it, I'm opening the wardrobe cabinet. Those old clothes are still hanging there. I grab the heavy coat from its hanger, pulling it on as I run out of the room. I put one arm into one sleeve, and I feel lightheaded. I shove my other arm into the other sleeve and a wave of dizziness makes me grab the wall for a second. I don't have time for this. I need to get to Libby. I stumble through the kitchen toward the still-open side door. Toward all that dark and ice and snow as I pull the coat fully around me . . .

. . . and everything goes white.

Snow. So much snow it's all I can see. Then . . .

A bright orange carrot sticking out of the ground. Libby laughs, throws her arms around my neck.

Blood rushes in my ears, and the thrum gets louder and louder. I stop and lean against Lola, my hands against her shimmery blond gas tank. I just need a few seconds to get my breath, but my thoughts won't slow down, thoughts and images and visions that pound me uncontrollably.

Scared green eyes stare into the fireplace.

"And if we were lost in the pits of hell . . . ?"

"I shall find you. The Devil himself cannot keep me away."

Another deep *THRUM*. Then a *CRACK!*

CRACK! My head whips around to see Libby at the end of the driveway, standing on the sidewalk, bringing the sledgehammer down on the concrete. *CRACK!*

"Libby!" I shout, and take off running. I'm almost to her when she raises the hammer again. I scream, "Stop! Libby, stop!" She brings it down, the heavy iron mallet racing toward the sidewalk. *CRACK!*

This time it rattles me to the bone. The concrete shudders, then splits. The sidewalk now has a thin broken seam that points directly to the green glass stone, to the numbers inscribed underneath: *2 3 6*.

"Tell me what it means," Libby says, breathing hard, the sledgehammer hanging in her hand like she's worn out. Like she's ready to give up. Like everything depends on my answer. "Two . . . three . . . six . . ." she repeats, prompting me, *begging* me.

Then the words are there. In my mouth. On the tip of my tongue. Three words, bubbling up, knocking at the back of my teeth. What the actual fuck is happening?!

Libby watches me, the snow falling thick between us, her breathing deep and heavy, white huffs in the cold air. She's waiting for me, so much hope in her eyes.

"Please. I know it's you. It has to be you," she pleads. "Tell me."

My tongue tries to move, but it's frozen. Three little words.

She raises the sledgehammer one more time.

I watch in fear and awe as it comes down, right over the inscription. Right over the green glass stone. Just before it strikes, my body jolts, a cranked-up version of the jolt I felt the first time I stepped on the stone, the first time I ever saw it, the first time I ever noticed this big house on Mulberry Lane. Then, like I'm watching it in slo-mo . . .

. . . snow falls on the inscription: *2 3 6* . . .

. . . the hammer comes down . . .

... the green glass stone peeks out, catching just enough light to glow ...

And it's all about to be gone.

So I stop thinking. I stop pushing. I stop trying. And I let the words come.

"Me! You! Always!"

48

LIBBY

Me! You! Always!

The sledgehammer crunches the sidewalk, directly on the inscription. I feel the impact all the way up to my shoulders. The concrete breaks; so does my composure. My legs turn to water and lose all their strength. I drop to my knees on the sidewalk, bury my face in my hands, and sob. In relief. In gratitude. In joy.

I look up to see her standing at the edge of the driveway, in her slouchy PJ pants and oh . . . oh, oh, oh . . . Patricia's coat. Seeing the garment on Tish brings the memory of that day right back to me. Our snowman. Our Christmas Day. Our gift exchange. I gave her that coat she's wearing. I gave her the Tagore poetry book. She gave me . . .

. . . the green glass stone.

I carefully move the shards of broken concrete. There it is. Perfectly intact.

An emerald-green perfume bottle.

"It matches your eyes, so I knew you had to have it."

The metal cap is gold-tipped, closed tight. The perfume is long gone, but I know the scent by heart. Gardenia Summer. The scent I wore on my Saturdays in the park, and on the overlook. My stolen Saturday hours with Patricia. I pick it up, gently brush off the gray dust, and hold the bottle up to catch as much light as I can. It's enough to see that the bottle itself is transparent, but there's something inside that makes the glass look opaque. I look at Tish. My tears make her look wavery, but she's *here*. With me. In the Mulberry house. She looks confused. And scared.

So . . .

. . . I smash that beautiful green bottle against the ground, watch it shatter into a thousand tiny pieces, watch it reveal its true treasure. Amid all that broken green glass is what looks like a tiny scroll. I pick it up . . .

My old, aching hands work to carefully create our very own message in a bottle, feeding the rolled item into the tiny mouth of the perfume bottle.

. . . and unroll a photograph.

Patricia and Elizabeth.

Tish and me.

There's no date written in pen, no names on the back, no identifiers. I don't need them. I know this day. December 26, 1925. I remember it. In the photo, we are standing with the snowman, our grins as bright as the sun. I remember hiring the town's newspaper photographer to come and photograph the house "for posterity," then grabbing Patricia for a quick shot with our snowman. Because *that* was the photograph I was really after. That was the moment I hired him for. I just couldn't tell him that.

They look like us, the young women in the photo, but different enough that we're not identical. My face is almost exactly Elizabeth's face, but for the eyes. Hers light, mine dark. Patricia's face is more finely drawn than Tish's, her features more refined. But it's her. It's *us*.

"What's—what's that?" Tish stammers.

I jump up and go to her. I give her the photo. She stares down at it, her hand shaking.

"Tish, listen, this is going to sound crazy, but—"

She backs away. Two steps, then three.

"No. No! What the fuck?!" she says, still backing away, staring down at the photo, at the faces that look so much like hers and mine. I see her throat working as she swallows.

"I didn't know, okay? I didn't . . . I just . . ." I start, then trail off. There's nothing I can say to even start to explain what is happening to us, and she doesn't really look like she'll listen anyway. She just keeps shaking her head back and forth. "Tish, come with me. I'll show you. Come with me," I say, and reach for her hand. She pulls away again.

I back off, careful not to startle her more.

"Okay, okay. That's fine, just . . . please come with me," I say. If I can get her upstairs, I can show her the entire breadcrumb trail. The key, the hope chest, the journal, the dresses, the poetry book, the note. How I was finally led to the truth of that photograph she's holding in her trembling hand. She'll have to believe me. She'll have to believe me because it's all right there.

She'll have to believe me because it's true.

"Just . . . please come," I say again. I hurry toward the house, grabbing the oil lamp on my way up the stairs, moving quickly, wanting so badly to just get into my room and show her. Show her that I'm—that *we're*—not crazy.

I'm talking the whole way, telling her how sorry I am that I didn't share the journal, but how could I have possibly known that *they* were *us*, that *we* were *them*, that something so unbelievable, so beyond the realm of possibility was, indeed, a possibility? I mean, who actually thinks they're walking around reincarnated, looking for the love of their life? Lives. Lifetimes?

Lifetimes. Omigod.

I turn back to Tish, but she's not there. The photograph lies on the stairs, where she dropped it. Then I hear Lola's engine start up, hear her rev, hear her roar. Before I can process what's happening, I hear her squeal away. I run to the door and back out into the snow. Lola's tire tracks are all I see. Tish is gone.

49

TISH

Lola's headlight barely cuts through the falling snow. I'm glad I at least grabbed my own helmet before I got the hell outta there. The visor gives me some protection, but I'm trying not to cry, so now it's fogging up. With that, and the coming tears, I see less and less of the road.

I followed Libby inside when she asked me to. I stood at the bottom of the staircase, holding that freaky photo, watching her hurry up the stairs with her oil lamp. She was all excited, talking fast about the past and the present. Every word she said sent a shock through me. I wanted to run, but I couldn't make my feet move. I could only watch her and her oil lamp move farther up the stairs. Then, in her chattering, she said "Elizabeth," and my mouth went dry.

When she said "Patricia," my legs remembered they belonged to me, and I took off.

I'm breathing too hard, too fast. I'm panicking. Only the sound of Lola's engine, my Lola girl, and the feeling of her rumbling beneath me, carrying me over the icy streets, is keeping me sane right now. Because the things I'm seeing, the thoughts I'm having, the images that are hitting me . . . I feel like I'm going to wake up in that tiny closet-room, in that small apartment with all my roommates. Like I'm going to wake up from the best dream I ever had, only to realize I'm still the same stupid girl who wanted something she couldn't have. My mistake. My bad.

Then Hasina's voice hits me. "Every life is a cycle . . . Time after time, again and again . . . We grow, we evolve, we get new chances . . . to do things better. To do things right."

I see Hasina staring down at that cake, hoping that after she and Paps are gone, they find their way back to each other. I can't imagine believing something like that.

Then I see green-eyed Libby, my head in her lap, Christmas all around us. She's reading from a small book of poetry, "'. . . *in life after life, in age after age, forever.*'"

Then that photograph flashes before my eyes, the snowman. Those girls.

"Have you found me?"

I try to shake it off, but it's not letting loose, its claws dug in deep.

"Two . . . three . . . six . . . Tell me what it means."

"I don't . . . I don't know."

But she was right. I did know.

"My brothers used to have a code . . ."

I don't have brothers! I'm the only child of a mother who doesn't even want me!

Three brawny redheaded boys tussle in a field of green grass and purple flowers. I can feel myself as a little girl. One of them swings me up in his arms. I squeal as he tosses me up, so high, and I sail upward, the air on my cheeks, up where I can breathe. Free.

The boys chase an older woman, her fuzzy red hair wrapped in a ragged cloth. She swats at them as they shout numbers at her, laughing as she tries to figure out what they're saying. Little me yells at them, "Leave her alone!" She scoops me up and kisses me, calls me her "wee protector." My mother. The mother who wanted me. The mother who loved me . . .

The images keep coming. My heart keeps pounding. My head keeps spinning.

. . . *the mother who cries as she shoves a cloth pouch into my hand, a few coins inside. I know without knowing that my brothers are gone. Killed in the war. My mother is sending me away because she loves me, because she wants me to have a better life. Our dear Ireland is a place of misery now. Of abject poverty and starvation. She wants me in America. The land of the free. I cling to her, wanting to stay—who will take care of her if I go?—but she pushes me onto the ship, whispering urgently, tearfully, "Your mother loves you, my sweet lass. No matter how far from me you are, I will always be loving you. Don't you ever forget that."*

A mother. Who loved me.

I push Lola faster, desperate to outrun whatever this is. She jerks under me like she's fighting me, but I twist the throttle and make her go. Go! Go! Go! It only makes the images come faster, though. Like the harder I run, the harder they chase me.

Walking up to the side door of the big Victorian house. Gathering my courage and pulling the bell. Libby, with green eyes and wearing an old-fashioned green dress—I love that dress—answering the door, saying softly, "Patricia?"

Standing on the way-too-patriotic sidewalk on Main Street, flags and bunting everywhere, looking into the window of a new perfumery, at an assortment of colorful bottles. Reflected in the glass . . . is me. My hair is long and braided. I'm wearing a plain dress. Libby is beside me, in her vintage clothes. But that was when I knew her as . . .

"Elizabeth," I choke out, feeling like I'm two people, ripped right down the middle.

Unfastening Libby's clothes, then laying them over a wingback chair. Lovingly running a brush through her hair. Her turning to look up at me with a smile. Green eyes.

Libby on her knees in front of the green glass stone, pulling it from the concrete, holding it in her hand like it's the most precious thing ever. It's the perfume bottle I bought her for Christmas. Our first Christmas together. Our only Christmas together.

Libby smashing the bottle. Unrolling that photograph.

Firelight. Garlands on the hearth. Libby's hands in my hair.

Confetti.

Snow.

Blood.

I'm not even paying attention anymore to where I'm going, just letting Lola keep us upright while I try and comprehend the images, the scenes, the . . . the . . .

"Time after time, again and again . . . we get new chances . . ."

. . . memories.

Was that what Libby was trying to tell me? On the stairs? About the past and the present, that they were us and we were them? She was trying to tell me this. All of this. That same fear shoots through me again, except this time, it's sharper than it's ever been. Like it's hunting, like it's hungry, like it wants to sink its fangs right into me. More flashes, like moving snapshots . . .

A silver dress. A gold dress. A countdown. That kiss. Screams.

I try to pull my arm away from him, scream at him, "Leave us alone!"

Something in his hand. He swings his arm.

On my back in the snow. Hurting. Bleeding.

Libby lying beside me on the cold ground. Crying. Begging me not to leave her.

I can't see more than that, and I don't need to. I don't *want* to. I don't care if it means the fear wins. I'm too scared to try. To risk. To *lose*. Lola shifts beneath me, leaning, turning. I snap to the present. We're at the road that leads to the overlook, but the bike is veering away.

No. No, that's exactly where I want to go.

I yank Lola toward the overlook road and hit the gas. She stutters, whines, resists.

I curse the freaking carburetor and torque the throttle harder, harder, until the gas clears whatever blockage it found, and Lola shoots forward, headed toward that windy, twisty, icy road. I shove the visor on my helmet up and let all that wind and snow hit me in the face, let it freeze my cheeks and lips, let it make me as numb as it possibly can.

50

LIBBY

I should have just finished reading the journal. I shouldn't have run from the pages. The pages gave me distance, a kind of barrier. Reading them would have been so much easier than *this*, being here, on my knees beside the scorch mark, reliving that night. New Year's Eve, 1925.

When I realized Tish had taken off, I was frantic. She was angry, upset, confused, out there in the middle of a snowstorm, on a motorcycle. As much as Tish loves and trusts Lola, it's just a bike. Two wheels and an engine. No kind of cover in this weather. I raced back inside to grab my car keys from the hook on the wall, intent on going after her, but . . .

. . . as soon as I came through the door . . .

. . . the oil lamp flared. And I heard music. From the Victrola.

The wick bloomed again, drawing me toward the parlor.

It was decked out for Christmas. Garlands everywhere. A huge tree, decorated with lights and ribbons and bows. A real tree. I could even smell the pine. A Nativity scene on the mantel. A fire blazing brightly. The Victrola was playing that song, "Auld Lang Syne," the record spinning, spinning. I saw it all, right there in front of me. I heard it. I wasn't simply remembering the past. I had walked right into it, as if somewhere else, this scene was replaying, repeating, over and over, waiting for the right ending.

And in a blink, it was gone. Just a glimpse. A hint of what came before.

The parlor is back to the way Tish and I left it: blankets, bookbags, laptops, shoes. The Victrola is silent. The fireplace is cold. During that brief step into the past, the parquet floor had been shiny, spotless, perfect. No scorch mark. But the mark is here now. On the floor. Still black, still charred, still immovable as I sit on crumpled knees beside it, my fingers tingling. I reach to touch it, to confirm its realness.

As soon as my fingertips brush its blackened edge, more memories rush forward, crashing through the veil of time and space as both of my lives converge. Elizabeth, from her journals, and me, alone on the parlor floor. The same, but separate. Her story. My story. Running parallel tracks, racing toward an ending only she knows.

. . . she will be destroyed she will be destroyed she will be destroyed . . .

The words drummed through Elizabeth's mind as she watched Honey make herself at home in her parlor, this beautiful parlor she and Patricia had painstakingly decorated for Christmas, this parlor that was Elizabeth's very favorite room in the house.

A fire burned hotly in the fireplace. They had been freezing when they got home, in a terrified panic, without their cloaks and gloves. Patricia hadn't even had time to move the fire screen into place before their uninvited visitors had ushered themselves in, Honey laughing delightedly and Chess simmering on a low boil, sloppy from the bottle of gin he'd brought with him.

Honey cranked the Victrola's arm and put the needle down on

the record, the same one Elizabeth had played earlier. "Auld Lang Syne." The song sounded sad now, an unwelcome reminder of that omen. Elizabeth could not keep her eyes from the fire, from the burning red coals growing hotter under the flames. Hell was on her way . . .

"Seems you found enough soap," Honey said, taking in Patricia's hair, her dress, her beauty. "What a surprise your mongrel turned out to be. I might be impressed if I weren't so . . ."

". . . repulsed," I hear Chess say, his voice surrounding me, the memory so alive that I can smell the gin that clings to his skin, that seeps from his pores. He's a mean drunk . . .

. . . mean mean mean . . .

"MEAN!" Elizabeth shouted as Chess grabbed Patricia's arm and hauled her from the sofa.

Patricia tried to jerk away, but he was stronger, growling into her face, "Get your things. You're leaving here. Tonight."

"*You* get out of my house!" Elizabeth lunged for him, the gin from his bottle sloshing onto the floor in front of the fireplace, wetting the hardwood and soaking the rug. He put the bottle on a lamp table, then turned to her with a vile smirk.

"This isn't your house. It's your father's house," he said, so calm in his privilege, so sure of his authority that my stomach turns. I can feel Elizabeth, feel her heart racing, feel her grabbing for him, trying to pry his hands off Patricia, but my eyes are on the fireplace, the fire, those red-hot coals that are starting to—

POP!

One of the coals shifts. No one is watching it. No one is paying attention.

My fingers trace the scorch mark beneath me. Cold. Black. An ancient wound.

"Chess . . . I don't like this," Honey murmured quietly, sounding uncertain now. Wavering. "It was supposed to be fun. Let's just go."

Elizabeth clawed at Chess's back. He swatted her easily away, knocking her against the lamp table as he pulled Patricia out of the parlor. Elizabeth shoved off the table and raced after them, leaving the gin bottle to teeter . . . teeter . . . teeter . . .

. . . and fall.

It landed on the corner of the rug, its contents dribbling steadily onto the parquet floor.

And the music, the music, the music. Playing, playing, playing.

"Should old acquaintance be forgot, and never brought to mind . . ."

The sound of the song warps in my head, slow and creepy, like one of those old calliopes.

Elizabeth chased after them as Chess dragged Patricia toward the front door, still open from his and Honey's unwelcome entry. Snow had blown in to cover the foyer floor, Patricia's feet leaving drag marks in the snow where she resisted him.

POP! The coal cracks, its red center hot, glowing . . .

"Leave her alone!" Elizabeth screamed, swiping at Chess's face with her fingernails, scoring two deep scratches across his cheek. He rounded on her in a fury, raised his fist—

"Chess!" Honey cried in outrage and shock.

"I'll go!" Patricia yelled, her voice colored by panic and desperation and a feral protectiveness. "I'll go! I'll leave. Just don't hurt her."

"No!" Elizabeth reached for Patricia, their hands clinging to each other, their eyes speaking a thousand words. Then . . . Patricia pushed Elizabeth's hands away.

"Let me go, my love. Let me go."

Elizabeth sobbed. "Anywhere you go is not with me."

"She'll go to the gutter, where she belongs," Chess said.

"I will be fine," Patricia said, pulling Elizabeth close for one long, fierce moment, whispering quickly in her ear. "I will be all right. I know you love me. I can bear anything as long as you love me."

Honey's eyes darted between Patricia and Elizabeth. Sudden tears filled the icy orbs, revealing a surprising hint of a heart underneath. "Chess. I think . . . I think this is real. Let's leave them alone," she whispered.

"It *is* real," he agreed, "and that is why it must end. Now."

Honey Harper was a bitch, through and through, a persona she wore as proudly as a new bespoke frock. Chess Pennington, on the other hand, was dangerous. A son of wealth and status. There were no rules for him. Honey reached for his arm, wrapping her fingers around it carefully, as if not to spook him or antagonize him any further.

The light cast from the fireplace grew brighter as the coals shifted suddenly, sliding and settling and cracking. No screen to stop them. Burning, burning, burning, redder redder hotter hotter hotter. *Pop . . . pop pop . . . . . . POP!*

Elizabeth straightened. Gave Patricia a watery but brave smile.

"I'll go with you, then. I hate this place anyway. We'll go somewhere big . . ."

". . . somewhere they'll never find us," I whisper to the cold, dark fireplace . . .

". . . somewhere we can be free," Elizabeth finished.

Chess's voice was rough, his pointy face sweaty, ruddy with rage and gin. "Have you thought about what you're doing? To your father? To *my* father? What this will do to them? To *all of us*? And for what? A quick roll with this Irish trash?! When you allow *this*"—he yanks Patricia closer—"to sully your bed, you sully us all!"

I know, finally, as I lie on the floor of my present-day parlor, what Chess meant when he said that. It wasn't *what* Elizabeth was doing. It was *who*. His objection was to *Patricia*. After all, he and Honey had been at the gin joint, too. They'd seemed perfectly at home there among the revelers. But they hadn't *been* the revelers. They had been voyeurs, drinking and watching.

But what Elizabeth heard, on that New Year's Eve in 1925, was yet another man deciding the terms of her life. She'd been free of her father's dictates now for months, long enough that she wasn't willing to let anyone tell her what to do. Especially Chess Pennington, who wasn't even invited into her house! Or into her life! This was her father's oppression, by proxy.

Anger rose up in Elizabeth for every time she had been dismissed or disregarded. For every time her own wants and needs had been downgraded in favor of a man's. So, in the midst of Chess's drunken diatribe about class and money and the responsibility of the wealthy to (at the very least) *fraternize* among themselves, "certainly not with their pets," Elizabeth turned on her heel and marched toward the staircase, intent on packing as much as she could carry. They would take the roadster to the city. They would sell it and use the money to buy train tickets to anywhere but here. It took only a few seconds for Elizabeth's plan to formulate as she hurried up the stairs. But Chess thundered up behind her.

"Don't you walk away when I'm talking to you!"

Elizabeth snapped and whirled on him, shaking with a fury of her own.

"Enough! Enough enough enough!"

She screamed it at Chess Pennington. She screamed it at

Nathaniel Post. She screamed it at the authoritarian world that was ruled by the iron fists of men who still lorded over them all, even in this modern day.

Chess grabbed her arm, his fingers digging deeply into her soft flesh.

Elizabeth shouted, "I will . . ."

". . . have no more of it," I mutter, trembling, wanting to stop this, wanting with everything inside me to fix it, to change what happened next . . .

. . . as Elizabeth shoved Chess as hard as she could.

Those soulless black eyes registered shock, disbelief, astonishment as he grasped desperately for the banister. In his drunken state, he was too off-balance. His back foot faltered, searched for purchase behind him, but as he landed hard on the step below, the wood splintered and gave way. He grabbed a banister post. For a moment, it held. Then it fractured in two, leaving Chess to plummet down the stairs.

Elizabeth stared at the jagged edge of the broken post, horrified by what she'd done.

Honey shrieked, her hands clasped over her mouth as Chess landed at the bottom of the stairs with a heavy *thunk*. There was a long, still silence as Elizabeth's eyes met Patricia's, then Honey's. All three of them terrified.

Then Chess moved. He got to his feet, suddenly agile in his anger.

Elizabeth stammered, "I didn't mean to . . . I was . . ."

". . . just so mad," I finish. I still hate him now, for the happiness he stole from me all those years ago. For the life he stole from her. He fled America after that night. Settled somewhere on the coast of Italy to live out his days free to do as he pleased. Free from justice. He never faced any consequences. Men like Chess never do.

. . . tshhhht tshhhht tshhhht tshhhht . . .

The song had come to its end, but the record continued to turn, the needle with nothing left to play.

The static covered Chess's first growl, but the second was heard by them all. His eyes locked on Elizabeth's where she stood, halfway up the staircase, shivering uncontrollably.

He took a step toward the stairs, toward her, then stopped, and turned to look at Patricia.

"There will be no protection for her. She has neither a name nor a family to defend her."

In a blink, Elizabeth realized what Chess was about to do. He forced Patricia outside, Honey grabbing at his arms, saying, "Chess, no!" as she was pulled along with them, out of the house.

Elizabeth bolted down the stairs, but she wasn't fast enough.

Honey's scream reverberated through the parlor, a sharp, shrill echo that slices through my mind, through time itself.

Elizabeth's knees buckled at the sound. Because she knew . . . she already knew . . . *"Patricia . . ."*

. . . my darling.

I can still feel how cold the ground was when I threw myself down beside her, can feel the wail coming from my own throat, can hear myself begging her to stay with me as I pressed my shaking hand to her temple, her blood warm on my fingers, my voice harsh and ragged as I pleaded, "Don't leave me. Please don't leave me."

I can hear Chess's car as he stopped behind us, demanding that Honey "Get in!"

I see Honey's eyes glued to mine . . . as she let Chess drive away without her. But when I stretched out my hand, a silent plea for help, she turned and ran.

I rip myself away from the memories and stagger to my feet. Woozy, still half here, half there, but Tish . . . Tish . . . Tish. She's out there. Without me. I need to find her.

I grab my car keys and stumble back out into the night as the memory shatters like a dropped mirror, reflecting the past back at me in disjointed pieces, jumping time, out of order . . .

One of the burning coals cracked, shifted away from its brothers, and leapt from the grate onto the floor, sparking the gin. Then . . . fire. A long, hot strip inching toward the parlor rug.

"For Pete's sake, Elizabeth, do you see why we never wanted to partner with you?"

Elizabeth, cards held loosely in her hands, pulled her eyes from the decades-old scorch mark as Honey flicked a playing card at her. Elizabeth laughed at her best friend. It was Honey's fiftieth birthday, and she was spending it here in Elizabeth's parlor, instead of with her (third) husband and their other friends. "Where's my cake?" Honey snarked. Elizabeth laughed again. Elizabeth had forgiven her fully. More fully than she would've thought possible.

I open my car door, about to get in, when I'm hit with more jagged pieces. I feel the wet of the snow on my shoulders as . . .

Elizabeth, defeated, freezing in her silver dress, curled herself around Patricia, trying to keep her warm. Both of them perfectly still but for the slight rise and fall of Elizabeth's chest.

"Darling, did you hear me? You can't stay locked in this house forever."

Honey said the same thing every Sunday. Elizabeth's answer every time was a smile and an offer of tea as she set up the cribbage board, a game Elizabeth still lost. Every Sunday.

Elizabeth clung to Patricia's limp form. She stroked the beloved fingers that would never again hold hers, buried her face in the thick red curls that she would never again see. Her heart broke over and over as she thought of all the moments they would never have, the things they would never do. Elizabeth held on as tightly as she could but it made no difference. Patricia was gone. Her wild, fiery, gentle, loving life . . . snuffed out by one angry act.

A glimmer of light inside the house caught her eye. She saw the glow of flames. In the parlor. Her very favorite room. She watched for a moment as the fire grew bigger, brighter, and then she dropped her head back to Patricia's chest. Let it burn. Let it all burn. She didn't care.

A car rumbled to a stop near them. The doors opened, men's voices shouting as they hurried into the house, and one soft voice in Elizabeth's ear.

"I am sorry, darling. I am so, so sorry. I didn't know," Honey whispered as she covered Elizabeth and Patricia in a warm blanket, then laid herself down behind them both, wrapped her arms around Elizabeth, and held her tightly.

Some people never change. Some people change over time, with years of learning and experience and wisdom. And some people change in an instant, their souls breached by something so profound, or horrific, that their pivot is immediate and eternal. This was Honey's change. She would always suffer the excitement of being wild, but her viper's fangs had been blunted forever.

"Honey," I whisper, "Honey Harper."

Our enmity was buried that night, and we were like sisters every day thereafter.

"You've seen me through the whole of my life. Let me see you through the end of yours."

Gray-haired Elizabeth smiled as Honey stood at her door, a

large suitcase beside her. Even with her wrinkled skin and silver hair, Honey was every bit as striking as she'd always been. And she was moving in. Her fourth marriage had ended "fairly spectacularly" a few years before. Now she was sick.

"Are you sure?" Honey asked, revealing a moment of uncertainty, so unlike her.

"Are you?" Elizabeth countered gently.

Honey gave it a quick think, then said, "Well, who else is going to wipe my ass?"

Elizabeth laughed and led her up the stairs.

I back out of the driveway, feeling the little dip under the tire as I hit the hole where the green glass stone had been.

"Let me call a doctor."

Elizabeth held a warm cloth to Honey's face, soothing her. Honey coughed roughly. "No, darling. This is done," she said, ragged and pained.

Elizabeth stroked Honey's damp neck, her hair, tears welling in her eyes as she watched a few of those bright strands fall from Honey's head and land on the pillow. *This is done.*

Then Elizabeth finally said what she'd been thinking all day. "You're going to see her before I do."

Honey's eyes turned toward Elizabeth, milky with age and sickness and regret.

"Yes. I will finally . . . get to tell her I'm sorry," Honey whispered.

Elizabeth shook her head, touched her hand to Honey's gaunt, pale cheek, and said, "No, no. None of that. You are forgiven. You have always been forgiven, sweetheart."

"I don't deserve it," Honey said, her tremulous voice filled with sorrow, guilt.

"We all deserve forgiveness, Honey."

They sat quietly, until Honey coughed again, harsh, heavy, and wet.

Elizabeth took her hand and asked, almost timidly, "Will you tell her that I love her?"

Honey began to cry.

"And take care of her for me? Until I am with her again?"

Honey squeezed Elizabeth's hand, held it tight. "I will. I promise."

Honey Harper. My sworn enemy. My dearest friend.

I pull myself back to the present, my eyes drawn to the spot on the sidewalk where the green glass stone had been, the spot where Patricia had been taken from Elizabeth, taken from *me*. I ache for Patricia, for Elizabeth, for what they lost.

But Tish. My Tish. There is nothing I would change, past or present, if it meant Tish would not exist. And as I stare at that spot, where Elizabeth's love story ended and mine began, I know, I *know* that Patricia would understand. That she needed this second time around as much as I did. I hit the gas and drive away from the house as fast as the ice and snow will let me.

51

TISH

Lola is almost uncontrollable beneath me, sputtering, spitting, skidding ahead, then slowing down, just plain resisting me. Completely uncooperative, like she doesn't want to run, like she's trying to stop. But I don't want to stop, so I keep pushing her. I'm a good rider, able to absorb her skids as we hit icy spots, manage the weird lunges and lurches she's doing, but this is the worst possible time for her to have an attitude.

"What the hell, Lola?! Calm down!" I shout at her.

I immediately feel guilty. I slap my visor down and try to pay attention, to see through the heavy snow, still coming down in solid sheets. It's not Lola's fault we're out here on this icy slope. I glance down at her precious honey-gold tank, repelling the snow and ice, working so hard to keep us on the road, with me pushing and pushing and pushing her. Lola. My best girl.

Then I remember Libby, behind me on Lola, hugged up tight.

Libby. Elizabeth. Patricia. Me.

It's like a movie I can't pause. I can't delete it or turn it off. Someone pushed play, and the whole damn thing is there. In front of me. Behind me. Inside me. I'm running as hard as I can, but this time, I'm getting nowhere. The snow doesn't help, muffling the world, making it blind white and dead silent—except for the sound of Lola's engine and my own breath inside my helmet—leaving me with only that photograph. With the images. With the *memories*. Elizabeth Mary Louise Post. Honey Harper. Chess Pennington. And me. Patricia Murphy. Who fled from starvation in Ireland, right into the arms of death in America.

Dancing. A hot, steamy, crowded room.

Silver and gold. "Give me this..."

Chess Pennington. Black eyes. A snarl. In his hand—a rock.

I remember it now. A deep cold, then numbness, then . . . nothing.

So Hasina was right. We do get second chances. I got a second chance to screw everything up again. I'm still that stupid girl who stepped out of bounds, who reached too far. Who wanted too much. Stupid, stupid, dumbass, stupid—

Lola bounces, skids, then swerves, snatching me from my self-hating tirade. Her headlight hits the backdrop of the snow and shines right back at me. It takes a couple of seconds for me to see through the light and the snow . . . a couple seconds too long . . .

The overlook! FUCK!

I clench the brakes. The ground is icy and slick. Lola skids.

I could lay her down, but it won't matter now. We're going too fast. The edge is too close.

Time slows to a perfect stillness as my whole life comes into clear view.

Stupid?

No.

Impulsive?

Maybe.

Hopeful?

Yes.

Did I do it all for love?

Yes, I did.

There is nothing dumbass about that.

Fear wouldn't let me tell Libby how I feel. Fear made me run tonight. Now, from here, I can finally see how small that fear really is, that the shadow of fear is always bigger and scarier than the fear itself. If I had just turned around and faced it, I would have seen that it was just a pissy little thing, only as strong as I made it. I fed it when I should have starved it. I should've faced that fear and given it nothing. That's all fear deserves anyway.

"I can bear anything as long as you love me."

Finally, I'm not afraid. But now I'm too late.

My last thought is of Libby, how beautiful she looked, right here on this overlook, the fresh snow just starting to fall. Sitting on the back of Lola. Wanting to kiss me.

And Lola. *Oh, Lola. I'm sorry. My fault. Again.* This time, though, it's gonna be more than busted-up butts. This time, we're through. I grip her handlebars. *At least we're together.*

Time resumes at supersonic speed, like it gave me the chance to know what I needed to know, to learn what I needed to learn, and now it's catching up with itself. As we near the edge of the overlook, Lola roars louder than I've ever heard her roar.

Her front wheel flies up off the ground. *Our last wheelie—*

—but then she tips roughly to the side, jerks upward, her rear end bucking wildly, and I'm thrown from the seat. I desperately reach for her, so bright and blond and beautiful, but she slips away . . . and I hit the ground. I land hard, still skidding toward that long fall. My fingers grab at the ground, and I dig in my heels, scrabbling to a stop just a few inches from the edge.

But Lola . . . Lola . . . my sweet . . .

"Lola!!!!!"

Her roar turns to a high-pitched whine as she launches off the edge of the overlook. Her body spins in the air, headlight shining up toward the sky. Then she swings around to shine that light on me, on my face, like a goodbye. I stretch out my hand, screaming for her, but she's gone.

I yank off my helmet, lie back on the ground, and sob, the snow falling on my face, just like it did all those years ago. Only this time, I'm alive. This time, I made it. Thanks to Lola.

52

LIBBY

The overlook. That's where she'd go. I drive as fast as I safely can, the Camry not yet prepped for winter weather. I'm almost to the turnoff when I see a bright light sail off the edge of the overlook up ahead, far above me, spinning in the air, snow swirling, reflecting the light so it looks like some kind of angelic laser light show.

But it's not a show. I know in my gut exactly what I'm seeing. It's Lola.

My whole body goes rigid as my heart stops beating, as my blood stops pumping.

"No. God. Not again. Not this time. Please."

Then . . . she falls. Her engine wails, like a helpless scream, as she plummets to the earth.

Everything inside me seizes as I watch her fall, watch her hit the ground, sending a shower of sparks into the air to mix with the falling snow. I'm frozen in place, the car coasting, my hands loose on the wheel, mouth agape, my eyes refusing to believe it. I don't believe it.

Then a surge of adrenaline dumps into my veins, and I go all hot and lightheaded, like I've just been dropped back into my body. I slam to a stop on the side of the road and practically fall out of the car. My open driver's side door ding-ding-dings into the night as I stumble around, frantically scanning the area. The fresh snow makes it easy. One shallow crater in the pristine blanket of white. Lola. Her headlight struggling to stay bright.

Please, please, don't let Tish be with her.

I scramble on shaky legs toward the smoke rising from the crumpled pile on the ground, the whole time terrified of what I'm about to see.

And when I see it—God. It's worse than I could have imagined.

Lola's body is twisted and bent, her rear wheel torn off, gone, like a shorn limb, the metal of her back end wadded up like so much paper. Her front wheel spins slowly as her headlight grows steadily dimmer, second by second, fighting a losing battle.

I look everywhere, calling Tish's name. The rest of the snow is clean, unbroken. A strange relief fills me. She's not down here. She's up there, on the overlook. I can feel her, like there's a thread that links our hearts together, pulsing electricity between us. She's okay. I know she's okay. Down here it's just . . .

"Lola." I drop to my knees beside her, my heart aching for her poor broken body. I put my hand against her slowly rotating tire, gently stopping it. Her headlight b-b-b-blinks . . . . b l i n k s . . . bli-bli-b l i n k s . . . . then she's gone. A sob wracks me as I rest my cheek against her twisted front fender. I press my hand against her golden gas tank, the only part of her that's still whole, and whisper, "Thank you."

The snow falls around me, the tic-n-tap patter of snowflakes settling on the ground and the steady ding of my car door the only sounds as I wipe my tears and stare up at the overlook, high, high above me.

The car's heater is still on, for which I'm grateful as I pull the heavy door closed and start the careful climb up the narrow, winding road that will take me to her. I switch my headlights to the fog setting. They go dim and undercut the falling snow, but I can still barely see the road.

It's a slow way up, ten miles per hour, but finally, finally, the headlights shine on something.

Tish's helmet, resting on the ground. The lights glint against the visor, flashing like a little signal. With my heart pounding in my throat, I see her legs first (not broken), then her hips (she looks intact), then her chest. I switch the headlight setting to normal and see all of her, hazy through the snow. No blood.

She throws up a hand to shield her eyes from the light, watching the car with a strange expression. I park and hurry out, running toward her. She holds out her hand to stop me.

I hesitate, confused. I had expected to run into her arms, expected her to hold me close, both of us crying, joyous at our reunion. Instead, she's watching me warily, and now I'm staring back at her, unsure. Maybe she doesn't remember. Maybe it's all me. How will I convince her? How can I make her believe that—

"No picnic basket?" she says.

Then Tish smiles, and I really *hear* what she just said. *No picnic basket?*

She remembers! I can see it now, all over her. The wildness that was Patricia, that strength that always made me feel so secure. And Tish is there, too, with her shy grin, rubbing her hand across the back of her hair, making that little clicking sound. I wonder if that's how I look to her now. Like Elizabeth *and* Libby. Does she see both of us at the same time?

"So. What did you bring me?" she asks.

My response bubbles up inside me on a laugh as bright as the new snow.

"Every good thing I could find," I say as I run to her and throw my arms around her.

She buries her face in my neck and whispers, "The best thing. You're the best thing, Libby." She takes one deep, heaving breath, then murmurs, "I love you."

The words strip the last of my strength, and I weep as I cling to her, even as I feel her own hot tears run down the skin of my neck. After a moment, I pull myself together and press my warm hands against her cheeks. "Oh, you're so cold. Why did you take off your helmet?"

"Lola . . ." she starts. "Lola was— She—"

She looks toward the edge of the overlook.

"I saw her," I say gently.

"She saved me, Libby. I mean it. I know it sounds crazy, but Lola saved me."

"I know. I know she did."

I can't fully process the how or why of that right now. All I care about is this moment. I bury my fingers in those red, red curls and shake the snow from her hair. Then I let my fingers trail down her cheeks, over those twelve precious freckles, down to her lips. "I love you," I say, looking right into those vibrant blue eyes, made sparkly with tears.

"Two . . . three . . . six," she says in return. "Till my very last breath. And ever after that."

And I would swear, just for a second, the words have a lilt to them. A tiny Irish lilt.

53

TISH

Libby's asleep, burrowed up next to me, her head tucked under my chin. As much as I don't want to move, I have to. Last night was the closing night of *A Christmas Carol*, and I promised Wallis I'd head up striking the set. He wanted to leave early for a romantic winter-break vacation with Dr. B. I mean, how could I say no? Besides, he's paying me double, so it was a no-brainer.

I'm going to spend the money on an antique green perfume bottle I found on eBay. It even has the gold-tipped cap, just like the green glass stone had. Libby pretends it doesn't bother her that it's gone, but I catch her all the time, looking out the window at that jagged hole she left in the sidewalk.

Maybe it's too sentimental, too "on the nose," as Dr. B would say—usually about some play she was directing—but I'm planning to give it to Libby for Christmas. I figure it's perfect, since it'll be our first Christmas together since, well, since our first Christmas together. I'll also have some tissues handy for when she starts crying. She cries a lot these days, over the littlest things. Things that make her think of us today, or yesterday, or so many yesterdays ago. Sometimes she'll just look at me from the vanity while I'm putting on my shoes, and she'll cry.

"Happy tears," she says. And I believe her.

I never really got the *happy tears* thing. My tears had always been from sadness, or sorrow, or pain. Or fear. Until Libby. Now I feel a lump in my throat every time I look at her, every time I wake up in this room, in her arms. All the things I ran from led me here, to the place I was always meant to be. We were in the right place at the right time under the right circumstances. The right two people standing right where we needed to be. Lightning does strike twice, I guess.

Thanksgiving with Hasina was hard. Our first without Paps. We told funny, sweet stories about him until Libby swore she felt like she knew him. So much so, that when the stories inevitably ended—because there were no more to tell—she cried with Hasina. And I cried with Bari. Bittersweet tears of goodbye. But then Hasina patted Libby's cheek and told her that it was all going to be all right, and Libby looked over at me and smiled, like she already knew.

In the car, on the way home from Hasina's, Libby took my hand and said, "Even if I forget you, I will never forget you." It felt like another vow, for next time, maybe, and my eyes filled with tears of joy. I was grateful, for the first time in my life, to be *me*.

I quietly reach for my phone, sensing that the alarm is about to blow. My fingers make quick work of canceling it before it wakes her. She needs to sleep. She's going to be a manic mess all day, what with her family dinner thing tonight.

I don't know what she was thinking, inviting them over here last-minute like that, but she just kind of melted when she saw them in the auditorium, handing their tickets to the usher. Her mom, her dad, even her brother. She'd sent the show poster to her dad by text. He hadn't answered, hadn't replied at all. But then he showed up. And now they're coming to dinner. Here.

Libby hasn't cried about that, though, like I expected her to. Her stress level immediately went beyond tears.

She asked me to invite *my* mom, but I'm gonna let that one stay on the shelf for a little bit, let it marinate. Truth is, when I think of *my mother* now, I think of the haggard Irish woman who selflessly shoved me onto a boat and pressed all the money she had into my hand, her eyes full of love and loss. That's what a mother should be, and if the mother I got this time around can't do that, then I'm not sure I want her any more than she wants me.

Besides, I'm plenty terrified at the thought of meeting Libby's dad and brother, without dragging my own momma drama into the mix. I'm not-so-secretly hoping Molly will bring by dinner ahead of time and Libby can just warm it up and pretend she made it. That would take some of the stress off. Libby said "That's crazy" and "Don't be stupid," but I suspect she's hoping the same thing.

I was worried about the elephant in the room, the first time I met Molly, but Libby just blurted it out. "*We* are an *us*." Molly, as trad as she looks, didn't blink an eye. She calmly went on sprinkling cheese over the lasagna she was making and said, with the straightest face I've ever seen on a parent, that she just wants her kids to be happy.

What a concept.

So now it's Dan I'm worried about.

Libby assures me that if Dan has a problem with me, it won't be because of my gender. It'll be that I wasn't part of his plan. And what can I say to that? Libby wasn't part of my plan, either. A house wasn't part of my plan. A *plan* wasn't part of my plan.

I gently untangle our limbs and slip from the bed, my feet immediately bouncing on the chilly hardwood floor. I need some cozy slippers, I really do, but I refuse to wear anything, slippers included, from the wardrobe downstairs. I get that Patricia's things were once my things, but still, to me, they're someone else's shoes. Anyway, that coat freaked me out. It's one thing to remember what happened before. It's another thing to *wear* it. I'm not like Libby that way. I can't walk around wearing a skin that's not mine anymore. She understands, but she still teases me about it as she decks herself out in Elizabeth's clothes.

Sometimes I wonder if that's where some of Libby's tears are coming from. From letting go of *that* life and moving on in *this* one.

We spent a lot of time reading the journal together. Seeing Elizabeth's handwriting the first time knocked the wind right out of me. It's so weird to be with Libby here in this time, and remember her in that time. She still hasn't told me everything. I'm not sure she ever will. I don't push. People don't need to know every single thing about each other for it to be true love. They just need to love each other no matter what, and Libby has that promise from me. Forever.

The sun shines through the window as I look down at her on the bed. She glows. It's not the oil lamp, or Elizabeth's pajamas. Bari was right, per usual. "That's her heart, dummy." I pull the blankets up around her, smiling as she snuggles into my pillow, grunting and mumbling.

It's been three weeks since that night on the overlook, since Libby pulled the green glass stone from the sidewalk, since she found the photograph that finally revealed to us the truth of who we are. Who we were.

Three weeks since the last time I slept in that downstairs bedroom. I started to go in there when we got home that night, but Libby took my hand and said, "I don't want to sleep without you for one more minute." And that was that.

Three weeks since we walked into the house, freezing and cold and exhausted. Confused, surprised, reeling. Happy. In love. A million memories swirling between us. Three weeks since Libby picked up the oil lamp and headed upstairs, and I heard her voice in my head, from another time, say, "I would light my oil lamp and let its flame lead you home."

That's where I am. Home. And I never intend to run again.

54

LIBBY

The oil lamp flickers on the floor beside me as I tuck Elizabeth's journal, the Tagore poetry book, Patricia's note, and the photograph into the back corner of the hope chest. I lay the folded silver and gold dresses carefully on top. The strange merge of time, past and present, is filling up all the little holes inside me, like the pores of a sponge absorbing water, until there is no room left for anything other than this complete and utter *oneness* with everything.

The house is feeling the joy, too. The sad room isn't so sad anymore. It's almost like remembering Honey—and most importantly, remembering that she had become my dearest friend in all the world—had somehow wiped the sadness right off the walls, lifted it from the floor, and flown it out the window. The whole house seems lighter now, brighter, like it's been cleansed.

And the black scorch mark finally came off the floor! Wiping it up had been as easy as taking a wet paper towel to it. But the fire left its mark. The parquet there is tinged a different color, like a healed wound, like a scar. Maybe one day Tish will repair it. Or maybe that's one of the scars we keep, as a reminder that we made it to the other side and back again.

Even the little outside light over the side door has been behaving. It no longer has a mind of its own. It comes on with the switch and goes off with the switch.

Tish and I went to my family's house for Christmas Eve, still taking baby steps, finding our way forward in this new paradigm. When Mom brought out an apple pie for dessert (with ice cream on the side), Dad suddenly asked Tish what she thought about Neapolitan. Tish, without missing a beat, said, "Three flavors for the price of one? Count me in. And also, it's delicious."

Peter stared at the pie, I stared at Dad, and Mom stared at me. Suddenly, Tish seemed to realize the question was more than just a question. She glanced at me, her eyes wide and nervous. Then Mom's hand landed gently on Dad's shoulder and squeezed. Molly being Molly, doing it her way. I held my breath until Dad finally said, "Delicious, it is." Mom smiled. That's when I knew, for sure, that everything was going to work out this time.

I was still floating on that bliss cloud when we came home and exchanged gifts by the fire, then built a snowman from a fresh midnight snowfall. When Tish plucked off her hat and looked up at those tiny white flakes falling like lace against the black sky, I thought my heart would burst. It did burst when, in bed, she surprised me with one more gift. An antique green glass perfume bottle. This one, I swore to her, would remain in its place on the vanity.

We invited everyone over for Christmas Day. The whole house was decked out with decorations we brought down from the attic, and we were eager for everyone to see it. Joe was the first person on the guest list, and the first to arrive. I was so excited to finally meet him. Old Joe, the man Tish never stops talking about. What I didn't expect was to *recognize* him.

I was sitting in the nook on Christmas morning, gazing over at the glimmering green bottle, nestled so perfectly among the others, when movement caught my eye outside the window. An old man was standing on the sidewalk, staring down at the small crater where the green glass stone used to be. I leaned closer to the window to get a better look at him. He must have seen me, too, because he raised his hand to block the sun and looked right at me.

Joe. The final piece of the puzzle.

A thousand chills skittered over my skin as I saw his old face, but I also saw *his young face*, the day he stood right in that spot after he'd repaired that very same sidewalk. That had been the night I pressed the green glass into the concrete. The night I called Patricia back to me.

It was also the night I died.

I stood up on shaky legs and stared down at the young man, the old man, Tish's Joe, my fingers pressed to my chest, rubbing at the phantom ache. And I remembered . . .

A heart attack. Right here in my nook. I had just finished putting everything in the trunk, had just finished placing the key on top of the bedpost. My oil lamp was burning low. I was leaning against the window, staring out at the green glass stone, the concrete not even fully dry.

When the sudden pain shot through me, I thought of her.

When my arms went numb and I couldn't raise them, I thought of her.

I saw the oil lamp's flickering light reflected beside me in the glass, and when my eyes locked on that flame, I thought of her.

When the last breath left my lungs, it was to whisper, "Lead her home."

Joe was the last person to see Elizabeth alive. I felt that knowledge sweep through me as I turned and bolted for the stairs. I flew down them, out the front door, across the snowy yard, and right into Joe's arms. I don't think he expected it, but he caught me easily and hugged me back, patting me sweetly as I said tearfully, "Joe? Are you Joe?"

"Squirt must be saying some pretty nice things about me, to get this kind of welcome."

I looked up into his craggy face, his kind old eyes, and said, "Oh, she says terrible things. But I don't believe her." He laughed and patted my shoulder again. I loved him already.

The dresses twinkle up at me from the chest. I'm not quite ready to make myself close it, but I know I need to let them go, as much as I can. I need to respect the demarcation of time between their pasts, Elizabeth's and Patricia's, and our futures, Tish's and mine. I don't want everything we do now to be dictated by what we did (or didn't do) then. The lessons we learned as Elizabeth and Patricia will stay with us. The rest we get to figure out now, as Tish and Libby.

I *am* keeping Elizabeth's clothes, though. I mean, they were literally made for me.

It's dark outside. A little before midnight. I turn up the oil lamp so the light bounces off the beads of the dresses, watching the glimmers dance across the inside of the lid, reminding me of the gin joint, of that New Year's Eve a hundred years ago.

Tish and I spent New Year's Eve alone last night, downstairs in the parlor. We will spend it alone every year. It is the one night of the year that we will give fully to Elizabeth and Patricia. We will remember them, let their memories play inside us, let them run free. December thirty-first will belong to them. All our other days, though, belong to us. It's going to be harder for me than it is for Tish, I think, since I lived so much longer as Elizabeth. But this is *my* life now. Not hers.

I laugh a little, thinking of Joe's face when he backed up and really looked at me. He stared at me, then looked up at my bedroom window, then stared back at me again.

"You come from up there?" he asked, and pointed to my bedroom. I nodded, waiting to see if somehow he knew, if somehow he recognized me, too. He took his time studying my face. Then he just shook his head and said, "Old man's getting old."

"Let me show you the inside. Tish says you've been wanting to see it," I said, and tucked my hand in the crook of his arm to lead him toward the front door.

He stopped, looked up at my bedroom window again. I waited . . . waited . . . but he just sighed.

"What is it?" I asked.

All he said was "I don't know. There's just something about you and this house."

Tish is on her way upstairs. Just hearing her footsteps sets the butterflies dancing. I kiss my fingers and press them to the journal, touching the gold embossed numbers. Then I close the lid and lock it. I pick up the oil lamp, stand up, and put the key on top of the bedpost.

I don't know if Joe will ever figure it out, but I'm not going to tell him. I doubt he'd believe it anyway. It doesn't matter. The story is ours. It doesn't need to be believed to be true. We just need to be free to love each other. This time around, we've got a real chance to do that.

Joe's right about one thing, though. There is definitely something about me and this house.

The bedroom door opens behind me and Tish walks in. She gives me that grin I love so much, the light of the oil lamp making her hair look redder than red, her eyes bluer than blue.

"There you are," I whisper to her.

"Here I am," she whispers back.

She crawls into the bed and smiles as she waits for me. I let myself just look at her, just watch her breathe, knowing that she is real, that she's here with me, and that she loves me. Just as I love her. I keep my eyes on hers as I cup my hand around the globe of the oil lamp, take a deep breath, and blow. The flame flickers once. Pops. Then goes dark.

ACKNOWLEDGMENTS

This book would have been a complete dumpster fire without the hand-holding, cheerleading, and safety-netting of Vaneta Viars Martin. Daily, and without fail, this woman was my lifeline, my sounding board, and my chief critic. She was integral to getting this story out of me and onto the page. Thank you, Biscuit. Your belief in me helped me believe in myself. I love you so much.

A huge thank-you to my agent extraordinaire, Liz Parker. Your steady hand and levelheaded guidance have been invaluable and are much, much appreciated.

A million thanks to the rest of my team: David Boxerbaum, Adam Kolbrenner, Sara Nestor, Scott Whitehead, Aaron Marion, and all of the Verve, Lit, MFW, and The Marion Group crew. Y'all keep me working, and for that I thank you, thank you, thank you.

Dante Medema, my sister from another life! Thank you for your friendship and patience and for sharing your knowledge of the authoring world with me. Thanks especially for taking my midnight "what the hell does this email mean?" calls. I believe in the magic of the Northern Lights! I always will. Love you much, lady.

Thanks, thanks, and more thanks to my friends and family. I am unfairly blessed to be surrounded by such a bounty of love and support. If I name one of you, I will have to name all of you, so in my desperate fear of leaving someone out, I'm going to acknowledge you as one. You know who you are, you know (hopefully) how very dear you are to me, and you know (hopefully, hopefully) that without any single one of you, I'd be lost.

To my dear ones on the other side, I feel your love and protection and guidance every day. You may be gone, but you've never left my side, not for a moment. There is no greater love than that. Until I can hold you again . . . thank you.

As always, thank you to Tobias Iaconis, my screenwriting partner and most trusted ally in this fight to stay creative while also staying sane. You are the tourniquet when I'm bleeding out, my friend. I rely on you more than you know. Ampersand forever!!

Finally, and most importantly, all the gratitude in the world to Jennifer Klonsky and Stephanie Pitts for taking a chance on me and for providing such a safe place from which to create. The absolute freedom of this experience has been exhilarating. And cathartic. More directly, to Stephanie, I will be forever grateful for your keen insights and your deep understanding of story. I have been spoiled, and I could not be happier about it.

That's not to leave out Matthew Phipps and all the Penguin Random House and Putnam early readers, editors, copyeditors, and proofreaders who thoroughly vetted every line of this novel. Y'all really put me through my paces, and it was the most fun I've had creatively in a long time. Thank you, all!

A heartfelt thank-you to Elaine C. Damasco for the beautiful cover art for the book. You are a gifted artist, and I am humbled by the gorgeous cover you created. Thank you so much.

And a special, special, special thank-you to my little Finny

Finn. Everything changed the day you came into this world. One day you'll be able to read this, and when you do, I want you to know that you are the light of your Aunt Mik's life. Everything I do for the rest of my days will be for you. I love you, my angel. Now put down the iPad, be my sweet baby, and try not to make your mommy pull her hair out. It's bedtime somewhere, isn't it?

ABOUT THE AUTHOR

Mikki Daughtry is the coauthor of the #1 *New York Times* bestseller *Five Feet Apart*, which was based upon her screenplay for the major motion picture of the same name, as well as the *New York Times* bestseller *All This Time*. In addition to *Five Feet Apart*, her produced film credits include *The Curse of La Llorona* and *Nightbooks*, with several other projects in development. Mikki currently lives in Los Angeles, CA.

Follow Mikki online:
@MikkiDaughtry